CATHERINE AND THE WIND

AMANDA GALE

for Dez
who always knew

The wind's way in the deep sky's hollow
None may measure, as none can say
How the heart in her shows the swallow
The wind's way.

Hope nor fear can avail to stay
Waves that whiten on wrecks that wallow,
Times and seasons that wane and slay.

Life and love, till the strong night swallow
Thought and hope and the red last ray,
Swim the waters of years that follow
The wind's way.

— SWINBURNE

CONTENTS

NOTE

The autism spectrum is just that, a spectrum. No two people are the same, and autism manifests differently in everyone. Catherine is not meant to represent all people on the autism spectrum, nor is every trait she possesses related to her autism. Her experiences are her own, and others' experiences may vary widely.

PART I
CATHERINE

CHAPTER ONE

$\mathcal{C}$atherine pressed the chocolate between her fingertips. It molded obediently into a smooth, symmetrical disk. She took the edges with the index finger and thumb of her other hand and pulled just gently enough to lengthen it without opening a tear. The disk was now denser at the bottom, almost papery thin on top. She dipped her brush into a bowl of white chocolate, dyed red, and lifted the disk higher, toward the sunlight that filtered in through the window behind the sink. Then, eyes alert, with the precision of a surgeon, she swept the brush upward in long strokes, covering with a warm coral hue the last of a dozen petals that would form the chocolate rose.

She went to gently place the petal on a tray, her long, slender fingers extended. A motley-colored cat jumped onto the windowsill and then scampered across the countertop, its amber fur glistening in the bright Virginia sunlight.

Catherine started and gasped, then bent over the cat as it hopped back down to the floor.

Hand on her hip, she shook her finger at it.

"Miss Dorothea," she scolded. "Once again you poke your

AMANDA GALE

nose where it doesn't belong. You know you're not allowed in my workshop. How did you get down here again, anyway?"

The cat skulked toward her, head lowered, and rubbed against her leg in a conciliatory manner.

Catherine's face softened, and she sighed. She laid the chocolate petal on the tray, replaced her brush on the lip of the bowl, and lowered herself to the floor. She sat cross-legged, and the cat scurried into her lap and purred.

"You're a good girl, Dorothea," said Catherine. The cat flipped onto her back, and Catherine scratched her belly obligingly. "I forgive you, of course. We all have moments of weakness, don't we?"

A song tinkled from the corner of the room. Catherine's cell phone.

Catherine rose from the floor, the cat cradled in the crook of one arm.

"Now, who is interrupting our peace and quiet?" She reached for her phone, looked at the screen, and hesitated a moment, frowning. She met the cat's eyes and lowered her voice to a whisper. "It's worse than I thought. Aunt Maeve."

The cat returned her gaze, wide-eyed.

Catherine took a deep breath and answered her phone.

"Where are you?" her younger sister chirped before Catherine could even say hello. "You were supposed to call me back hours ago."

Catherine's eyes darted to the clock on the wall, and she inhaled sharply. "Oh, that's right. I'm sorry." Catherine bent to release the cat, who scampered upstairs. She washed her hands at the sink, then dried them on a dishtowel. "I must have lost track of time."

"You'd better get with it. We have to be there in an hour. Are you even dressed?"

"Sure I'm dressed." Catherine glanced down at her paint-stained skirt and faded blouse. "I've been dressed all day."

4

"I'm hearing an echo. Why am I hearing an echo? Are you in your workshop?"

"I'm supposed to be getting ready, right?" she said noncommittally, glancing nervously back at the spackled walls of her basement as she carefully slid the tray of chocolate petals into the baker's rack against the wall, then headed for the stairs.

"Oh God, you're not dressed." Catherine could almost hear Maeve shaking her head. "What are you planning on wearing? Do I need to help you choose what to wear?"

Catherine emerged from her basement workshop and into the hallway. She shut the door behind her and strode toward the living room, her slippers silent on the hardwood floor. Dorothea the cat scuttled between her feet, and she stumbled.

"Whoops!" she cried.

"What's the matter now?"

"Nothing." Catherine bent forward and scooped Dorothea into her arms, then pattered up the stairs.

"So what are you wearing?" asked Maeve, as Catherine entered her bedroom. Daylight was already fading, and the setting sun was visible through the trees that lived outside the window. "Please tell me you're not wearing Grandma's gray suit again."

Catherine's face drooped as she gazed at the gray suit she had just removed from her closet. She replaced the hanger on the rod.

"Honestly, Catherine," said Maeve, eerily reading Catherine's thoughts. "I don't know why you love that suit so much. It's drab as hell, and it's old."

"It's a 1930s Elsa Schiaparelli," said Catherine, the reverence in her voice bordering on horror at her sister's blasphemy, "and it's not drab at all. Quite the contrary, in fact. It's meant to be romantic." She fingered the ribbon of green fabric that outlined the pocket. "Schiaparelli is famous for bringing back the more graceful, feminine lines that had disappeared in the '20s."

"It's so conservative."

"Only in that it subtly emphasizes the wearer's womanly form.

5

You see, in the 1930s, designers didn't want to ignore the progress women made in the 1920s. They only sought to—"

"Save it, sis. You win. Wear whatever you want. You can give me another history lesson later. Just be there on time."

Catherine bit her lip. She was busy and distracted, and she'd forgotten to keep it succinct. More importantly, now she didn't know what to do about her outfit. She frowned as she pulled the suit back out of the closet and held it in the air.

Her sister seemed to sense her faltering. "Sorry," she conceded, her voice softer. "You look lovely in the Schiaparelli suit. You should wear it if that's what you like."

Catherine's frown dissipated. She held the suit against her body and looked downward with satisfaction. Of all her 1930s dresses, this suit was her favorite. Having belonged to her mother's mother, who had passed away several years before, it was the suit that had sparked her love of 1930s clothing. Its straight lines were so elegant and classic—perfect for Catherine's long, lean limbs. Catherine so often felt awkward and out of place because of her height. But this suit, with its slim silhouette, seemed to celebrate her tall form and long legs. And as its modesty ensured she wouldn't be the center of attention, she felt comfortable wearing it.

She reached for a hatbox at the bottom of her closet. She removed the lid and withdrew a forest green cloche hat with a tall feather jutting from the side. Catherine cherished this hat; it had been given to her by her best friend Hei. It would look perfect with her Schiaparelli suit.

Maeve's voice regained its urgency. "Just hurry up and get there on time. This is important to Mom and Dad. Okay?"

Catherine was already pulling off her blouse and tossing it to the floor; it landed on top of her nightgown from the previous night, which had landed on a pile of books.

"You can count on me," she said as she stumbled to her dresser to exchange her simple cotton bra for something lacier, her last words shaking as she swiftly sidestepped Dorothea, who had scurried between her legs.

Maeve seemed wary. "As always," she said. "Remember to lock your door," she added, and hung up the phone.

~

SHE PULLED UP TO HER PARENTS' massive colonial home and swung too quickly into the driveway, coming to an abrupt stop behind her father's pristine black vintage roadster. She threw the door open and climbed out, then slammed the door shut, ready to run into the house. She was met on the walkway by her sister Maeve, who evidently had been waiting for her. She was approaching as quickly as she could in her tall heels and slender-fitting straight skirt.

"Okay, you were right about the suit," said Maeve, eyebrows raised as she shamelessly looked her over. She tugged Catherine's arm to hurry her into the house, and the two scampered toward the door. "You're a knockout, you bitch."

Catherine's brow furrowed. She let Maeve pull her up the steps.

"It's a compliment," said Maeve when Catherine didn't respond. Catherine removed her hat as they paused on the front stoop, breathless from running. Maeve neatened Catherine's shoulder-length honey-colored hair, then plumped her own dark bob from the bottom. "It means you're gorgeous and I'm jealous."

Catherine's already soft, doe-like eyes softened further. "But you're beautiful."

Maeve's usual impassive expression momentarily warmed. "Eternally kind, as always, even when it isn't deserved." Her eyes studied Catherine's features. She sighed. "I'd kill for your cheekbones."

Catherine remained silent as Maeve squared her shoulders and opened the door.

They were greeted by the muffled sound of laughter and conversation; Mr. and Mrs. Sheering and their guests were in the formal living room to the left. Catherine's eyes took in the stately antique furniture, dark woods, and elegant wallpaper that composed her childhood home. She took a deep breath against the tug of anxiety that always stalked her at social events, already feeling claustrophobic as the cacophony of voices and clinking of glasses assaulted her ears. She fluttered her eyelashes a few times, a nervous tic she'd tried to eliminate for years and finally just learned to tolerate.

"Don't do that," whispered Maeve.

"I'm sorry."

"Shh," Maeve said, holding her finger to her lips. She cast her sister a warning look and strode into the living room.

Catherine sucked in her breath and held it for three seconds before exhaling and following in Maeve's footsteps.

The scene that greeted her was familiar. Twilight's blue glow seeped in through the large-paned windows, which were flanked by heavy gold drapes, and onto the walls and hardwood floor. About a dozen people lounged in armchairs and on love seats that rested on a Persian rug in the center of the room. They were silver-haired and elegant, their clothes impeccable and their bodies trim. They held wine glasses and tumblers in manicured hands. The room smelled of perfume and pipe tobacco, and it glowed with the cozy light of banker-style lamps. As Maeve and Catherine entered the room, the people turned their heads. Instantly their smiles broadened, and her mother stood to meet them.

Catherine stood on the periphery of the room and waited for her to approach, grateful for the precious extra moments before she'd need to insert herself into the crowd.

"Ah, my dear elder daughter," her mother cooed, taking Catherine's hands in hers. Her fingers were warm as they squeezed Catherine's hands, her grip firm. She leaned in to kiss

Catherine's cheek. Catherine breathed in the floral scent of her mother's perfume. She had always felt that if her mother's perfume were a color, it would be a soft, muted red. Like rosewood, or blush.

Her mother pulled back and looked at her daughter with a sunny smile. "At last, you're here. I was just telling the Bickharts how you love to be fashionably late."

"I'm sorry," Catherine whispered somberly, leaning in toward her mother.

"It's okay," her mother whispered back, kissing her cheek and patting her hand.

"As fashionable as your suit," offered a smooth, pleasant voice from the center of the room. Catherine's eyes followed the voice. It had emerged from an attractive older woman with a pleasing, handsome face and a neat bob of silver hair. The woman smiled and stood. She was petite and slender, dressed in a tasteful cowl-necked navy sweater dress that belted around her waist, modest and sophisticated but complementary of her curves. She approached with easy, elegant steps; her fingers clasped a glass of white wine. "Is it Chanel?"

"Schiaparelli," Catherine corrected. "Chanel is a good guess."

"It's lovely," the woman said, reaching to gingerly touch the fabric of Catherine's sleeve. Her eyes met Catherine's. They were round and sharp, a rich slate blue. The woman smiled, the lines of her face indicating she was used to smiling. "It appears tailor-made for you. Oh, how I'd love long legs like yours." She sighed, but the comment bore none of the bite of Maeve's comment only minutes before.

"Catherine, this is Sarah Bickhart," interjected Catherine's mother, gesturing toward the woman in the navy dress. "She's a professor at University of Virginia. Sarah, my daughter Catherine."

"Hello," Sarah said pleasantly, holding out her hand. "It's so nice to finally meet you, darling. Your mother has such nice things to say about you."

"Oh," said Catherine, raising her eyebrows, then smiling. "What does she say?"

Catherine's mother laughed, a rich, throaty sound. She rubbed Catherine's back. "Our Catherine is nothing if not blunt," she said. She turned to Catherine, and her face turned more serious. "It's impolite to ask such questions, honey."

"I'm sorry," Catherine whispered again, lowering her head as her eyelashes fluttered.

"It's not impolite at all," said Sarah. "As you know, Lois, a bold woman is my favorite kind of woman." She turned to Catherine. "Well, for instance, I hear you're a chocolate maven." Sarah lifted her eyebrows in a girlish gesture of delight. "How lucky your family must be!"

"Yes, that is true," said Lois. "Catherine's chocolate is delicious."

"And beautiful," added Sarah. "I looked at your website, darling. How intricate are your designs! You must have quite a steady hand."

Catherine felt the knot in her stomach relax just a little, and she smiled. "I have patience, is all."

"And rather a lot of time," said Lois, downing a sip of wine.

"You have talent," said Sarah, leaning in and tapping Catherine's arm. "Don't sell yourself short. We women should acknowledge our accomplishments, and should proclaim them proudly."

"Thank you, Sarah. That's kind of you."

"Very kind indeed," said Lois.

Maeve had been tending to something in the kitchen. She reentered the doorway holding a glass of red wine and swept grandly with her arm.

"Come one, come all," she announced, with a brilliant smile. "Now that we're all here, we can sit down to dinner."

The three women made their way to the dining room, and those still seated rose and followed.

"Dear girl, you're breathtaking," said her father, his hand on her back as he led her from the room. "I was hoping you'd wear the gray Schiaparelli."

Catherine's heart warmed. She turned toward her father, a gray-haired, dignified gentleman in a black suit and tie. His smile soothed her anxiety like balm.

"Thank you, Dad," she said. "I almost didn't."

"Next time you tell Maeve that if she wants to dress other people, she should buy herself some paper dolls."

Catherine stifled a laugh and pulled out her chair. Her father kissed the side of her head and took his own seat at the head of the table.

The party instantly launched into bright, hearty conversation.

"Maeve, Catherine," said their mother, unfolding her linen napkin and laying it over her lap, "I am so pleased for you to finally meet Sarah and Charles. They're our new favorite people." She laughed lightly and patted Sarah's hand as it rested beside hers on the table.

Sarah and the kind-looking gentleman beside her joined in her laughter. "What an honor," Sarah said, her eyes crinkling with good humor. "And what an honor it is to meet your daughters, Lois. I'd say it's long overdue."

"Please remind us how you met," said Maeve, bringing her wine glass to her lips.

"Yes, I'd like to know, too," said Catherine. "Did you meet at the university?"

"Catherine," Lois said in a hushed tone, with a little laugh. "Give us a chance to answer, now."

Catherine leaned back in her chair and was silent.

"It was at Harold Beck's speech at the university," began Lois. "We were about to head to the luncheon we were holding in his honor, when—"

"When a pushy lady clutching a copy of Mr. Beck's book interrupted them and demanded an audience," said a smiling Sarah. She turned her head and spoke directly to Catherine. "I usually don't like to be so rude, darling. But this was a once in a lifetime opportunity, and I had no intention of letting it slip by. And I'm glad I didn't. I not only got to meet Harold, but I was invited to the luncheon, where I sat in a starry-eyed stupor while my most favorite journalist shared never-before-heard opinions and personal anecdotes, all while sitting so close I could feel the breeze as he swept his arm up." Sarah closed her eyes and shook her head, and placed her hand on her heart. She opened her eyes. "It was the experience of a lifetime. And I made some wonderful new friends."

"And where was Charles in all this?" laughed Catherine's father.

The man beside Sarah smiled. "I was following Sarah's lead, as always, Fred." He rubbed his wife's shoulder, looking at her fondly. "I've learned by now that she'll never lead me astray. And this time was no exception."

"Sarah and Charles have grown quite cozy with Harold," noted Lois, lifting a spoonful of soup to her lips. "They've become good friends."

"I had been an admirer of his for many years," said Sarah. "I read his column religiously every week until he retired. I had been hoping to meet him last year because, by a happy twist of fate, my son Wes was dating his daughter. Unfortunately their relationship ended before I had a chance. How wonderful that I've met him anyway. Isn't it funny how things work out?"

"That is very funny," agreed Catherine. "Chance meetings are fascinating. It reminds me of the story about Willa Cather, how in the 1930s she by chance ran into a woman named Caroline, who turned out to be Flaubert's niece. The women then—okay," she sputtered with a start as Maeve kicked her under the table. Her mother shook her head.

CATHERINE AND THE WIND

Abandoning her story, Catherine bent her head down and returned her attention to her salad, her hair concealing her fluttering eyelashes.

"She seems chatty," she whispered subtly to her sister. "I thought it was okay."

"Flaubert?" Maeve returned. "Really?"

"Speaking of Willa Cather," said Sarah, pouring a thin stream of cream into her coffee. "I've always adored her *O Pioneers.* There's so much conflict in her characters, from both inside and out." She looked at Catherine and smiled brightly. "Don't you agree?"

Catherine nodded and gratefully returned her smile.

They chatted in pairs and small groups for a time, until Sarah turned to Fred once more.

"Fred," she said, spearing a bite of salad with her fork, "have you heard anything about this landfill situation? You know, that corporate monstrosity. What was the name of the corporation?"

"Ah, yes. J. J. Munson Industries."

"So is it real? Is it happening? I've been so worried."

"You're right to be worried, Sarah," Fred replied solemnly. "It appears to be a real concern."

"What's going on?" asked Catherine tentatively, deliberately not looking at her mother.

"A big corporation wants to buy some state surplus land right on the outskirts of Charlottesville," said Sarah, with a frown. "They want to build a landfill there. It would house toxic and hazardous waste. At least, that is my understanding."

"How awful," Catherine said, before she could stop herself. "Aren't there safety standards for such facilities?"

"Yes, there are," answered her mother, too cheerily, it seemed. "And I'm sure that if we wait patiently, your father and Sarah will share all pertinent information."

Catherine shrank in her seat, resigned to remaining silent. She knew her mother and sister were only looking out for her, but their chastisements tonight seemed particularly heavy-handed. It seemed to her that they were so used to stepping in that they were imagining a need where there wasn't one—but then again, she never could trust her own opinion.

Fred swallowed a bite of bread. "J. J. Munson has another such facility in Texas. It receives waste from thousands of industries—chemicals, oil sludge, all sorts of nasty stuff. He didn't seem to care much for safety standards; his place was poorly planned and shoddily constructed. There was talk of bribery, people speculating Munson had bought the permits and brought in his cronies as contractors." He stuck his fork into some potato salad and shook his head. "It's a shame. The local residents have reported chemical smells in the air and water. There's no reason not to believe Munson would pull the same stunts here."

"Is there anything we can do?" Sarah asked.

"Well, Marks will be no help," Fred muttered morosely, with a grumble, referring to their state senator. "He's all in for it."

"But why?" asked Sarah, hands raised. "I'd think even Marks would be against hazardous waste seeping into his backyard."

"Marks doesn't give a damn. The land is situated next to low-income housing, no one he deems of any importance. Surely he'll say it'll bring in jobs."

"Would it?"

Fred shrugged. "It depends. If it's anything like the Texas site, not that many. Munson promised a thousand jobs at that site. When all was said and done, it was fewer than two hundred."

Sarah frowned in thought. "Wouldn't Marks worry about not being able to keep that promise, then?"

"You're assuming he's capable of thinking long term, which he's not. Frankly, it wouldn't surprise me if there were a kickback for him in all this. In any case, I'll look into it and see what I can find."

"Thanks, Fred. In the meantime, I think I'll try to get the word out. If people don't know what's going on, they can't fight it.

The folks whose homes border that site might not like the idea very much."

"That's a good idea, Sarah. I think it's wise to start fighting as early as possible."

"Oh, how I wish you were still our state senator." Sarah sighed. "You were such a champion of the people, and Charlottesville flourished under your lead. Why did you have to retire from the General Assembly, Fred? And if you had to retire, why did Harrison have to lose to Marks?"

"Harrison was a weak candidate. He was too difficult to work with. And Marks made all the usual promises."

"Well, I have just the person to defeat him next election," said Sarah, brightening. "My son. He's been tossing around the idea of running for office. It wouldn't surprise me a bit if he decided to oppose David Marks for state Senate. Would you mind talking with him, Fred? I'm sure he'd love to pick your brain."

"Why, sure, Sarah. I'd love to talk to Grady."

"No, not Grady. Grady's a quieter soul, not one for the public eye. Besides, Helen is pregnant. No, I mean Wes." Sarah's eyes sparkled as she discussed her elder son. "He's moving back down here from Washington. He'll be here next week. He's recovering from his breakup and in need of some distractions. A campaign for state Senate might be just what the doctor ordered. Why don't you join us for dinner one night? You and your family?" Sarah's eyes darted to Catherine, and sharpened. She didn't look away, and the two stared at each other in silence until Catherine attempted an awkward smile.

"You know," said Sarah, leaning forward with her elbow on the table, a sly grin crossing her lips, "my Wes is quite a charming fellow. Smart, successful, and handsome as the devil. A little older than you, perhaps, but that's all right. I wonder if—"

Lois interrupted with a friendly laugh. "That's a lovely thought, Sarah. But Catherine wouldn't be interested."

Sarah's face fell. "Rats. You're seeing someone." She smiled ruefully. "I should have known it. A woman as lovely as you surely wouldn't be available."

"Oh, she's not seeing anyone," said Lois. "She's just not... Your son wouldn't... Well, you see..."

"She's not his type," Maeve offered, mumbling through a mouthful of bread. She washed it down with a large gulp of wine.

"Now, now," said Sarah. "That's just silly." Her eyes bore into Catherine's. They were warm, crinkled in the corners and bright with good humor. "How about Catherine answers for herself?" she said kindly. "Catherine, darling—shall I connect you with Wes?"

Catherine's heart was pounding. Everyone was watching her and waiting. Her fingers twisted the napkin under the table. She didn't even care whether she met Sarah's son; she merely wanted this moment to be over. "Sure," she managed to utter, unsure what else to say. She fluttered her eyelashes. Maeve kicked her under the table, and she frowned.

Sarah settled in her seat, took up her knife, and began smoothly cutting her roast beef. "Then it's settled. I'll have Wes call you next week." She smiled brilliantly. "There now! A campaign to run and a woman to call. My motherly duty is done."

Everyone laughed at that. Catherine made herself smile. Sarah was nice. Catherine felt she had an ally in her, and was grateful. But Sarah didn't know her like she knew herself. She didn't understand that it just wasn't that simple at all.

CATHERINE PRACTICALLY FELL OUTSIDE, so quickly did she exit the house after the Bickharts and her parents' other friends had filed into their cars and gone home. She inhaled the sweet, fragrant air of summer in Virginia, the lush green leaves and the oncoming evening mist. The sky was now a rich indigo, clusters of stars smattering the sky like rhinestones on a velvet dress.

She stood on the walkway, just before the steps, waiting for Maeve, who was kissing their parents goodbye in the open doorway. The warm light from inside the house contrasted with the darkness. It made Catherine sad, but she couldn't pinpoint why.

The front door closed, and Maeve turned to Catherine.

She rolled her eyes. "Whew. That's over."

Catherine stood still while Maeve approached. Then they ambled toward their cars, breathing in the fresh night air.

Maeve opened the conversation. "So I think that went well," she said. "Mom's been talking about the Bickharts forever. And now Dad has someone new to mentor. All in all, it was relatively painless."

Catherine thought about the night's events and the interesting characters who had sat at her parents' dining room table. "Do you really think Mom's told Sarah my chocolate is delicious?"

"Oh, for God's sake, Catherine, what does that matter?"

Catherine continued looking downward toward her feet. Any second now would come the apology.

"Sorry, you didn't deserve that," Maeve muttered. "I'm stressed out, and I'm taking it out on you."

"What are you stressed out about?"

"Oh, just work stuff. There's drama at the office. We always seem to get along better when Senator Wright isn't there. Things will settle down again, I hope."

"I hope so, too."

They arrived at their cars. Catherine dug into her little feather-lined vintage purse and retrieved her keys. She was surprised when Maeve brought her in for a quick hug.

"Okay, then," Maeve said, her voice now softer. She looked her sister over and allowed herself a small smile. "You do look nice tonight. And you did good in there, too."

"Thanks," said Catherine, a subtle warmth enveloping her heart.

"And look, your chocolate is the best. Who cares what anyone else says? You know?"

Maeve opened the door of her car and made to get inside, but she turned back to Catherine instead.

"Say, are you going to go out with Sarah's son?"

Catherine's eyelashes fluttered. She didn't try to hide it, grateful for the cover of the darkness.

"I don't know. He hasn't even called me yet." She took a breath to calm herself; at this reminder, her heart had begun pounding. "Maybe you should go out with him."

"Eh," said Maeve, shrugging. "My job is my love life."

"You just said your job is stressing you out."

"And your point is what?"

Catherine remained silent.

Maeve pulled her keys from the pocket of her coat. "Well, if you do go, just make sure you clean your house first."

Maeve waved, climbed into her car, and drove off. Catherine returned home, exhaling with relief once surrounded by her safe, familiar walls. She flicked on her music and prepared for bed, and anxiety melted from her as Brahms's swaying melodies eased like magic into her soul.

CHAPTER TWO

*C*atherine selected the photo and clicked the "send" button on her phone. Not three seconds later, she received a text back from Maeve.

Too much. Don't go vintage tonight.

Catherine frowned. She selected the photo again and sent it to Hei.

Look at you, girlfriend! Is that new? was the reply.

Yes. Do you like it?

You look fabulous! Best one yet.

Catherine smiled. That meant a lot coming from Hei, the only person in the universe who supported her in her love of 1930s suits.

I don't usually wear red, she texted back. *But this one called to me.*

It's a really pretty red! What color red is that? Crimson?

I think it's fair to call it crimson.

Please let me know how it goes. Okay?

Catherine started as she heard the sound of a car door closing outside her house. *Okay. Thanks. Love you.*

Love you too! Have fun!

Catherine slid her favorite ring onto her finger—it was a

cameo of coral and cream stone, handsomely set in an ornate gold band—and quickly stepped before the mirror, checking that her makeup was still perfect. She rarely wore makeup, but this was a big night, and the suit seemed to call for it. It was a form-fitting suit with a nipped-in jacket, which was topped with a round black velvet collar. But the keynote feature was the curves. The edge of one side of the jacket fell not straight but in a wide half-circle, black velvet buttons following around from the collar down to her waist. The jacket continued to curve along her side and over her hip, following around her lower back and meeting the other side in a symmetrical rounded edge. Catherine hadn't intended to purchase a new suit, but the owner of her favorite vintage store had called her earlier in the week and told her she had just the suit in just her size. And indeed, it fit her like a glove, the soft feminine lines accentuating her narrow waist and ample hips, and complementing the fullness of her modest breasts. It was the height of elegance. Catherine loved it.

Also she had a hunch about her date. She instinctively felt he was someone to dress up for.

He had called her the previous weekend to introduce himself. Catherine was the first to admit that reading people wasn't her forté. But even in the five minutes they had spoken, Catherine could tell he was smart and sophisticated, just like his parents.

He spoke in crisp, clear sentences, an upbeat lilt in his voice. If his voice were a color, she thought, it would surely be gold. He sounded to Catherine like someone used to talking to people.

"My mother tells me you're 'divine,'" he had said. "That was exactly the word she used. My mother's a smart woman. So I know what she tells me must be true."

She hid her face a little, even though he was only speaking through the phone. "Oh," she had muttered. "That's so nice."

"And I hear you're a chocolatier. Is that right?"

"Yes," she had replied, clearing her throat. "That's right, I am."

"Well, Catherine, chocolate happens to be my favorite. You'll have to teach me all your secrets."

"I'd be happy to," she had said, her voice brightening. She had almost begun describing the process by which she dried, roasted, refined, and conched the beans when Maeve's disapproving face had popped into her head. She had swallowed and bitten her lip.

He had asked her about her favorite restaurants, and they had settled on a day and time. Before he called, she'd been nervous, and part of her had been hoping he wouldn't. She had been through this process so many times; it always ended in disappointment, and it was almost easier not to even bother. After speaking with him, she became simultaneously less nervous, and more.

She touched up her crimson lipstick and threw on another layer of mascara for good measure. She stepped back from the mirror just in time to hear the doorbell ring from the front of the house, pleased that she had given herself plenty of time to ensure that she wasn't late.

She glided toward the front door and swung it open.

He was sandy-haired and tall, slim and impeccably dressed, standing casually in a perfectly tailored gray suit. The casualness of his stance—and his captivating smile—contrasted with the formality of his appearance, and the contrast was glorious. His hair was wavy but short and professionally cut, swept backward slightly and held perfectly in place. He gave the impression of confidence and elegance, and Catherine was instantly charmed.

"Hi, Catherine," he said, and his smile warmed. He held out his hand, and she took it. "It's a pleasure to meet you, finally."

She looked at their clasped hands, his straight, angular fingers wrapped firmly around her delicate ones. "It's a pleasure to meet you, too."

His smile now softened. "What a stunning suit," he said. "I hope that's not too presumptuous of me."

"Thank you." Blushing, she tilted her head forward and

brushed her hair out of her face, a pretext to hide the fluttering of her lashes. She felt she should return the compliment. She looked him over, her mind working furiously to choose among the many nice things she could say to him. "Your mother was right. You're handsome as the devil."

His eyebrows rose, and his smile grew wider. "Why, thank you, Catherine," he said pleasantly. He chuckled once. "Mothers sure love to sing our praises, don't they?"

Catherine was grateful for his levity, and she smiled in return. "I just need to grab my purse. Would you care to come in?"

She regretted the words as soon as she turned and saw the condition of her house. It had never bothered her before, but now she wished she had heeded Maeve's advice. Piles of clothes were everywhere. Boxes of chocolate supplies sat in tall columns by the door, waiting for her to bring them downstairs. Stacks of papers tumbled over themselves on nearly every surface. His footsteps sounded in the foyer, and she panicked. Tripping over Dorothea, who had run between her legs, she quickly scooped up her purse from the table and faced him.

He was bending down to offer Dorothea his hand. "Good evening to you," he greeted her brightly, now rubbing her spine. Dorothea bristled with pleasure and purred.

Wes straightened as Catherine rejoined him in the foyer. Crisp and dashing, he looked totally out of place in the mess. He met her gaze and smiled, but not quite quickly enough for Catherine to miss that his eyes had taken in his surroundings.

"My workshop is neater," she blurted.

"Pardon?"

"I mean, let's go," she said, and hurried him out the door.

CATHERINE SAT across the table from him, nodding as he spoke, fidgeting with her fingers under the table, willing her eyelashes not to flutter. She absorbed the romance of the restaurant but barely noticed any of it—the wide-planked hardwood floor, the wrought iron tables and chandeliers, the dim lighting, the soft lavender light of the dusk outside. A single candle burned between them, and its delicate light cast graceful shadows over his face.

His face. What a face it was. It wasn't just that he was handsome. It was the rapt attention in his eyes, the way they focused and held her gaze, the way they sharpened when he made an important point, the way they smiled at her even when he wasn't smiling, as if the two of them shared a secret. It was a sophisticated face, but a friendly one too. The combination was utterly charming. Catherine watched him, enraptured.

She was happy to listen as he told her a little bit about himself —where he had gone to school; why he had decided to go into law; how he had been married, years ago, to a very good woman, from whom he had grown apart; how at forty-six he was ready to start this new chapter in his life, and was eager to feel settled once again. He was fascinating. His voice was eloquent and smooth, his smile inviting. She had already monopolized the early part of the conversation, after he had made the mistake of asking her to tell him about her chocolate. To his credit, he had listened alertly, and to her surprise had seemed genuinely interested. He had even asked her to elaborate. Delighted, Catherine had accommodated, but even she had been able to sense when she had heard too much of the sound of her own voice. In the back of her mind, she saw Maeve kicking her under the table.

A waiter came and took their orders. Wes relaxed a little in his chair and favored her with a warm smile. "Tell me more about your business, Catherine," he said. "Do you make chocolate full time?"

"Oh, yes," she said emphatically, nodding. "I sell enough to earn a modest living. I was working for my father. I didn't like the job much, though I enjoyed working with him. Now I can focus exclusively on my chocolate. Although," she said, tilting her head in consideration, "that's not quite fair. I inherited my grandmother's house when she passed away eight years ago, so I don't have a whole lot of expenses. I probably have it a little easier than most people."

Wes nodded somberly and picked up his water. "I admire your honesty. I often think the same about myself."

"Did you inherit your grandmother's house too?"

Wes chuckled into his water. "You're very funny." He sipped his water, then laid the glass back on the table and smiled. "Actually, I'm lucky to still have my own grandmother. She turned one hundred last year, in fact. She's quite a spitfire."

"Oh," said Catherine, with longing. "She sounds wonderful. Maybe I can meet her one day."

"Maybe." His own smile warmed, and Catherine's heart flipped. "Anyway, what I meant is that I'm a fortunate person. Money was never an issue for my family. I was able to attend good schools and then go into a profession where I could make a great living, which I did."

"Did?"

He nodded and swallowed a bite of bread. "I'll be working with my brother now, starting a consumer protection and public interest law practice. Not as good for the wallet, but much better for the soul." He rested his arm on the table and leaned back casually. "I spent years in corporate and construction law. I made a ton of money. But I'd been doing pro bono work that felt much more satisfying. Obviously I enjoyed the money. I told myself that was just how life worked, that you're idealistic when you're young, and you're practical once you've been around the block."

"Is that not true?"

"That's certainly what we're taught, isn't it?" He smiled. "I'm not so sure it has to be true—at least, not anymore. As the years went on, as I grew older and older, it grew harder and harder to tell myself I was on the right track. I found myself feeling more connected to my pro bono work." He shrugged. "I figured as long as I was uprooting myself, I might as well go whole hog."

"Whole hog is good."

His smile spread. "I guess you'd have to go whole hog to accomplish what you have. Congratulations to you on following your passion," he said jovially, tipping his water toward her in cheers. "Clearly, you excel at it."

"How can you be sure? You haven't tasted it yet."

Wes raised his eyebrows and grinned. "No, I haven't. But to build a business from the ground up, and keep it running all this time—that's quite an accomplishment. It isn't something everyone can do. Wouldn't you agree?"

"Oh," she said. "I suppose that's true."

"So what's your secret? What sage advice would you impart to those of us seeking to follow our passions?"

"I have excellent business sense. And I'm not good at very much else. There's a lot I can't do, but what I can do, I can do really, really well."

Wes studied her but did not respond. Their waiter came with their wine and hurried off.

Catherine took a sip of wine and closed her eyes a moment, enjoying its headiness. When she opened them again, he was holding his glass out toward her.

"Cheers," he said as she met his glass with hers, and clinked it.

"Cheers," she echoed, and took another sip.

They both relaxed in their seats, looking around the room for a few moments.

"You're close with your brother?" she asked.

"I am." His face brightened, and he nodded. "Grady's a very good man. He was a major factor in my moving back down here. And now his wife Helen is pregnant. I wanted to be part of my niece's life."

"I think it's admirable of you."

"What's that?"

"The way you left a lucrative career to do something more satisfying. To give back, to help people."

He took a long sip of wine, then smiled. "Thank you, Catherine. But I don't know that it's admirable as much as it is being a citizen."

"Your mother wants my father to talk to you about running for his seat. Now I know why."

"Ah, my mother," he said, and grinned. "She isn't one to sit quietly on an idea, and she's usually right."

"I really liked her when I met her the other day. She was so kind."

"My mother is a wonderful lady, I agree. And she adores your parents. She's practically giddy."

"Well, they have a lot of common interests, and some common friends. In fact I hear you recently dated Harold Beck's daughter."

"I did. We were briefly engaged, actually. I never met Harold, though. They were constantly traveling overseas. Our time together never overlapped with one of their visits home."

"You were engaged? How long were you engaged for?"

"About twelve hours," Wes laughed. "It's kind of a long story."

"A long story about a twelve-hour engagement?"

"That's right—long story, short engagement. Ironic, isn't it?"

His voice had grown dark, but not dark enough for her to feel certain it wasn't just her imagination.

"Why did it end?" she asked.

Wes inhaled deeply, appearing to consider how to respond. "Well," he said, "let's just say our visions didn't align."

"Did you end it, or did she?"

"She did," he said, his voice a little quieter. His smile had dimmed, but his eyes remained kind. "She did."

"Did it end on good terms?"

"There were no hard feelings. Well, not too many," he said with a laugh. "Separations aren't easy, of course. But now that the dust has settled, we're on good terms. I think we'll stay in touch. She contacted me after she got married."

Catherine sat back and thought about this.

"But you're so charming and wonderful," she said. "I can't imagine why she would end it."

"She had her reasons, evidently," he said flatly into his water, his eyes off to the side. He cleared his throat and replaced his water on the table. He looked at her, and his smile warmed. "These things are always more complicated than they appear."

"Still."

His expression softened, but she couldn't identify the emotion behind the softness.

"I'm sorry," said Catherine, her mouth drooping. "It seems I'm always putting my foot in my mouth."

"No," he said, reaching forward and placing his hand on hers. "Please don't apologize."

She glanced briefly at their hands overlapping on the table. Heat flooded her. He removed his hand, and her hand felt cold and lonely.

Catherine's jaw set. She wanted to tell him. Why shouldn't she tell him? He seemed like he could handle it, and she was tired of games.

"Um, I'm autistic," she said, the last word lifting upward as if it were a question. "I mean I'm just inquisitive and forthcoming by nature. So it's not always relevant. But sometimes it is. Social situations can be challenging." Now that she had told him, she didn't know how much to explain; it seemed like every statement required further qualification, in an endless cycle of disclosure. "I wasn't diagnosed until I was an adult. Not that that matters." She swallowed and took a deep breath, allowing herself a split second before braving a glance at his face.

He looked as amiable and pleasant as he had all evening, his smile warm, his eyes sparkling.

"Thank you for sharing that, Catherine," he said gently.

Catherine took a little breath against a not unpleasant tightening in her chest.

"Do you want to leave now?" she asked.

"Why would I want to leave?"

"I don't know. Sometimes they do. Sometimes they at least make it through dinner but never call me again."

"I'd say that speaks volumes about them."

Their waiter returned with their dinners. Beautiful steaming plates were laid before them. They arranged their napkins on their laps and dug in.

"Henry Clive," said Catherine.

Wes looked up from his plate and swallowed, then paused. "Excuse me?"

"Henry Clive," she repeated, enunciating more deliberately. "There's a Henry Clive picture here." She nodded toward the wall behind him.

Wes raised his eyebrows and turned, then looked back at Catherine. He pointed to a large painting of a glamorous woman that hung along the back wall. "Right there?"

"Yes."

He turned around again and rested his arm on his chair, his elbow sticking out casually. Catherine indulged in looking him over, the way his slick suit jacket hung along his half-turned torso, the angular lines of his neck and jaw.

He turned back around. She made sure to meet his gaze and smile.

"It's beautiful," he said. "What period is it? The '40s?"

"The '30s. He was Australian, but he lived in Hollywood later in life after supporting himself as a magician. He acted in silent films and even knew Charlie Chaplin. After that he painted the Ziegfeld Follies women. His artwork even appeared in many—"

Catherine stopped abruptly and closed her mouth.

Wes had been watching her intently. His brow rose when she went silent mid-sentence.

"Catherine?"

She sank back in her seat. She was usually more adept at masking, but she was nervous, and he seemed to want to hear what she had to say. "I'm sorry. I tend to get carried away. I shouldn't go on and on like that."

"Why not?"

Catherine opened her mouth to reply, then closed it.

"Does your passion for Henry Clive's art have anything to do with your suit?" he asked astutely, pointing a moment with his knife as he cut into his dinner. "It shares the painting's glamor."

"Yes, it's from the '30s. And you're right, there are similarities. 1930s women's clothing tends to be slim-fitting, reminiscing for a more neoclassical shape. It's more sophisticated and modest than clothing from the '20s, probably because of the economic downturn."

"Ah, you're a history buff, then."

"No, I really only know about the '30s. I find that decade fascinating."

"Why the '30s?"

"Because of the loss of innocence. It was a time when we were forced to grow up, as a nation. The Great Crash ended a period of excess and optimism and showed us the repercussions of our naiveté. That new awareness manifested itself in every aspect of our culture, from our art to our fashion. It all eventually culminated in World War II." She shrugged. "The struggle has always fascinated me."

"I find it interesting that clothing became more modest. One would think fashion would grow less modest over time."

"Well, remember that there was so much cultural upheaval during this time. Women's roles were changing. First there was suffrage. Then there was an increase in women receiving a college education. Between that and the Great Depression, the country was looking for reassurance, to slow progress, which is always unknown. A return to modesty makes sense in that context."

"So you're saying it was an effort to keep women in their place."

"Maybe not consciously so. But yes. Of course, the effort was futile. Women already were eyeing more freedoms. Like birth control. Women were in the midst of a sexual revolution, and birth control was in higher and higher demand. They couldn't frame it as sexual revolution, though."

"How did they frame it?"

"They said birth control would be better for marriage."

"I see. It didn't rub their traditional sensibilities the wrong way."

"Precisely."

Wes smiled and returned his attention to his plate.

Catherine imagined Maeve shaking her head at her. *Now look what you did,* she would say. *You talked the poor man's ear off, and now he's bored.*

"Next I'll be telling you about my own birth control," she muttered.

Wes paused in mid-chew.

"Sorry," she said, straightening in her chair. "That would probably be too much information."

The corner of his mouth turned up slyly. "Not at all," he uttered, then took a sip of water.

Catherine drank her wine, closing her eyes as it glided down her throat.

She opened her eyes and looked at him. Her head was spinning from the wine. What was she doing? This man was totally out of her league. He was sophisticated and worldly, smart and devastatingly charming. He could probably have any woman he wanted—why the heck would he want to be with her? She couldn't believe Sarah actually thought they'd be good together. She shook her head, wondering why she had agreed to this.

Wes met her gaze and looked at her questioningly. "What's wrong?"

"I'm sorry," she said. "I know you're just here to please your mother. I don't want you to feel guilty."

"Guilty about what?"

"About not taking me out again. About not having a good time."

"Who says I'm not having a good time?"

"Well, I just thought—"

"I'm not here to please anybody. I make my own decisions. How about you stop criticizing yourself and let me determine my own feelings?" His words were stern, but his voice and eyes were kind. "I think maybe you're letting other people's opinions have too much of an effect on you."

"But you're so handsome and charming. And I ramble about the 1930s. I have a messy house. I overshare. You must think I'm so awkward. You must think I—"

Wes interrupted her by reaching across the table and laying his hand on hers.

"Not at all," he said, his eyes intent on hers. "I find you delightful and sweet and utterly sincere." He squeezed her hand, then patted it a few times for good measure. "And I adore it."

Catherine was reeling from the warmth and comfort of his hand surrounding hers. A little gasp escaped her throat, and she fluttered her eyelashes. She put her hand up to hide her face, but too late: Wes had seen it. His lips had straightened, his eyes widened.

"I'm sorry," she said. "It's this thing I do."

"What is? The eyelashes?"

"Yes," she whispered. "It's awful."

"It's one of the sexiest goddamn things I've ever seen."

A tingling sensation spread outward from her belly. She squirmed a little in her seat, but said nothing.

"Who told you it was awful?"

"No one. I mean, it..." She swallowed. "It doesn't matter."

They didn't say anything for a moment or two. Catherine sat

still and watched him as he took a sip of wine and slid his knife into his beef.

"You're a very interesting man," she said.

Wes looked up from his plate and smiled, looking amused. "Is that right? Is that a good thing?"

"Yes. Yes, it's a good thing."

"Well, you're interesting, too. Remarkably so." He paused to lean forward a little across the table. "So let me assure you that you're doing just fine. Just bat those pretty eyelashes at me, and I'll be wrapped around your finger like your 1930s ring." He flicked his finger toward her hand, then smiled again and winked.

He then relaxed in his seat as he finished his dinner.

Catherine took another sip of wine. *Very intriguing*, she said to herself as she drained her glass. He noticed immediately and motioned to the waiter, then asked for another glass. *Very intriguing indeed*.

THEY WERE AMBLING up the walkway to her door. The air was fresh, the trees abuzz with crickets chirping. They hadn't said anything in a minute or two. She rather wished he'd say something. Her eyes darted in his direction. He was walking with his hands in his pockets, his suit jacket pushed behind. She rather wished he'd take her hand.

He stopped at the bottom step, and faced her.

"This was nice, Catherine. Thank you." He looked at her with a pleasant smile. His hands were still in his pockets. "I hope I can see you again soon."

"I'd like that." Her voice was a little brighter than she would have liked. She tried to temper her enthusiasm. "When?"

"How about I'll take a look at my calendar and give you a call?"

"Okay. That sounds good."

He watched her a moment, his smile sobering. His eyes narrowed thoughtfully.

"May I ask you an awkward question?" he said.

Catherine blinked. "Please do."

"Are you averse to being touched?"

Catherine stared at him. "No one's ever asked me that question before."

"Let me rephrase that," he said, a little too quickly. His eyes had widened, and his brow had creased upward. For the first time all evening, he looked unsure of himself. "I apologize if that was insensitive. I've just heard that—"

"It wasn't insensitive at all. It was considerate. And you're right that some people on the autism spectrum are averse to being touched." She relaxed, shifting her weight to one hip. "Generally, I'm not, though. I'd say the opposite is true for me. I sometimes have trouble discerning boundaries. So I've been told," she added. She hesitated. There was more, but she felt it was too soon to say it. "I can be averse to touch if I'm stressed. Then all my senses go haywire, and I need quiet and personal space. But I think that's the case for everyone, isn't it?"

"Yes, I think that's true."

Her eyes searched his face. A gentle smile was on his lips, but she couldn't read the emotion behind it.

"I really appreciate your asking me that question," she said. She was surprised by the prickling of tears; she never cried. She ignored them, and they retreated. "I appreciate it more than you can know."

"And I appreciate your honesty. I just want you to be comfortable."

"Oh, I am. I'm very comfortable."

He watched her for a moment in silence. Then he leaned in toward her, took her arm in his hand, and kissed her cheek. A soft breath left her. So close...He was so close to her now. The pressure of his lips on her cheek felt so lovely; it sent a delightful tickle down the back of her neck and spine. His skin was freshly shaven, but not completely smooth, the promise of a five o'clock shadow beneath. Catherine closed her eyes and inhaled, chin lifted. By God, did he smell good. He smelled like—like freshness, and spice, and leather, and velvet—everything clean—and everything blue. If his smell were a color, it would definitely be blue. Blue like cobalt, or an evening sky. Her lips parted and drifted toward his. He pulled away, and she followed him, opening her eyes and catching herself as she nearly stumbled on top of him.

He straightened and smiled. "Goodnight, Catherine. I'll call you."

She nodded, turned, and walked up the steps. She fumbled a moment for her keys and stuck her house key in the lock, only to realize she had forgotten to lock her door again. She turned back to look at him one last time.

He stepped back a few paces and waved. She waved back shyly and stepped inside, closing the door behind.

CHAPTER THREE

$\mathcal{H}$ei took a seat at her little round kitchen table, sitting on one foot with the other propped on the bar between the chair's legs. She settled in, opened her laptop, and typed a few words. After a couple of seconds, her eyes widened.

"Yowza," she said. "Jackpot."

Catherine had been standing behind with her hands on the back of Hei's chair. She now slid into the seat beside her and leaned across the table on her elbow, her hand propping up her face.

She looked at the screen of Hei's laptop. Staring back at her was a picture of Wes's face.

"He worked for this law firm in Washington, DC," said Hei, clicking through the tabs on her browser. "Now he and his brother have this practice all to themselves."

Catherine lifted her coffee mug and gingerly took a sip. The mug was white, with a photograph of Hei, her husband, and their little boy and girl dressed in Christmas-colored clothing. It said "WORLD'S BEST MOMMY" in big green letters.

Hei's eyes darted upward from the screen. She raised one eyebrow. "Not bad."

The ghost of a grin touched one corner of Catherine's mouth. She took another sip of coffee and said nothing.

Hei took a few moments to read her screen, then sat back and relaxed cross-legged in her chair. She was wearing yoga pants and a silk bathrobe, and her dark hair had been swept hastily into a high, messy ponytail. She looked peaceful and pretty in this white, sunny room. It was a cozy, lived-in room, with cascading plants in painted clay pots and bulletin boards full of notices and children's artwork. It smelled of cooking and finger paint, chocolate chip cookies and freshly washed laundry. They sat in a cheerful breakfast nook with tall windows and hanging shelves of books and picture frames. It was almost a ritual, Hei and Catherine sitting at this table over coffee, exchanging advice and figuring out their lives. Catherine indulged in a deep, soothing breath, basking in the comfort.

Catherine and Hei had met in a candy shop ten years before. Catherine had been tossing around the idea of turning her chocolate-making hobby into a business. For years she had made chocolate informally for friends as gifts, and she had been hired for the occasional event. But working for her father was exhausting her, and the yearning to focus more on her passion had been tugging at her soul. She had visited this gourmet candy shop to poke around and absorb inspiration. That's when she had met Hei, who was six months pregnant at the time.

They were standing beside each other looking at the glass counter, which displayed golden trays of chocolate hearts, seashells, and swirl-topped truffles.

"Wow," Hei had said, staring wide-eyed. "It all looks good."

"Mmm," Catherine had agreed, her eyes wide with excitement. "I like these starfish, over here."

She had pointed at a plate of white chocolate starfish. Hei had leaned forward to take a closer look. She had straightened once more and sighed.

"I don't know what to choose," she had said. "It's all kind of the same to me."

"What do you need it for? Is it for something special?"

"My baby shower." Hei had instinctively rubbed her belly. Her expression of consternation had softened. "I'm helping my sister plan it. I told her I'd let her know what I liked."

"What do you like?"

"I like chocolate. That had always been enough."

Catherine had studied Hei and rubbed her lips together, thinking. "What do you like to do?"

Hei had been silent a moment, in contemplation. "Well, my husband and I like to go bird-watching."

"I can make bird eggs out of chocolate. I can make nests, too. I've never done it before, but I'm sure I could try. It would be easy. The eggs could be white chocolate. Do you like robins? I could color them robin's egg blue, with a natural red cabbage food dye, which would be better for the baby. All I'd need is an egg-shaped mold and some—" She had abruptly stopped. "Well, you get the idea."

Hei had been watching her with a smile. "You make chocolate?"

"It's more of a hobby, but yes."

"Is there any way I can see some of your work?"

"I have lots of experiments at my house. Do you want to come over?"

A half hour later, Hei and Catherine were standing over Catherine's grandmother's dining room table which, as her grandmother never entertained anymore, had been confiscated by Catherine for use as a work station.

"Such a pretty house," Hei had said, her head turning this way and that. Her eyes grazed over the dozens of peacock statuettes and figurines that sat on end tables, bookshelves, and windowsills. "I love your peacock collection."

"Those are my grandmother's. She loves peacocks. She's been collecting them for decades."

"They're beautiful. Does your grandmother live here?"

"Yes, this is her house. I live with her. I keep her company and drive her to her appointments, and make sure she's taken care of and safe. I help her stick to her routines, which are really important to her. I don't cook for her, though. I have a gift for chocolate, but I'm a terrible cook. A lady named Agatha comes a few times a week."

"That's such a sweet story. You and your grandmother must be very close."

"Yes, we get along well. People say we're a lot alike. It works out for both of us."

"My grandmother passed away years ago. I still miss her every day."

"I'm very sorry to hear that. I can imagine how sad it must be. I try to cherish every moment with mine."

Hei had turned her attention to the motley array of chocolate creations before her. "What's this?" she had asked, pointing.

"That's my feeble attempt at a chocolate castle. There's not enough detail. I'm going to try again next week."

"I think it's gorgeous," said Hei, bending over to get a closer look. She took a few steps forward, scrutinizing the objects one by one.

She had stood and faced Catherine. "I like the idea of the bird eggs and nests. Can you make fifty?"

And thus had begun Catherine's most cherished friendship.

"Should we look up the ex-girlfriend?" Hei was now asking, drawing Catherine back to reality.

"Oh," she said, taking a sip of her now-cold coffee. "Sure."

"What's her name again?"

"I'm not sure. She's Harold Beck's daughter. The journalist. I don't know the last name because she's married now."

Catherine was silent as Hei typed into her laptop. After a few moments, Hei turned the screen in Catherine's direction.

"Here she is," Hei said. "Her name is Meredith."

Catherine looked in silence at the face on the screen.

"She's pretty," said Hei. "Not as pretty as you, of course."

It was an official-looking picture, a headshot of some sort.

"Looks like a yearbook picture," added Hei, apparently reading her mind. "Looks like she was a teacher."

She was dark-haired, with a friendly looking face. She had wide green eyes and delicate, feminine features. She was smiling, and the smile looked genuine: it sparkled in her eyes.

"Didn't they just break up?" Hei was asking. "How could she be married already?"

Catherine shrugged. "I don't know."

"Hmm," Hei muttered, turning back to her laptop with a furrowed brow.

Hei was a developmental pediatrician at the children's hospital in Charlottesville. She was the one who had set in motion the chain of events that had led Catherine to the realization that she was neurodivergent.

"You're always apologizing for yourself," Hei had told her that day. She and Hei had been sitting in her kitchen, as they were now. Hei had been breastfeeding her brand new son, a half-moon shaped pillow wrapped around her waist for support. "You don't have to apologize. Just be yourself. You're a great person."

"I know that. I have trouble, though."

"Everyone has a little trouble."

"Yes, but I have *so* much trouble."

Hei had looked up from her baby and studied Catherine with thoughtful eyes. "What do you have trouble with?"

Catherine had shrugged. "Everything, I guess. I have trouble understanding what people are saying, like I can't read between the lines. I misinterpret them a lot, so I end up offending people. I also have no filters. People don't know what to make of it." She had shrugged again. "It's fine. I like myself. I guess I apologize to acknowledge that I'm different."

"Everyone's different, sweetie." Hei's face was tender, her smile bright and full of kindness. "I work with so many different children, a whole rainbow of personalities. Everyone has their place in this world."

"Hmm," Catherine had murmured, watching as Hei tucked her now sleeping son into her arms. "Say, Hei?"

"Hmm?"

"I'm wondering if you see any similarities."

"Similarities?"

"With any of the kids you see."

"Well," said Hei, settling in her chair, "I only work with kids. I'm definitely not qualified to give you any diagnosis. But I suppose I see some similarities."

"You do?" asked Catherine with interest, her brow raised. "Like what?"

"A lot of my kids have trouble interpreting social cues and knowing what to say. Natural back and forth can be more difficult for them. Many of them learn tools to guide them."

"Are they nervous around people? I'm so nervous around new people. Even old ones, really."

"Oh, sure. They can feel sensitive to overstimulation. They can feel panicked in crowds or places where there's too much noise. But of course, every child's different. There's no one rule that everyone follows. And of course this is true of many people, not just of the kids I see."

"What do you think about me?"

"Well, it's tough because you're an adult. If you were a child, I could give you a series of assessments. It's not so easy with adults. The answer is much more subjective." She hitched her baby over her shoulder now, to burp him. "But from what you're describing, and what I know of you, if you're asking me for my opinion, I'd suggest it might be worth looking into further."

Catherine had nodded, thinking. Her heart was beating more quickly, her senses alert. She had always felt she saw the world differently, that she was simultaneously seeing more than everyone around her, and less. She saw the world as a good place, containing countless details of beauty and joy. And yet people constantly seemed to be in on a secret, a secret of which she was not a part. She longed to learn more about herself. She was interested in hearing about how her brain worked, about how to tap into the best of herself, about why other people's behavior just didn't seem to make much sense.

Hei had referred her to another children's doctor in her hospital—most doctors in this specialty worked mainly with children, and many would not diagnose an adult—and the three of them had sat together to talk.

Hei and Dr. Brown had asked Catherine dozens of questions. They asked her about her childhood, her relationships with her family, her relationships with her friends, her fears, her hobbies, her strengths and weaknesses. They had wanted to know what school had been like for her, how frequently she dated, how she felt about her job, and what her hopes were for the future.

In the end, Dr. Brown had offered that Catherine was on the autism spectrum.

"It doesn't change anything about you," Dr. Brown had told her. "You're still the same person you were when you walked into this room."

"Oh, I know that," said Catherine. "Except now, I have a name for it."

Something about the doctor's words brought a sense of finality that Catherine had had to sit with for a while. Still, she hadn't expected the relief, the sense of feeling finally at home. Now that she had a name for it, she could understand herself better. She read as much as she could and learned to identify her challenges. She determined how to ease her way in the world without changing who she fundamentally was. And she grew more decided than ever that a hunch she'd developed was correct—that her grandmother was autistic, too.

"Look, I found his ex-wife."

Catherine snapped out of her reveries and refocused her eyes on her friend. "You did?"

Hei gestured toward her laptop screen. "I have the newspaper announcement right here. Her name is Claire. She's a surgeon. Here's her profile."

Hei clicked to a hospital's website. Dr. Claire Robinson, living in Washington, DC. Blond hair, square face, soft, feminine eyes.

"He knows how to pick 'em," said Hei. "You're an impressive bunch, all three of you."

"It's no surprise. He's very attractive, and nice."

"And all over the internet." Hei closed her laptop, then leaned back in her seat and picked up her mug of coffee. "So do you think he'll call you?"

They both jumped at the sound of Catherine's phone ringing. They stared at each other a moment. Then Catherine picked it up from where it lay on the table.

"It's him," she said, and answered it. "Hi, Wes."

"Hi there, Catherine. How are you this morning?"

"I'm great," she said, straightening in her chair, and smiling in spite of herself. "I'm at my friend's house. How are you?"

"Couldn't be better. I had a wonderful time last night. I'm getting ready for my weekly tennis game. But I wanted to call and thank you again."

"I should be thanking you. You picked me up and paid for the whole thing."

"That's nothing. It's my pleasure. In fact, I'd like to do it again, maybe next weekend. Does that work for you?"

"Definitely." Catherine looked at Hei and scrunched her

shoulders with glee. Hei's smile widened, and she gave Catherine a thumbs up. "Where should we go?"

"How would a concert do for you? The university's hosting a string quartet. Let's enjoy a nice dinner and then soak up some culture. What do you say?"

"I say that's perfect."

"Fine, then. I'll call you this week and we'll iron out the details. Okay?"

"Okay. Thank you, Wes. Thank you for calling."

"The pleasure's all mine. Talk soon."

"Okay. Have a good day."

She laid her phone on the table and lifted her shoulders a moment as a pleasant chill rolled through her.

"Catherine has a boyfriend," Hei whispered with a grin.

"Even I know one date doesn't make a boyfriend, Hei."

"I'm just saying," said Hei, standing. "I have a good feeling about this one." She turned toward the countertop and reached for the coffee pot, then sat back down and refilled their mugs.

Delicate fairy wings seemed to flutter in Catherine's belly as she recalled the heavenly scent of Wes as he had leaned in to kiss her cheek. She imagined his tall, lean form, his dapper appearance, his sparkling smile. His eloquent conversation, the confidence in every word and every gesture. She couldn't imagine him being her boyfriend. It was too much to ask for, really. And anyway, she was too old for boyfriends. Boyfriends were for prom dates and kids in their twenties. Catherine was thirty-six. Women her age had partners. They had husbands.

"I don't want to get my hopes up," she said, holding her fresh mug of steaming coffee to her nose and inhaling with a closed-eyed smile.

"Not all men are Brian."

"Or Colin. Or Dan."

"I think this one's special," said Hei. "I can see it in his eyes."

Catherine sighed softly but said nothing. She took a sip of her coffee, rejuvenated by its punchy bite—she always took her coffee black—and rubbed her lips together thoughtfully. Hei knew her history. She had walked her through a couple of breakups, though truth be told, most breakups weren't awful; Catherine hadn't grown too attached to any of them, and she never really expected them to stay. But even Hei couldn't truly understand.

Unlike some others on the spectrum, she didn't start dating later in life. She'd jumped in impetuously, like every other teenager, in her naiveté thinking it would be as easy as they all made it look. She'd soon found it was the furthest thing from easy. It was a jungle of cryptic innuendos and suggestive comments, of playing hard-to-get and knowing just the right moment to wear your heart on your sleeve. As a teenager, she couldn't even decipher her own feelings; how was she supposed to figure out everyone else's, when they weren't even saying what they meant?

She had only grown more frustrated as she grew older. Dating was exhausting. Flirtation felt like a labyrinth, and she had no compass or map. Already at a disadvantage having difficulty reading facial expressions and interpreting comments with hidden shades of meaning, she felt ill-equipped and lost. When dating, one was supposed to be coy. Catherine didn't know how to be coy. She didn't know how to say something she didn't mean, and make it mean what the other person wanted to hear. She didn't understand the point of subtlety or sarcasm. The idea that someone would want her to be dishonest made no sense. And yet her honesty and bluntness seemed to annoy, and even offend, her dates. Invariably they mistook blunt for rude or uncaring. Explaining that it was part of her diagnosis only alienated them further.

Dating required that she be constantly on her toes, disrupting her safe schedules when she was staunchly a creature of routine. And while she bravely forced herself to try new things, to go out on "in" days and attempt new activities, at the end of the night, she had nothing to show for it but a headache. In short, dating was a game of mind reading and hat tricks, and she never knew whether she was following the rules—that is, until they never called her again—or until they told her it wasn't her, it was them.

Catherine didn't cry at the end of relationships. She moved on with her life, and in a practical way she took the lessons she had learned and vowed to assimilate them into her general being. She didn't miss any of the men to whom she had said goodbye. She couldn't imagine incorporating any of them into her life. But it didn't mean the loss didn't sting. It didn't mean she never analyzed herself with a critical eye. She was only human, after all.

These days, Catherine found it easier to simply live her own life and be alone with her thoughts, which were actually quite delightful, full of chocolate and flowers and pretty vintage fabrics. She enjoyed being alone. She watched her classic movies with Dorothea snuggled in her lap. She made her chocolates, experimenting with colors and techniques and making people happy with creations just for them. She liked the quiet of early mornings with a cup of strong coffee. She liked aromatic bubble baths and cozy cotton nightgowns. She liked going for walks in her gardenia-scented neighborhood, coming home to a place all her own.

"I hope he kisses you for real this time," said Hei, scanning her laptop again, her coffee at her lips. "You need to tell him it's okay. You aren't some delicate flower."

That was one good thing about relationships, thought Catherine. She didn't mind the kisses. She didn't mind the sex. In fact she might have even gone so far as to acknowledge that she missed those things. But getting there was so difficult. One had to endure cat-and-mouse conversation and the reading of signals. Catherine had misinterpreted sexual advances on more than one occasion. She always seemed to think men were inviting more than they actually were, or not understanding that they were inviting anything at all. It required questions and explanations, which were neither spontaneous nor sexy. The experience was at best, frustrating, and at worst, humiliating.

Catherine sighed as she watched Hei stir some more sugar into her coffee. Before her date with Wes, she hadn't been out with anyone in over a year. She had accepted her celibacy, had even embraced it. Even after meeting him, she had been smart enough to avoid developing any expectations. Talking to Hei, however, she couldn't help feeling hopeful. She found herself feeling giddy and restless, and aggravated.

"You shouldn't encourage me," she reprimanded her friend, but with a smile. "If he breaks my heart, I can lay the blame at your feet."

"I'll take the risk."

She and Hei turned at the sound of shuffling footsteps. In walked a lanky pajama-clad boy, his dark hair mussed, his fingers rubbing the sleep from his eyes. He was followed by a little girl, her nightgown rumpled from sleep, her hand clutching a clearly much-loved blanket.

The little girl laughed and hopped toward Catherine. Catherine hugged her tight, rubbing her back. The boy approached Hei, who held out her arms for him.

"Good morning, sleepyhead," she said, her voice muffled as she kissed his head.

"Morning," he said. He smiled at Catherine. "Hi, Catherine."

"Hi, John."

"Would you like your breakfast?" asked Hei, standing.

"Yes, please."

Hei went to the pantry for a box of cereal. John and his sister Alison sat at the table, squinting in the light.

"How's school, John?" asked Catherine.

"It's good."

"You still like your teacher?"

"Yes."

"What's your favorite subject?"

"Art."

Catherine nodded. "Art is good. It was always my favorite,

too." She turned to Alison. "You have a ballerina on your night-gown. And look at her dress. It reminds me of a photograph of a famous ballerina. Do you want to see?"

Alison nodded eagerly, and Catherine punched a search into the browser on her phone.

"Here," she said, holding out her hand. "That's Harriet Hoctor. Look at her dress."

"She looks like an angel," Alison breathed.

"Yes, she does," Catherine agreed. "But she's not as angelic as you." She playfully tweaked Alison's nose, and Alison giggled.

John yawned and rested his elbow on the table, then laid his face in his hand.

"Are you all ready for that job this week?" Hei asked Catherine as she grabbed a spoon from a drawer and stuck it into a bowl. "The one with the roses?"

"Oh yeah," said John, perking up and holding his head straight. Fully awake now, he smiled. "Good luck with that job, Catherine."

"Thanks. I'm ready. It's all packed up and set to go." Catherine thought of the trays of coral-colored chocolate roses that now sat neatly packaged in her living room. She was to deliver them to a bridal show on Thursday. She'd also been asked to stick around and talk about her business with potential clients.

The four of them chatted a while longer, and the children scampered off to play. Catherine drained the rest of her coffee and stood, mug in hand.

"I guess I'm going to head out," she said as she pulled down the dishwasher door and stuck the mug up top. She straightened and pulled Hei into a one-armed hug. "Thanks for the pep talk, friend."

Hei hugged her back and kissed her cheek. "No problem. It was fun. I'm so excited for you," she told her, with a girlish grin. "I can't wait to see where this goes. Keep me posted."

CHAPTER FOUR

*C*atherine passed a happy week. She woke up each day at seven o'clock to the aroma of coffee wafting up from the automatic coffee maker in the kitchen. She slipped into her bathrobe, tied up her hair, and moseyed downstairs, where she replenished Dorothea's cat food and poured an oversized mug of steaming black coffee, which she drank as she perused the morning news online. She then showered, dressed, and checked her email, sometimes skimming backward through a few days' worth of unread messages, making sure she hadn't missed anything important: Catherine was diligent with her business account, but the inbox of her personal account, like her bedroom, was often disorganized and unruly.

She then, weather permitting, embarked on her morning walk. This was one of two walks she would take during the day, the other being in the late afternoon, before dinner. Her walks helped get her mind churning and her heart pumping; they awakened all her senses, the fragrance of the foliage and the warmth of the air filling her. In between, she worked tirelessly in her workshop, breaking only for lunch, which she ate in her dining room, a hastily thrown together plate of food squeezed between boxes of supplies and stacks of papers. Catherine ate a sandwich or hearty protein-topped salad for lunch. She had to, to make up for the morning—she never ate breakfast.

Her work time was quiet and meditative, a time of precise handwork and ritual in her dank but tidy and adequately lit basement workshop. She played classical music to inspire her mood. Her brushstrokes seemed to mimic the soft, sweeping gestures of the melodies. Catherine was not a musician, but she loved classical music. She preferred Brahms. She had a penchant for the violin.

She was a fast but thorough worker, with a sharp eye for detail and a perfectionist's painstaking persistence. The persistence was worth the time and effort. There was nothing like neat rows of flowers or sailboats or pleasingly round truffles, each completely identical in size, shape, and form. There was nothing like the bowls of brightly colored chocolate, just waiting to be applied to the blank slate of her creations.

Then there was making the chocolate itself. This was a task Catherine did not take lightly. She bought the beans from a fair trade vendor and had invested in only the cleanest, most efficient tools. She made her chocolate in large batches, for while the work was gratifying, it was tedious, and she didn't want to repeat the process more than was absolutely necessary. Of all the steps in the process of making chocolate, Catherine most liked the tempering, which made her chocolate smooth, shiny, evenly colored, and beautiful. It also served to keep it from turning grainy and crumbly, instead ensuring it melted in one's mouth and snapped off in one's hand with a satisfying pop. Of course, there was something to be said for the roasting of the beans, which filled her home with the heady, sensual aroma of warm chocolate.

Catherine liked the instinct involved with making chocolate. It was an art as well as a science, and she knew she had a knack for it.

She had finished a fresh batch of chocolate early in the week and had delivered her coral-colored roses to delighted applause and profuse compliments. It was time for her to relax.

Saturday night was her second date with Wes. Before that, though, on Friday, her father picked her up mid-afternoon so they could have lunch together.

They sat outside at a café in Charlottesville, on wrought iron chairs under a lavender-striped awning that shielded them from the sultry July sun. The sounds of bright chatter and of silverware clinking against porcelain plates imparted to the air a feel of cheerfulness and life.

"You did good this week, my girl," Fred told her as he unfolded his napkin and placed it on his lap. He smiled at her. "I saw the pictures you texted us. Those roses were out of sight, maybe your best work yet."

"Thanks, Dad."

"I mean it. They were gorgeous, just gorgeous. The level of detail was incredible. I'm proud of you, Catherine. You've made it. You're the cream of the crop."

"I'm so happy you liked them. That's nice of you to say."

The conversation halted as a waitress placed a glass of white wine at each place, took their orders, and hurried off.

"Here's to my girl," said Fred, raising his glass. Catherine lifted hers to meet it, and they clinked in cheers before settling into their chairs to wait for their meals.

"How was your week?" asked Catherine.

"My week was good. I talked Maeve down off the ledge. She was bent out of shape over office politics."

"She mentioned it the other day, but she was vague about it."

"It's nothing of note, my dear. Maeve will be okay. What it really boils down to is that she prefers state politics. After I retired, she was out of a job, and Wright has an office in Charlottesville. Obviously she wasn't going to work for Marks."

Catherine took a long, smooth sip of her wine, closed her eyes a moment, and smiled.

"Mom was very proud of you, too," said her father. "She showed the photos to all her friends at luncheon."

"That's so sweet of her. I'll have to thank her the next time I see her."

"Then you can thank her tonight. I'm supposed to ask you over for dinner. Can you come?"

"Okay." Catherine relaxed in her chair and took another small sip. "Sure, I can come over tonight. Thanks."

"The Bickharts' son is coming over, too. The one you went out with the other night."

Catherine choked on her wine and coughed into her hand, her face contorted as she gasped for breath.

"My goodness, are you okay?"

Catherine nodded and clutched her throat. "Wes is going to be there?" she asked, now dabbing the side of her mouth with her napkin.

"Yes." Her father was watching her curiously. "You don't have a problem with that, do you? I heard you two hit it off."

"We did. I don't have a problem with it. Why is he going over to your house for dinner?"

"He called me this afternoon. He wants to talk about running for my seat."

Catherine nodded and took a deep breath, her elbow resting on the table, her long fingers wrapped around the stem of her wine glass. "Ah, right. Yes, that makes sense."

Her father's face softened, a gentle smile curving his lips. "So how did it go the other night? Did you really hit it off?"

"Mmm," Catherine said, nodding vigorously as she took another sip of wine. She licked her lips, enjoying the last remnants of the sip. "Yes, we did. He's so nice, Dad. He's a real gentleman. And he's very handsome, too."

"I hear you're going out again tomorrow night. Is that true?"

"Yes, it's true. We're going to dinner and then a concert at the university. I'm so excited!"

"Well, this certainly is interesting." Her father raised his eyebrows at her. "I don't think I've ever seen you this excited about a man before."

"That's because I haven't been. But I'm excited about this one."

"Just watch yourself," said her father, reaching his hand across the table to pat hers. "I'd hate to see you get hurt if it didn't work out."

"Why wouldn't it work out? What do you mean?"

"It doesn't mean anything. It's just a gentle reminder not to get your hopes up."

The brightness in her face dimmed. "I'm allowed to be excited."

"Sure, you are. It is very exciting, certainly. I'm happy you're having such a good time. Try to enjoy it as long as you can."

Their meals arrived, and the discussion ended. Soon they were chatting blithely on this topic and that, from the success of a new local restaurant to controversial bills in the General Assembly.

"Has there been any news on the landfill?" asked Catherine.

"Nothing really, except that Munson's hired Rick Tremaine to represent him."

"Who's Rick Tremaine?"

"He's an attorney, of the slimy variety. A big proponent of dirty tricks. Knowing what I know of Munson, I'm not at all surprised."

"Maybe that's good, then. You know what they say: birds of a feather flock together. When people see that Munson's hired someone like that, they won't want to let him build his landfill."

"You're an idealist to the end, dear girl. I wish I had your faith in humanity."

The waiter returned with the bill, and her father paid it. They stood and walked from the patio, into the golden warmth of midafternoon.

They spent a couple of pleasant hours tooling around Charlottesville's Downtown Mall, with its red-brick pedestrian pathways and towering oak trees, poking in and out of shops and taking in the bustle of life. They stopped in a chocolate shop and emerged holding chocolate-covered orange peels wrapped in wax paper.

"Very good," observed Fred as they sat on a bench by a tall flowing fountain, "though it doesn't hold a candle to yours."

"They seed temper. I silk temper. It makes a subtle difference. It's a matter of personal preference."

"I think they could take a lesson from you, my dear."

Eventually they returned to the car and made their way to her parents' house. As they grew closer and closer, Catherine tried more and more desperately to act normal. Her heart was thumping, and she had begun sweating a little. She hadn't expected to see Wes today. She looked down at herself. She was thankful she had worn her 1950s Claire McCardell lavender and periwinkle floral sundress with the halter top and the gathered full circle skirt. When she wore vintage clothing, she usually stuck with the 1930s. But she liked 1950s dresses for those halter tops and full circle skirts. They were pretty. They showed off her shoulders, one of her best features. And they were well-suited for her lanky figure and too-long legs.

This dress was appropriate for an impromptu dinner with Wes. Yes. It was quite appropriate indeed.

Catherine exhaled slowly through puckered lips to calm herself. She could control, somewhat, the speeding of her heartbeat, but she couldn't help the tingling warmth that was rolling through her blood. As they pulled into her parents' driveway and parked beside Wes's immaculate black car, Catherine moved slowly, taking her time getting out of the car and lagging behind her father as they walked to the door.

Stepping inside, they were greeted by the soft light of the lamps in the hallway, casting the cream-colored paint and russet-patterned wallpaper in a warm glow. More vibrant light reached them from the living room, and it was into this room they wandered, finding Lois and Wes engaged in chipper conversation.

Wes stood as they entered the room.

"Good evening, sir," he announced jovially, with a wide smile. He turned to Catherine, and his smile gentled. "And good evening to you, Catherine," he said then, more softly.

Catherine smiled in return. His comfort and ease were infectious. He was wearing a gray suit, expertly tailored, a powder blue shirt, and striped tie. He approached and extended his arm, his other hand holding a drink, then brought his hand to her bare shoulder; delightful tingles prickled under his fingers. He leaned in to kiss her cheek, and she lifted her chin to let him, only realizing after he'd pulled away that she'd closed her eyes.

Wes and Catherine's father shook hands and instantly broke into robust conversation.

"I received an interesting call from your mother," said Fred. "She tells me you're tackling the Munson landfill debacle."

"News sure does travel fast," Wes laughed. "Indeed, the ball is rolling."

Lois had stood and walked toward the group, and was standing by Catherine's side. "Now, now, gentlemen. There's plenty of time for that. What do you say we sit down for dinner first?"

"My wife knows best, as usual. Come on, Wes, join us for dinner. We'll get down to brass tacks later, over scotch."

They moved to the dining room and sat down for dinner, the spacious room bathed in late afternoon light. Catherine was determined to make a good impression on Wes and perhaps was thinking too carefully about what to say; she said nothing for a good few minutes as conversation swirled around her, ultimately resigning herself to playing it safe by remaining silent, until Wes turned to her with a charming smile.

"So Catherine, tell me. What delicious projects have you been working on this week?"

Straightening, Catherine returned his smile, shyly. "Well, I finished my chocolate roses. They came out beautifully, and they were received very well. Would you like to see?"

She scrolled through the photos on her phone and held it before him.

"Simply incredible," he said. He took the phone from her hand and zoomed in to look more carefully. He studied the photo for some time before returning it. "What a gift you have. I'm speechless. And as anyone will tell you, I'm never speechless."

Everyone chuckled. Catherine blushed, turning her head as her eyelashes fluttered.

"What else is on your agenda?" he asked. "What will you be moving on to this week?"

"I have several new projects, actually. Some of them I've already started. I'm making some wedding favors, and also some specialty boxes for the new gift shop in town. I had a trial run last month. The boxes sold well, so the shop is going to have me make seasonal displays for them on a monthly basis. I'll be very busy. It's good. I'm happiest when I'm busy."

"That's fantastic," Wes said. "Congratulations are in order."

"That's our Catherine," said Lois, elbow on the table and her chin resting in her hand, looking at Catherine with a smile. "Bringing pretty things into the world, even at the ugliest of times."

"What a blessing," said Wes. "We most need artists during those times."

Fred nodded and tipped his glass. "Hear, hear."

They all clinked glasses.

"Wes, I hear you know Harold and Patricia," said Fred.

"Actually, I never had the pleasure of meeting them."

"Really?" Fred speared a tomato with his fork and regarded Wes with interest. "Harold's one of a kind. How did it happen that you never got to meet him?"

"Meredith left me before I had the chance. That is," Wes added quickly, "our relationship ended before then."

"Now, that's a shame."

Wes said nothing. A few moments of silence passed.

"Anyway, you were saying, Wes," said Fred, finishing off the last of his chicken and laying his knife and fork on his plate, "about the Munson ball rolling. Your mother's asked you to take on the case?"

"Ah, yes." Wes smiled and leaned back in his seat, stretching his arm around the back of Catherine's chair and assuming a relaxed position. "I've been enlisted to join the battle. And not a moment too soon. Munson's lawyer, Tremaine, paid a visit to the Department of General Services. Talks are in the works for the purchase of that land. Next we'll see them submit a rezoning request with the Planning Commission so Munson can build on it."

"Tremaine," grumbled Fred. "Do you know him, Wes?"

"I'm sorry to say I do. Rick and I go way back. We worked for the same firm, many years ago. I didn't like his methods."

"What do you mean?"

Wes's face darkened slightly. "To be frank, he was a bully. And a lecher. A female paralegal I worked closely with complained to me that he'd made some sexist jokes and inappropriate comments about her appearance. It turns out she wasn't the only one. A couple of women were concerned that he appeared to be following them around. I brought the issue to the management committee, and we ultimately expelled him from the firm."

"And what happened?"

"He was reprimanded by the state Bar Association and black-balled by other firms."

Fred nodded thoughtfully. "That explains it," he said. "He's got his own office now, handling small real estate closings and disputes between homeowners and kitchen remodelers. Hardly the big deals he was accustomed to."

"Hardly," agreed Wes. One corner of his mouth crooked upward. "I'm not his favorite person."

"I'd imagine not," said Lois, emphatically. "Have you run into him since?"

"Nothing to speak of. I moved north shortly after."

"Well," Fred said, leaning back in his chair, "it looks like you're about to meet again."

"It'll be interesting, that's for sure. And that's not the half of it."

"You mean there's more?"

"Oh, there's more. By sheer coincidence," said Wes, with a devilish grin, "Tremaine happens to be David Marks's brother-in-law."

Fred's mouth dropped open. "Now that I didn't know. That's outlandish."

"Not really. Ten to one it's exactly why Munson hired him."

"I'm sure," Fred boomed, with a cynical laugh. "And Marks will certainly benefit from this."

"That's nothing. Are you ready for this one? Marks has another brother-in-law."

"Who is it? Munson?"

"No, not Munson. William Carmichael. The contractor."

Lois gasped. Fred shook his head and crossed his arms. "Well, I'll be damned." He sat in contemplation for a couple of moments. "Looks like a little good old-fashioned nepotism. That was a sharp move, to look into the contractor of the Texas site."

Wes shrugged and smiled. "It seemed a promising place to start. Nothing surprises me anymore. Besides, I was already looking into the safety violations at the Texas site. I would have stumbled across the information eventually."

"So what's your next step?"

"Well, my mother's gathered a small group of local opposition. I'll take a trip to Texas to check out Munson's landfill and talk to the Texas Department of Environmental Protection, maybe look at the public records on the site. I'll also take out an ad in the *Herald* to make our case and let people know about the Planning

Commission hearing. In the meantime, my mother will be making some calls."

"To Munson?"

"To Munson, and also to the local news." He grinned again. "Munson's surely prepared to fight the Planning Commission and the state. But he had no idea he'd be up against my mother."

Catherine was struck with an idea. "What if we contact residents near the Texas site? They might be willing to help. Maybe they'll write some letters to the Planning Commission, telling them all the problems they've had since Munson built his landfill there."

"That's a lovely idea," said Fred, "and in an ideal world, it might do some good. But the Planning Commission won't care. Nor will the state, once it gets that far. Most elected officials don't give a flying fig about the opinion of anyone who isn't a constituent."

But Wes nodded, studying her. "No, I think there's something to that. If nothing else, those letters might inspire our own residents to be more vocal. Great idea, Catherine. Thank you."

Catherine smiled, her heart fluttering. "I can make some calls, too. I could call the Planning Commission."

"Excellent," said Wes. "Go for it. Let's give 'em hell."

After dinner, Fred and Wes made their way to Fred's study; Lois and Catherine took coffee out onto the patio, then walked through Lois's sprawling garden. In the lavender light of the oncoming dusk, butterflies rose and dipped into the azaleas, and unseen crickets called to each other through the gardenia-scented summer air. Lightning bugs made the garden seem to sparkle with magic, their soft glow floating in the air like fairies and then disappearing in a playful game of hide-and-go-seek.

"Your father seems very impressed with Wes," said Lois, fingering a stalk of jasmine as they strolled by. "I think he'll be a great candidate to try to defeat Marks."

"Yes, he's very smart and wonderful," said Catherine, brightening. "He seems like a natural politician."

Lois was watching her, her brow turned down thoughtfully. "You like him, don't you."

"Wouldn't you?" Catherine turned toward her mother for a moment, but her mother had faced forward once more. Catherine paused momentarily to pick a red rose from the bramble, then fiddled with its petals as she resumed walking. "I know what you're going to say. You're going to tell me not to get my hopes up, that you don't want me to get hurt. You think he's too good for me."

"What makes you think that?"

"Dad told me not to get my hopes up."

"And why do you interpret that as his thinking Wes is too good for you?"

"How else should I interpret it?"

Lois linked her arm through her daughter's, and patted her arm with her hand. "You're absolutely wrong about that. There is no man on this Earth who wouldn't be lucky to have you. You're a very special person. Your father and I simply worry about you."

"Yes, I'm quite aware."

"We're just looking out for you, you know."

Catherine sighed and leaned her head against her mother's. "I know."

"We only want you to be happy. We love you. We'd never say any man was too good for you. To be honest, Catherine, what you said hurt my feelings."

"I'm sorry," Catherine muttered, frowning. She tilted her head downward. Her hair fell to the sides of her face like curtains, hiding the fluttering of her eyelashes. "I didn't mean to hurt your feelings."

Lois patted Catherine's hand once more. "It's all right. I've learned to take your words with a grain of salt." She smiled. "It's one of the charms you inherited from your dear grandmother."

Catherine said nothing more. They walked a moment in silence before Lois spoke again.

"Truth be told, your father and I would love to see you with a man like Wes. We want to know you'll be taken care of."

"Do I need someone to take care of me?"

Her mother laughed lightheartedly. "Well, you know. Your chocolate is lovely. But a little hobby won't be able to sustain you."

Catherine walked a few paces before speaking. "It already is, though, really."

"Don't take it personally. It's a mother's job to worry." She squeezed her daughter's hand and sighed. "I worry about Maeve, too. For some reason I can't fathom, she seems intent on remaining single."

They walked back toward the house. Catherine stuck the rose stem through the strap of her dress. They were soon joined by Fred and Wes, who emerged from Fred's study boisterous and animated and smelling of cigars. They shook hands as they finished the last of their conversation, then faced forward as they caught up with the women. Wes gazed at Catherine and smiled.

"How was your chat?" asked Lois.

"Marvelous, very marvelous indeed," Fred answered, watching Wes with a cheerful grin. "Wes was made for this job. He'll be a fine candidate."

"It was fortunate that we met your parents, Wes," said Lois. "This couldn't have worked out any better."

"I'll say," said Wes, his face beaming. "A mentorship with our best state senator, and a divine evening with this lovely woman right here." He brought his hand to Catherine's back and rested it there for a moment, then retracted it and stuck both his hands into the pockets of his slacks. "What a week I'm having."

"Well, let's continue that momentum and meet again next week," said Fred, swiping his keys from a porcelain bowl on a small dark wood table. "In the meantime, Catherine, I'll drive you home. It's getting pretty late."

"Say, now, Senator, why don't you let me have the honor?" Wes turned to Catherine. "I'd be delighted to take you home, if you don't object."

She smiled. "I don't object at all. Thank you."

"That's good of you, Wes," said Fred, "as long as you don't mind."

"Nonsense. It would be my pleasure."

Fred held out his hand for another firm shake. "What a guy."

Catherine exchanged kisses with her parents, thanked them for dinner, and left on Wes's arm.

"Your parents seem like good people," he said, his hand on the back of her headrest, his body twisted toward her as he looked out the back windshield to pull out of the Sheerings' driveway. He glanced at her and smiled. "Not that I'm surprised."

"Yes, they're good people."

He pulled out onto the street and straightened, and they drove off toward Catherine's house.

"They certainly seem to like you," she added. "I don't think they have much hope for us, though."

Wes raised his eyebrows. "Why do you say that?"

"They know relationships generally don't work out for me." She stopped. "I'm sorry. I probably shouldn't have said that."

"No, it's good. I'm glad you did."

"They don't believe in my diagnosis," she said, surprised by her candidness; her parents, and her diagnosis, were the only topics she was reluctant to talk about. "My mother would prefer not to accept that it probably fit my grandmother, too."

Wes glanced at her with serious eyes. "Have they said as much?"

"Yes. They think I should work harder at fitting in with genteel society. They think it's my way of justifying my lifestyle."

"Does your lifestyle need justifying?"

"I quit my job in politics for something fun and fanciful. And I'm not married."

"Well, I'm not married, either," he told her with a smile. "Besides, you're very talented. And you're happy."

Neither said anything for some time. Finally, he turned to her.

"You know, when it comes to how you feel about yourself, the only one you have to listen to is you," he said gently, his eyes sincere. "You do know that, don't you?"

"I know that. It's hard sometimes."

"I know it is. But it's the truth."

He extended his arm and patted her shoulder. Catherine smiled, feeling giddy and glad.

"I'm very excited about our date tomorrow night," she said. "I've been looking forward to it all week."

"Well, I'm certainly glad to hear it. I am, too. Do you go to concerts often?"

"No, hardly ever. Who are they playing?"

"Brahms, I believe."

Catherine straightened and smiled. "How serendipitous. He's my favorite."

"Is that right?" He glanced at her with a smile. "I should try to impress you by telling you I knew all along, and take credit for it."

"No, then I'd wonder how you knew that and think you'd been spying on me."

Wes laughed. "All right, then. Serendipitous it is."

They arrived at Catherine's house. Wes pulled up to the curb and had barely put the car in park before Catherine turned to him and placed her hand on his thigh.

"Will you come inside, Wes? I'd like to give you something."

Wes's eyes darted from her face to his thigh.

Catherine frowned. "You don't want to? I think you'll really enjoy it. But we can wait until tomorrow night, I guess."

He stared at her, a crease forming between his brows.

Catherine's own brow creased. "I think you might have misunderstood me. What I mean is that I actually have something for you, a physical, tangible thing. A present."

A puff of air resembling a laugh escaped him. He glanced skyward, then grinned and shook his head. "I'll tell you, you certainly keep me on my toes."

"You're welcome." She smiled and patted his thigh. "Let's go inside, shall we?"

They climbed out of the car and made their way up the walkway toward the house. Catherine went through the motions of pretending to unlock her door even though she had remembered she'd left it unlocked. Once inside, she didn't turn on any lights; it was mercifully dark outside, and the darkness hid the mess. She closed the front door behind them. The glow of her porch light illuminated the entryway as it poured in through the three small windows at the top of her door; the contents of the rest of the house were mere indigo silhouettes.

"Wait here," she said, and left him standing in the doorway.

She returned a moment later holding a red box wrapped with a shiny gold ribbon.

"I made this for you," she said.

She held it out for him, and he took it.

"I'm touched," he said. "Shall I open it now?"

"Please do."

He gently pulled the end of the ribbon so it untied neatly in his fingers. He lifted the lid of the box, and the scent followed.

"Chocolate," he said. He stared at her. "Catherine, thank you."

She shrugged. "You said it was your favorite."

"I did. How kind of you to remember."

He was looking intently inside the eight-piece box she had put together for him a couple of days before. His brow creased. He met her gaze, his eyes wide. "It's the scales of justice." His lips puckered a little as if he were stifling a grin. "The scales of justice are on these chocolates."

"Yes. Neat, isn't it?"

"It's out of this world. How did you find a chocolate mold of the scales of justice?"

"Oh, I made the mold myself. I make most of my molds. It's not hard."

His expression had softened. "Is that right?"

"Sure."

She stopped.

Wes regarded her carefully. "Was there something else?"

"There's always something else." She shrugged. "It always seems like too much. I've gotten pretty good at keeping it to myself."

"Don't keep it to yourself. What were you going to say?"

Catherine took a breath. It really was nice that he was so interested. Masking took so much energy. It was a relief to relax a little.

"Well," she said, "you mix the silicone plastique, apply a thin layer to the object you want to mold—in this case scales—insert it into a thicker layer, and carve off the excess. You have to work quickly, though, to ensure it bonds properly. You don't have much time, not more than fifteen minutes. Then you wait an hour and peel the object out. And voilà. You have your mold."

"Where did you find the scales?"

"I, um, carved the scales into some wax," she stammered, feeling anxious over what he'd think about her spending so much time and going to such great lengths to make him these chocolates. Eager to continue making a good impression on Wes, during the week she'd found herself fretting over their next date, and she'd sensed the gray cloud of anxiety encroaching into her consciousness. In response, she'd thrown herself into her work with even more gusto than usual, working longer hours and turning up the volume as Brahms echoed through her workshop walls. Creating this special present for Wes had had the added benefit of occupying time that otherwise would have been spent worrying.

"What do you use to carve the wax?" he asked.

"There are special carvers and spatulas. You know." Her voice had grown quiet. She rubbed her lips together and folded her hands, and rocked back and forth on her feet. Her eyelashes fluttered, and she instinctively turned away.

"Are your eyelashes fluttering?"

"Of course they are." She sighed. "At least it's dark."

"I wish you wouldn't hide it. I told you how I feel about that fluttering."

They fluttered again. She didn't turn away, but she tucked her hair behind her ear, taking a deep breath.

"Do you think we could turn a light on, Catherine?"

"Oh, no," she said adamantly, alert now. "I wasn't expecting you. My place is a mess."

"I don't care if it's a mess. We all have our messes, don't we?"

She looked at him skeptically. "I don't believe you could possibly have a mess."

"Some messes can be easily concealed."

His tone was flippant, but his voice had changed; it sounded somehow quieter, more serious. Catherine was intrigued.

"So what is your mess?"

He took a breath and offered a little smile. "I'll tell you what. Let's not mar this pleasant evening with talk of my messes."

"It wouldn't mar the evening. I think it's good to get to know each other."

"That's not untrue."

He didn't say anything more, however. They stared at each other in silence.

She took the opportunity to look him over. Even in the darkness he was dashing and dapper, his eyes sultry and his form straight and tall. "Well, you most definitely do not look like you have a mess."

He laughed now, recovering his usual upbeat tone. "You haven't seen me partake of any messy activities yet." His smile turned crooked. "Like eating chocolate, for instance."

"We should change that."

"I concur."

He reached into the box for a chocolate just as she did, and their fingers bumped. He retracted his, letting her in first. She took a milk chocolate square between her fingers, lifted her hand, and slowly brought the chocolate to his lips.

His face turned serious. He opened his mouth, and she carefully placed it inside, the warmth of his breath on her skin.

He closed his lips and held her gaze as he pressed his teeth into it. His eyes half-closed, and his body visibly relaxed.

"Good lord," he moaned, chewing slowly.

"You like it?"

He said nothing, but nodded, eyes closed, as he chewed once more and swallowed. Catherine watched with delight as his chest rose and fell beneath his unbuttoned suit jacket. He opened his eyes and stared at her with wide, alert eyes. "What's in that chocolate?"

"Oh, you know," she said giddily, with a whole-body shrug, "just a little of this, a little of that."

"It's amazing. What texture. It's soft and creamy, but solid too. Pillowy, almost. Is that the right word?"

"Pillowy's a very good word."

He didn't say anything in response, and they stood still in the darkness for a couple of moments. She was reliving over and over again the vision of his mouth sucking on her chocolate, the way the angles of his jaw had moved this way and that. Her entire body felt restless and alive. The sound of her breath seemed to cut into the darkness.

"I want to thank you again for this, Catherine," he said,

replacing the lid, breaking the spell. "I don't know what to say. That you took the time to do this, that you put such heart into it." His hand found the small of her back, and he leaned in and kissed her cheek. "It means a lot to me."

Before he could pull away, she took his upper arm in her hand and held firm.

"You don't have to go yet," she said, her chin lifted, her voice deeper than she had expected.

She didn't remove her hand. He said nothing for several moments. He lifted his hand and brought it to the side of her face, and neatened a stray lock of hair around her temple. His fingertips brushed along the outline of her jaw, making her skin tingle. Molten heat crept through her, amassing low in her belly. She exhaled deeply and swallowed.

He smiled. "I really should go. I have a strict three-date rule."

"Does this count as a date?" she asked, her eyes hazy.

In response, he looked her in the eye and let his fingers trail downward toward her throat, resting them under her chin, tilting it further upward. With an inhalation of breath, she closed her eyes and waited, and then his lips were on hers. He took her jaw in the palm of his hand, his fingers burying into her hair; thus enveloped in him, she released a soft sigh.

He withdrew gently, but remained close, laying a final kiss on her lips.

"Do you think it does?" he whispered.

Her mind seemed clouded by a pleasant pink fog.

"You taste like chocolate," she replied.

He grinned slyly. "You're quite a firecracker. You know that?"

Dorothea slinked into the room. She rubbed herself against Wes's leg. Wes bent to pet her, then patted her side. Dorothea purred and sauntered off.

"Cats have a sixth sense about people," said Catherine. "Especially mine. She lived with my grandmother, who was very wise. She used to talk to Dorothea for hours on end. Dorothea's heard all sorts of stories and secrets. The fact that she likes you says a lot."

"Well, I'm certainly glad to hear I've made the cut."

Catherine shivered with delight as he now brought his hands to her waist, squeezed her hips, and held her close.

"So what do you think?" she asked. "Is this a date?"

He kissed her forehead and patted her hips. "What do you say we answer that question tomorrow night."

She nodded, accepted one last kiss with a sigh and a smile, and watched as he headed for the door.

"Goodnight, Catherine. And thank you," he told her, indicating the gold box by lifting it in the air, his voice sweet and silky as the chocolate in his hand. He waved once, winked, and left, closing the door behind.

CHAPTER FIVE

"The rest of the chocolate was spectacular," he said with a smile, unfolding a linen napkin after the waiter had delivered their wine and taken their orders. "I'd never had anything like it."

"I hadn't, either. I added a special ingredient I'd never tried before."

"Oh, is that right? What was it?"

"Cardamom."

He raised his eyebrows. "Cardamom. Really. What made you go with cardamom?"

"It's an aphrodisiac."

Wes nearly spit out his wine. He swallowed, brought his napkin to his lips, and muttered something inaudible.

"What did you say?"

He cleared his throat, replaced his napkin on his lap, and grinned at her. "I said a lesser woman wouldn't have admitted it."

"Oh." She smiled, settling in her chair. "I don't see a reason to hide it."

"And that, Catherine, is what I love most about you."

Catherine stifled a grin of her own. Her fingers fiddled with the stem of her wine glass.

"How do you eat chocolate?" she asked.

He said nothing for a moment. "Is there more than one way to eat chocolate?"

Catherine took a long swallow of her wine and licked her lips. "I mean, do you eat a lot of it at once, or do you space it out, and savor it?"

Wes laughed, and nodded once or twice in understanding. "Well, now. That's an interesting question."

"I think it says a lot about a person."

"It does." His smile softened. "Normally, I'm rather regimented, as a rule. I don't like to overdo it."

"But?"

He chuckled. "But I have to admit your chocolate didn't last long."

A pianist began playing an easy, mellow tune from a grand piano in the corner. Both Wes and Catherine turned to watch for a moment, then faced each other once more, with content smiles.

"How do you like being back here?" she asked. "How are you adjusting to the change?"

"I'm adjusting well," he said as he buttered a slice of warm crusty bread. "It's a very different kind of work for me, but the kind of law I practiced back in Washington offers a useful perspective. Years ago, before I moved to Washington, I was active with the Charlottesville Legal Aid Center and Virginia for Fair Housing. I have meetings set up for this upcoming week so I can get back in the game." He smiled. "It's nice to feel that I'm on the right side of the issues, finally."

"How wonderful." Catherine smiled. "And you're also helping to fight the landfill. That'll help a lot of people. J. J. Munson doesn't have a chance with you on the case."

Wes laughed good-naturedly. "Why, thank you. I certainly hope you're right."

A waiter brought their orders. They clinked glasses, smiled, and sipped their wine.

"When will you start campaigning? It's a little early yet, isn't it?"

"It's a little early, yes. But I can talk to your father and begin the necessary rounds of hobnobbing. I'll start campaigning seriously next year."

"That will be nice for you. You can settle down and establish yourself, then jump into it when your life has calmed down."

"I agree with you. In any case," he said, "I've started falling into a comfortable routine. It's good to be back home."

"Do you miss Washington at all?"

He swallowed a bite of bread. "There are aspects of it I miss. I enjoyed the city. I lived there for years, and I had friends there. But it was time for me to leave. I had too many memories in that house. I bought that house with my ex-wife."

"Why did you two divorce?"

"We were young when we got married. Well, not young," he added, with a smile. "But young for two professionals building challenging careers. We just drifted toward our own paths. Maybe we were too much alike."

"I can't relate to that at all. I never felt like I was anything like any of the men I dated."

"I wouldn't sweat it. I can't speak for anyone else, of course. But I've been with women like myself. And when I think about the failure of those relationships, I can only theorize that opposites must attract."

They chatted happily over their dinners, barely breaking to eat over bright, hearty conversation.

"What a nice time I'm having," said Catherine, after their dessert plates had been cleared. "I'm sad for this dinner to end."

"Despair not," he told her, pulling his wallet from the inside pocket of his jacket. "We're just getting started."

CATHERINE LOOKED about her at the grand auditorium, built in the warm, formal Jeffersonian style. She looked upward at the domed ceiling...around at the white pillars that lined the balconies and the still, silent, well-dressed guests...and before her, at the reproduction of Raphael's *School of Athens*, which loomed breathtakingly before them, dwarfing the members of the string quartet on stage. She looked to her left at Wes, his face in profile, his expression content but his eyes alert, relaxed but stalwart in his straight charcoal suit, crisp white shirt and gray tie, the picture of style and masculine elegance. Like the music, he was perfect in structure and composition. Taking a breath against the brisk staccato fluttering in her chest, she turned back to the music, feeling vibrant and alive.

Brahms. Catherine loved him so. Her heart seemed to beat with the music as the melody galloped steadily, then looped into a slower interlude and came back, jumpstarting her senses and propelling her forward with renewed fervor. The highest notes sang like the voices of angels, then drifted back downward like falling leaves, into a dramatic passage in a minor key.

The voices of angels, individual voices, asking questions and then answering them...Individual voices, following the same rhythm, a rhythm that built up and lifted up the whole, separate but dependent on each other, each moving on its own, but creating a song together, until its finish...

The beauty overwhelmed her, and she closed her eyes, letting her body sway a little, this way and that, allowing herself to be swept away. If the music were a color, it would definitely be silver. It was so romantic, the intermingling of melodies, like the intermingling of hearts...or souls...or breaths...or limbs...

She was compelled to open her eyes, and she looked at him. He was watching her, a smile on his lips and in his eyes. He leaned in toward her, imperceptibly, but just enough to be clear he felt it too. He took her hand and squeezed, and she squeezed his in return. She gazed at their joined hands with wonder and delight, this wordless connection, her slender wrist against the angular lines of his suit sleeve...the intermingling of fingers...

He stroked the top of her hand with his thumb, the soft motion so tender, and Catherine couldn't help but sigh aloud. She lifted her chin, letting the melody guide it; she tilted her head and closed her eyes again, the music painted on her face, the fullness of her heart reflected in the parting of her lips.

SHE WAS MOVING AGAIN to the music, this time, on a dance floor.

She was wearing a 1930s ankle-length cream satin dress with a deep plunging neckline and sleeveless bodice, rhinestones sparkling in floral patterns on the bust and skirt. It was the perfect complement to his charcoal suit and gray tie, and Catherine indulged in peeking at their reflection as often as she could as he drifted with her past an ornately framed mirror or dipped her backward, offering her a splendid view of the glass-paneled ceiling. She loved the way her long limbs looked against his, their hands clasped and their arms outstretched, their hips nearly touching as their legs matched each other's movements with fluid grace.

"You're very good," he told her, with a quick lift of his eyebrows and a devilishly handsome grin. "I'm very impressed."

"I'm actually quite a good dancer. I have good coordination on the dance floor."

She laughed as he dipped her low to the ground, her hair nearly sweeping the floor. He pulled her up swiftly, spinning her around, pressing her close once more.

She continued. "I know you wouldn't think it, because I'm so uncoordinated everywhere else."

"You have yet to prove that to me. You keep saying that, but I just haven't found it to be true."

He held his arm forward and stepped back to twirl her. She obliged, feeling the satin around her calves lift and float outward, the fitted fabric around her waist tightening around her straightened form.

They met once again in an easy embrace, Wes guiding her in a smooth, swaying rhythm.

"I generally don't like a lot of attention," she said. "The one time I don't seem to mind it is when I'm dancing. And when I'm wearing vintage dresses, of course."

"Well, you do both splendidly."

She smiled. "Thank you. You're a very good dancer, yourself." Her blood tingled pleasantly as his hand once again found her lower back.

"Thank you. I've worked pretty hard at it."

"It's paid off. You're the best dancer in this room."

"Now, if that's true, it's only because my partner makes me so."

The music slowed, and the dancers' movements turned quieter and more intimate. Wes and Catherine slowed, too, rocking together in graceful, lilting motions.

"I have to tell you, Catherine," he said silkily into her ear, pressing her close. "The way you feel through this dress." He gripped her a little with his fingertips, and the cool satin massaged her skin. "Good lord. I can't even keep my head on straight."

Catherine melted into him, her breath deepening as he rubbed his hand from her back to her waist. Her eyes closed, and she smiled, letting him nuzzle his cheek against hers.

"How do I feel?" she whispered.

"Like heaven."

She slinked her arms over his chest and wrapped them around his neck, taking the back of his head in her hand.

She looked up at him dreamily.

"It must be because that's where I am."

They embraced and continued dancing, wrapped in each other, the room swirling with their movements. Catherine closed her eyes and breathed it in, the most glorious night of her life. Her arms around him, supported by his hands, hips pressed to his and her head tilted upward as they exchanged sweet nothings, she felt like a princess—special, beautiful, the most important woman in the room. Her senses alive and full of romance, she registered the sparkling white lights and the glowing flames of candles, the warmth of the wood-paneled walls and the shine on the black and white checkered floor—but her eyes were focused on him, the confidence in his movements; his handsome face and his warm, perfect smile; the kindness in his eyes and the way his attention never left her, making her feel desired, valuable, loved. It was breathtaking and magical, the loveliest of dreams.

The song ended, and they clapped for the band. Then they walked off the dance floor toward the bar, her hand on his arm, to refresh themselves with a drink.

"Whiskey neat for me, sir, and another Chardonnay for my gorgeous date," Wes cheerfully told the bartender. He turned to Catherine. "Is that right? Or would you like something else?"

"No, that's fine. Thank you." She wasn't really paying attention —she had caught sight of a treasure that had absorbed all her attention. She pointed toward the back of the bar. "Is that real?" she asked, turning to the bartender. "Is that lamp real?"

The bartender stared at her blankly. "Is it real?" One corner of his mouth turned upward. "Yeah, I'm pretty sure it's a real lamp."

"I mean is it a real Jean Perzel. It sure looks like it. Do you know if it's real?"

"I have no idea."

She paused, eyes sparkling with wonder, as the bartender handed her and Wes their drinks. She stepped to the side to let in the couple behind them. Wes moved along with her, slinking his arm around her back.

"Which lamp are we looking at?" he asked her, leaning in close. "That one? The sconce?"

"Yes." She clasped her hands together. It definitely was real. She'd seen one just like it on an auction site. The sconce had clean lines and featured geometric shapes, interspersing metal and frosted glass to create a sleek and elegant look. "Isn't it beautiful?"

"It is." He was rubbing her back. She pressed into his hand, enjoying a little shiver of excitement. "Who's Jean Perzel?"

"He was a French designer and a prominent figure in the Art Deco movement. He was born into a glassworking family and ultimately founded his own company, which came to be known for modern design. His company still exists. They make lighting fixtures based on his original designs."

"Is this piece representative of his work? How did you know it was his?"

"There's a certain aesthetic, one of simultaneous simplicity and functionality. His work often used frosted glass to diffuse light, which created a kind of atmospheric glow." She leaned over the bar to get a closer look, and pointed. "There's such craftsmanship and attention to detail. If you look at—"

But her arm had swept too far, and it knocked her glass of wine in the direction of the woman beside her. Everyone in the vicinity jumped as the glass tipped over, spilling wine across the bar and onto the floor.

The woman's partner threw his hands in the air and glared at her. "What the fuck are you doing?"

"Oh my goodness, I'm so sorry." Eyelashes fluttering, Catherine snatched a napkin from the bar and attempted to contain the spill. "I'm just so sorry."

"Did she get you?" the man was asking his date. He looked her over with a frown, then turned to Catherine. "If her dress is stained, you're paying for the cleaning."

"Forget it, Dave," the woman muttered. "She didn't get me. It's fine."

"No, it's not fine. I don't know what the hell's the matter with some people."

Wes had swiped a pile of towels from the bar and by this time had nearly contained the spill. At the man's words, he halted.

"Hey," he said, his eyes hard. "It was an accident. There's no need for all that."

"Maybe you should teach your date how to act in public."

"That's enough. I think you need to lay off the drink."

The woman was nudging her intoxicated partner, attempting to make him walk away. "Stop it, Dave. Let it go."

But Dave evidently was under the influence of the puffed-up bravado alcohol often instills in men. "You're lucky you didn't ruin my wife's dress," he spat at Catherine. "Pay attention next time, instead of gawking over a goddamn lamp. I mean, it's a lamp. Who cares."

Wes lifted his hands and lowered them slowly in the direction of the floor, suggesting Dave calm down. "Hey, relax, all right? There's nothing wrong with being passionate. May we all have something to care so deeply about."

Dave snorted. "Yeah, good luck with that, buddy. She seems like a headache, if you ask me."

Wes's face iced over. He faced the man fully and pointed his finger. "I don't know who you think you are, but you are way out of line," he said firmly, with a low, clipped tone. "I didn't ask you. Now back off."

Dave grumbled and allowed his wife to push him quickly away. Catherine felt a tap on her shoulder: it was the bartender.

He held out a fresh glass of wine, and smiled. "On the house."

Catherine thanked him shyly, then stumbled dazedly away as Wes took her shoulder in his hand and drew her from the crowd, leading her away, stopping a few feet down near an alcove in the wall.

He looked her in the eye, his expression grave.

"Don't you ever let anyone tell you you're not good enough," he said. "Don't let anyone tell you who to be. You stay just the way you are, and love yourself for it. Do you understand?"

Catherine nodded, dumbstruck.

He straightened, and his expression became less severe. He rubbed her shoulder, then her arm, and then stroked the side of her face with his fingers. "I want you to know how stunning you are, Catherine. Inside and out."

Catherine's jaw clenched as she struggled to fight back tears. What was wrong with her lately?

His face softened further, and finally he grinned. "Now, would you please do me the honor of joining me on the dance floor? I'm with the most beautiful woman in the room, and I'd like to show off a little."

She couldn't help but smile in return. She watched as he took her drink from her hand and placed it next to his on a nearby table. Then she let him lead her back onto the dance floor, where he swept her around the room and swept her off her feet, making the world around them disappear, and replacing it with a fairytale.

CATHERINE HAD CLEANED her house that day. She had neatened piles and relocated them to out of the way corners, she had shoved boxes of supplies into closets, she had washed all the dirty dishes and put them away, and she had picked up all the laundry and random accumulated items on her bedroom floor. It wasn't perfect, certainly, but it would do—just in case. As Wes drove her home that night she suppressed a little grin. Maeve had finally given her some good advice.

They arrived at her house. Wes strode to the passenger's side to help her out of the car. The night was chilly, and she had no jacket or shawl. Goosebumps bristled from underneath her satin dress. Noticing her shiver, he removed his suit jacket and wrapped it around her shoulders. It was warm from his body, and it smelled of his cologne. A molten feeling gathered deep in her core, and she exhaled slowly, feeling weak in the knees.

They walked up the steps to her door and faced each other. Catherine retrieved her keys from her purse, then turned her head and inhaled with her eyes closed.

"Your jacket smells so lovely," she said. "Do I have to give it back?"

Wes laughed. "For you, I'd gladly give it up. Though it's not in the 1930s style, I'm afraid."

"I don't care."

They were silent a moment, smiling at each other.

She decided to be bold.

"How about," she began shakily, heart pounding—even she couldn't believe she was saying this, "I keep it a little longer—until, say—tomorrow morning?"

His smile dimmed; in its place, a subtle grin formed. He reached for her face and stroked the underside of her chin, then took a lock of hair and twirled it around his fingers.

"Are you asking me to stay?"

She held her breath as his fingers brushed over her neck and across her collarbone.

"Yes," she said, through half-closed eyes. "It's our third date, isn't it?"

She watched as his face turned grave; she shivered with anticipation as his fingers made their way over her shoulder to her side, where they traced the curve of her breast, his thumb toying with her nipple through the satin until it was firm and taut. The air left her lungs in a slow, deep breath.

He leaned toward her; her face was now at the base of his throat, and her eyes drifted shut. Then his breath was on her neck, his lips brushing the sensitive skin behind her ear. She tilted her head to the side, her lips parted with rushed breaths.

"My jacket and I would love to stay," he told her, his soft kisses sending fire through her veins. His hand drifted toward hers, where he gently pried the keys from her fingers. "So what do you say we open the door."

CATHERINE RUBBED his back with one hand and his arm with the other as he fumbled a moment with the lock. Her blood was racing; her nerves were on fire. She couldn't believe this was actually going to happen. She bit her bottom lip to avoid smiling too widely.

He turned to her.

"Catherine, your door was unlocked."

"It's fine."

"Is there a chance someone is in your house?"

"I just forgot to lock it again. It's fine."

"I'm concerned about this. You really—"

"I will, I will." She nudged his back to hurry him in.

The door flew open, and they pushed inside, where he slammed the door shut with his foot. They met swiftly in a firm, heady kiss, her hands pressed to his shoulders and his fingers gripping her hips through her dress. She shrugged out of his jacket, letting it fall to the floor, and they stumbled up the stairs and down the hall, arms and legs entangled, lips locked.

Once in her room, they fell together onto the bed, their silhouettes illuminated in the dark by silver moonlight that streamed in through the open blinds. Catherine lifted her knee, letting him fall into place on top of her; her chin pointing to the ceiling as his lips caressed her throat, she wrapped her arms around his back, relishing the pressure of his hard body on hers.

His kisses trailed down her neck and across her chest. "This dress," he groaned, his fingers pulling the front of her dress and delicate silk bra from the center, exposing the soft fullness of her breast. "This goddamn dress. It's been driving me wild."

"That's the idea," she told him, breathing hard, watching him through half-closed eyes over the rising and falling of her chest. "Just don't rip it, please."

He kissed his way back up, and grinned at her. "I'll be gentle with your dress, sweetheart," he said silkily, laying a kiss on her nose, and in response to this little pet name Catherine's heart did a dramatic flipflop. His eyes darkened sensually. "Just tell me how to take it off."

A carnal thrill stirred at the gentle command in his voice. "Zipper's in the back," she breathed, then paused to catch her breath. His hands. One was on her face while the other now stroked her thigh, cupping her backside in his fingers. "You called me 'sweetheart,'" she managed to squeak.

"I did," he murmured into her neck as his hand slid upward toward her shoulders. His fingers found the zipper, and she propped herself onto her elbows to give him room to pull it down. She felt the delicate fabric falling from her back, and exhaled against the anticipatory fluttering of her heart. "Is that okay?"

"I love it. You should do it again."

Catherine felt him grin. It tickled her neck; she smiled and tilted her head into his.

"Will do," he said. "Go ahead and lie back down."

"Your voice sounds really sexy when you tell me what to do."

"Good. Now lie back down so I can take off this dress."

She fell back to the bed and watched him, excited to find out what he'd do next.

He took the sleeves of her dress in his hands, and pulled. Slowly the cool satin brushed over her shoulders, caressing her skin.

"Now lift your arms for me."

In a breathless daze, she lifted her arms. "I've never been with someone so forthright in bed," she whispered as he slipped the bodice downward over her chest. "It's very refreshing. I try to be forthright, too, but it's hard. There's one thing, people sometimes have trouble understanding, because it's difficult for me to—*oh*," she gasped, then arched her back as he took her nipple in his mouth, circling and pressing until every nerve in her body pulsed from the touch of his tongue and lips. He tugged a little with his teeth, and she moaned aloud.

All thoughts now evaporated. Half-clothed and exposed, her long hair sprawled beneath her, she brought her hands above her head. He took her in his hands and traced the curves of her waist and breasts. She sighed at the feel of his skin on hers, the intimacy of his touch. She wriggled beneath him on the bed, enjoying the coolness of the sheets on the bare skin of her back. His hands now cupping her face, his fingers in her hair, his eyes took her in, turning hazy and dark. She felt sensual and erotic, like a goddess.

His lips were closed, but the hardness of his breathing was evident in the heaving of his chest beneath his shirt. She brought her fingers to the collar and pulled him into a kiss, then pulled the shirt from the waist of his pants. He swiftly undid the buttons and threw the shirt to the floor. Catherine swallowed and sighed inside. He was so perfect, strongly built and trim, his chest firm and his waist slender, his entire body sleek and straight. She touched her fingertips to the tight, rounded muscles of his arms, then ran her hands up and down his back. He slid his fingers through her hair, now pressing his bare chest to hers, and she emitted a soft, shaky sigh.

His lips found hers once more. His hand was behind her throat, supporting her head; the other was at her leg, pulling her dress up in satiny bunches. With the hem of the dress at her waist, he hooked his finger into her scant lace panties and lowered them over her thighs and knees until she kicked them off with her feet. His hand now slid between her legs, where he began teasing her with his fingers, kneading and stroking while his thumb massaged her most sensitive flesh. She cried out, eyes closed, as tight sensation surged into fiery ripples through her blood. She writhed in time beneath him, her voice high and desperate, and leaving her with each breath.

Dorothea leaped over the edge of the bed, making them start. Catherine's eyes widened as the cat climbed onto Wes's back and settled into a comfortable ball, resting her head between his shoulders.

"Hey there, Dorothea," he said, twisting his head back and then reaching behind himself to pat her on her haunches. "Nothing personal, but this really isn't a good time."

"Dorothea, go!" Catherine ordered desperately with a wave of her hand, heart pounding. The cat scuttled off the bed and out the door. "I love you, though!" she called after her, watching her tail end vanish around the corner.

Wes's face wore an amused grin. He turned back to face her, his expression sobering and his eyes darkening.

"Now, where were we?"

"You were doing wonderful things with your fingers, and I was contemplating how to suggest you could begin at any time without scaring you off with my boldness."

His eyebrows rose and his lips curled upward, his face taking on the look of wicked delight. "You can't scare me with boldness, sweetheart," he responded, his voice raspy and deep. He let his finger trail along the side of her face, alighting a glowing tingle in all her most delicate places. "The bolder, the better."

Humiliating visions of past dalliances flashed before her eyes, dampening her excitement. "You might think it's too much."

This made him laugh. "It won't be too much. I promise you. More is more."

"You'd be surprised."

"Prove it to me."

Her hesitation melted as his hand tugged her dress upward, his fingers brushing against the bare skin of her waist. She helped him slip it over her chest and head and lay there aching, his warm breath on her lips and his fresh, cool scent in her lungs.

He looked at her, dress in hand, the sparkle of humor in his eyes.

"Shall I hang this up, or toss it?"

"Toss the darn thing, for God's sake, toss it."

He dropped it to the floor and went for the button of his slacks. Catherine watched eagerly as he pulled them off in a flash, revealing a pair of gray silk boxers beneath. She was delighted: it was quintessentially, unequivocally him.

"Of course you do."

"Pardon?"

"Nothing," she blurted, and pulled him into a kiss.

Catherine ran her hands over the silk and smiled with glee. It was smooth and supple, blissfully fine between his muscles and her hands, between the soft skin of her midriff and his hard, rigid fullness. She gripped him from behind, eliciting a low grunt from his throat. She gripped him tighter, the perfect roundness of him; he groaned again, and laughed.

She paused a moment, self-conscious. "Is that too hard?"

"Jesus Christ, no."

As if to prove it, he took her face in his hands and kissed her firmly, his fingers gripping the back of her head and his thumb pressing her temple. She tilted her head to deepen the kiss, sliding her fingers under the waistband of his boxers; he wriggled out of them and kicked them to the floor. She grinned, encouraged by his voraciousness. There was nothing between them now, nothing to do but wait for him. She lifted her hips to urge him forward, relishing the delicious bliss of his skin on hers.

Her eyes half-closed as he lay sultry kisses on her neck and settled neatly between her thighs, her body bracing in delicious anticipation as he pressed to her tender aching center; her finger-tips curled into his back as he entered her in one swift motion, releasing his breath with a low groan, his tense body gliding forward and then relaxing into a low, smooth rhythm. She enclosed him further in her arms, squeezing him tight, letting herself be moved with his movements. She constricted her arms, greedily absorbing the taut, firm feel of his back, and pressed her thighs into his hips, bringing her knees closer together, wondering if she should say what she wanted to say. He broke their kiss and gazed at her, his eyes searching, seeming to read her thoughts.

"You're trying to tell me something," he whispered, his fingers cradling her neck and his thumb brushing her lips. "Just tell me."

Her lips parted as his thumb trailed across her cheek. "Tighter," she whispered shakily. "It might help if you hold me tighter."

He brought his arm down and slid his hand between her shoulder and the bed, pressing her close. "Is that tight enough?"

"You could go even tighter." She swallowed. "If you can."

"I think I can go tighter," he assured her, and a warm quiver rolled through her at the playful lilt in his tone. "Let's see..." He brought his hand lower, until it was under her backside. "How is that?" he asked her, grasping her hard and crushing her hips to his, filling her in her loveliest, most unreachable places. "Is it tight enough now?"

"Yes," she gasped, consumed by sensation, her body seeming to scream with sweet relief. "Yes, yes, oh God, like that."

Finally, she sighed, in satisfying bliss; finally, completion she had sought but could not find. *This. This is what it's supposed to be.* Her muscles relaxed and loosened under the dizzying spell of his rhythm. Her eyes fluttered shut; all thoughts seemed to dissipate in a beautiful, fuzzy pink dream. He seemed to sense where to press and squeeze her, when she needed him to augment his pace, and with the deep pressure of his body on hers, and the tight, firm grip of his hands, every nerve felt calm and focused, every sense in perfect order. She lay back, euphoria overcoming her, and let herself move with his movements, unyielding but graceful, like the music, sure and steady, like his dancing. She held him more desperately as tension began building, tight like a rosebud that hasn't yet bloomed; her breath caught as all at once, the blossom burst open, luscious tendrils of rapture spilling from the innermost center of her. She let her voice ring uncontrolled. The room was spinning, her body flying—she lost all self-control, and it was glorious.

Through a delirious haze she relished his hands, which were clutching her hips and shoulders, then clenching her hair with his fingers; his movements quickened, his breath deepened, and his body shuddered and relaxed into slower, lighter glides until he finally was still. For some time, they lay pressed together, warm and panting, silent as their heartbeats slowed. Finally he withdrew his face from the side of her neck, and kissed her gently with soft lips, his fingers raking back her hair from her sweat-drenched hairline. She felt as tranquil and balanced as she ever had in her life. As he lifted his face and looked at her, his eyes warm and alive, she smiled placidly up at him, completely and totally besotted.

She turned to her side as he shifted from on top of her, and they embraced comfortably, limbs entangling and faces nuzzling.

"That was heavenly," she breathed.

He took a deep, calming breath and exhaled slowly, rubbing her lower back. "Damn sure was."

"It was perfect, just perfect. Like a rosebud."

He paused, and his eyes searched hers. "A rosebud?"

"Yes, like a beautiful, pert little rosebud, exploding into a radiant flower."

He studied her a moment, then closed his eyes and kissed her again, lingering long enough for her to wrap her arm around his neck and hold the back of his head.

He pulled back and settled his head into the pillow, now smoothing back her hair with an unbearably handsome smile. "What a charming thing to say. A rosebud, huh?"

"Roses are my favorite."

"Interesting."

She brought her hand forward and stroked his chest, admiring its angular strength.

"You should know," she said, "that's never happened to me before. Not with a partner."

"What's that?"

"I'd never reached orgasm with any partner. You're the first."

He raised his eyebrows and grinned slyly. "I'm happy to oblige." His expression turned serious then. "I'm sorry you had to wait this long. Why do you think that is?"

She shrugged and exhaled. "Lots of reasons. I felt self-conscious. The sweat bothered me. And I was always so distracted by everything in the room."

"And that didn't bother you tonight?"

She smiled and caressed the side of his face with her fingertips. "Thank you for pressing so tight. I had a feeling that would do the trick. And thank you for making me feel like I could ask."

"The pleasure's all mine."

"I'm serious." She cradled his jaw in her palm and looked deep into his eyes. "I've never felt like I could ask. There was already so much pressure." She swallowed. "It's hard to explain."

His eyes warmed; he brought his fingers to her face and tenderly brushed her lips. "No need to explain, sweetheart. You should always feel free to ask. I want you to ask."

He shifted again until he was on his back, and stretched his arm out to pull her in close. She snuggled into his side, resting her head in the nook of his shoulder and spreading her hand around the side of his waist.

"Wes?" she said tentatively.

"Yes, sweetheart?"

She ran her fingertip up and down the line in the center of his chest.

"You're the sexiest man I've ever been with," she said. "You're the sexiest man I've ever seen."

She felt him take a deep breath and watched as his chest rose and fell. After a few moments had passed, his fingers found the underside of her chin and gently tucked her face upward. She watched dreamily as he gazed at her in silence.

"Thank you for saying that. I'm flattered, sweetheart." He smiled then, but the smile was somber. "And thank you for being a spot of sunshine. The world seems a nicer place now that you're in it."

He took her in a kiss, and the world disappeared. *Don't ever leave me, please*, she thought, satisfied and content, before he pulled her in close, nestled his face in her hair, and then fell asleep with her enclosed securely in his arms, not letting go until morning.

CHAPTER SIX

*W*es left early the next morning to meet his brother for their weekly tennis game, then picked her up and took her to lunch that afternoon, a dozen red roses in hand.

She gasped and took the roses from his outstretched hand, and hugged them close, inhaling with closed eyes and a happy smile.

"My favorite," she said, opening her eyes and taking his hand. "How thoughtful. Ooh, and look. A rosebud."

"How risqué," he said slyly, and pressed her close for a kiss.

The two spent the rest of the day together, enjoying lunch and seeing a movie, then going back to Wes's house to relax over dinner and wine. Catherine with effort contained her excitement. She'd been imagining the previous night all afternoon, and had felt tingly and warm, and impatient. When he held her hand, her body remembered the firmness of his grip; when he kissed her cheek, she could taste his breath on her lips. The need was almost oppressive. She was happy to finally be alone with him again.

Wes lived in Wellbourne, right outside Charlottesville, in a large, charming Tudor-style brick house with steep pitched roofs, multi-paned windows, and half-timber second story framing. It was enclosed by a white picket fence and surrounded by sprawling foliage. Catherine hadn't expected anything less. Still, she was impressed. As they walked together toward the arched recessed doorway, which housed a heavy mahogany door with an ornate iron knocker, she had to acknowledge its splendor.

"This house," she murmured, peeking inside as he swung the door open. "It's just spectacular."

"Thank you," he said, his hand on her back, leading her inside. "I have to admit, I do love it."

Catherine placed her purse on a little table in the entryway and looked around at the interior of the house, the shining herringbone hardwood floors and heavy antique furniture, the exposed beams and handsome wood paneling. It was elegantly decorated with warmly colored drapes, tasteful fine art, and wing-back chairs in luxurious fabrics. It was cozy, sophisticated, expansive, and immaculate.

"How did you furnish this so quickly?" she asked. "You've only been back a few weeks."

"I had to hire a decorator. I bought this house months ago. He started working long before I moved down here."

She let her fingers graze the mahogany banister. "Why don't you give me the tour."

He took her upstairs and showed her the bedrooms. Catherine admired his four-poster bed and pristine white sheets and pillows, all perched upon a Persian rug-covered floor. Her eyes scanned the room, taking in the pale mint paint and more delicate furniture, the golden glow of sunset pouring in through white blinds and crisp linen curtains. She imagined lying beneath him in the bed, the sheets crumpled and askance. Heat flushed her skin. She turned to him.

"Your bed looks comfortable."

The corners of his lips rose subtly. "It is."

She'd been hoping he'd take her hint. She didn't often drop hints; subtlety was not one of her strengths. She'd been impressed by her attempt and was disappointed that it hadn't seemed to work. The exciting flurry of her heart faded.

"Come on downstairs, sweetheart," he said, patting her hips. "Let me make you a nice dinner. If I do say so myself, I'm a pretty good cook."

He proved that statement true after another hour had passed, when they were sitting across from each other at a little table in Wes's splendid kitchen, with shiny new appliances and white paneled cabinets, the light smoky walls complemented by a rounded brick archway leading into the formal dining room. The room boasted a tall bay window, under which was a ledge with a pin-cushion settee. Catherine enjoyed watching him cook, the natural flow of his movements and his obvious comfort as he reached for this utensil or that. She tried not to stare or to lose her focus as they chatted about their day, and she smiled as he approached the table, laying a steaming plate of aromatic food by each place. He sighed with satisfaction as he took his seat, and clinked his wine glass with hers. She sank her fork into her pork chop with sautéed peaches, taking a moment to inhale the savory scents of the herbs and vegetables before popping a piece into her mouth.

She nearly melted in her seat, and closed her eyes.

"Oh, good heavens," she crooned, chewing slowly, savoring the buttery texture and earthy taste of the meat. But the sweetness of the peach put her over the edge. "You're a genius in the kitchen. Do you know that?"

He chuckled and took a bite of his own. "Thank you, sweetheart. That's very kind."

"How did you learn to cook like this? Did anyone teach you?"

"My father's an excellent cook. I guess you could say I was inspired by him. It just takes practice. I like to cook, so I practice a lot."

"I'm a terrible cook. I don't have the instinct for it. I can slaughter a slice of toast."

"You make up for it, though, with chocolate. Does anyone really need anything else?"

Catherine sat back and enjoyed his company, eating his dinner and drinking wine from a thin-stemmed crystal glass. She helped him clean up, their lively voices filling the room with cheer, then tingled with anticipation as he dried his hands on a dishtowel and surveyed the room, satisfied.

"Well, that appears to be everything," he said, turning to her with a smile. "Thank you for your help."

"You're welcome. We make a good team."

He took her waist in his hands. "Thank you for joining me for dinner, sweetheart. I enjoyed the company."

She blinked a few times. "I'm still enjoying it."

He kissed her once, gently. She breathed him in, and her nerves seemed to awaken at his nearness, his now familiar scent. She waited for him to kiss her again, or to lead her upstairs, but he didn't. She swallowed, fearing the evening was already over.

"I'm not sure if I'm supposed to make another overture," she told him, her face still nearly touching his. "You're going to have to tell me."

He clasped his hands behind her at her lower back, his face turning sly as a grin touched his eyes. "I wouldn't object to an overture. Overture away."

"I think I just did."

Catherine shivered with expectation as he pressed her close. "Well, then," he said smoothly, laying a soft trail of kisses from her shoulder to her ear, making her breath catch. "I suppose this is the part where I respond."

She followed him upstairs to his bedroom, where moonshine illuminated the bed in long rows as it streamed in through the blinds, and sank with him into the blankets. She eagerly enveloped herself in him, sighing with gratitude, as if given a long drink after devastating thirst; later, she snuggled cozily against him, reveling in the comfortable security of his arms. At sunrise, he drove her home before heading to his office. He was even more handsome than usual, crisp and freshly shaven, smelling mildly of cologne as his workday began. They exchanged warm, intimate kisses on her doorstep, and finally separated, Wes holding her hand and lifting her arm as he stepped backward, only letting go when he could no longer reach. He smiled, winked, and told her he'd call her, and she turned to open the door. She watched him with pleasure as he sauntered toward his car, then waved as he hopped inside and drove off, the smell of him on her clothes and in her hair, the thought of him ever present in every detail of the rest of her day.

SHE SAW him a couple of times that week, once at his house, and once at hers, and continued to see him frequently over the next few weeks. He texted her every so often to find out about her day or to tell her he was looking forward to seeing her again. She grew comfortable in his house, and she enjoyed having him in hers. Catherine felt as giddy as a teenager. She was so used to spending her days alone with Dorothea, and her chocolate, and Brahms. Sometimes she might meet Hei for lunch. She'd always found unexpected changes difficult; she depended on her routines, which made her feel safe, and she was comforted by the quiet of her days. But Wes's little intrusions were delightful; they filled her days with sunshine. She found herself practically skipping on her walks, and humming along with the music as she worked.

"Hei," she told her friend as the two sat in Hei's cheerful kitchen one Sunday morning, cups of coffee in hand. She and Wes had spent the night together, then visited Hei so the two could meet. Wes was now at his weekly tennis game with his brother. "It's been almost a month. It's just going so well. I'm so incredibly happy, in ways I never imagined were possible."

"I told you," said Hei. "I knew this one was different."

"He doesn't make me feel anxious or nervous. I don't worry about saying the wrong thing all the time. I feel like I can really be myself. That's never happened to me before."

"I know, and I'm just so excited for you." Hei smiled and squeezed her hand. "I just love him, Catherine. He is so good to you, so sweet and so caring."

"Agreed. I just wish there were a little more of the physical. The last couple of weeks, he's said he's been tired, or he's had to leave too early the next morning."

"How often does it happen?"

"Maybe once a week."

"And how often do you see him?"

"A few times a week, I'd say."

"Hmm," said Hei. "It could be more, but it's not too bad."

Catherine frowned. "Even for a new relationship? I thought now was the time when it would happen the most."

"Well, he works really long hours. Maybe it'll get better once he's more settled in."

"Maybe." Catherine shook off her thoughtfulness and smiled at Hei. "So what's the next step? Do we just keep going like this until—what?"

"It would be nice for you to spend some time with his family. I think the next step is becoming part of each other's lives."

That opportunity came one Saturday evening in August, when Catherine dressed in a fuchsia Schiaparelli suit and applied bright lipstick to her lips. She slipped into tall black heels and fluffed up her hair, playing Brahms at full volume to distract her from the flipping in her stomach. Tonight she and Wes were having dinner at his parents' house in Wellbourne. She was used to the anxiety that accompanied meeting new people or mingling in groups; tonight, however, there was the added pressure of wanting to impress, to fit in with his family and live up to expectations. She decided to pretend it was a political event for her father—she'd attended enough of them and had developed the tools to cope.

Her parents and sister were going to be there, as were Wes's brother, sister-in-law, and grandmother. Though it was the perfect chance for Catherine and Wes to meet each other's families, the true purpose of the dinner was to celebrate the presence of Harold Beck, revered professor and opinion writer for the *Philadelphia Times*, and his wife Patricia.

Harold had retired years before, but he was still active in the political circuit, giving talks and lectures and attending charity events. He and Patricia resided in Philadelphia but spent most of their time traveling across the country and abroad, sight-seeing and touring and visiting with the many respectable people they had met in Harold's years on the front lines of politics. The Becks had recently spent several months in Washington, DC, rubbing elbows with Harold's associates in government. They were now traveling southward toward Atlanta, where Harold was to speak at Emory University. They had graciously accepted Sarah's invitation to stay with them overnight to break up their drive.

"So you've never actually met the Becks?" Catherine asked as Wes pulled onto the road and drove them toward the Bickharts' home.

"No, I never have. Isn't that funny?" He smiled, his hand draped over the steering wheel, his posture relaxed. "For all my mother talks about him, and for all the coincidences that connected us, we've never actually met."

"Do he and Meredith not get along?"

"She was reluctant to talk about her parents. But as far as I could tell, I'd have to say no. She certainly doesn't see them often."

"It's kind of strange how this all worked out. I hope it isn't too awkward for you."

"Oh, thank you, sweetheart, but I'll be fine. The past is in the past."

They pulled into the driveway of the long white colonial manor home. Her first impression was of the expansive front yard, meticulously landscaped with shade-bearing trees and lush flowering shrubs. The house itself was the picture of elegant grandeur, the first floor boasting large windows with black shutters, a second floor gable crowning each. In the dimming glow of the setting sun, it was magnificent, cozy and romantic.

Catherine stared forward, mindlessly fidgeting with the bow of the box of chocolate butterflies that rested in her lap—the stress of anticipating this gathering had sent her anxiety into overdrive, and she'd once again found an outlet in her chocolate-making. She sensed his eyes on her, and she closed her own, taking a deep breath to calm herself.

Her eyes still closed, she felt his hand on her thigh.

"How insensitive of me," he said. "All this talk about whether I'd feel awkward, and I didn't even ask how you were feeling."

She opened her eyes and exhaled. "I'm anxious. I'll be okay."

"Do big groups bother you?"

"Yes, they do. Even more so when the people in them are important to you and I want them to like me."

He smiled, his eyes shining with kindness. "Just remember, sweetheart. You've already met my parents. And they already love you."

"But now it really counts."

He brought his hand around her back and squeezed her shoulder, placing his other hand over hers. The nervous fidgeting of her fingers slowed; the racing of her heart faded to a quick but steady canter.

"How are you doing, sweetheart?" he asked her softly. "Any better?"

"Yes," she said, meaning it. "Yes, thank you. Let's go inside."

He met her on the passenger's side and helped her from the car, then took her hand and walked leisurely with her up the neat brick path, rounded mounds of flowers on either side. They stepped up to the doorway, and Wes squeezed her hand, winking once and casting her a playful smile before reaching for the door-knob and opening the door.

They were instantly met by the sound of boisterous voices and the enticing aromas of home cooking. Together they walked through the hallway toward the back of the house, which was warm and welcoming, with white walls and dark wood molding, antique furniture that was stately but not oppressive. They entered a comfortable kitchen with wooden beams on the ceiling and ample dark wood cabinets. A chandelier hung above an elegant table with intricately carved feet. Standing about were Catherine's and Wes's parents, Maeve, and a number of people Catherine had never seen before. Maeve spotted her from over the rim of her glass of wine, raised her eyebrows, and made a beeline in her direction.

"Thank God you're here," she said through a long sip of wine, taking Catherine's arm and standing just behind her. "I couldn't take another moment of Mom and Dad."

Maeve's closeness somehow soothed her; she was familiar, and Catherine took what comfort she could get. "Are they being hard on you again, Maeve?"

"What? No, they've barely even noticed me. I mean the way they're fawning over Harold Beck." She glared in the direction of Lois and Fred, who appeared deep in conversation with a couple Catherine took to be Harold and Patricia. Harold stood straight, and he nodded somberly, round glasses resting on the bridge of his nose and salt-and-pepper hair combed neatly back. He wore a sports jacket and bow tie, with a dress shirt and khaki-colored slacks. Patricia had a chin-length chestnut bob and fragile, delicate features; she wore a long gray skirt and flatteringly fitting gray sweater, with a gray and red scarf. The two were short in stature and slight in frame, but their presence was mighty. "It's almost like they want to convince him they're nice people." Maeve grimaced and took another sip. "It's ghastly."

"Maeve, you haven't met Wes," said Catherine, changing the

subject. She stepped back and settled into Wes's side, and patted his arm. "Here he is. My new beau."

"Ah, hello," said Maeve, eyes wide as she looked him over. She took his outstretched hand and shook it. "Aren't you a tall drink of water."

Wes laughed. "Well, now, that's a first. I've never been called that before. And I've been called many things."

"I find that hard to believe," said Maeve. She grinned and arched an eyebrow, shifting her weight to one hip.

"Maeve," said Catherine in a hushed, frantic voice, the kind she used only when her sister had had too much to drink.

"Oh, relax, Cat. Wes knows I'm joking."

Wes turned to Catherine with a smile. "Is that what people call you? Cat?"

"Only my sister, and only when she's drunk."

"I like it," said Wes, reaching for the short tumbler glass being handed to him by an approaching Sarah. "I may commandeer that, in fact."

"Commandeer what, darling?" asked Sarah, lifting her chin to kiss his cheek. She wrapped her arm around her son's waist and hugged him close. "Are we commandeering things already? Because if we are, I'll start with Catherine's gorgeous suit." She offered Catherine a warm smile. Catherine smiled back, already feeling more comfortable. "Schiaparelli, right?" Sarah winked and grinned knowingly. "How lovely you look, Catherine. I'm so glad you could join us. Is that what I think it is?" she asked, glee in her voice, her eyes on the box of chocolate in Catherine's hands.

"I assume you mean chocolate. And yes, it is." Catherine passed the box to Sarah. "They're butterflies, with Meyer lemon filling."

"How delightful! Someone had better take these from me before I devour them all myself. Grady," she called with her finger outstretched, to a man standing by the table a few feet away.

"Take these to the kitchen. And please fetch Catherine a drink. What would you like, Catherine?"

"White wine would be wonderful."

Catherine and Sarah leaned forward and kissed each other's cheeks, then stood back in their cozy foursome.

"Catherine, I'm so pleased to hear how well you and Wes have been hitting it off." Sarah paused as Grady, with a tiny elderly woman shuffling along on his arm, returned and handed Catherine a glass of wine, with a smile. "This is Ethel, my indomitable mother-in-law. And this is Grady, Wes's younger brother. Now look at these boys and tell me I'm not the luckiest mother in the world."

Catherine shook Grady's hand and returned his smile. He looked much like Wes, but his hair was darker and his frame more slight. His face was more hollow, and his features sharper—but his smile was warm, and his eyes kind, and Catherine liked him instantly.

"Good to meet you, Catherine," he said, his voice steady and sure like his brother's, but quieter. "How are you tonight?"

"I'm very well, thank you. And yourself?"

"Fantastic. Couldn't be better."

Catherine turned to Ethel and smiled warmly as Wes bent to kiss her. "I'm happy to meet you, too, Ethel."

Ethel accepted Wes's kiss and then playfully slapped him away. Wes laughed. "And I, you," she said. "A friend of my grandson's is a friend of mine. I hear you make chocolate."

"Yes, I do."

"Ah. Spectacular." She patted Wes's arm. "Settle down with this one, won't you?"

Catherine was delighted. She turned as she noticed a woman approach, and watched as she joined Grady and rested her hand on his back. She was sweet-looking and unassuming, with long mousy brown hair, which she had pulled into a low, floppy ponytail. Her clothes were plain but tidy. She was pregnant, obviously rather far along.

"You're Helen," said Catherine. She offered the woman her hand. "It's really nice to meet you."

"It's nice to meet you, too," Helen responded in a reticent voice, a flush creeping into her cheeks. *She's shy*, Catherine thought, encouraged. *She and I will get along nicely.*

"Catherine, your parents and I were just talking about all the good things on the horizon for us," said Sarah. "A budding romance between their daughter and my son, and now your father is about to pass his baton to the most talented attorney in the state of Virginia. Well, one of them, anyway," she added, rubbing Grady's arm.

"My mother, the perpetual cheerleader," said Wes, his face wearing a jovial smile. "In her world, I've already won the election."

"Oh, you'll win. I'm sure of it. I'm an optimist, darling. We optimists just know these things."

Catherine began to relax. Wes's family was wonderful, warm and friendly and earnestly welcoming. She exhaled, relieved to feel so quickly at home.

She turned her head and caught sight of her parents. Her mother noticed and waved her over.

"We should say hello," Catherine whispered to Wes, and the two headed in her parents' direction.

"Good evening, my girl," Fred greeted her cheerfully as they approached, holding his arms out for a hug. She leaned in and embraced him, kissed his cheek, then pulled away. "And there's the man of the hour! Harold Beck, meet Wes Bickhart. He's the fellow to watch next year."

"Yes, yes, I've heard about you." Harold took Wes's hand and shook it firmly with his other hand on top. With the handshake over, he stood back to look at Wes. "You have big shoes to fill, young man. But you already know that."

"Certainly. It doesn't get any better than Senator Sheering. It's an honor to follow in his footsteps. And it's an honor to meet you and Patricia, at long last." Wes shook Patricia's hand in greeting, then stood back, sipped his drink, and smiled charmingly. "Yours was a voice that truly stood out, Harold. Your column changed the conversation. I'm not sure your influence is quantifiable."

Harold emitted a laugh that was more like a snort; he raised his eyebrows and smirked. "I wish words were as powerful as you seem to think they are. I might have shaken things up, maybe pissed off enough of our ostensible lawmakers to force some discussion. But nothing really happens without money. You're a lawyer, now, you should know that."

Wes laughed in earnest. "Yes, I suppose that's true. Shall we at least agree you gave them a run for their money?"

"We shall. I only wish they hadn't taken the money and run."

Catherine's eyes were diverted to Harold's side, where his wife Patricia stood in silence, her hands folded in front of her waist. Catherine thought she had seen Patricia roll her eyes, but by the time she looked at her, she had turned toward Sarah and Lois, who were joining their little group.

"I have to say, Harold, you're as pithy and impenitent as I'd imagined," said Wes, raising his glass. "And thank God."

"Amen," answered Harold, and clinked Wes's glass with his own.

They all sipped their drinks. Catherine drained hers. Within a moment, her mother's lips were at her ear.

"You might want to slow down tonight," she whispered.

Catherine was preparing to apologize when Wes's hand found her lower back.

"Harold, Patricia—I understand you haven't yet had the pleasure of meeting Catherine," he said.

"Yes, our daughter is quite an interesting girl," said Fred. "Politico turned chocolatier, aficionado of all things 1930s."

"1930s, eh?" said Harold, eyebrows raised as he studied Catherine. "Why the '30s?"

"Well," Catherine began, encouraged by the support of Wes's hand on her back, "it's a subject that reveals the strength of humanity and of our country. The way we pulled through the Depression, the way our citizens made do with what they had."

She stopped speaking at the feel of her mother's hand on her arm. She felt that was a little unfair. She had caught herself early, and also, she'd barely even said anything, this time.

Wes was watching her. "Go on, sweetheart," he said softly, with a tender smile.

Catherine returned his smile gratefully. "Anyway," she finished, tipping her head downward and straightening her hair to hide the fluttering of her eyelashes, "I wish I could have witnessed it."

"How apropos," Harold muttered, draining the rest of his drink. "With this administration's policies, the way things are going, you may just get your chance."

Everyone laughed and carried on their conversation. Catherine stood in silence, not paying attention: she was enjoying the warmth of Wes's hand, which was around her waist, holding her protectively.

The conversation turned to current events. Harold listened attentively as Sarah and Fred told him about the Munson landfill.

"Bastards," spat Harold, shaking his head. "Cronyism at its finest. There's always someone looking to sell out the little guy."

Sarah took Wes's arm and updated Harold on the case, proudly showing off the son she was convinced would save the world.

"Good for you," declared Harold, nodding. "Tell me about your plans. There's nothing like talking to a fearless sharpshooter to soothe one's worries over the state of the Union."

Vibrant chatter ensued, and the tone lifted. Wes outlined the obstacles and opportunities, and Harold seemed pleased.

"My blood pressure's through the roof these days," said

Harold. "This conversation helps. Wes, it's a shame you and I never met when you were dating my daughter. I would have discouraged her from casting you off."

Wes smiled mildly and took a long sip of his drink, saying nothing.

Harold patted his shoulder. "I'm serious. I think I'd enjoy having you in the family."

Catherine took exception to this idea. She was rather glad Wes hadn't ended up in Harold Beck's family, and was about to tell him so, but Wes responded first.

"Ah, well." He lowered the glass from his lips and watched it as he swirled his drink a few times. "Things happen for a reason, as they say."

"I have to agree," said Sarah. "Your daughter is lovely, Harold. I adore her, but it wasn't meant to be." She took Catherine's arm and hugged it. "As sorry as I am for your loss, your loss means we now have Catherine. I'm enamored of her. I'm not giving her up without a fight."

"No matter. Meredith wouldn't have listened to me, regardless. She's headstrong as hell. She and I don't see eye to eye."

"Your daughter, headstrong?" Sarah playfully slapped his arm. "I can't imagine where she gets it from."

Harold snorted again. "Point taken." He turned to his wife and held out his glass. "Say, Patty, would you mind, terribly?" Stone-faced, Patricia took the glass and walked away.

Harold watched her for a moment, then turned back to Sarah and sighed. "The ship has sailed, anyway," he said. "Meredith's married now and living in Maine."

"How is she, Harold? Is she happy?" asked Sarah.

"I don't have the faintest idea. She plays her cards close to her chest with Patty and me. We don't even know the guy. He could be a serial killer for all we know."

"He's a good guy," said Wes. "I met him once."

"That's good to hear. It's news to me. Have you talked to her,

Wes? Maybe you can enlighten me as to how my daughter is doing."

"We've emailed once or twice. It was pretty brief." He took a long drink and looked about the room, his eyes darting here and there. "But I can assure you that she seems very happy."

Wes's father Charles emerged from the kitchen and announced that dinner was ready. Wes, his hand rubbing Catherine's back, led her in his direction, and they all greeted each other brightly. Charles was friendly and kind, with a laid-back demeanor, quieter than Sarah but no less warm. It was apparent to Catherine which son took after which parent.

Wes pulled her aside as the other guests trickled into the dining room. He kissed her tenderly, then massaged her shoulder with his hand.

He leaned in so he could speak quietly in her ear.

"Harold Beck is a piece of work, isn't he?" he said.

"He's definitely opinionated."

Wes smiled. "I don't know how familiar you are with his writing," he went on. "But he's known for his bite and his bluster. So if he said anything to give you pause, I hope you'll dismiss it as Harold being Harold."

"You mean what he said about having you in the family?" said Catherine, eyes closing and then opening as he planted a kiss on her forehead. "It didn't bother me too much. It isn't like you said you wanted to be part of his family."

"Well, I'm glad you're okay. I was worried the conversation might have upset you."

"It didn't. Thank you for worrying about me. Thank you so much." Abruptly she was overtaken by a sensation that was cozy and warm, but devastating too. Though it was massive in weight, it lifted her up. She felt it deep in her gut and around her heart; it was rosy in color, and intoxicatingly happy. "I love you."

Wes's face softened imperceptibly, and he said nothing for a moment or two. Then his eyes crinkled, and he pulled her in close.

"Sweetheart," he said. "I love you, too."

She closed her eyes and let him hold her, her heart pattering, almost in song. *There is nothing more*, she told herself, and sighed in the comfort of his arms and chest. *There is nothing more than this.*

AFTER DINNER, the guests, coffee cups in hand, mingled in pairs and small groups. Catherine and Wes made the rounds, chatting with everyone in turn. Catherine appreciated how Wes never let the conversation leave her behind, drawing her in and asking her questions, making her feel important. With his hand on her back and his protective aura around her, Catherine relaxed and participated in the discussions, and even enjoyed herself.

Regardless, conversation was always exhausting, and when Wes asked if she would mind if he joined Grady on the patio for cigars, she was almost relieved. She refilled her coffee in the kitchen, then strolled through the formal living room into a sprawling sunroom at the back of the house. It was a luxurious enclosed porch with paneled windows that rose from the floor to the ceiling, though as the evening had grown late, the view was obscured by darkness. The room was rich and handsome, with leather furniture and dark woods, even the ceiling composed of the beautiful linear planks.

Catherine stepped into the room and started, surprised by movement to her right. Helen was sitting in a chair by a little table, a glass of water in hand. She looked up and smiled as Catherine approached.

"Hello," said Helen, her voice reticent, but bright. "Feel free to join me, Catherine. Grady and Wes stepped outside, and I just needed to rest a moment."

Catherine smiled and took a seat by Helen, already comforted by Helen's raw sweetness. "This is a beautiful room. It's cozy in here."

"Oh, yes. I love this room. It's my favorite room of the house. The rest of the house is lovely, too, of course. But I love this room the best."

The two sat in silence for a moment or two.

"I'm sorry if I've seemed quiet tonight," Helen said then. "I'm awfully shy in social situations."

"I know how that is," Catherine assured her. "There's no need to apologize to me."

"The good news is, we're friends now." Helen's smile widened. "So now I don't have to be shy."

Catherine was touched. "You're absolutely right." She settled in her seat and folded her hands on her lap. "I can relate to what you said. I feel shy, too. I've had a lot of practice, though, because my father's in politics. It's gotten easier over the years."

"Oh, I know what you mean. It's gotten easier for me, too. Mostly because the Bickharts are so wonderful. I love them so much. It's really hard not to be comfortable with them."

"They're a very loving family," agreed Catherine, vaguely aware of a profound, unidentifiable emotion steadily rising from deep within her. "Have you known them long? How long have you and Grady been married?"

"We've been married for about five years. We met at a wedding in Charlottesville and fell in love immediately. I'm from Wisconsin, and I moved down here to be with him. I was excited to do it, but I missed my home. The Bickharts made it so easy to be happy here." She smiled and rubbed her pregnant belly. "They're so kind to my family. My parents don't have a lot of money. Grady and his parents make sure they can come visit as often as they want to, and we fly home to see them, too."

"That's so great," said Catherine softly, warmed through and through. "What a nice story."

"Thank you." Helen smiled again and watched her. "Catherine, I hear you make chocolate. What a fun job."

"It's a lot of fun, yes. I love it."

"Do you work in a store? Where do you make it?"

"Oh, I do everything in my house. I have a workshop in my basement."

Helen's face was bright and eager. "Would you tell me all about it?"

Catherine launched into an energetic description of her chocolate-making business, telling her how she got started and how she acquired the knowledge, the equipment, and the business sense. Helen was an attentive, enraptured listener. She nodded and smiled and even clapped her hands. Catherine felt comfortable with Helen and found herself hoping Wes and Grady stayed out as long as possible.

At the end of Catherine's explanation, Helen said, "I really admire you, the way you built this business all by yourself. I know I couldn't do it."

"Sure you could. You can do anything you put your mind to."

"I don't even think I would want to. I think I'm much happier with my charity work. It's not a lot, of course. But it seems to suit me."

"Oh, well, then you should do that. Business isn't for everyone. We all have to do what's right for us."

Both women smiled.

"I hope you don't mind my saying this," said Helen, and Catherine could see the nervousness in the flush in her face. "But I feel...I just feel like I can talk to you."

"Me, too." Catherine felt more and more of a kinship with Helen and had begun to suspect, in fact, that she had some form of neurodivergence, herself. It would explain, in part, her need to take this time to regroup by herself, as well as their ease together. "I hope we can be good friends."

"Oh, I'm sure we will be." Helen smiled. "So how serious are you and Wes?" she asked. "Things are going well?"

"Yes, very well," said Catherine, heart flipping as it always did when she talked about Wes and their time together. "He is..." She paused, unsure how to describe her feelings about a man who was infinitely more wonderful in infinitely more ways than any man she had ever met in her life. She settled on, "I'm very happy, too," and stopped herself before she became too gushing.

Helen's eyes were wide and eager. "I'm so glad," she said, latent excitement in her voice. "Wes is a really good brother-in-law. You two make such a nice couple."

"Thank you." Catherine was delighted, and happy to have a new friend in Helen. "I think we do."

"Sarah says you're just perfect for Wes. You're very different from Meredith and his ex-wife Claire, and you're a much better fit. That's what Sarah says, anyway."

"Really? How so?"

"Well..." Helen frowned, appearing stumped. "I never met Claire. And I just met you." She smiled once more. "But I believe Sarah. Sarah's never wrong!"

When Wes and Grady returned, accompanied by the earthy scent of cigars, the guests began wishing each other goodnight. They shook hands and shared good wishes, and left the Bickharts and the Becks to retire for the night. Outside, in the crisp autumn night, Catherine stood waiting by Wes's car as Wes exchanged pleasantries with her parents. She felt a presence behind her; before she could turn, Maeve was tapping her shoulder.

Maeve crooked her finger and motioned toward herself, suggesting Catherine should lean in for a secret.

"You hit the jackpot," she whispered. "Congratulations."

"Thank you, Maeve."

"He's a damn good catch. I'm happy for you."

Catherine looked at her. "You are?"

"Of course." Maeve's brows snapped together crossly. "I'm your sister, aren't I?"

"Yes," said Catherine, with trepidation. "It's just that—"

"All sisters bicker, Catherine. Come on, I'm trying to have a moment."

Catherine didn't know what to say. She stood in silence, with her hands folded and eyes fluttering, waiting for Wes to return.

"Does he seem a little hung up on his ex?" Maeve asked suddenly.

Catherine stared at her.

"Of course you wouldn't think so," said Maeve, tossing her hand up. "You always see everyone through rose-colored glasses."

"I don't think he is," said Catherine warily, brow furrowed. "Do *you* think he is?"

"I'm just saying it's possible."

"Do you think I missed something?"

"It wouldn't be the first time."

Catherine frowned. She didn't know how to interpret the low, grayish-green feeling in the pit of her stomach, but she wished it would go away. "But he's so charming and wonderful."

"He sure is charming. Maybe a tad too charming." Maeve shrugged. "Maybe he's trying to hide it."

"Don't say that about him," Catherine insisted, growing frustrated, and rushing to his defense. "He's the best man I've ever known."

"Of course he is. I never said he wasn't a good man." Maeve rolled her eyes; her tone had become impatient. "I'm not criticizing him, Catherine. I like him. Calm down. Just don't be naïve, okay? Nobody's perfect."

"But he told me he loves me."

"He seems to. But he can love you both at the same time, can't he?"

"I don't know." She could feel her mind retreating; she was growing increasingly incapable of organized thought. "I guess I have noticed his expression change a little when she comes up in conversation. It happened on our first date. But that doesn't mean anything. I probably misinterpreted."

"Yeah, that's it. It's subtle, but it's there. It's the look on his face when he—"

Their conversation halted as Wes and her parents went their separate ways, her parents to their car, and Wes toward his. Wes extended his hand toward Maeve and favored her with a charming smile.

"Maeve, it was so nice to meet you," he said. "I hope I have the pleasure again soon."

"Likewise," Maeve replied, leaning in as he kissed her cheek. Maeve turned to Catherine. "See you, sis," she said, after a slight hesitation, and playfully punched her on the arm. "Keep me posted."

They waved, parted, and hopped in their cars to drive home.

WES AND CATHERINE enjoyed a pleasant drive to Wes's house, commenting a little on their evening and planning the day they'd spend together tomorrow. Catherine felt enchanted by the darkness and by the quiet of the night, as if they were the only people on Earth. She stole frequent glances at him and sighed inside at the way he turned briefly to her, on occasion, to meet her gaze as they chatted. A smile rose to her lips. She reached toward him and stroked his neck, letting her fingers toy with his ear. He returned her smile and patted her knee. It was a tangible presence, the affection between them, and it was undeniable. Catherine's face softened as she watched him. Maeve was wrong. That was all there was to it. Even Catherine could see how real this was. In her heart, there was nothing but happiness.

He pulled into his driveway and met her on the passenger's side, then held her close as they made their way to his door. They stepped inside and walked side by side upstairs, Wes goosing her from behind and making her yelp and laugh. They undressed in the soft lighting of his bedroom, where Catherine took strange pleasure in watching him perform little personal rituals, like removing his watch and his socks. He turned out the lights, and they slid into bed together, warm skin settling into cool, smooth sheets. They lay beside each other. Catherine touched her foot to his, running her toe up and down his calf, letting it slide ever higher until he started and laughed. She slipped her arm around his waist, coaxing him closer, and they lay intertwined, legs slinking and arms engulfing. She brought her lips to his, and fell with him into a kiss; his breath in her ear, his hands in her hair, and his body in hers, she shed everything that bound her, basking in the ecstasy of night and then waking to the comfort of him when daylight crept along the walls and onto the bed, kissing her cheek.

CHAPTER SEVEN

The heady, sweet air of summer faded into the crisp air of autumn. Orders for chocolate seashells and butterflies ceased, and orders for chocolate leaves and pumpkins rolled in. Catherine's paint palette changed as she switched out teal and lavender for russet and bronze. Her daily walks grew brisker, and she donned a cardigan as she enjoyed the foliage, which hung over her street like a canopy and made her neighborhood appear to glow with gold.

She and Wes enjoyed the season together, going on wine tours and tooling around downtown Charlottesville, taking advantage of the fresh, clear weather, holding hands as fallen leaves danced in the breeze around them. Catherine was a frequent guest at the home of Sarah and Charles, and it wasn't long before she felt like part of the family. Sarah and Charles were so kind to her, and her cheerful chats with Ethel buoyed her spirits. Of particular joy to her was the birth of Olivia, Helen and Grady's daughter, in the beginning of September; the family swarmed around the new baby, and Catherine soaked it all in, feeling wrapped in love and happiness. She always looked forward to visiting Helen and Grady with Wes and the rest of the family, snuggling the baby and falling into an auntly role for a time, until she and Wes retreated to Wes's house. Most of their nights together were spent at his house, and Catherine was happy with this arrangement: Wes's house was beautiful, and besides, it meant she didn't need to worry about the disarray in her own.

Catherine adored Wes's house. She loved the dark woods and sophisticated colors, the classic decor and cozy corners. There were books everywhere, neatly arranged on built-in bookshelves and tucked between bookends on end tables. The entire house was neat and tidy, precisely organized and perpetually clean. It was the loveliest, prettiest, most wonderful home she had ever had the pleasure of getting to know.

"I feel like a princess in a castle," she told him one Sunday morning as they sipped coffee on the stone patio in the back of the house. It overlooked a generous backyard spilling over with flowers and sprawling shrubs, behind which sat the green expanse of the forest. The sky was still pale with the new dawn, the dew still sparkling on the grass, and the cheerful twittering of birds serenaded them from the trees. Catherine was in a particularly good mood: though she'd spent the night many times, there'd continued to be less sex than she would have liked. They'd retired early the previous night and had made up for lost time.

Wes laughed heartily. "I'm glad you feel that way, sweetheart, but this is hardly a castle."

"It is to me."

Wes had a study in the house, and it actually looked like a castle. It was an oak-paneled room, lined with bookshelves, with exposed beams and a heavy oak desk. It had a sitting area and a distinguished-looking fireplace. But the best feature was the window—a five-sided bay window, with small crisscross panes, which faced directly westward and admitted glorious amounts of light. Outside the window, among the sycamores and maples, was a gnarled old white hawthorn tree, its thick, twisted branches sprawling outward and sagging at the ends under the weight of its clustered blossoms. It was always full of action, that tree, its leaves rustling with the flutter of songbirds or the scampering of chipmunks and squirrels. At dusk, the sun set through its branches, and its rays poured into the room in warm radiant streams. Wes and Catherine often sat in this room together, either chatting side by side on the love seat in front of the fireplace, or more quietly as Wes worked at his desk and Catherine read in a chair by the window. Catherine felt she could gaze forever at that hawthorn tree; draped in white flowers, with its knobby trunk, it looked like the home of fairies as it shifted softly in the breeze.

One Friday night toward the end of November, just before Thanksgiving, Catherine strode up his walkway, eager to begin a quiet night together. She twisted the doorknob and opened the door, which he left unlocked for her when he returned home from work and was expecting her. She entered the house and dropped her keys and purse in the foyer, then stepped toward the formal living room on the right, where she heard his voice and registered the shadow of his form in the flickering light of the fireplace. As she stepped into the room, a warm, welcoming room with richly colored rugs, elegant antique furniture, and fabrics in shades of cream and crimson, she saw Wes standing on the far end with his cell phone at his ear. He had already changed out of his suit; he was dressed casually, in jeans, a t-shirt, and a plaid shirt, unbuttoned, with the sleeves rolled up. He shot her a smile and held up his finger, suggesting he'd only be a moment. As she waited for him to finish his conversation, her attention was drawn behind him to the dining room, where he had set two place settings with two wine glasses, and a single candle between them. A fire leaped in the fireplace in the living room, its smoky scent mingling with the savory scent of dinner.

"Okay, sweetheart," he was saying. "Good to talk to you, too. I've got to run. Congratulations on the baby, again." He pulled the phone from his ear and hung up.

"Was that Helen?" asked Catherine.

There was a long pause as he stared at the screen, stone-faced. He then he lifted his gaze to meet hers. "No, it wasn't Helen, actually. It was Meredith."

Catherine stared at him blankly. "Oh?"

"Yeah. She's pregnant. Isn't that great?"

Catherine hesitated. "That is great."

He slipped his phone into the back pocket of his jeans in silence, then approached. She lifted her chin to meet his kiss and instinctively edged closer as he took her shoulders in his hands.

"Does it bother you?" he asked. "Are you uncomfortable with my keeping in touch with her?"

"No," she said thoughtfully, shaking her head. "No, we're all adults. Did you call her 'sweetheart'?"

He put his hand to his forehead and closed his eyes, nodding. "You know, I guess I did. Old habits die hard, don't they?" He chuckled. "Not to worry. It won't happen again. Hey, I'm so happy you're here." He looked at her with a smile. "I've been looking forward to seeing you all day." His smile brightened further, and he patted her shoulders. "Are you ready to begin our weekend?"

He hurried away and bounded toward the dining room, where he picked a bottle of wine up from the table and began pouring.

"What's wrong?" she asked.

"Wrong, sweetheart?"

"You seem a little manic, to be honest. Are you okay?"

"I'm good. I'm great. I'm fantastic. Nothing's wrong." He held his hand out, indicating the table. "Look, I set this up for us. Dinner's almost ready. Beef Wellington. Isn't that incredible? Even I'm a little surprised I pulled it off."

"What's the occasion?"

"I just felt like beginning the weekend with a bang. But also," he added, with a smile, "we won the Barnes case."

"Oh!" she exclaimed, and went to him swiftly. "I'm so happy!"

"Thank you, sweetheart. I am, too. I admit, I had really gotten my heart wrapped up in that case."

"Understandably. I had, too." She gazed at him fondly, affection flooding her; the case, which sought to curb the discriminatory practices of a landlord, was one of the first Wes had taken on after his move back to Charlottesville, and though in recent weeks he had been as cheerful and chipper as ever, Catherine knew the stress had been enormous. "I'm just so very proud of you."

He held her waist and kissed her lips, then patted her hips and headed for the kitchen.

"Have a seat, now, sweetheart. I'll be right back with the most delicious dinner you've ever had."

"Can I help?"

"Absolutely not. Have a seat and relax."

Catherine sat down and took in the coziness of the room. A moment later, he returned with two plates of steaming beef Wellington, perfectly cooked and beautifully presented. He laid a plate at each place and sat, then lifted his glass. She clinked it dutifully, and they tucked into dinner.

"This is outstanding, Wes," she muttered through a mouthful. "You've outdone yourself."

"Thank you. I have to admit, I'm quite pleased."

Catherine chewed and swallowed. "I'm so glad you won your case. I want to hear all about it."

Wes launched into an animated recap of his day. He seemed to Catherine to be more excitable than usual, his facial expressions more intense and his hand gestures more profuse. Catherine couldn't shake the feeling that he was somehow overcompensating, that he was hiding something that had upset him. He'd insisted he was fine, however, and Catherine knew she often misinterpreted body language. She guessed he was releasing stress, having prepared this case for weeks and investing so much of his heart and soul.

"Also," he said, his voice turning serious, "I had a chat with the county attorney. It won't be long before the rezoning request is submitted. Once that happens, it'll be game on."

"Oh, no. What will you do?"

"I've been reading up on the environmental issues at the Texas site. I think stressing the likely health risk to the residents adjoining the site will be the most effective approach. And indeed, the most important."

She helped him clean up after dinner, enjoying the homey sounds of water sloshing and dishes clinking. Then they snuggled on the couch in front of the fireplace, a warm blanket around them, glasses of wine in hand.

"Wes," she said, "you never really told me why you and Meredith broke up."

He was silent for a moment. Catherine waited until finally he spoke.

"Cat, sweetheart...The truth is, I haven't told you about it because the story is a little unflattering."

The statement, and the contrite tone with which he said it, caught her off guard, and she said nothing for a moment or two. "It's okay," she said finally. "You can tell me."

His jaw worked a little as his eyes studied her. "The long and short of it," he said, "is that we didn't agree on a timeframe. After my divorce, I felt the passage of time a lot more keenly. I was forty when Claire and I divorced. I still wanted a family. But work was very demanding, and there was just no time." He took a breath and continued. "With Meredith...I was excited to settle down, and I took it too fast. It appears that in my haste, I made too many decisions assuming she'd be okay with them."

"I take it she wasn't?"

"No," he said, laughing. "No, not at all. I misjudged the situation, splendidly."

"And what was the situation?"

He took a deep breath as he considered. "First there was the fact that deep down, she was still in love with her ex. Ultimately they reunited, and they got married shortly after. But perhaps even more importantly, she needed time to think. She was very opinionated. It isn't that I didn't respect her opinion. I was simply too eager to see it. Truth be told, I put her in a pretty tough spot. I've had time to reflect on it, and I can say that now in hindsight. She wasn't in a position to make any of those decisions—at least, not yet."

"What kinds of decisions are you talking about?"

"Well, for one, I proposed pretty quickly. She said she'd accept after more time had passed, so after more time had passed, I proposed again and bought this house, figuring it would be here for us when she was ready. I guess I jumped the gun a little, huh?" He laughed again. "It was all for her, but it wasn't what she wanted. It was foolish, in retrospect."

Catherine stared at him. "This house was supposed to be Meredith's house? You moved into the house you bought for Meredith?"

He said nothing for a moment. "Yes, I suppose that's true."

Catherine looked around at the house she had grown to love. "Hmm," she said. She turned to him again. "How long was it before you proposed?"

"Two months. It was absurdly fast, I know." He took her hand and looked at her earnestly; Catherine was surprised by the emotion that clouded his features. "Honestly, sweetheart, it's painful to think about. I had grand plans that didn't work out. I handled it badly, but I've come to terms with it. You have the right to know these things, and I'm glad we cleared the air. But if it's all right with you, I'd really prefer not to talk about Meredith."

Catherine's lips turned upward into a soft, somber smile. "It's okay," she said. "I understand. I am glad to know what happened. And I'm glad it wasn't anything serious." She watched him curiously. "Why did you think you couldn't tell me this before? You didn't do anything awful. You didn't lie or cheat or act out of malice. You followed your feelings, is all. It's really not that unflattering a story."

"Well, you know, sweetheart, it's hard to admit one's flaws, especially in matters of love. And even more so in subsequent relationships, when they involve strong feelings."

"Honestly, Wes, for what it's worth? I don't see those things as flaws. I wouldn't mind if you did those things with me. I'd welcome it."

He leaned his elbow on the back of the couch, held his face in his hand, and smiled. He brought his other hand to the side of her face and tucked her hair behind her ear. "Would you, now," he said.

She nodded. "I would."

"And why is that?"

"Because I think it's attractive, that you're so sure of yourself and strong. And because I love you."

His eyes sparkled with something between amusement and appreciation. "You have a heart of gold, sweetheart. Do you know that?"

She shrugged, happily enjoying a pleasant tingle as his fingers brushed against the skin of her neck. "I'm a little old-fashioned, I guess."

"It's delightful."

He cupped her face in his hands and kissed her with warm, soft lips, gently, but slowly, with a subtle promise of more. She closed her eyes and sighed.

"In any case," he said, pulling back and watching the motion of his fingers as they resumed playing with her hair, "you're probably right that I shouldn't have worried. It's nothing awful. I'm not a liar or a cheater. I've made mistakes, but they're with the best intentions."

"I know." Catherine leaned in and kissed him, and he reached his arm around her to pull her in close. She had never seen him vulnerable before, and it had moved her. "Thank you for sharing this with me."

"Thank you for listening, sweetheart. And for being a kind companion."

He kissed her again, and she rested her head on his shoulder. He rubbed her arm, and they passed a few moments in cozy silence.

"You said you first proposed after you had been together for two months?" she asked him.

"Yes. That's right."

Catherine thought about this.

"So then why haven't you proposed to me?"

He became completely still; he didn't breathe, and the motion of his hand on her arm ceased.

She lifted her head and looked at him. "We've been together for five months now."

He looked down at her and smiled. "Yes, we have. Five delightful months."

After a moment or two, she rested her head on his shoulder once more, and his hand resumed its motion.

"As to your question," he said quietly, after some time had passed. "It might be time to rectify that."

Catherine's heart stopped, and her voice caught in her throat. He touched his finger to the bottom of her chin and gently tucked it upward.

"What do you say, Cat?" he asked, his expression quite serious.

Her eyes drowsed under the soft stroking of his finger on her face. "To be clear," she said hazily, "are you proposing right now?"

"Yes. I think you're right. I think it's time."

He separated from her and slid from the couch, where he rested on one knee and took her hands. She straightened, eyes wide, her heart battering against her chest. She bit her lip to stop the tears. She sniffled, sucked in her breath, and fortified her face.

"Catherine, sweetheart...will you marry me?"

"Of course," she whispered, barely able to find her voice. "I can't believe you even think you have to ask."

A single burst of laughter erupted from him, and he smiled up at her, his brow creased, his entire body tense with emotion. He took her face in his hands and kissed her firmly several times, then looked at her, his thumb brushing away her now falling tears.

"Thank you," he told her softly. "I'm going to give you a happy life. And a ring. You deserve the perfect ring."

"Truth be told, I don't need a ring. Don't get me a ring. I'm just so happy, I'm just already so happy."

"You're going to have a ring, sweetheart."

"Okay, I'll have a ring."

They embraced warmly, Catherine closing her eyes with her face lifted toward the ceiling, squeezing her arms around him and savoring every moment of his hands rubbing her back. They spent the remainder of the evening chatting and laughing, exchanging kisses by firelight—indeed, a wonderful start to the weekend. By night's end, her world was only bliss, filled with love and tender touches in the silvery darkness.

CHAPTER EIGHT

Catherine and Wes's engagement was a happy event, much fussed over and much celebrated by all—and by no one more than Sarah Bickhart, who within an hour of being informed had already contacted the country club for available dates.

"I can't think of anything to be more thankful for," she told Catherine, bringing her in for a warm hug. "You're everything I could hope for for Wes, and I simply can't wait until you're officially part of our family."

Catherine's heart was bursting. She had never felt this way before, so loved and doted on by so many, so important and so central to everyone's happiness. If this feeling were a color, she thought, it would most definitely be red—not a bright, alarming red, but a red that was tinged with pink, like cardinal, or ruby, or rose.

"Thank you, Sarah. And you're everything I could hope for in a mother-in-law."

Sarah sighed and pulled her close again. "Oh, what a happy Thanksgiving," she crooned. She pulled back and looked at Catherine with watery eyes. "When shall we get you two married? Do you prefer a long engagement?"

"No, I don't think so. I feel too old for a long engagement."

"I'm so glad to hear you say that, darling. Let's bring on the happy day as soon as possible!"

Wes bought her what was indeed the perfect ring. Catherine had grown accustomed to Wes's almost impossible competence. But even she was amazed.

"It's a 1930s Raymond C. Yard art deco ring centering a shimmering oval-shaped opal with a pavé diamond surround and a diamond-accented split shank, all in an ornate rose gold setting," she told Hei breathlessly over morning coffee, holding out her hand. "Isn't it great?"

"It's gorgeous," Hei gasped, bringing her fingers to Catherine's hand and moving it this way and that, letting the opal catch the light. "How did he find this?"

"He said he has his ways."

"He sure does."

Catherine smiled happily at the obvious awe on Hei's face. "Do you know what he told me? He told me the opal is a stone of inspiration, for creativity and for healing. He said it's a soothing stone, to bring about inner peace and pleasant dreams. It's thought to have a larger proportion of water than other stones, so it aids the flowing of the spirit. But mostly, it's a stone of love—of sensual love, of unconditional love. It represents loyalty. It's said to inspire passion, warmth, and serenity in love." She paused for breath. "Those were his exact words."

Hei brought her hand to her heart and swooned, then brought Catherine in for a tight hug. "I'm so happy for you, my dear, sweet friend. You so deserve this!"

The only dark spot was Maeve. Maeve texted her one day as she was working in her basement workshop. Catherine tried to ignore the ping that sounded from her phone beside her, but curiosity got the best of her.

Don't you think it's odd that he proposed right then?

Catherine's eyebrows knit together. *What do you mean?* she texted back.

Right after his ex had told him she was pregnant.

Her eyes darted to the side as she thought about it, then back at her screen as she texted back.

He proposed because we were talking about it. Because he realized it was time.

That's my point. He realized it was time.

I don't understand what you're saying.

I'm saying it sounds like he's not over his ex.

Catherine didn't respond. She texted Hei instead to ask her for her thoughts.

OMG Catherine, Hei responded, almost instantly. *Your sister is a sourpuss. He proposed because he loves you! Enjoy this moment!*

Catherine smiled and thanked her, then put her phone down and resumed her work.

They planned an early March wedding. Catherine liked the idea of her wedding ushering in the spring. And she adored the fact that it would be brisk enough for her to wear long sleeves: she had just the dress in mind.

No, texted Maeve, when Catherine sent her a photo. *Not Grandma's dress. Please, Catherine. Just go contemporary this time.*

Catherine much preferred Hei's reaction. She showed her one morning over coffee in Hei's cheerful kitchen.

"Oh, I just adore it," Hei breathed, her hand on her heart, leaning back in her seat as she stared at Catherine's phone. "It's magical, like a fairy queen's dress."

"I can wear my hair down. I can curl it a little, maybe, and use my grandmother's pearl and ivory combs."

Thus the wedding planning began, and one of the first tasks was to decide where Catherine would have her shower. With the wedding less than four months away, they had little time to decide.

Restaurant, texted Maeve. *A fancy one. Taylor's?*

My house! texted Hei. *It'll be so cozy.*

For once, Catherine had to agree with Maeve.

I'm so appreciative, she texted Hei. *But Taylor's will be easier. And I like the idea of something fancy.*

Your wedding, your call! Hei responded. *It'll be beautiful at Taylor's!*

Maeve and Hei planned her shower together. They texted back and forth with each other, occasionally bringing Catherine into the discussion to ask for her opinion.

Your sister is all business! Hei texted her one morning. *That girl gets the job done!*

Hei loves exclamation marks, Maeve texted her that night. *Just an observation.*

Catherine's mother escorted her to the florist's shop so Catherine could decide on the flowers.

"Calla lilies," Catherine breathed, her hands clasped in front of her chest. "I love them. They're so elegant."

"Magnolias are just as elegant," Lois stated, pointing to an exuberant bouquet on the table, "and the scent is lovely."

"That's true," Catherine said with a frown, holding her chin in her fingers.

She snapped two photos and texted them to Maeve and Hei.

Magnolias, Maeve texted back.

Callas! replied Hei.

There were many other decisions to attend to. But the most serious of them all was what Catherine would do with her house, the house she had lived in with her grandmother and had inherited when her grandmother passed away. Though she was eager to move in with Wes—she couldn't wait to wake up with him every day, to incorporate each other into their daily routines, and she so loved his house—she was heartbroken by the idea of no longer having that connection to her grandmother.

"Keep your house, sweetheart," he told her tenderly as they sat together on the love seat in his study, the hawthorn tree swaying in the breeze outside. "There's no need to let it go if it means that much to you."

"But it's such a sweet house. I don't like the idea of it sitting there empty."

"We can rent it out, if you'd like. That way it won't be empty, and you can keep that connection to your grandmother."

"Hmm," she said, her eyes on two chipmunks chasing each other through the hawthorn tree. "I'll think about it."

Catherine ultimately decided to keep her grandmother's house. For the time being, she'd leave her workshop there; it was set up so perfectly, and she'd grown used to her midday walks. She could even bring Dorothea with her on days when she made her chocolate. With all the change in her life, she found comfort in something remaining the same, something as personal and important as her workshop. And besides, this way, she could retreat somewhere in private, without worrying Wes with the true extent of her anxiety: the wedding planning, while exciting, was stressful, and Catherine was finding an outlet in hard, constant work.

"I hope Dorothea enjoys living here," said Wes, with a playfully handsome smile. The cat had climbed into his lap, and he stroked her back as she purred. "Do you think she'll get used to it?"

"Oh, yes," Catherine assured him solemnly. "Dorothea's very adaptable. And this house will appeal to her regal nature."

Even though she was keeping her workshop, she was still going to be living with Wes—which meant she had to pack up her things and clean her house. Catherine balked at the idea of packing. It required that she go through her piles and boxes, that she make decisions over where things would belong in her new home and which things shouldn't go with her at all. The task was daunting and overwhelming.

"Let's get to work," Hei told her as the two stood in the entryway of her house one Saturday afternoon. "Where should we start?"

"Might as well start right here," Catherine said glumly, throwing her hands toward the piles that sat in the corner right in front of them. As they sat on the floor and began pulling objects from the pile, Catherine was disheartened. She vowed that she wouldn't let things grow out of control at Wes's house. It wasn't a house for a mess. And she wanted him to see the very best side of her.

In the meantime, Rick Tremaine had submitted Munson's rezoning request, and the Planning Commission hearing drew near. A notice appeared in the local newspaper, as required, alerting nearby residents of the requested change. And notices were sent by mail to individual homeowners whose property bordered the site. Sarah had been busy making flyers calling for protest. Wes's full-page ad in the *Charlottesville Herald* encouraged people to attend the hearing. Wes himself flew to Texas to check out the Munson site, look at records, and talk to people at the Texas Department of Environmental Protection. He then prepared his case to present to the Commission.

"This is where my past life comes in handy," he told Catherine over dinner one night. He'd been interviewed for the local news that afternoon, his third interview that week, and Catherine, Sarah, and Helen had gathered gleefully to watch him. "It's just the kind of law I practiced up north, only from the other side. I know just how these corporate machines run."

"My hero," Catherine said, gazing at him with a starry-eyed smile. "Swooping in to save the town. You were brilliant today on TV. You were so smart and confident."

"You flatter me," he replied with a laugh. "Keep it up, sweetheart."

The weekend before the hearing was the first annual Beating

Heart Charity Christmas Gala, a fundraiser benefiting many of the area's charities. The Sheerings and the Bickharts all were attending. For the occasion, Catherine chose a 1930s black velvet sheath gown with a Brussels Duchesse lace collar that draped over her shoulders and met in a deep v-cut halfway down her back. But for all her excitement about dressing up in her fanciest of dresses and dancing in the most beautiful hall in town, everything paled in comparison to Wes, who in his crisp, well-tailored tuxedo looked as dashing and handsome as she had ever seen him. He was at his most amiable and his most charming, his confidence evident in his every movement and his sophistication in his every word.

Catherine couldn't stop looking at him as he held her on the dance floor. He was the picture of perfection, from his perpetually neat sandy hair to the bottom of his feet, which danced with flawless rhythm. She moved her body closer to his as he pressed her in close. Melting, she closed her eyes at the warmth of his hands.

It was a boisterous, grand time. Catherine enjoyed the interactions between families. Everyone had complimented and congratulated her, even her parents, even Maeve. Their laughter echoed through the ballroom, rising above the din of the guests and the music. It seemed to signify a new, fuller era of Catherine's life, and she welcomed it warmly.

"I'm so happy you're going to be my sister-in-law," said Helen. They were seated next to each other, eating the first course of dinner. It was Helen and Grady's first night out together without Olivia: the baby was with Helen's parents, who were visiting for the week. "You're such a good friend."

"Thank you so much, Helen," said Catherine. "That means so much to me. I'm very happy, too."

"I'm so excited that you get to be Aunt Catherine to Olivia." Helen smiled, then sighed. "Oh, my little baby. I miss her!"

Catherine returned her smile, kindness in her eyes. "That's so sweet. But it's good for you to go out and have some fun with Grady. Olivia's in good hands with your parents."

"Thank you, Catherine. I know you're right. You're very wise." She sighed again and shook her head knowingly. "It's so hard to be separated when the baby's this young." A little grin touched her lips. "You'll find out, I'm sure."

"Probably. Not for a while, though."

"I don't know," said Helen. "Wes is pretty anxious to have kids and start a family. It was all he could talk about with Meredith. Has he brought it up?"

Catherine shrugged. "We know we want kids, but we don't know when."

"I'm surprised he doesn't have it all planned out. That doesn't sound like Wes." Helen leaned against the back of her seat and closed her eyes. "I'm so tired. The baby isn't sleeping well at night."

Catherine smiled and let her sister-in-law-to-be take a little rest. She felt it would be wrong to share her thoughts on this matter. The fact was that it made sense to her why Wes hadn't pushed her into planning when they'd have children. After their conversation about Meredith, Catherine suspected he was reluctant to make the same mistakes he'd made before and that he was consciously attempting not to rush—even though in her eyes, he could never rush her, for any discussion about their future was a discussion she eagerly wanted to have. Helen hadn't been privy to this private conversation, of course, and had no way of knowing.

Her eyes caught Maeve's from across the table. Maeve was slouching casually in her chair, a nearly empty glass of wine at her lips, listening to their conversation in silence.

At one point Catherine excused herself to use the powder room and refresh her drink. She asked the bartender for a glass of Chardonnay and was waiting for him to fill her order when her eyes were drawn toward the far wall of the ballroom. A man was standing there, with a drink in his hand, watching her. He was of average height, thick and strongly built, with dark hair. His face wore a brooding expression. When their eyes met, he did nothing —didn't smile, didn't flinch. Catherine's brow drew downward, and a sick kind of feeling overturned in her stomach; all the nerves in her body seemed to stand at high alert.

"Thank you," she murmured to the bartender as she took the glass from his outstretched hand. She scuttled off to rejoin her party.

She was intercepted by a former client and her client's friend, who sought to hire her. Catherine forgot the man in the corner, delighted to talk about her work and to think about some fresh new ideas for a brand new person. The three gaily chatted for a few minutes, then dispersed. When Catherine looked up, the man from the corner was standing before her. She jumped, and the sick feeling returned.

"Some dress," he told her, his drink at his lips, his eyes scanning her up and down.

Catherine withdrew a little, clasping her hands before her waist in a feeble attempt to hide herself. "What do you mean?"

"You don't have to be coy. A woman doesn't wear a dress like that if she doesn't want to be looked at."

Catherine was taken aback. "I wore this dress because I like it."

"Ah, so you want to play games. I get it." He shrugged. "I can indulge you if it'll make you feel better."

"Do I know you?" she asked, desperate to be away from him, but inexplicably glued to her spot.

"Not yet," he replied with a crooked grin. He looked her over again and lifted an eyebrow at her. "Would you like to?"

"No," she said, shaking her head. "No, I wouldn't."

She turned on her heels and hurried away.

She found her family at their table. She fell into her chair beside Wes and sat there for a moment, flustered.

Wes brought his hand to her back and leaned in toward her.

"Are you okay, sweetheart?"

Catherine fidgeted under the table and took a deep breath. She mentally counted to three, trying to calm her nerves. "I'm a little anxious. I just met a man I really didn't like."

His face clouded. "What happened?"

"He made a comment about my dress. I didn't like the way he was looking at me."

"Who was it?"

Catherine looked around the room but couldn't find him.

"I don't see him anymore. I hope he's gone. He gave me such an awful feeling. I just can't calm down."

Wes held her as she sat, pressing her close and rubbing her back until her heartbeat had slowed.

He placed his hand on hers and leaned in to speak to her softly.

"How are you doing, sweetheart? Do you need to leave?"

She inhaled and smiled a little, meeting his eyes with gratitude. "No, I don't need to leave. Thank you, though."

"Well, if you see him again, point him out to me. Okay?"

She nodded again and let him pull her close once more, smiling as he kissed her forehead.

They enjoyed an elegant dinner, and Catherine put the encounter out of her mind. She reveled in the smiles of her family. Everyone was in such a good mood—even Maeve.

"I want you to come to me for advice, Cat," she told Catherine, leaning in, with her hand on her arm and the other hand holding a glass of wine.

"Advice about what?"

"About anything. As sisters do. We're sisters, Cat. Sisters. Why don't you ever come to me?"

Catherine was simultaneously touched and confused. "But I've been letting you plan my shower. I've been asking you for all sorts of opinions."

"But you never did before that, Cat. You only ever ask me

about what to wear. Not about anything important. And I try, Cat. I try."

"I don't know, Maeve," said Catherine. "I always kind of had the feeling you thought I was silly."

"Well, you are silly. That doesn't mean I don't love you, though. Because I do, Cat. I love you, and I don't like to see you hurting. You know?"

Maeve hugged her. Catherine let her, awkwardly bringing her hand to her sister's back and standing still for a moment until Maeve pulled away.

"I hope you're not driving home tonight," Catherine said.

"Don't be stupid. Mom and Dad drove me. I knew I couldn't be sober tonight."

They mingled with the other guests. After a while, Catherine grew tired and looked for Wes. She spotted him standing by the bar, talking to the dark-haired man from earlier in the evening. Wes was in his usual casual stance, one hand in his pocket and the other hand holding a drink, an easygoing smile on his face. The dark-haired man glared at Wes with a scowl in his eyes.

She stopped in her tracks, staring. She leaned in toward Maeve.

"That's the man who made those comments about my dress."

Maeve squinted in the direction Catherine indicated.

"Wow. Yeah. He looks mean. But why are there two of him?"

Catherine sighed inwardly and left Maeve in the care of Lois, who was gliding toward them. Then she slowly approached Wes and the unknown man, trying to remain unseen.

"You're going to cost the county jobs, you know," the man was saying gruffly. "I don't think that'll look too good when you run for state Senate."

"So the cat's out of the bag," Wes replied. "How did you hear?"

"Doesn't matter. I'm just saying it would be a shame for you to get the reputation of being anti-jobs."

"I appreciate your concern," Wes said, sipping his drink, his voice tinged with sarcasm. "Let's just say I'm not worried about it."

"You should be worried. You've set yourself up for attack. I'd rethink trying to stop this deal if I were you."

Wes leaned back and raised his eyebrows in mock disbelief. "You wouldn't be threatening me, now, would you?"

"Do you think I'm threatening you?"

"I can't imagine that you would. It would show pretty poor judgment."

The man sniffed and shook his head. "You sure are a cocky bastard. Always have been."

"Well, that may be," Wes said with a grin. He took another sip of his drink. "But it doesn't change the fact that the jobs argument is bullshit. It was bullshit in Texas, and it's bullshit here. You and I both know the jobs won't come through on that landfill. And it'll destroy people's lives in the process."

Both men turned as Catherine drew near. Wes's face brightened, and he held his arm out for her; the other man started and stared.

"There you are, sweetheart," he said. "Rick, this is my enchanting fiancée, Catherine Sheering. Catherine, this is Rick Tremaine."

Catherine's eyes widened as the man reached out his hand. She gave him the tips of her fingers and barely moved them up and down once before pulling her hand away in disgust.

"So you two are engaged," said Rick.

"Yes, this angel on Earth consented to marry me. Can you believe it?" Wes smiled and rubbed Catherine's back.

"Congratulations," Rick said dourly.

"Thank you. Was there anything else I could help you with tonight, Rick?"

Rick swigged from his glass and held up his hand. "You two take care of yourselves," he muttered, and slipped off into the crowd.

Wes turned to her fully. "Quite a charmer, isn't he? I'm sorry you had to meet that scoundrel." He rubbed her shoulders. "He really shouldn't have even tried to talk to me."

"That's the man I was talking about earlier."

The brightness left his face, his mouth straightening and his eyes blackening as they darted over her head to where Rick had retreated. After a moment of silence, in which he visibly composed himself, his eyes met hers again, and he attempted to smile. "Don't worry about Tremaine," he said. "I don't think you'll cross paths much."

"Do you really think he was threatening you?"

Wes laughed good-naturedly. "People say funny things when their money's at stake. He's acting like a tough guy because he wants this deal with Munson to go through. But you can rest easy about that, Cat. Rick Tremaine is all bark and no bite."

"Wes, I don't like him. He gave me a creepy feeling."

"Your feeling is warranted. He's rather unlikable. Please don't go near him, sweetheart." He patted her shoulders and kissed her. "Come, now—let me take your mind off it."

Catherine danced the night away with Wes, occasionally glancing over her shoulder for Rick; she passed a lovely evening, but the magic had been marred. She always felt he could be watching, like she was an unwitting performer in a twisted kind of play. She felt less free to move as she liked on the dance floor, less able to indulge in a discreet kiss with Wes. The energy required by the constant vigilance was exhausting, and she was relieved when their party disbanded and went their separate ways for the night.

Wes flicked on some classical music in the car, and the ride to his house was largely silent.

"Well, that was some event," he said cheerily as they undressed for bed. "For a first effort, they did a remarkable job. Don't you think?"

"Yes. It was great."

He stepped toward her and rested his hands on her shoulders. "You seem thoughtful. And I have a feeling I know why." His expression somber, he kissed her forehead. "I haven't forgotten about what Rick said to you. Are you very upset, sweetheart? What can I do?"

"It's not just that." She shuddered as she remembered the way Rick had looked at her, the repulsion in her stomach, the way she had felt exposed. "It's what he said to you, too."

Wes chuckled. "That's nothing to fret over. Please don't give it another thought. Rick Tremaine's just got his feathers ruffled because he knows logic and reason aren't on his side."

Catherine gazed at his face: his eyes were round and kind, his smile sincere. It was full of calm and confidence, the charmingly handsome face she had fallen in love with. She sighed inside, desperate to ensure she'd see this face every day for the rest of her life.

"I don't know. He seemed pretty mad. And his words were so sinister."

"He's full of hot air, sweetheart. That's all."

"But you said he doesn't like you because of your role in his leaving the firm." Catherine's heart wouldn't stop pounding. She frowned, unable to suppress the sick feeling in her gut. "It sounds like he's holding a grudge."

"Whether he is or isn't, it's not my concern. I'm not losing any sleep over what happened to Tremaine."

"I love you, Wes. I'm just...I'm just worried about something happening to you."

"My sweet, darling Catherine." He held her close and nuzzled his face in her hair. "I love you, too. And I love you for your concern. I won't let anything happen to me. I promise." He smiled. "Okay?"

Catherine nodded and returned his smile weakly as he patted her hips and walked away, disappearing into the bathroom. She stood still for a moment, thinking. Wes was sharp and perceptive, keenly attuned to the people around him. She hadn't ever known him to be wrong about anything. She relaxed somewhat. If he wasn't worried, if he said nothing would happen, it must be true. *Okay*, she thought. *I'll believe him.* And she climbed into bed to wait for him, feeling better, putting it out of her mind completely when he slid beside her and turned out the light.

CHAPTER NINE

*M*onday evening Catherine met Wes at the county building for the Planning Commission hearing. Wes had secured the testimony of several expert witnesses who would talk about environmental dangers and the substandard safety conditions at the Texas site. Sarah had done her part to reach the residents: they packed the building, holding her flyers, and filled the room until it was standing room only. Catherine was impressed by the energy in the crowd. Sarah held her hand and insisted that she sit up front with the rest of the family. Catherine preferred to stay in the back, where there was a little more air; reluctantly, she let Sarah lead her to the second row. As she sat between Wes and Sarah, she caught sight of Rick Tremaine across the aisle: he had been watching her squeeze through the crowd. Naturally recoiling closer to Sarah, she frowned at the lurching in her stomach. She averted her gaze and took her seat.

As the room settled and the hearing started, the excited din mellowing into a soft buzz, Catherine looked around the room at the array of people who had shown up to protect their homes and their environment.

"This is a wonderful turnout," she said to Sarah. "The Commission will never say no to all these people."

"We'll see, darling," said Sarah somberly, patting her hand.

Catherine turned to her. "I thought you said you were an optimist."

"Best to be optimistic without being naïve, I'm afraid."

The meeting came to order, and the agenda was announced. After a few minor orders of business, attendees were asked to speak about the planned zoning change of approximately two hundred acres of Virginia surplus land for the purpose of selling to J. J. Munson, who sought to build a landfill there. The first to speak was Rick Tremaine.

He stepped to the front of the aisle and cleared his throat, then spoke with his lips very close to the microphone.

"The Planning Commission's job is to advise the Board of Supervisors in matters relating to the development of land in this county. Your task is to make sure decisions are in the best interest of the residents of this county. In this case, your priority is to secure and preserve jobs. With this landfill, J. J. Munson has promised to bring a thousand jobs to this area, a much-needed boon to the county. If you walk around the neighborhoods surrounding the landfill site, you can see, it's a disaster. Houses are rundown, schools are struggling, people are unemployed. People's jobs are being sent overseas, factory jobs are being lost to technology, and coal jobs are vanishing every day. The tax dollars brought in by the landfill would help revitalize failing communities. Munson's Texas location pays nearly $3 million a year in taxes, money our towns would be deprived of if the Board fails to act. We need it to revitalize the community and foster growth that's a long time coming. It would be irresponsible of this Commission to fail to act on an opportunity to lift up these communities..."

Rick spoke for a minute or two about the virtues of Munson's Texas site, then curtly thanked the Board and stepped back. There was a murmur in the room as he took his seat.

Wes was to speak next. He stood and approached the microphone.

"Good evening, Commission members. I really am grateful to be speaking here tonight not only as a representative of this community, but also as a resident. As anyone who knows me will tell you, I'm always happy to take an opportunity to share my opinion"—he laughed here, and was joined in his laughter by most of the room—"but in this case, the situation is quite serious, so I'm perhaps even more eager than usual. Mr. Tremaine felt it incumbent on himself to remind you of your job. I know you good people take your jobs seriously and that you're just as vested as the rest of us in making sure this community remains the safe, desirable community that it is. So when Mr. Tremaine speaks of revitalization, I can't help but grow a little upset. I can't help but imagine what his motives are when with only the most cursory examination of Munson's site in Texas, one can see that building a Munson landfill here would be detrimental to the residents of this community. You see, when Mr. Tremaine talks of jobs, what he neglects to mention is that the unemployment rate in this county is lower than the statewide average. What he doesn't tell you is that Munson promised a thousand jobs at his Texas site and delivered only two hundred. And when Mr. Tremaine talks of tax revenue, what he doesn't say is that the operation, maintenance, and cleanup costs of the Texas site have exceeded its revenue and that as a result, Munson's requested from the town a deferment on his city tax payment. And it's not just about jobs and money, folks. In Texas, residents have reported a chemical smell in the air and in their water. They're reporting a myriad of health issues, everything from dizziness and nausea to accelerated heart rates. Already an environmental remediations group has been called in to the Texas site to examine safety failures and compel compliance with environmental regulations. A month ago, nearly two dozen families were evacuated from their homes at a moment's notice in the middle of the night because methane gas had been detected in their neighborhood, methane gas that was found to contain vinyl chloride. Now, for those who don't know, vinyl chloride is an industrially produced chemical used to produce PVC, and is a known carcinogen. As we speak, these families are displaced from their homes, unsure whether their homes will be safe for them to return to. Countless other families remain in harm's way. The human cost of this landfill could be tremendous, and that's to say nothing of the degradation of the value of their homes. But that's what you get when you hire subpar contractors like William Carmichael, who himself has been sued for breach of contract and cited for the illegal dumping of toxic waste. Look, I understand the temptation to grab hold of a chance to bring in jobs. But at what cost? As Mr. Tremaine derisively noted, the neighborhoods surrounding the site tend to be low income. Many of those folks are indeed struggling. Are we now to sell them out for the sake of the almighty dollar? Are we to take advantage of their voicelessness, to commit what ultimately amounts to environmental discrimination? That's not the Virginia I know and love. We need to protect the vulnerable among us, not exploit them. I couldn't put my head on my pillow at night having done such a thing, knowing I had hung those folks out to dry. I couldn't raise my own children here knowing I hadn't fought for their future. And so, I'm asking you, on behalf of the good people you see behind me, many of whom you'll hear from next, to recommend against this rezoning request, for the sake of my children, your own children, and all the children in this community. Thank you for your time tonight."

The room erupted into applause, and Wes shuffled through the row to his seat. Settling in beside Catherine, he smiled and patted her knee.

"That was so beautiful," she told him, the corners of her eyes prickling with tears. "You're a brilliant, decent, magnificent human being."

He kissed her gently as the applause settled down. "Thank you, sweetheart. I sure am a fortunate one."

"I love you," she said, leaning against his shoulder.

"I love you, too," he responded, and patted her knee once more.

The meeting continued for over two more hours as resident after resident rose to speak, many of them vehemently, about the dangers of the landfill. It was a raucous meeting, the passion almost palpable. Well into the night, after everyone had said their piece, Catherine, Sarah, and Wes rose and stretched, and made their way outside.

"What happens next?" asked Catherine.

"The Planning Commission has sixty days to make their decision," said Wes. "Then they'll pass their recommendation to the Board of Supervisors."

"Does the Board have to do what they say?"

"No, they're free to do what they wish. But the Commission's recommendation carries a lot of weight."

"I'll be on pins and needles," said Sarah. "It's all I'll be thinking about, that's for sure."

"Well, there's a lot more to think about," Wes said. "We need to start talking about what our plans will be if the zoning is approved. That'll involve protesting the sale of the land, and it'll take the fight to Richmond."

"I'll try to fire up the residents. I'll encourage everyone to call to complain."

"Me, too," said Catherine. "Maybe we can organize a citizens' trip to Richmond."

"Now you're talking!" cried Sarah. "That's the spirit."

"Have I mentioned how I love having activists in the family?" Wes placed one hand on his mother's shoulder and the other hand on Catherine's, and grinned. "You make my job so much easier."

"Well, you just keep working hard, darling," said Sarah, as she leaned up to kiss his cheek. "We'll win this battle together."

Sarah hugged Wes and Catherine, waved, and climbed into her car to drive home.

Wes and Catherine faced each other, standing between their cars.

Catherine wrapped her arms around his waist, her hands coming together at his lower back.

"Can I go back to your place tonight?"

"Of course. You're always welcome. It's not just my place anymore." He held her hips in his hands and kissed her. "Although, there's a good chance I'll be gone when you wake up tomorrow. I'm heading out extra early in the morning. I have to visit a client almost two hours away."

"That's a shame, but I understand." She smiled slyly and pressed herself close, slinking her hands up his back to his shoulders. "At least we still have tonight."

He grinned as she kissed him, coaxing his lips to part, and now moving her hands to the back of his head.

"You're very tempting," he said, his voice soft and silky. "But I need to get right to sleep. I have a long day ahead of me tomorrow."

"Oh." She frowned in disappointment. "Well, I might as well go home, then, and let you get your rest. I'll come over tomorrow night."

"That sounds wonderful." He kissed her again, his hands supporting her back. "I'll take you out for a nice dinner to make it up to you."

"You don't have to make it up to me." She smiled up at him, her hands clasped behind his neck. "You make it up to me every day by being the smartest, strongest, kindest, most handsome man in the whole entire world."

"Well, shucks, sweetheart. You sure are good to me."

"That's because you're good to me."

"You make it easy."

They both turned as someone walked by them in the dark

parking lot. It was Rick Tremaine. Catherine shrank into Wes as Rick's eyes met hers. She shivered as he turned and continued on toward his car.

Wes and Catherine kissed once more and drove home separately, Catherine's mind swirling with the intensity of the evening.

The next few weeks passed happily, including the holidays, which were a grand affair. The Bickharts hosted the Sheerings for Christmas, and once again Catherine basked in the warmth between the families. The Bickharts' home was festive and elegant, draped in white lights and glowing with a massive, fragrant blue-needle Christmas tree in the sunroom, from which the family had strung crystal globes and glass figures, and topped with an antique angel in a white lace dress.

The house boomed with conversation and laughter, and smelled of coffee and wine. Charles had cooked an indulgent breakfast and an even grander dinner, and the families now milled about in pairs and small groups, chatting easily with each other.

Catherine was holding Olivia, rocking her back and forth. The baby had fallen asleep and lay peacefully in Catherine's arms. Catherine couldn't stop staring at her perfect face, her long lashes and smooth skin, her tiny nose and heart-shaped lips.

"You have a natural touch with her," said Sarah, approaching, and taking a sip of her Irish coffee through a warm smile.

"She's so sweet," Catherine gushed, laying a gentle kiss on the baby's forehead. "I could hold her all day."

"Perhaps you'll have one of your own, soon, darling."

Sarah patted Catherine's arm and smiled. Catherine nuzzled her face against the baby's head, inhaling the soft scent of slumbering newborn.

For New Year's, Wes and Catherine took their first overnight trip together, to an inn in the heart of Virginia wine country. They passed the day on a winery tour, then spent a quiet elegant evening together at the inn, holding hands and kissing over champagne as the ball dropped in Times Square. There was nothing else she felt she'd rather do, ringing in the new year and her new life, enjoying cozy, intimate time with the man who had given her a life she'd never even imagined.

After the new year began, wedding preparation took off in earnest. Maeve and Hei planned a beautiful shower at Taylor's, an upscale restaurant in Charlottesville. Also in attendance were Lois, Sarah, Ethel, Helen, Olivia, and a handful of acquaintances. For the occasion, Catherine wore a mauve wool Milgrim suit with gold-encased fabric buttons and a short rolled collar: it seemed perfect for a shower just before Valentine's Day.

Catherine wasn't used to being the center of attention, of having everyone gather for her. She was nervous and apologetic, fearful of putting anyone out—but touched by everyone's desire to give her a day all her own, during which they crooned and doted over her, throwing gifts at her and not letting her lift a finger.

"Thank you," she said to Maeve and Hei when it was over, feeling frustrated by her inability to translate the magnitude of her appreciation into words. "I don't know what to say. Just—"

"You don't have to thank us," said Hei, bringing her in for a hug. "We love you, and you're getting married. It's a big deal."

"I'm sorry. I have a hard time being pampered, apparently."

"Guess what? You deserve it."

By the time the wedding approached, Catherine had moved her things to Wes's. She had already been spending most nights there anyway.

"I can't believe I'll be living here," she said one evening, hands clasped in front of her chest, turning around in a circle to take in the scene. "It's so glamorous!"

"Well, I'm glad you feel at home, sweetheart. Maybe one day you'll move your workshop here, too. I must admit I like the idea of having a chocolate factory right under my nose."

Wes's phone buzzed. He pulled it from his pocket and read the screen.

"It's Grady. He says the Planning Commission recommends in favor of the rezoning."

Catherine gasped. "I can't believe it! How could they? After your beautiful speech, and all those expert witnesses."

He punched in a quick response. "Money," he told her, and returned his phone to his pocket. "It always has the last laugh."

"You must be so disappointed."

"It's disappointing, but it's not over yet. The Board of Supervisors has to approve it. If they do, we'll appeal to Superior Court."

"Aren't you discouraged?"

"Me, discouraged?" He wrapped his arm around her and kissed her, then tickled her and smiled when she laughed. "Not to worry. It takes more than this to knock me off my game."

Finally, the wedding week arrived. They were to be married on Saturday morning. Friday evening, the families gathered at the country club for the rehearsal dinner.

"It's going to rain tomorrow," Maeve lamented into her wine. "Torrential downpours. A tropical storm."

"That's okay," said Catherine. "According to folklore, rain on your wedding day is good luck. It signifies renewal and cleansing, as well as fertility. In fact, in some cultures, the bride and groom—"

"Rain is good luck," Maeve interrupted tersely, holding up her hand. "Got it."

"That's our Catherine," said Hei, hugging her close. "She only sees the silver lining."

Catherine had been following the weather closely, not so much because she cared, but because she wanted to make sure they were fully prepared. Instead of setting up outside—they were supposed to be married in the gazebo, nestled deep in the church's colorful, fragrant garden—they arranged to have the flowers adorn the inside of the church itself.

"It will be just as beautiful," said Sarah. "I think you're lucky."

145

"I agree," Catherine answered emphatically, nodding. "I definitely agree."

They ran through the ceremony. Catherine's belly fluttered with nerves as it always did when she knew she'd be looked at and required to perform in front of a crowd, but otherwise, she was strangely free of anxiety. She'd been planning this for months. It was exactly what she wanted. Their families got along famously. She and Wes were practically living together already. They'd be married tomorrow, sure. Really, what difference did it make?

"You're so weird," said Maeve. "Most women freak out right about now."

"I already did all my freaking out, when I didn't know where my life was going. Now I do. Why would I freak out now?"

"I don't know, Cat. I'd think one would feel some emotion at the thought of marrying the love of one's life. I mean the man wants to spend his life with you."

"Oh, I feel plenty of emotion about that." Catherine instantly turned solemn. She looked at Maeve with wide brown eyes. "I feel so much emotion I almost can't feel it."

It was a deeply colored emotion, something between indigo and garnet. It was a color she wanted to wrap herself in. It was something soft and serious, with the richness of velvet but the whimsy of silk.

"I do worry about being a good wife," she admitted, thinking of Wes's grand home, the new life she'd be leading, and all the wonderful things about him that made her want to impress him. A vague tremor of anxiety tugged at her gut. "I hope I'm cut out for it."

"What does 'good' even mean? He's marrying you. You're cut out for being you, aren't you?" Maeve's voice was annoyed, but a sudden flash of emotion crossed her expression. The two sisters looked at each other, and Catherine thought she sensed warmth in her sister's usually inscrutable eyes. In just as short a moment, it was gone. "Don't worry about that stuff," she said, and turned to replenish her drink.

Catherine kissed Wes goodbye that night on the club's grand porch, the iron sconces bathing in light the white paneling and white-painted wide-plank floors, casting them in a warm glow that contrasted cozily with the darkness outside.

"Enjoy your night with Hei," he said, his arms wrapped around her, his hands clasped at her lower back. He looked down at her with that smile, and she swooned inside, as she always did. "I'm sure you'll have a marvelous time."

"Oh, it will be very tame. There won't be any shenanigans. Besides, Maeve will be there."

"Quite a motley trio." Wes grinned. "Those two could not be more different. I'll bet you feel pulled every which way."

"It's good to have them both for perspective. They always disagree. Usually the right answer is somewhere in the middle."

His face turned more solemn. "I'm truly looking forward to our life together. Thank you for marrying me, sweetheart."

"Oh, gosh. You don't have to thank me. I couldn't be any happier. This is the best time of my life. You're like—you're like —" The depth of her feelings was almost too great for words, and she struggled to find a suitable comparison. "You're like a Schiaparelli gold lamé gown with a low draped back and long bell sleeves, complemented by a panel of ruched fabric. And a train," she added emphatically, with wide, knowing eyes.

Wes was watching her with playful amusement in his eyes. "That good, huh?"

"Better."

He leaned in and kissed her slowly, taking his time, brushing his soft lips against hers and caressing the side of her face with his fingertips until she was warm and giddy.

"I love you, Cat," he said. "Tomorrow will be a wonderful day."

"Tomorrow, and every day after."

They kissed again and parted, the air around them brisk and sweet, and joyful with the singing of night's lively creatures.

CHAPTER TEN

*C*atherine hadn't known rain could fall sideways, but on her wedding day, she discovered that it did.

"Wow," marveled Hei, standing at the window of the makeshift bridal suite at the church. Everyone in the room—Hei, Maeve, Lois, Sarah, Helen, Catherine, and the hairdressers—had turned with surprise at the sound of the rain pelting the building in a strong gust of wind. The bridal party had intended to prepare at Lois's house, but they changed their plans to avoid being caught in the rain with their wedding hair and makeup. "I'm glad we're getting ready here. Good call, Sarah."

Sarah ticked her finger against her head and smiled coyly. "I've still got some good ideas in this old brain of mine."

"I like this weather," said Maeve, holding completely still as a hairdresser pinned up her dark brown locks. "It's like a movie. Very dramatic. Lots of emotion in this weather."

"I tend to agree," said Catherine, with a little smile. She was sitting in a comfortable armchair, sipping a cup of black coffee, her eyes closed. She concentrated on the trickling melody of Brahms as it sailed up from a speaker on the dresser. She had been the first to have her hair done, and she was trying to relax before the makeup.

"I fear it won't let up by the end of the ceremony," lamented Lois. "Leaving to go to the club is going to be a challenge."

"It'll be okay," said Catherine, glancing at herself in the mirror, admiring her vintage-style hairdo. Her soft honey-colored hair fell straight, with an added wave in front; the lower half had been meticulously curled into large round ringlets, à la Lauren Bacall.

"We'll just wrap ourselves up in plastic," said Maeve. "Problem solved."

"It'll be okay," said Catherine again, smiling as her makeup artist approached.

The church, with its tall steeple and exposed wooden beams, was decorated elegantly with calla lilies and white candles. They lined up outside the chapel, and Catherine watched in solemn awe as Hei and Maeve fell into order before walking down the aisle, both looking so beautiful in their Prussian blue dresses and pulled-up hair.

After Hei had marched forward, with an excited little squeal and a glowing smile, Maeve turned to Catherine and Fred.

"Dad, can I have a minute alone with my sister?"

"Of course." Fred patted Catherine's arm and stepped away.

Catherine looked at Maeve expectantly. "What is it, Maeve?"

Maeve's eyes were glassy, and her rose-painted lips quivered. She blinked, her dark eyelashes shining with tears. "You, um—you look beautiful in Grandma's dress. I'm sorry I told you not to wear it. You were right to be yourself." She swallowed. "I'm really glad for you. I wish you and Wes nothing but happiness for the rest of your lives."

Catherine waited for the inevitable criticism, but it didn't come. Maeve merely stood there, sniffling.

"Maeve," she said, touched. "You're not even drunk."

Maeve burst into laughter, and Catherine laughed too.

"Jesus, Catherine," Maeve sighed, shaking her head, but smiling. She then dabbed her eyes with a tissue handed to her by a frantic usher, and headed off down the aisle.

Fred stepped beside her and held out his arm. She took it, tears in her eyes.

"You really did it. I'm so proud of you, my girl. And I couldn't love you more."

"Thank you, Dad. I love you, too."

And at the nod from the usher, they stepped into the aisle.

Catherine would always remember her first look at the inside of the church, calla lilies everywhere, a cooing crowd smiling as they turned their heads to see, the grand stained glass window above the altar. Hei and Maeve stood on the left, Grady and Wes's friend Mitch, from Washington, on the right—and Wes, tall, slim, and perfect, wearing a crisp tuxedo and a dazzling smile. It was almost too much, the noise of so many people, so many beautiful things to look at, so many people looking at her; for a devastating moment, she believed she couldn't enter the room, thinking herself a fool for failing to predict how difficult it would be. She forced herself to put one foot in front of the other, making herself master the fray. Every person here, every flower—this was all for her. It was wonderful, and terrifying. Sweat was beading along her hairline, under her arms, and down her back. She gripped her father's arm, and he placed his hand on hers. Beginning to panic in the disorder, she closed her eyes. *One, two, three.* She opened them again, and locked eyes with Wes. She gradually approached him, focusing on his smile, and glided evenly through the noise as if gazing at him through a tunnel. By the time her father kissed her cheek and stepped back to take his seat, she felt calmer and more at peace.

Wes took her hand and looked at her, his brow crinkled upward and his eyes wide. Catherine smiled tearfully and squeezed his hand.

The ceremony was cheerful and upbeat, full of warm words and smiles. The crowd gasped and laughed when the rain slammed against the outside of the church, seeming to agree with the proclamations and predictions of happiness. Catherine had imagined she'd feel beside herself, that her wedding would seem surreal. But it was definitively real, and she very deeply experienced the sensation of being in the process of being married. In her mind, she ticked off the items on the program, calculating how many more minutes it would be until she was bound to him in marriage.

They said their vows. Catherine held onto his gaze as if it were her lifeline. His eyes were bright and his voice steady, and he slipped her ring onto her finger with the assured tenderness that had made her fall in love with him. When the marriage was pronounced, Catherine looked up at him with eyes full of tears. He was smiling brilliantly, his own eyes glistening. He brought her in for a kiss, and the room broke into applause.

"We did it, sweetheart," he said, his lips at her ear. "Are you ready?"

"I am so ready," she said, and reveled in his laughter. He took her hand and held it up toward the ceiling, then offered his arm and glided with her back up the aisle, to begin the rest of their lives.

THEY STOOD at the entrance of the church, staring at the limousine that awaited them in front. It was only about a hundred feet, but with the intensity of the storm, it looked like a mile.

"We may have to forego the picture-perfect exit," he shouted above the din of the wedding party and assorted guests who had filtered out of the chapel. "There's a private exit in the back. We can hop right into the car from there."

Catherine peeked through the crack in the doors, listening to the tumult of the storm. She turned to him.

"Let's have a little fun," she said.

Before he could respond, she opened the doors fully, picked up the skirt of her dress, and stepped outside into the rain.

"Holy—" she heard him exclaim, but the rain drowned out the rest.

Instantly she was drenched—her hair, her shoes, her dress. She squinted against the onslaught of wind and chilly water, looking for him inside the church. There he was, mouth open with shock, surrounded by equally shocked-looking guests.

He was shouting to her, but she couldn't hear what he was saying. She waved him over. After a pause, with a backward glance, he ran out to join her, unable to see the guests he had left behind, who were holding their hands to their faces and screaming.

He slowed as he approached, looking upward at the sky.

He looked back down at her when he stood before her. He was soaked from head to toe. His tuxedo stuck to his form in wrinkled clumps; his impeccably neat sandy hair fell in dark slabs over his head. He brushed it backward, and he somehow looked even more handsome than he had before.

"What were you saying in there?" she yelled, the sound of the rain muffling her voice.

"I said you've certainly made this a day to remember. This takes the cake, sweetheart."

"Isn't it wonderful? It's just like *Singin' in the Rain*."

"I'd say it's a little more than that."

She smiled as he took her arms and began dancing with her in the rain. Behind them, the crowd cheered and laughed.

"Your grandmother's dress," he said as they stood still once more, his hands on her waist. "It isn't ruined, is it?"

She shrugged. "It's just water. They had water in my grandmother's day."

He smiled soberly and shook his head. "You sure are something special, Cat."

They hugged each other close, to the buoyant applause of the crowd.

"What do you think?" she asked him, more seriously. "Isn't this wonderful?"

"Well, it's not what I'd envisioned, but sometimes plans are best when they've gone awry." He rubbed her back, his hand an oasis of warmth in the cold, merciless rain, and met her gaze with a smile. "It's perfect. It's lovely in its own special way."

He leaned in for a warm, watery kiss. She smiled and wrapped her hands around his neck. She raised her leg, and the guests cheered again. The photograph that was taken of that moment would be her favorite for the rest of her life.

AFTER DANCING IN A RAINSTORM, one dries out surprisingly quickly in a room full of people. It doesn't hurt if friends and family frantically rub one down with towels and shove one under the restroom hand dryer.

The wedding reception at the country club was lovely but overwhelming. There were so many people, most of whom she didn't even know. She was used to big events like this, to being around a lot of well-dressed, talkative strangers. But this time, they were here for her. She was obligated to meet them all, to shake their hands and pretend to be interested in what they were saying. Worse, she was expected to remember them. Much of it passed by in a blur of bright lights, faces, and voices, coming at her from all sides in confusing spurts of flashes and noise. Wes stood beside her at all times, rubbing her back and squeezing her shoulder, whispering encouragement and asking if she was all right. Regardless of the whirlwind around her, his nearness fortified her; the calm of his demeanor, the concern in his eyes, brought her comfort and reset her equilibrium. She held onto his arm, grounding herself in his physical firmness, closing her eyes as he squeezed her hand to mentally retreat from the chaos.

In the stressful hubbub of the evening, three events stayed with her in clear, vivid detail.

The first was her first dance with Wes—when she was introduced as Mrs. Bickhart, when she stepped onto the dance floor with him as his wife. Despite the fact that everyone was watching, that cameras were flashing and lights were glaring, it was a cozy, intimate moment, one in which the chaotic environment disintegrated around her. Staring into his eyes, where so much love resided—resting her head on his shoulder as he held her against the rhythm—it was her own little version of paradise, one of the happiest times of her life.

The second was an improvisation, a spontaneous group hug with all the important women in her life. Hei, Maeve, Lois, Sarah, Ethel, and Helen happened to surround her at exactly the same moment, and they all leaned in to kiss her. The resulting photograph—in which she smiled more widely than she ever had, in this feminine circle of support and well wishes—always made Catherine's heart leap.

The third was when she met Dr. Claire Robinson, Wes's ex-wife.

"So you're the new Mrs. Bickhart," Claire drawled, leaning in to kiss each cheek. She then stood back to look at her, her hands still on Catherine's arms. Catherine watched her, in awe: she was gorgeous—slender, curvy, and blond—with round, soft features. Her voice was eloquent and smooth. She exuded a calm confidence that Catherine could perfectly imagine in someone who used to be Wes's wife.

"Yes," said Catherine.

"Well. Clearly, Wes has impeccable taste."

Wes laughed jovially and leaned in to kiss Claire's cheek. "Thank you for coming, Claire. It's good to see you. You, too,

Patrick," he said to the man behind Claire. The two men shook hands amiably.

"It's the least I could do, supporting you in your new marriage as you supported me in mine." She turned to Catherine. "Wes and I don't believe in animosity. He was at my wedding. We all had a grand old time."

"It was a fantastic wedding," Wes agreed. "I wouldn't have expected anything less."

"Thank you," said Claire, taking a sip of wine. She looked around their little circle and grinned. "Look how mature we are."

"Yes, we're models of civility. It helps when both parties are sincere and understanding."

"Amen," said Claire, holding out her drink. "And cheers."

They all clinked glasses and sipped their champagne, Wes with his hand on Catherine's lower back.

Claire pointed discreetly toward the center of the room. "That's Harold Beck."

"Yes, it is," said Wes, glancing backward, then back at Claire. "He and Patricia were gracious enough to come."

"You didn't invite Meredith?"

"We did," said Wes. "She couldn't make it last minute. She's had some complications in her pregnancy. Her doctor nixed the idea."

"That's a shame. I would have liked to see her again."

Catherine's brow rose. "You met Meredith?" she asked, breaking her silence. Though Claire was friendly, Catherine was intimidated, and she hadn't known what to say before this moment.

"I met her once, yes. Smart, savvy woman. I somehow knew it wouldn't work, though."

This piqued Wes's interest. "Did you, now," he said wryly.

Claire took a long sip of wine. "She wasn't your type, just like I wasn't. You just didn't know it at the time."

"I presume you're about to tell me what my type is."

"I think you already know." Claire smiled at Catherine, then laid her hand on her arm. "I'm delighted for you both, Catherine. And I wish you both a lifetime of happiness."

"Thank you," said Catherine, blushing from such kind words from such a splendid woman.

"You've got yourself a very good man, there. Wes will be good to you. He's nothing if not chivalrous."

"Oh, I know." Catherine instantly warmed, happy to be talking about her relationship with Wes. "He's magnificent. It's almost surreal, how perfect he is in every way. I'm utterly smitten."

Claire's face seemed to transform; her strong, more guarded expression melted into something soft, almost vulnerable. "How beautiful," she said, with an earnest smile. She turned to Wes and tipped her glass. "Congratulations, my friend." Her smile grew crooked, seeming to turn a little sly. "This one's perfect for you."

Finally the party was over. Wes and Catherine retired to a suite in a nearby hotel. The next morning, they'd leave for a two-week St. Lucia honeymoon. But before that, they'd spend their first night as a married couple in one of the most luxurious rooms in Charlottesville, and Catherine had plans.

He carried her over the threshold and set her down inside the room. It was dimly lit, the lamps and sconces set to a romantic half strength—elegantly decorated—and blessedly quiet. They embraced in front of the bed, sighing with exhaustion and relief. Wes took her face in his hands and kissed her gently, then parted her lips with his and deepened the kiss, making her insides flutter. To his evident surprise, she excused herself and retreated to the corner, where their suitcases had been deposited; she withdrew a special box, large and wrapped with a wide gold ribbon. She brought it to him, and he took it in silence, then set it on the bed and pulled open the ribbon. He lifted the lid and gazed inside, standing still a moment as he absorbed what he was seeing. She nudged his hand with her fingers, encouraging him to explore the contents. Slowly he reached for the first object within his grasp, and lifted it. It was a small box of four chocolate-covered strawberries, plump and luscious, their red flesh glistening. He laid this small box on the bed and removed another object: a chocolate feather, so fragile and fine, encased in a thin, clear case. He studied it a long time, then laid it, too, on the bed. Out came the next object, a dainty glass jar full of rich, syrupy chocolate. He unscrewed the lid and sniffed, his chest swelling with his breath. Catherine watched his face: it was sober and serious, but his eyes were sharp, taking it all in. He replaced the lid, then set the jar on the bed. He peeked inside the rest of the box, moving his hand around the objects still inside. His eyes darkened, and a grin touched the corners of his mouth. He turned to her in silence, for nothing needed to be said: she'd worked for weeks on these objects, painstakingly crafting them with him in mind, her gift to her husband on their wedding night—the gift of chocolate, the gift of herself. In the softening of his eyes, in the tender touch of his fingers on her face, Catherine knew he understood. Without a word, he kissed her, deeply, unhooking the clasps of her dress, from the nape of her neck to the small of her back, working effortlessly against the rising and falling of her chest. She held her arms for him as he carefully pulled her from the sleeves, and she stepped out of the dress when it crumpled to the floor. He found the button of her petticoat, and she closed her eyes as he let it fall over her hips to her feet. She stood before him in ivory-colored lingerie, silky and smooth, and cool under his touch. His fingers grazed her shoulder, her nipple, the curvy crease where her thigh met her bottom, and delicate prickles rose to the surface of her skin; he guided her downward, and she slipped between the covers of the bed, watching as he untied his bow tie, and tingling with delight. His bow tie, his jacket, his cufflinks, his belt—then his vest, his shirt, his trousers. Catherine inhaled as she gazed upon his form, until he extinguished the lights and was a mere silhouette; she exhaled as he slid beside her, his bare skin warming hers. He wrapped her in his arms, like a present, special and safe, and kissed her hungrily, like a morsel of chocolate. Catherine moaned aloud, eyes closed, heart open. She'd taken so long to find him, but by God, he was worth the wait. *I love you*, she told him in her mind, her breath overpowering her voice. *I love you, I love you, I love you, I love you.* She clung to him, and he held her fast, driving away all thoughts and making her feel how good it was to be his wife.

CHAPTER ELEVEN

*T*he new Mr. and Mrs. Bickhart enjoyed two weeks on St. Lucia, taking in the scenery and sipping cocktails on the beach. It was a small thing, but Catherine was delighted that Wes never once wore a suit. Though Wes definitely knew how to wear a suit—his suits were stylish and well-tailored, and they always fell perfectly on his straight, fine form—he looked equally dashing when dressed more casually, and Catherine had no trouble admiring him in his shorts and polos or short-sleeved dress shirts. It was wonderful to see him sleep past sunrise for a change, and relax with his feet up in the sun—especially since halfway through their stay, they received some bad news.

"Damn," he muttered, looking at his phone when it beeped one evening as they sat down for dinner. They were seated at an outdoor table at a restaurant on the water, and the sky melted from blue to lavender to russet to gold.

"What's wrong?"

He scrolled through the message a moment, then returned his phone to his pocket.

"Well, we have a decision from the Board of Supervisors," he said, pushing back his sunglasses and opening his menu. He'd acquired a healthful tan, and Catherine found it attractive against his sandy hair and handsome features. "They've approved the rezoning. Looks like we're going to have to appeal after all."

"How disappointing," Catherine said with a frown, her shoulders drooping. "I thought they'd see how bad it would be for the residents and deny it. I was sure of it."

"I'm not too surprised. When the Planning Commission recommended in favor, I didn't hold out much hope."

"What happens next?"

"We'll appeal to Circuit Court."

"Do you think we'll win?"

"I don't know, sweetheart, but I certainly intend to try."

They paused a moment as a waiter poured their water, then stepped away.

"I wish you didn't find out on our honeymoon," she said. "What a rotten thing to have to deal with now."

"No worries, sweetheart." He closed his menu with a smile and laid it down, then took a sip of water, his arm resting on the table. "I'll deal with it when we get back. I'm not stressing about anything now—work, Munson, or otherwise."

They didn't mention it again; they chatted gaily and held hands across the table, breathing in the fresh sea air and the sweet, musky smell of the beach. They clinked glasses and indulged in a gourmet dinner, then danced under the stars until retiring to their room.

By the end of the two weeks, Wes seemed restless and ready to get back to work. Though Catherine was sad for her honeymoon to be over, she liked her husband's need to be active, the fact that he was constantly moving. His eagerness to resume helping his clients was admirable to her. He'd never taken such a long vacation; Catherine felt glad to have had his full attention for so long.

They returned home to the house she loved. Dorothea rushed to her side and nuzzled against her leg, then Wes's.

Catherine scooped her up and kissed her. She rubbed her cheek against her fur.

"And now, our new life truly begins," she said, returning her to the floor and sighing with happiness.

Though she lived in a different house, Catherine's routine remained largely the same. Wes left for work early, and Catherine kissed him goodbye before sitting in the kitchen with her cup of black coffee. She then drove the short distance to her grandmother's house and her workshop, where she made her chocolate and took her walks, just as she had before. She tried to be home by the time he was: she didn't want to miss even a minute with him.

She wanted to be a good wife for him. She kept her piles and stacks to a minimum. She tied a string around the door knob on the inside of the front door so she'd remember to lock it, and she only forgot a handful of times. She attempted to cook him dinner —which didn't turn out as well as she'd hoped.

"How are you eating that?" she exclaimed, flinching as another bite of unrecognizable chicken marsala passed his lips.

"Sweetheart, it's not that bad," he mumbled through a mouthful, before taking a large gulp of water.

"Really?" she asked him hopefully, the divot between her eyebrows creasing with surprise.

"Really." He smiled at her. "In fact, I rather like it."

She watched as he ate a few more bites, then rubbed his hands together and placed his napkin on the table.

"You're already through?"

"Yes, I think so. I had a late lunch with Grady today."

"Well, there's a real lot left. I can pack it for you to take to work tomorrow."

"That's a great idea, sweetheart. How very kind of you."

She thought about him all day long and lived for him to text or call her. The sight of his name on her phone was enough to make her jump from her seat. The sound of his voice made electricity shoot right through her, from her head to her toes and all the wonderful places in between.

"I'm so glad you're home," she'd announce cheerfully upon his arrival, her arms wrapped around him, bopping up and down a little on her toes in her excitement. "I missed you so much today!"

"I'm glad to be home, too, sweetheart. How was your day?"

"It was good. I finished my project. I made a new dish tonight for dinner, do you want to try it?"

They'd eat dinner and sit for a while in his study, either in comfortable conversation or cozy silence. Sometimes they'd walk through the beautiful tree-lined neighborhood. Sometimes they'd sit in the garden. But no matter what they did, Catherine would wonder how the night would end, whether her prayers would be answered or she'd be disappointed once again.

He works around the clock, Hei assured her. *And he's no spring chicken. Maybe you need to start doing it in the morning, when he's fresh.*

I tried that, but he leaves so darn early. Unfortunately it's just not enough.

It was never enough. Not for as much as she thought about it, which was always, night and day, in the morning as she made her coffee and the afternoon as she worked on her chocolate, in the evening as she attempted to cook dinner and at night as they prepared for bed. Catherine felt obsessed, but she couldn't help it. She was passionately, desperately, consumingly in love with him. His intelligence and competence were almost unbearably sexy. The important nature of his work essentially made him a hero. His vigilance of her comfort, his embracing of her eccentricities, made her weak in the knees. He was just so attractive, so dashing and handsome; he was just so good, so considerate and kind. It just felt so good to be in his arms. She so loved to hold him, to feel his tight muscles beneath her fingers, to take his body into hers and be one with him. Her favorite place on Earth was underneath him, feeling his strength and being in his power. He held her just right, said all the right things, in a way that she'd never imagined. He was a drug, an idol, a beautiful work of art. And being with him was all she wanted, all day long, in every waking moment.

"Oh no, really?" she lamented in bed one night, receiving a kiss on the nose, the surest sign, she'd learned, that he was going right to sleep.

"Sweetheart, I'm so sorry. I hate to disappoint you again."

"Then don't," she moaned softly, pulling him close, her hand in his hair.

"There's nothing more I'd love than to oblige. But I had a fourteen-hour day today. Grady and I just got back from Richmond an hour ago, and I'm exhausted. I'm going to knock off work a little early tomorrow. I'll make it up to you then. What do you say we go out to dinner and then call it an early night?"

"Okay." She kissed him. "Promise?"

"I promise," he said, a smile in his voice. "And I never break my promises."

When her prayers were answered, they were answered in full, and in ways that made the dry spells worth it. He was enthusiastic in bed, with remarkable stamina. He had a firm, decisive touch, but also gentleness that made her swoon. He was attentive and loving and sensitive to her needs, and he met those needs, with mind-blowing efficiency, without fail. His dedication and expertise, and the resulting breathtaking ecstasy, indeed made up for the nights when she went without. *What was I so upset about?* she'd ask herself the next day, grinning into her coffee, bristling pleasantly as she remembered the events of the previous night. And sure enough, that evening, she'd be praying once again.

Before meeting him, she'd never known what it was like to feel satisfied, and now that she did, she felt she could grow used to it. Which was why she was so frustrated by the infrequency of these dalliances.

Maybe he's having an affair, texted Maeve.

Catherine had made the mistake of telling Maeve about her

problem. She hadn't intended to, but Maeve had asked her how things were going, and she'd taken a leap of faith.

Wes isn't like that.

That's what they all say.

Catherine always took everything Maeve said seriously, at first, because she didn't trust her own opinions and because Maeve was smart. But she couldn't truly believe Wes was having an affair. He had too much integrity, and he was so good to her. And then came his question about babies.

It was after dinner at his parents' house one night in April. Helen, Grady, and Olivia had been there, too. Sarah had told them she'd talked to Harold Beck. Meredith was doing well, despite the complications in her pregnancy. She was due in August. She and her husband didn't know the sex of the baby, but she suspected they were having a boy. Harold hadn't heard any of this from Meredith, of course; she never told him anything, he said. They'd heard it secondhand from their son Vince, who lived in Maine like Meredith and who was very close with her and her husband.

"I was thinking we should speed up our timeline," Wes said in their bedroom that night, slipping out of his clothes and climbing into bed in his boxers.

Catherine stopped fussing with the waist tie of her 1930s pale blue silk nightgown with the cap sleeves, lace trim, and keyhole bodice and looked at him curiously. "You were?"

"Yes." He smiled at her from bed and held out his hand for her to join him. "What do you think? Too soon?"

"Not necessarily." She scrambled into bed with him and cuddled into his outstretched hand. "What brings this on?"

"Well, neither of us is getting any younger, sweetheart. I'm forty-seven. At this rate, I'll be geriatric by the time our child's in preschool."

Catherine giggled. "No, you won't."

"So what do you say? Should we go for it? Are you ready to be called 'Mommy'?"

Catherine bit her lip in thought. "Well, we'd have to have sex to get pregnant."

"You don't say," he replied in an exaggerated manner as he leaned over her and grinned, then pinched her playfully from behind, making her squeal.

Catherine didn't care either way. She hadn't thought much about children, but taking care of Olivia had changed her. She was drawn to the sweet baby girl and suddenly could imagine having one of her own. She liked what Olivia brought out in her. She was pleasantly surprised to find that the motherly instinct came naturally to her. She was so used to living on her own, to taking care of only herself. Helping with Olivia reminded her of the days when she took care of her grandmother, and made her miss them.

Even more than that, though, was the fact that the thought of having a child with Wes thrilled her. She craved the bond and the connection with him. They'd discussed the issue, and they'd planned to wait a year. But if he wanted to speed up the timeline, that was fine with her. And besides, she was thirty-seven. She wasn't getting any younger, either.

It wasn't the only important issue in their lives. The Munson landfill took center stage as Wes prepared for their rezoning appeal and fought the sale of the property. Catherine and Sarah met frequently to send flyers and call representatives in the General Assembly, asking them to intervene. Wes worked even longer hours than usual—examining records, seeking out witnesses, giving interviews with the press. He flew to Texas a second time to gather more information from the Department of Environmental Protection and speak with residents; he even flew a few of them to Virginia to speak at a rally in Richmond. The rally was a protest against the sale of the surplus land to Munson. It had been organized by Sarah and took place in front of the Department of General Services, next to the Capitol. In attendance were hundreds of county residents, as well as some from surrounding counties who feared the effects the landfill would have on their water and air supply. Sarah, Charles, Helen, Grady, Catherine, and Wes were all there, though not all were in the crowd: Wes was inside, pleading his case, at that moment.

"So many people!" Catherine shouted above the din of protesters, resisting the urge to cover her ears and close her eyes. She glanced around, observing the news cameras and helicopters reporting on the scene. "This will be all over the news."

"We've all done a fabulous job," replied Sarah, clapping her hands as a speaker took to the podium. "You and I definitely did all we could! And Wes has been working his heart out, as you know."

"I can't wait until this is over. I've barely even seen him."

"I know he feels the same." Sarah wrapped her arm around Catherine's shoulder and squeezed.

At the end of the protest, Catherine cheered with the rest of the crowd as Wes emerged with a variety of others involved in the case—witnesses, reporters, and other attorneys, including Rick Tremaine. State senator David Marks, a slim, balding fellow of middle age and average height, followed a few steps behind.

"Marks," muttered Sarah, leaning in toward Catherine. "I wouldn't think even he would have the gall to show his face here."

"Is it really that bad?"

"I think it's in poor taste, and a little suspicious. Why does he care about this deal so much?"

Catherine watched the group, deliberately not looking at Rick Tremaine lest he glance her way and meet her eyes.

"I'm more worried about...him," Catherine said to Sarah, not even wanting to say his name. "He gives me such a funny feeling."

"Who? Rick Tremaine?" Sarah asked, looking with her. "Yes, he's awful. As you know, he was ousted from Wes's firm. He had a habit of harassing women, but somehow that was Wes's fault."

Catherine watched as a microphone was shoved in Wes's face and he began talking, one hand in his pocket, the other hand gesturing as he made his points. A wave of pride flooded her, and she grinned widely.

They waited as Wes was interviewed, then a grumpy-looking Rick Tremaine. David Marks spoke next, and the crowd dispersed.

The protest rally was over, but the excitement it generated lingered. Wes placed several more ads in the local newspaper, urging people to share their feelings with the county and to contact their state representatives. He worked tirelessly on his case for appeal, which he'd present to the Circuit Court in September.

In the meantime, Catherine's life continued as normal. She loved living in Wes's house, and Dorothea loved it, too—especially now that the weather was so lovely and she could enjoy the outdoors, like Wes's patio and perfectly planned garden, and their beautiful street and neighborhood, which was shady and romantic under a canopy of trees. She sometimes took a blanket to the front yard and sat beneath the hawthorn tree; her hands behind her back, she gazed upward, where sunlight trickled through the clusters of white flowers. She was always amazed by the birds and small creatures that played there, for the flowers were guarded by thick thorns. She admired the creatures' persistence and courage, the way they'd adapted to the dangers so they might live somewhere so beautiful.

It was a funny thing, she thought. She was used to living by herself. Even when she'd lived with her grandmother, she'd kept her own routine, and after her grandmother passed away, she'd been happy to spend so much time by herself. Now that she had Wes, however, spending time alone wasn't as satisfying. She was lonely during the day. She found herself lamenting his long hours. And when he did come home, she wanted to be close to him. He was affectionate and loving, and their intimate nights were extraordinary, when they happened. But these sporadic occurrences couldn't match the demand of her craving for him. She began to grow frustrated, and was surprised by her negative emotions. She didn't know if her feelings were legitimate, or if she just didn't know what a real relationship felt like.

"Are you having an affair?" she blurted one evening over dinner.

Wes froze with his fork halfway to his lips. He stared at her with an expression she'd never seen on his face, one with sharp eyebrows and stern lips. "Excuse me?"

Catherine flushed. "I..." she began, but for once, she couldn't finish her thought.

He continued staring at her with the same serious expression. "I'm not a cheater, Cat. I thought you knew me better than that by now."

She sat up straight. "I do. I mean, I know I do. It's just that—"

"I work over seventy hours a week. I'm still growing my practice with Grady, and I'm trying to fight this damned landfill. I'm beginning my campaign for the Senate. And, I'm nearly fifty."

"I'm sorry." Her voice was small, and she shrank back in her seat. Her face was on fire. Had Maeve been teasing her with her suggestion? She chastised herself for being so stupid. "I hope I didn't make you mad."

His expression softened, and he lowered his fork. He reached across the table for her hand, and she took it.

"Sweetheart," he said, his voice now patient and tender. "I love you. You know that. Do you really think I would have an affair? That I'd inflict that pain on you, and on myself?"

She shook her head, tears prickling the corners of her eyes. "I don't, Wes. I don't."

He offered a rueful smile, then took a deep breath and smiled more warmly. "I'm not having an affair, Cat. I've never cheated in my life, and I certainly don't intend to start now. You're my wife, and I adore you, and I'll do everything in my power to preserve what we have. And may God strike me dead if I'm lying."

"I'm so sorry," she said quickly. "I'm so sorry."

His eyes turned mournful. He stood and approached her. He knelt next to her chair and placed his hands in her lap.

"No, sweetheart. I'm sorry." She folded her hands over his, and he looked at her with earnest eyes. "I know it's hard. I know you get lonely. And I want to try to be there for you more often, because you deserve it."

"Oh, Wes," she gushed, turning to him fully and stroking his face with her fingers. "I respect you so much for how hard you work. And I know you're trying to help the town. You give me so much, Wes, and it's enough. It's more than enough. I'm just being silly. Please, please, forget what I said. You must do what you must do."

Wes's hard work paid off. The Circuit Court heard his case and decided in his favor, and the sale fell through. The Munson landfill was officially dead, and the people's joy knew no bounds. Celebrations were held across the town. Wes and Catherine were invited to all of them: Wes was now a local hero, the public face of their cause. And the timing was perfect, because he had just kicked off his campaign. Everyone felt more confident than ever that he'd defeat Marks, that his good work on the landfill would propel him to the Virginia Senate.

And that wasn't the only reason to celebrate. In October, as the leaves were turning once again, Catherine found out she was pregnant.

CHAPTER TWELVE

*C*atherine knew the next year would be her most exciting yet. She'd lived a relatively quiet thirty-eight years. Now suddenly, she was preparing for motherhood, and her husband was running for political office. Her life, previously quiet and predictable, was now consumed by change and uncertainty. Barely a day went by when she wasn't meeting someone new or going to a new place. She took deep breaths and told herself she could handle it. Only good things were on the horizon. And the last year had shown her how much she could gain when she stepped outside the safety of her boundaries.

Her pregnancy was remarkably smooth. She had been under no illusions about pregnancy, as Hei had suffered from devastating morning sickness and postpartum depression. But as her pregnancy progressed, all she felt was fascination.

"Look," she said to Wes one night as they undressed for bed. She stood in front of the mirror with her hands on her back, her tummy pushed outward. "I'm getting round! There's a baby in there!"

He smiled, approached from behind, and wrapped his arms around her, resting his hands on the soft curve of her emerging bump. He nuzzled his face into her neck and kissed her. Her eyes drifting shut, Catherine sighed and tilted her head to the side, enjoying the warm tingles.

"You look," he said, kissing her neck, "so lovely."

"I do look lovely, don't I? I feel lovely."

He chuckled and wrapped his arms tighter. "You should, sweetheart. You damn well should."

Wes was over the moon about the pregnancy. He told everyone they knew, and he wistfully wondered what their child would be like and what they would grow up to be one day. His joy was almost intoxicating to her; she was delighted by the tender, careful way with which he treated her, but what truly touched her was his enthusiasm. She was also pampered and fawned over by Sarah and Lois, who now had their grandmotherly bond between them, in addition to their friendship.

"I bought this for the baby!"

"Show us your bump!"

"Sit down and let us make you a nice cup of tea!"

These and other proclamations were a frequent part of her everyday life, and Catherine embraced it. She felt important and cared for, the happiest she'd ever been.

It was her second holiday season with the Bickharts, and Catherine loved them more than ever. She had grown used to the happy family dinners, the outward displays of affection and the respect they had for each other.

Also exciting was Wes's campaign, which had ramped up in the fall and was now in full swing. Now that the landfill work was over, he had more time to dedicate to his run for state Senate, and his campaign capitalized on the role he'd played in the landfill's demise.

Maeve and Catherine volunteered for the campaign. Maeve wrote press releases and managed the social media. Catherine served as an assistant, helping to organize Wes's schedule and to correspond with constituents. She also researched policies and statistics, which she'd done for her father years before. Back then, it had seemed miserable work; though she was good at it, with her eye for detail and knack for numbers, she had loathed the low-creativity, monotonous work that had forced her to sit at a desk. Now, however, she was excited to participate. She was so proud of Wes, who'd made quite a name for himself in so short a time. And the pride she felt when she knew she had helped him made the work interesting and enjoyable.

Wes appeared made for politics. With his sharp intelligence and wit, his charisma, and his dazzling smile, he was a natural from the start. His good looks and his comfort in front of the camera didn't hurt. He flowed effortlessly from one task to the next, never seeming to tire or to lose his zest or his passion. He charmed reporters during interviews and wowed constituents during rallies and town halls. He shook hands and held babies and ate pancakes in mom-and-pop coffee houses. He listened intently to concerned parents and spouses, his eyes locked on theirs and his voice full of compassion and understanding. He promised to continue fighting for their safety and welfare, and took countless photographs, in which he looked every bit the part of the beloved elected official.

He didn't show a hint of intimidation in the face of David Marks, who tried to use Wes's corporate law background as evidence of his insincerity. Wes laughed off these accusations, standing casually, as always, one hand in his pocket, the other gesturing warmly, suggesting he'd not a care in the world.

"I suppose if one looks for something, one is going to find it," he said. "But the facts, though stubborn, remain. Even in my Washington law days, I took on huge loads of pro bono cases, everything from family law to fair housing to consumer rights. It's this pro bono work that's become the basis of my practice today. My work on the Munson landfill is perhaps the most well-known example of my dedication to Virginians, but it's by no means the only example. Now that I'm back in my hometown,

I've resumed work for a variety of non-profits and charities, and I'm absolutely committed to ensuring fairness and equality for all Virginians."

Catherine sighed and swooned when he talked like this. She beamed with pride at his interviews, listened with amazement to his off-the-cuff responses to questions from constituents, and cheered him on as he gracefully fended off oppositional attacks. Nothing, it appeared, could stop him. He was poised for great things, and Catherine loved following him on this journey.

Catherine attended as many of Wes's events as she could. She was often joined by her father, who in his mentorship role had emerged from retirement to speak vociferously on Wes's behalf and to pronounce Marks's tenure in his Senate seat a complete and utter failure. Even Harold Beck had put retirement on pause; a close friend of Sarah and Charles, he wrote an editorial about the Munson landfill, praising Wes and the residents for fighting off corporate interests and proclaiming that government needed more people like Wes.

The only problem was that she rarely saw him. As his scheduler, she knew how busy his campaign kept him—to say nothing of the fact that he still worked with Grady at the practice. His long days had turned even longer, and while she was proud and enamored of her husband, she missed him terribly. On the bright side, she sometimes saw him at his campaign office. He sent her flowers and offered his input on how to decorate the nursery and on what they should buy for the baby. And he always made time to join her at her appointments with the obstetrician.

"It's a girl!" Catherine announced excitedly one night just after Christmas as she and Wes walked through the door of his parents' house. She was still wearing her coat, the lapel of which Wes held in his fingers, prepared to help her take it off.

"A girl!" Sarah shrieked, hands in the air, and she rushed to Catherine and hugged her tight. "Oh, a girl! Oh, darling! My heart is so full, I can't even stand it!"

Wes laughed as he pulled Catherine's coat from her back and went to hang it in the closet. "Well, that didn't take long."

"Sorry," Catherine said, clasping her hands together. "I was just so excited to tell her, the news just burst from me!"

"Oh, darling," said Sarah, now standing on her tiptoes to kiss Wes's forehead, his face in her hands. "Another granddaughter for me. How did I ever get to be so fortunate?"

"You've had your fill of boys, have you?"

"Never. But now I have both!"

Catherine rubbed her belly with glee. She was delighted to know the sex of the baby, to be able to envision her daughter's face. She and Wes had agreed to find out, rather than wait until the baby was born. He was a planner by nature. And she didn't like surprises.

During the day, when she wasn't making chocolate or working at Wes's office, she spent time with Hei and also with Helen and Olivia, who was just over a year old and now waddled across the floor with a proud smile. Catherine loved Helen. She could relate to her quiet, tender nature, and the two were fast friends. She also adored the dark-haired toddler, with whom she had a special bond. She played with her and fed her and sang her beautiful songs. She was so excited to have a daughter of her own, to watch the little girls grow up together.

The good news was that, since Wes was not often home for dinner, she didn't feel pressure to cook. She didn't enjoy it, wasn't good at it, and was anxious about failing so spectacularly at something she wanted to do for Wes. Though he pretended to enjoy her cooking—bless him, he always ate it with a smile, though even Catherine was astute enough to notice the tension in his face as he swallowed—and though he assured her he didn't care, she knew cooking was important to him. She wanted to assimilate into his life. She had a vision of what the perfect wife should be, and she felt she couldn't be one if she couldn't cook him dinner.

But in every other way, she longed to see more of him, especially since her second trimester brought on an increase in her sex drive. Catherine hadn't thought she could long for him any more than she already did, but amazingly, she could. She yearned painfully for him when he was gone and felt electric when he was home. Her fingers yearned to touch and please him; her hands seem to take on a life of their own.

"You...are...very...sexy," she told him between kisses one Friday evening, when after a long week he'd decided to come home early. They were sitting on the couch together by the fire. Catherine had tried to refrain from seducing him—as badly as she wanted him, she would have liked to have been pursued for once, truth be told. But his proximity to her, the heat from his body and the way he looked in his clothes, consistently proved her undoing.

"Mmm," he murmured with a smile, closing his eyes a moment, and smiling. "You are so darn good to me, sweetheart."

"You're good to me, too." She slipped her hand between his thighs, a jolt of pleasure shooting straight to her core. She lost her breath and added in a whisper, "Let me be good to you, right now."

This was the way it went. Catherine longed, and found herself begging, and was sometimes rewarded for her efforts. She tried not to be discouraged. In all other ways, her life was blessed and perfect. Besides, it wasn't like they never had relations. After all, she was pregnant, wasn't she?

It's like he's living his life and squeezing you in when he has to, texted Maeve after, in her desperation, Catherine had unloaded to Maeve about her frustration. *He's so distracted.*

He's sooooo busy, Hei told her. *This is the most he's ever had going on in his life. It has nothing to do with you! Sorry, Catherine. Don't listen to your sister. Why is she always thinking the worst, anyway?*

In any case, there were a lot of other things to think about. The nursery had been decorated, and it was so lovely. The walls had been painted in a faint taupe, and the curtains and accessories were a tasteful shade of blush. There was a pale taupe chair and a delicate chandelier, and stuffed animals tucked into the night-stand and bookcase. Wes and Catherine had chosen a name for the baby—Amy Seraphina, two old Bickhart family names. And though Catherine's back was hurting, and though she'd been plagued with sciatica, all her aches and pains were overshadowed by the most blessed aspect of pregnancy, the constant kicking of the baby. She felt that she was never alone, that she had a companion with her every moment of her day. And best of all, she loved that she was providing a safe home for the baby. It was something for only her, something important. It made her feel special and proud.

One day in April, a few months before her due date, Catherine was tidying up some papers she'd let accumulate in a pile—though since moving in with Wes, she'd gone to great pains to be less messy, her pregnancy had exhausted her, and she'd let things slide. She came across a little unopened envelope with neat, pretty handwriting. It was addressed to Mr. and Mrs. Bickhart. According to the return address, it was from Meredith Kelly, in Dearham, Maine.

Catherine immediately ripped open the envelope and pulled out the card inside. The outside of the card had a picture of watercolor flowers, with the words "Thank You" in gold print. On the inside was a note written in tidy script, in blue pen. The note was dated September 14.

It read,

Dear Catherine and Wes,

Thank you so much for the wonderful gift for Gabe. It took my breath away. It's the most unique, most beautiful baby gift I've ever seen. The fact that you went to the trouble to find an artisan right here in Maine to make it—and that you thought to have him make something so special and personal—means so much to Nick and me. There aren't any words to express our gratitude.

I'm so sorry we had to miss your wedding. I was devastated not to be there to celebrate with you. Please know how delighted we are for you both and that we wish you all the happiness in the world!

Perhaps we can all meet soon. You are welcome any time.

With love,

Meredith, Nick, and Gabe

Catherine read the note four or five times, then lowered it and sat there in thought. She had no idea what Meredith was talking about; she hadn't been a part of any baby gift, much less a specially commissioned one from an artisan in Maine. Though the note itself was innocuous enough—it was addressed to her and Wes, and it was from Meredith's entire family—it gave her a funny feeling. It wasn't a darkly colored feeling, like charcoal or gray; it was a questioning, in-between color, like turquoise or chartreuse.

"Hmm," she said, setting the note aside. She went back to her cleaning.

When Wes came home that night, especially late, having had a late dinner with Fred and a group of other veteran senators, she was waiting up for him, despite being exhausted. Most days, now, she moved as little as possible, and fell asleep early, having little energy for seduction.

She was sitting in bed with a book when he walked in.

"Well, good evening, sweetheart," he greeted her cheerfully, his eyes brightening upon seeing her. He immediately went to her and laid his hand on her belly, cupping her face with his other hand and kissing her softly on the lips. "I'm glad you're still awake. You and Amy sure are a sight for sore eyes."

God help her, Catherine couldn't help but melt. "So are you," she told him, her eyes greedily taking him in as he removed his jacket and his tie, unbuttoned his shirt and his pants, stripped down to his boxers and slid into bed with a groan. She turned to him with a smile as he embraced her fully, her belly, and baby girl, nuzzled between them.

"Tired?" she asked, massaging his head with her hand as he kissed her again, eyes closed.

"Mmm," he moaned loudly, making Catherine's heart drop with need. "Exhausted. That feels so good, sweetheart. Thank you."

Meredith's note flew out of her mind. "Does it?" she asked, breathing him in, his reaction to her touch making her instantly alert.

"Yes." He sighed, over and over, his face so beautiful as he accepted this pleasure from her.

She was practically breathless. "I'm glad. Because I want to make you feel good, Wes. It's very literally nearly all I want to do."

He opened his eyes and looked at her, then propped his head in his hand, his elbow over his pillow. He stroked her face with his fingers. "You've been so patient, sweetheart," he told her tenderly, his eyes kind. "I know you've felt a little neglected. Frankly, I can't blame you."

"Oh, it's okay," she said, with sincerity, his acknowledgment already making her feel better. "I've been missing you, of course. But I understand. Your campaign needs you."

"Well, I truly appreciate it." He took a moment to gaze at her earnestly. Her heart skipped a couple of beats, and she exhaled. He pressed her closer, and she felt the firmness of his need against her hips. "You've been so selfless and supportive. I think you deserve to be rewarded for your patience."

Catherine grinned, her pulse picking up speed as his hand trailed over her nightgown and settled at her breast, his fingers toying with the taut nipple underneath the ivory silk.

"Just being with you is its own reward," she whispered, her lips so close to his that his breath mingled with hers.

"You're an angel," he said, and kissed her with passion, his lips soft and supple and his hands roaming freely.

She tugged at the waistband of his boxers, and he pulled them off and kicked them to the floor. She took him in her hand and tightened her hold, nearly coming apart inside when he stiffened beneath her fingers and released a long groan.

"I'm so glad I stayed up for you," she said, hiking up her nightgown. "And to think I never would have, had it not been for that note."

He opened his eyes. "Note?"

Darn it, she muttered to herself. "It's nothing," she said aloud. "Kiss me some more."

"Catherine, what note?"

She sighed and pulled away, then reached to her nightstand and withdrew Meredith's thank you card.

She handed it to him. "I found this today."

Brow furrowed, he took it, opened it, and read its contents in silence. His expression remained unchanged. Catherine watched as his eyes moved back and forth across Meredith's neat handwriting.

"Where did this come from?" he asked finally. "It says it was written in September."

"I found it in a stack of old papers. It must have gotten shoved aside and lost."

He studied the note a moment more. Catherine waited for him to say something.

"Did you find an artisan in Maine to make Meredith a special baby gift?" she asked finally.

"Oh. Yeah," he said offhandedly, handing the note back to her. "We received the birth announcement in the mail. You remember. I thought I'd send her a baby gift, as one does."

"How did you find the artist?"

He shrugged and yawned, closing his eyes. "It wasn't that hard. A fifteen minute Google search took care of it."

"She said it was personal. What was it?"

"It was nothing." He turned and faced her, wrapping his arm around her and cuddling close, eyes still closed. "Just a hand-crafted snow globe, but with sand and seashells in replication of the beach where they live, and an engraving with the baby's name and date of birth."

Catherine raised her eyebrows. "That's very specific."

"You know me, sweetheart," he said, yawning again. "I always go all out."

She was silent a moment. "You didn't tell me you were going to do this."

"It wasn't that big a deal. I didn't think you needed to be involved."

Catherine thought about this, then reached back to replace the note on the nightstand. She clicked off the lamp and turned back to Wes, whose breathing was slow and even.

"Are you ready, sweetheart?" he said, patting her backside.

Somehow Catherine's mood had been dampened. Her body ached, but her mind was pensive. "Maybe you should just get some sleep," she said.

"Are you sure?"

She didn't respond. Within seconds, he was snoring.

Catherine lay awake in silence, in his arms, for a long time. Finally she kissed his forehead and rubbed his back gently, to avoid waking him up.

"I love you," she told him, then turned her back to him and fell asleep.

LIFE WENT on like this for weeks. Then, in early June, Catherine had a very bad day.

She was working at the desk in Wes's campaign office. Wes himself wasn't there; he was at work with Grady, preparing a case revolving around a company that had failed to meet emission standards. Maeve was there, too; her boss, a US senator who had endorsed Wes for state Senate, was understanding of her desire to volunteer and was lenient with her schedule. Maeve had left Wes's office briefly to pick up lunch for herself and Catherine, leaving Catherine temporarily alone.

She was sitting behind the desk going over some paperwork when the door opened. Catherine looked up, expecting to see Maeve. Instead, she saw the brooding face of Rick Tremaine.

She straightened in her seat, heart pounding. It seemed that poison suddenly flowed through her veins; she felt sick and alert, the hairs on the back of her neck prickling.

"Mrs. Bickhart," Rick said, nodding.

Catherine's eyes darted toward the window, desperately seeking Maeve.

"Can I help you?" she asked timidly.

Rick smiled, if one could call it that; though the corners of his mouth turned upward, his face looked tense and full of dark feelings.

"I just thought I'd pop over and check out Wes's new digs."

Catherine looked around the room. "Well, this is it. Please help yourself to a flyer."

Rick approached the desk. Catherine recoiled, pushing her chair back as he placed both hands on the table and leaned downward, making a show of turning his head this way and that.

"Nice place," he said. He looked right at her. "How do you like working here?"

Catherine didn't know what to say. She felt that Rick was trying to trick her, or mock her, or both.

"I love it."

Rick nodded again. One corner of his mouth ticked upward into a dangerous-looking grin.

"So Wes actually thinks he can defeat David Marks, does he?"

He shook his head. "He always did have a high opinion of himself."

"Wes wants to make a change. He'll be a terrific senator."

"You're a good little wife, now, aren't you?"

Catherine was silent. Under the desk, she fidgeted with her fingers.

"You know, Catherine, I knew your husband many years ago. We didn't get along, he and I."

"I know."

Rick raised his eyebrows and smirked. "I should have known. Leave it to old Wes to run his mouth. What did he tell you?"

"He said you were expelled from the firm."

"Damn sure was. I ended up taking on ridiculous cases, working for nothing, listening to people bitch about leaky plumbing all day." He huffed. "It wasn't even a big deal, what I said to that paralegal. Wes just wanted me out the door so he could steal my biggest client. He always loved to be a hero, and he made sure everyone knew about it. He must be mighty proud of himself for blocking Munson's landfill."

"Mr. Tremaine," said Catherine, nearly choking on air, "I really don't think I should be alone with you."

He paused a moment. "And why is that?"

"Because it isn't..." She knew she couldn't tell him she was afraid of him, that being in his presence made her feel like vomiting. "It isn't proper."

He leaned in farther and grinned more widely; Catherine could smell his breath. "What do you think might happen?"

Catherine's eyes widened, and she placed her hands on her belly. "Are you being sexually suggestive?"

Rick laughed. "No one gets anything by you, do they, Catherine? Okay, sure. Yeah, I'm being sexually suggestive."

"But I'm pregnant."

"So? You know the thing about pregnant women, don't you?"

She grimaced and turned away, repulsed.

Rick removed his hands from the desk and stood straight, his eyes wandering over her from head to toe. "What a shame you're with cocky old Bickhart," he said, practically spitting the name. "I have to tell you, that really lowers you in my estimation."

Just then, the door flew open. In walked Maeve, her arms laden with bags of food. She took one look at the scene before her, and her face drew downward. She placed the food on a nearby table and began shuffling Rick out the door.

"I'm sorry, Mr. Tremaine, but I have to ask you to leave. Catherine has a doctor's appointment. We need to lock up the office."

"Such coincidental timing," Rick said, allowing himself to be ushered away. He stopped then and turned, waving to Catherine. "Good to see you, Mrs. Bickhart. Send your husband my regards. Tell him I'll see him soon."

Maeve shoved him through the threshold, then closed and locked the door. She hurried over to Catherine and put her hand on her shoulder, her face stern with concern.

"Are you okay?"

Catherine turned her head to look at her. "Thank you," she said.

Maeve's expression softened. "You're welcome."

Maeve rubbed her shoulder. Catherine placed her hand on her sister's hand, and squeezed.

"What a creep," said Maeve. "I shivered just looking at him."

"Me too. He's awful."

"He certainly doesn't seem to like Wes very much."

"No, he doesn't," said Catherine, taking a breath, beginning to relax. "And it's the highest compliment Wes could receive."

ONCE SHE RETURNED HOME, Catherine called Wes and told him what had happened.

"That bastard," Wes said when her story was finished. "Same Rick as always. For God's sake. Looks like he's got nothing better to do with his time than go to my office and harass my wife."

"Wes, he really seemed mad. He said you wanted him out the door so you could steal his biggest client."

"The McDonnell case? Are you serious?" Wes laughed. "I can't believe he's hung up on that. That has absolutely nothing to do with it. Sure, I picked up that case. But I damn sure didn't conspire against him to steal away his business. I didn't make him corner a paralegal and tell her she looked sexy in her sweater. I didn't make him follow her out to her car at night or accost her outside the women's bathroom. No, he did that all on his own. If he expected that I'd look the other way, he was very sorely mistaken."

"I know," Catherine said solemnly, her heart warming with pride. "But still. He said to tell you he'll see you soon. I'm scared for you. I don't want him anywhere near you."

"Sweetheart, don't worry about me. I'll be fine. What makes me not fine is the entitlement he seems to claim over you."

"Maeve was wonderful," said Catherine. A soft smile crossed her lips as she remembered her sister's firm defense. "I was lucky she was there."

"Agreed on both counts. But Maeve shouldn't have to hold down the fort like this. Rick Tremaine's been harassing women ever since I've known him. Well, he's sure as hell not going to intimidate my family. He won't be allowed back in the office. I'll take care of it, sweetheart. Don't worry."

Catherine spent the rest of the afternoon feeling nervous and ill at ease; once again, she was disgusted by the way Rick looked at her, and she was terrified by his sinister comments about Wes. She was relieved when Wes arrived home that evening. He was taking a quick break before attending a town hall meeting that night.

He walked in the door and dropped his briefcase on the

ground. Catherine was instantly upon him, holding his face in her hands and kissing him, wanting to feel his warmth and comfort after the unnerving experience she'd had in his office.

He returned her kisses and inquired how she was feeling, then bent at the waist and kissed her belly. Catherine laughed and followed him into the kitchen, where he grabbed an apple and sat at the table, relaxing in a chair with his foot over his knee.

"I talked to Tremaine," he said.

"You did? Already?"

"Yes. We had firm words. He won't bother you again."

Catherine smiled. "Thanks."

"I'm just sorry you had to endure that. It makes me sick to think of it."

"Me, too," she said, shuddering.

"Anyway, on to happier things. Tell me about the rest of your day, sweetheart. How's your back today?"

"It's good. I'm feeling great. In fact, Helen is coming over soon so she can help me in the garden."

Wes smiled. "Is that right? What are the two of you going to do?"

"Well, I've never been much of a gardener. But I want to learn, to help keep the house pretty. Helen has such a green thumb. She told me she'd help me plant some new flowers."

"What a nice idea. Just don't work too hard, sweetheart. I don't want you overtiring or gardening yourself into early labor."

His cell phone rang from the table. He picked it up and glanced at the screen.

He straightened in his seat and furrowed his brow. "It's Meredith," he said, and answered it immediately.

He greeted her brightly and leaned back in his seat, asking after her health and the health of her baby. Catherine sat listening and watching his face. He was smiling, his eyes intent; he sometimes looked downward to concentrate more fully. Catherine guessed she'd inquired about the campaign; he launched into a lengthy description of where things stood and what the campaign's approach had been.

Catherine grew bored and looked out the window. She perked up: Helen's car was parked in front of the house, and Helen herself was ambling up the walkway, Olivia's little hand in hers.

She stood and met Helen at the front door, leaving Wes to his conversation.

Helen stayed about an hour. It was a perfect early summer evening, and the air was fresh and fragrant. By the time she left, the air had cooled, and the sky had darkened with the setting sun. Catherine thanked her—and her little helper, too, of course—and returned inside, in search of Wes.

She found him in his study, seated at his desk. He was staring into space, out toward the window, his expression serious and thoughtful.

She took a few steps into the room before he noticed her, after she'd said his name twice.

He looked up with a start. "Oh. Hello, sweetheart."

He swiveled toward her and attempted a smile. Neither spoke for a moment or two.

"How was..." he began, but his voice trailed off, as if he'd forgotten. "How was gardening?"

His voice sounded funny. "It was good," she replied. "What did Meredith want?"

"Meredith? Oh, good news. She's coming down here to visit."

Catherine's eyes widened. "She is? Why?"

"I invited her."

Catherine felt faint. She thought she should know how to respond to this; she wished she could text Maeve or Hei. She didn't know if the reaction she was having was appropriate, and she needed someone to tell her how to feel. She wanted to be okay with what he had told her; she wanted to be mature. But the feeling inside her was ugly and dark.

"I…" She didn't know how to finish the sentence; she couldn't parse out her own feelings. She changed her approach. "Why?"

"Well, you know, with the baby, and all. She's going to be driving south anyway because her best friend's having a baby girl, too. Isn't that funny?" When Catherine said nothing, he went on. "Anyway, we keep saying we're going to see each other, to introduce each other to our families, but we never do." He shrugged. "We decided to just do it. They'll be down sometime in August."

He smiled again, but it was short-lived on his face. He turned back toward the window and slapped his thighs.

"Well, I'd better get ready to go."

"Why does she keep calling you?"

He swiveled back toward her and stared at her, eyes wide.

"What?"

She blinked a few times. "I just asked why Meredith keeps calling."

He continued to watch her. "Does she keep calling?"

"It seems like it."

He seemed to consider. "Well, I had told her not to be a stranger. We promised to keep each other up to date."

"It wouldn't bother me, except that her calls always seem to upset you."

His expression remained unchanged. Catherine couldn't tell what he was thinking.

"I just think," she forced herself to say, the words seeming to push through molasses to exit her throat, "that maybe she shouldn't be calling you."

"She didn't do anything wrong—let's not blame her."

Catherine was taken aback. "I'm not blaming her," she said, blandly, for lack of anything else to say.

He rose and approached her, placed his hands on her shoulders and kissed her forehead. "Catherine," he whispered tenderly into her hair. "You do know I love you. Don't you?"

Catherine did. She nodded.

He pulled away and smiled, stroking her face with his fingers. "Good. Because I do. Very much."

"I love you too, Wes."

He kissed her again and rubbed her belly. "I really do need to go. Can't be late for the town hall."

She smiled wanly and accepted another kiss, then stood still as he walked past her through the study and out the front door.

But you can love us both at the same time.

Maeve's words had been echoing through her mind since she said them so many months before, standing in the dark in the Bickharts' front yard. Though she knew Maeve loved her, she'd always felt Maeve looked down on her, that maybe, on a subconscious level, she had wanted—or expected—her to fail. But maybe Maeve had just been looking out for her. Maybe Maeve had been right; maybe she had her best interests at heart, after all.

For the very first time, Catherine wondered if her sister's cynicism was more realistic than Hei's idealism. She felt something in her shift in that moment, and she shed a few tears for the loss.

She was skeptical of her ability to parse the hidden meanings, to interpret his expressions and read between the lines of what he said. As she stood there in the study, surrounded by his books, his desk, his scent, his life, she recalled the clues she'd registered but ignored, always assuming she was misreading signals. But what if she wasn't? What if she saw more than she'd thought? Catherine's mind was swimming; his study walls seemed to close in around her. She turned and walked out, toward her bedroom, scooping Dorothea up into her arms as she went.

She flicked on her music—Brahms's neat, orderly melodies always helped center her when her world threatened to overwhelm her—and sat on her bed petting the cat's soft mottled fur. She knew he loved her. But did he love another woman more? Was he settling for her because his first choice was out of reach, telling himself he was happy but wishing she were somebody else?

"We'll see," she told Dorothea, surprised by the coldness in her voice. "We'll see when she gets here."

CHAPTER THIRTEEN

*A*my Seraphina Bickhart was born in July to adoring parents and a host of other ecstatic friends and family. Sarah liked to say the birth was just like Catherine herself: happy, magical, and to the point. One of Catherine's greatest fears was going into labor while Wes wasn't with her, or worse, giving birth before he could arrive. But Catherine went into labor at home, on a Sunday morning, when Wes had his entire day free. Her water broke at the hospital. She was given an epidural and labored for three hours before delivering Amy, in no pain and with no surprises.

Wes wept when Amy was born. Catherine would never forget it, nor would she forget the way he brushed back her hair and cheered her on, telling her what a great job she was doing and thanking her for giving him the greatest gift of his life.

"You were so strong for me," she told him as the baby was lifted from her chest to be weighed, measured, and cleaned.

"Are you kidding? Jesus Christ, I'm a goddamn mess!" He ran his fingers through his hair and laughed, releasing the tension of the day.

All the family came to the hospital and clinked champagne

glasses over her hospital bed. Congratulations, laughter, and tears were shared all around. Her parents were loving with her and the baby. Even Maeve seemed overcome.

Maeve held her baby niece, staring at her with wonder as the little girl slumbered in her arms. She sang "Twinkle, Twinkle, Little Star" with tears in her eyes, telling her to shush, Auntie Maeve was here to take care of her. Hei hugged and kissed Catherine and told her she loved her. She tickled the baby and oohed and aahed, making Catherine promise she'd let her babysit.

Back home, Catherine and Wes connected as new parents, taking turns waking with Amy in the middle of the night, asking each other for opinions on this or that, going together to the first pediatrician appointments. They snuggled together in bed each night, in new parental bliss. Catherine loved to watch Wes coddle and comfort their daughter; he was a loving, doting father, and he seemed to cherish every moment and every task. Moreover, true to form, he ensured Catherine didn't want for anything. He brought her water when she was nursing, made her gourmet dinners, massaged her shoulders and rubbed her back and did all the things one hopes for when one makes someone a father.

"Thank you," she told him, for the millionth time, after he'd brought her a cup of tea and a plate of cookies. He propped her feet up and rubbed them sensuously, making her lean her head back and sigh.

"It's my pleasure, sweetheart. Consider me your servant. There is nothing too good for the mother of my child."

Even when Wes went back to work, Catherine was never alone. Amy had two doting grandmothers and several aunts, all of whom helped Catherine with laundry, cared for the baby so she could sleep, and, thankfully, cooked dinner.

Her mother was gracious enough to offer many opinions about how Catherine should care for the baby.

"No, make sure the swaddle's tighter when you—oh, dear," she said with a sigh, nudging her out of the way. "You're too gentle, in true Catherine form. You'll never get her to sleep this way. Let me do that for you. It'll save us a whole lot of time."

Catherine was exhausted, but she was living in a blissful haze and didn't care. Her daughter was perfect, beautiful and sweet. She smelled delicious. And everyone said she looked like her.

"She's so pretty," Helen sighed. "Just like her pretty mommy."

"The world could use another Catherine," said Sarah. "I could look at this baby all day!"

Catherine was now in charge of the life of another person, a tiny, helpless angel who had grown inside her and would look to her as her caregiver for the rest of her life. She welcomed motherhood and all that came with it. Part of her had worried that she wouldn't be able to handle the change, that the disruption to her routine—the uncertainty of her days—would be intolerable. But in fact, the unpredictability of motherhood forced her to grow comfortable further outside of her boundaries; it showed her she was capable of change. She adapted to a new sleep schedule. She accepted that some days, she'd be covered in spit up, or worse.

In short, she felt the gravity of her responsibility, and she hadn't put much thought into her unanswered questions about Meredith. She didn't have time or energy for anyone outside her immediate circle. Besides, Wes's devotion to his daughter—and the bond it fostered between them—made the question obsolete, at least momentarily. As Meredith's visit grew near, she wondered what she had been so worried about. Wes so clearly loved her and their daughter; their life was as wonderful as always. She must have misinterpreted. It appeared to Catherine that she was woefully incapable of reading people after all, and for once, she was happy about it.

Finally the visit arrived. The night before, Catherine examined her kitchen calendar, but for an entirely different reason.

"And, zero," said Catherine, crossing off the date on her calendar with a thick red marker. She turned to Wes, who was finishing cleaning up from dinner. She disposed of her marker and clasped her hands together, smiling with glee. "Amy was born six weeks ago today. That means zero more days."

From the sink, he glanced over his shoulder, casting her a sly grin. "Is that right."

"That's right."

While his attention was on the dishes, she took the opportunity to eye him up. He hadn't changed from his suit that day, and he stood in light gray trousers and a white dress shirt, his sleeves rolled up as he tended to the chores. His weight rested on one leg. Catherine admired the beautiful contrast, the straight lines and curvature of his form.

She stepped forward and stood beside him, slinking her arm around his back. "You're not too tired tonight, are you?"

"Hell, no. You're not the only one who's been hurting, sweetheart. Six weeks is a long time. I'll be glad to get back in the saddle again."

He tossed the dishtowel into the sink and took her hips in his hands. Catherine kissed him through a wide-mouthed grin: she was surprised to be appeased so quickly. He hurried her upstairs and accommodated her without delay. It was fast, frenzied, and furious, just as expected after a six-week wait. They fell asleep happy and rejuvenated, Catherine smiling into the crook of his arm.

When Amy woke in the middle of the night, Catherine rose to take care of her. She was surprised to find that Wes was not beside her in bed.

She tended to Amy and slipped on her bathrobe, then shuffled downstairs in the darkness.

A lamp was on in his study. She padded down the hallway toward the light, then stood in the doorway looking at him. He was sitting on the love seat before the now cold fireplace, leaning forward with his elbows on his knees and his hands clasped in front.

She knocked softly.

"What are you doing down here?" she asked, looking around the tidy, elegant room, which seemed to slumber in the quiet and the dim lighting.

He turned to her and smiled, then turned back toward the fireplace. "I just couldn't sleep."

"I would have thought you'd sleep soundly after exerting yourself as you did earlier."

He chuckled but said nothing.

She entered the room and sat beside him, wrapping her robe around her lap and legs.

"Is everything okay?"

"Sure. I just needed some quiet time to think."

"What are you thinking about?"

He shrugged. "A little of this, a little of that." He pulled his phone from his pocket and handed it to her. "But mostly, this text."

Catherine looked at the screen. It was a long text message from Grady. She read the message and looked at him, then read the message again.

"It can't be."

"It can. And it appears that it is."

"But how did you know?"

"I had a hunch. There's always more to the story, and money's always involved. Evidently my hunch was correct."

Catherine inhaled and read the message again. At Wes's request, Grady had looked into the investors of Munson's landfills. They were a hodgepodge of shell companies, layers and layers deep. And behind the whole deal were two main players: Senator David Marks and his attorney, Rick Tremaine.

"Lord," she breathed. "Then that means..." She didn't want to finish her sentence—the fallout seemed too good to be true.

Wes seemed to read her thoughts. "I don't want to count my chickens, but yes, that's what it means. He's done, sweetheart." He patted her knee. "David Marks is done."

They sat in silence for a while. Catherine looked out the window, where her favorite tree stood guard, its lush leaves at their summer fullest.

"You should come back up to bed. We have a busy day tomorrow."

"You go ahead, sweetheart. You need your sleep. I'll be up soon, I promise."

Catherine kissed his cheek and received a pat on the knee in return. She then went back up to bed. She tried to wait for him to join her but fell asleep promptly.

Meredith and her family were expected around noon the next day. Wes and Catherine rose and dressed early. Around noon, Catherine went in search of Wes. She found him once again in his study. This time, he was standing by the window, his hands in his pockets, staring outside at the street. As she watched unseen, he pulled his hands from his pockets and crossed his arms, then uncrossed them, looked at his watch, and stuck his hands in his pockets once more.

"They should be here any minute," she said.

He checked his watch again, then turned and faced her. His face was white, his eyes wide and his lips straight. They looked at each other across this space, in deafening silence.

"You look like you've seen a ghost."

He ran his fingers though his hair and looked outside again.

"I..."

She waited, but he didn't go on.

"You what?"

She saw him take a deep breath before responding.

"I'm beginning to think this visit was a big mistake."

A car pulled up along the curb outside and stopped in front of the house. Wes started, straightened, and pulled his hands from his pockets.

"Oh, my God."

Catherine followed his eyes. A man and a woman were

emerging from the car. The man met the woman as she opened the backseat and unbuckled a child from his car seat. Catherine looked back at Wes. He was staring, eyes sharp, lips parted, chest rising and falling.

A feeling took over Catherine's body and soul. It was a more darkly colored feeling than she'd ever felt before, one that overwhelmed and consumed her, that was black like burned up ashes. She'd never known such a hateful feeling, could never even find anything or anyone to hate. It wasn't hate, exactly—it was something much worse. It was something that demanded her attention, something that inflamed her, something that became her.

Jealousy.

The woman was walking toward the house. The man held the hand of a little boy and was trailing just behind. Catherine looked at Wes. The line of vision between his eyes and the family on the other side of the window was almost tangible.

They didn't have much time. Catherine got to the point.

"Does she know you're still in love with her?"

He spun on his heels and stared at her.

"I'm not in love with her."

"I'm not stupid."

Wes said nothing, but looked at her blankly. He took a deep breath and turned back to the window.

"I know you're not stupid, sweetheart. And I'm not in love with her."

"You are. You're in love with her. I suspected at first, but now I'm quite sure."

"Damn it, Catherine. Please. Now is not the time."

Catherine was quiet.

The woman had seen him in the window: she was waving at him from the walkway. Wes stood straighter and inhaled deeply. Catherine stepped aside as he then stalked past her out of his study and toward the front door.

CATHERINE WENT TO THE WINDOW. He was walking swiftly to meet her, and he opened his arms as she approached. The two embraced warmly, holding each other for a very long time. Catherine didn't like the way his hands splayed across her back, the way his head dipped into her neck.

She watched as the two pulled back, holding hands for a moment before separating. Wes's back was to her. But the woman was smiling up at him, listening to something Wes was saying. She responded, dabbing her eye. She then looked at the man and little boy, extending her hand in introduction. Wes and the man shook hands. Wes then bent at the waist and waved to the child.

Catherine turned away. She went upstairs to fetch Amy.

CATHERINE DIDN'T LIKE crowds or new people. They made her feel overwhelmed and disoriented, and they left her off balance and exhausted. But as a politician's daughter, she knew how to play the game. She was good at putting on a smile, at pretending to be charming, at pretending to be charmed.

She reminded herself of this as she rocked back and forth on her bed, holding herself, stifling the sound of her cries, her vision blurred and her cheeks stained with tears. Her heart was pounding in alarm, her pulse hammered in her ears, and her breaths let in precious little air. It had been a long time since she'd had an anxiety attack like this. With her newfound strength and confidence and all the happy things in her life, she'd thought she'd been beyond breakdowns. She felt foolish and naïve, as Maeve had said. She hadn't been prepared for any of this; she'd simply been playing house. Maybe she was better off alone, after all. Why had she thought she could do this?

No. I can do it. And I must. She loved him, and she wanted to fight for him. She hadn't come all this way, made so many changes and found so much joy in those changes, sacrificed her routines and absorbed a new way of life, only to give up. She'd never known she'd needed this, and now that she did, she didn't want to lose it. She felt lost and in-between, like her old life was no longer enough but her new life was unattainable. How was she to function, not even knowing who she was? How was she to defend herself? What was she to do?

This time, there was no one to rub her back or comfort her; there was no one to lean on but herself. She'd have to push through this—that was all there was to it. She'd simply have to endure, and then talk to him, and assess.

She pulled in her breath and stood. Then she washed her face and willed away all evidence of her panic: the only thing worse than an anxiety attack was revealing the intensity of her anxiety, especially to Wes, to whom she so desperately wanted to appear competent and in control. As she removed the sleeping baby from her bassinet, cradling her in her arms as the little girl fussed and fell right back to sleep, she fortified herself to play the game again. Her heart was frantically beating; her entire life, it seemed, was at stake. She would decorate herself with a smile; she would make her voice calm and controlled. And she would take comfort in the presence of her baby, whom she knew to be on her side.

She returned downstairs and stepped outside to greet her guests. They were standing in a circle, everyone smiling and laughing. The little boy was looking around, his hand chasing a dandelion seed as it floated through the air just above his head. Despite her nerves and the darkness in her heart, Catherine warmed at the sight.

Meredith had spotted her and was watching her with a smile. Wes, who'd been watching Meredith, followed her line of vision and extended his hand for her to stand beside him. Catherine joined him and smiled, letting him bring her in close and rest his hand on her shoulder.

"Oh my goodness," breathed Meredith, gazing at Amy with her hand at her heart. She then brought her hands to her face and looked between Catherine and Wes. "Amy is so beautiful! What a perfect little angel!"

Catherine studied Meredith. She was petite in frame, with dark brown hair and wide green eyes. She was pretty, and her face seemed genuinely kind. She was nicely dressed, in a white floral skirt and a baby blue cardigan sweater, a single string of pearls around her neck. Catherine imagined this woman in bed with her husband, the two of them naked and calling each other's names. He'd done to this woman the things he did to her, on the rare occasion she was able to entice him. This woman had lain underneath him, her hands on his back and in his hair; he'd gripped her and kissed her and made her feel loved. She'd touched him, pleased him, seen his face constrict in ecstasy. Did he wish they could still do those things together? Did he think of this woman while he was with her? Had he thought of her last night?

"Thank you," Catherine said pleasantly, returning Meredith's smile. "It's so good to finally meet you, Meredith."

Meredith brought her in for a hug, careful of the arm holding Amy. "It's so good to meet you, too. I'm so sorry I couldn't meet you at your wedding. Nick and I fully intended to go, but my doctor said no. I had a high-risk pregnancy with this little guy." She looked to her son and smiled.

"He's adorable," said Catherine. "How old is he?"

"He's just over a year."

"He looks exactly like your husband."

"I know." Meredith rolled her eyes and laughed good-naturedly. "I was just the vessel, right?"

Catherine turned to Meredith's husband Nick, who was standing with his hands in the pockets of his jeans, a warm smile on his face, quietly observing. He was a tall, well-built man, strong and lean, with sharp features and longish blond hair. He patted the head of the little boy, who with his blond hair and earnest blue eyes, looked like a miniature version of his father.

They were a nice-looking, friendly-seeming family, Catherine thought. She wanted to know what they were doing there, why they felt the need to intrude upon her life and shake her world into chaos.

"Well, let's go inside, shall we?" pronounced Wes, indicating with his hand their beautiful Tudor house. *Your house*, Catherine told Meredith in her mind, wondering if the thought had occurred to her, too.

"Your house is gorgeous," said Meredith as they ambled up the walkway. "I wouldn't expect anything less."

"That's exactly what I thought," said Catherine, "when I first saw the house."

Meredith's fingers brushed the hanging blossoms of the hawthorn tree on her way toward the house. "What a beautiful hawthorn," she said. "And how nice that it's still in bloom. Usually they're bare by this time of year."

Catherine smiled in spite of herself. "I love that tree. It's my favorite."

"Do you know the folklore of the hawthorn tree? It used to be said that they were protected by fairies."

Catherine had always imagined fairies living in that tree and adored the idea that this was part of its folklore. Her heart was delighted, but devastated, all at the same time. She was confused and flustered by her contradictory feelings, and she resented it. She continued walking in silence.

"Hawthorns are one of my favorites, too," said Meredith. "They can bend with the wind. Have you ever seen the photographs? The wind moves and shapes them, but the hawthorns never break. They simply adjust and grow stronger. It's really quite beautiful, when you think about it."

"Mmm," said Catherine, her eyes on the ground.

They reached the doorway and stepped inside. Meredith

glanced back at the yard once more before Wes closed the door behind her.

"I couldn't help but notice your landscaping," she said, following Catherine into the living room. "It's so beautiful. Do you do it yourself?"

"No," said Catherine, "we have a landscaper. And Helen comes by to help me with maintenance, sometimes. I lack the elusive green thumb."

"It's just as well," said Meredith lightly, sitting on the couch with Nick as Wes and Catherine sat in two chairs. "I do all our gardening myself. I love it, but it's exhausting, especially now with Gabe. Really at this point it's just a massive headache."

Catherine couldn't tell what Meredith meant, whether she was bragging about her gardening skills or genuinely trying to make Catherine feel better. She'd missed so many signals; there were layers to her life she was only now seeing. She didn't know how to interpret anything. She had even less faith in her perception than before.

"What else do you like to do?" asked Catherine, trying to make polite conversation.

"Well, my first love is cooking. I've actually been catering parties here and there, whenever I have the time."

Catherine's heart seemed to shudder and cry.

"Will you excuse me a moment?"

She stood, smiled, and hurried upstairs.

CATHERINE TRIED NOT to be angry with Meredith. It really wasn't Meredith's fault. After all, she'd left Wes, not the other way around. Meredith wasn't there to steal away her husband. If either of them had regrets over the end of their relationship, it wasn't Meredith.

As they sat outside on the patio enjoying the sunny afternoon, eating sandwiches and drinking lemonade, Catherine watched Meredith with something like awe. It was surreal, in a way, like going back in time, only it wasn't her life. What a strange feeling it was—bluish silver, perhaps, an unearthly, alien color—to know her husband had loved this woman so much he'd proposed to her twice. He'd set up their life together, to the point where she'd felt she had to leave him. Catherine had told him it wasn't a flaw, that she'd like him to propose to her, to set up their life, too. But why hadn't he? Why had she had to ask him to do it? And why hadn't she realized any of this before?

The pieces were falling into place. They'd been there all along, but she'd been too enamored to see them.

Maeve hadn't, though.

Don't you think it's odd that he proposed right then?

The wheels in Catherine's head were turning. Everything was a farce. Every step they'd taken, they'd taken because of Meredith.

I was thinking we should speed up our timeline.

He'd said these words to her in bed that night, the night after Sarah had told them she'd talked to Meredith's father. Harold had said Meredith was doing well, despite the complications of her pregnancy. They didn't know the sex of the baby, but Meredith thought it was a boy.

I'm surprised he doesn't have it all planned out. That doesn't sound like Wes.

Helen's face floated through Catherine's mind. It was the night of the Christmas gala, and Catherine had told her they didn't yet know when they planned to have kids. At the time, Catherine had assumed he hadn't pushed her into making big decisions because he didn't want to make the same mistakes he'd made with Meredith. But that wasn't it at all. He didn't wait longer with her because he was worried about repeating mistakes: he waited longer with her because he'd loved Meredith more.

It was like he couldn't be left behind, like with every milestone in Meredith's life, he'd felt more intensely the need to move on. It wasn't that he'd wanted to propose; it wasn't that he'd wanted a baby. It was a race against the clock, and nothing more.

Maybe he's having an affair.

Maeve's words came back to haunt her, though Maeve hadn't gotten it quite right.

I'm not a cheater, Cat...I'm not having an affair.

He wasn't. Catherine believed him. As he'd said once, he never broke his promises. He'd promised to love and care for her, and he did. In his actions, he was honest and upstanding. But in his heart, he lived a whole different life.

Catherine watched him watching Meredith. She couldn't read his expression. As always, he was impeccable—calm, controlled, and charming. But his eyes were lingering an extra moment; when she spoke, he smiled, no matter what it was she was saying.

Meredith herself, for her part, seemed comfortable and unaware, meeting his gaze when it was natural to do so, and no more. She was affectionate with her own husband, holding his hand and resting her hand on his thigh, casting him discreet little smiles and occasionally sneaking a kiss. They sat close together, his arm around the back of the couch; he'd sometimes rub her shoulder or tuck her hair behind her ear. They seemed content, serene, and happy, like two people truly meant to be together.

First there was the fact that deep down, she was still in love with her ex.

Ah. Of course. It was all so very obvious. Meredith had loved Wes, but her heart had been in the past. Just the way Wes himself loved Catherine now.

Wes was now Meredith. And she herself was Wes.

"Ironic," she said aloud.

They all stopped talking and looked at her.

Catherine blushed, and her eyelashes fluttered.

Wes leaned forward and smiled. "What's ironic, sweetheart?"

"Oh," she replied, looking frantically about. "I was just thinking, it's ironic that we're out here in the garden, when I made us chocolate flowers."

They all responded brightly, nodding and smiling and talking with enthusiasm.

"You two are in for a real treat," said Wes, emphatically, gesturing toward Catherine. "My wife is a master chocolatier. She makes the best chocolate you'll ever have in your life."

"You and your chocolate," said Meredith, smiling. "You and Catherine are meant to be."

Catherine excused herself and fetched a vase of chocolate flowers. They were painted bright, summer colors and arranged into a bouquet. Meredith gasped and cooed at it. Even Nick, reserved and quiet, commented on its beauty.

"This is unbelievable!" Meredith exclaimed, examining each piece carefully. "I'm floored. I'm so impressed."

"Amazing," said Nick, nodding in agreement. "How long does it take you to make something like this?"

"Well, it's a rather long process," said Catherine, carefully removing a chocolate daisy and sitting back in her seat. "It's hard to say how long it takes because the steps are so removed from each other. Making the chocolate can take days if it's done right. Then there's the molding and the painting. I'd say, when it's all said and done, this took me a couple of weeks."

"It's a work of art." Meredith poked around the bouquet. "It's so beautiful, I don't even want to eat it!"

"It's meant to be eaten and enjoyed. Please help yourself."

They all picked their chocolate and resumed their conversation. Catherine wasn't feeling very talkative, so she sat back and observed. She was fascinated by Nick, Meredith's husband, who was clearly the passive partner. He was reticent but not impolite; he was introverted by nature, that much was abundantly plain. He was warm and loving with Gabe, often taking it upon himself to check in on him as he played in the yard, crouching before him and patting his back. His expression was serious, but a smile touched his eyes. They crinkled kindly when he looked at her. Catherine found that she liked him quite a bit.

At one point Wes had taken Meredith to the far side of the yard to show her a special rose bush. Catherine took the opportunity to inquire into something she'd been curious about.

"How do you feel about being down here?" she asked Nick.

Nick smiled and leaned forward, resting his elbows on his knees and clasping his hands together. "I'm really happy to be here."

Catherine couldn't help but return his smile. Though a man of few words, he was a very nice man. Evidently glad to let others do the talking, he was soft-spoken but content and at ease. With his angular features, too-long hair, and casual dress—he wore light faded jeans, a white t-shirt, and navy blue flip flops—there was an outdoorsy, rugged air about him, and he made Catherine feel more relaxed.

"Wes said the two of you met once before."

"We did. It was right after Merry and I got back together. Around the time Wes moved back here, I think."

"Why did you and Meredith break up?"

Nick's face turned serious, and he looked at his hands thoughtfully. "It's kind of a long story. Back then I didn't have a lot of confidence. I thought she could do better." He looked at her and smiled. "That's the short version."

Catherine saw the kindness in his eyes and wished she hadn't asked that question. She smiled back and thought a bit about what say to him next.

"So Meredith and Wes are still friends."

"Yes. It's nice, isn't it?"

Catherine stared at him. "You think so?"

"For sure. I've always encouraged her to keep in touch."

"Why?"

He tilted his head and furrowed his brow. He watched her a moment in silence.

"Well," he said, shifting in his seat a little, "I think it's good when people get along. It puts positive energy into the universe."

Catherine felt like screaming. She'd wanted to ask him if it bothered him that her husband was in love with his wife. But he was too nice to even see it. She'd hoped he could help her brainstorm, that he'd have some words of wisdom. But she realized quickly he would be no help. It appeared he was even more clueless than she was.

They spent the rest of the day at Wes and Catherine's house, relaxing on the patio and taking a walk around the neighborhood. Catherine wanted to hang back, to retreat into her thoughts, but Wes was his usual attentive self. He held her hand, or placed his hand on her back, or invited her to share her opinion. Ordinarily, Catherine would adore his infallible ability to make sure she felt included and important; it was one of the reasons she'd fallen in love with him. But the meaning was gone if she had to share his heart. And the idea that there was part of him to which she had no access, was almost more than she felt she could bear.

As confused and dark as she felt, she was amazed, as well. Watching Wes with Meredith was like viewing the world through sunglasses, then taking them off and seeing the world as it actually existed: she learned a lot about her husband by watching him with Meredith. Their interaction was different from what she'd expected, different from what she herself had experienced.

Meredith challenged him and disagreed with him, on many topics, from gardening techniques to foreign policy. It was something Catherine rarely did; she'd never felt the need. And as a result, perhaps, his conversations with Meredith were livelier—his comments sharper, his jokes wittier.

"I just finished Bill Wentworth's new book," he said. "Have you read it?"

"Funny you mention it. I started it last month, but I couldn't make it through. It was so pretentious, I had to stop."

"Well, Wentworth is pretentious. You kind of know that going in."

"I think he's gotten more pretentious over the years. I just don't have time for it anymore."

"It doesn't detract from his genius, though. It might even be part of it."

"Sorry, Wes. I can't agree. His job is to make me want to read him. If he can't be bothered, then neither can I."

In the evening, they sat around the dinner table with Wes's homemade dinner.

"The soufflé is incredible," Meredith told him. "What kind of cheese did you use to line the mold? It isn't gruyere."

"I cheated," he said, with a wicked little grin. "I used Parmesan instead because it grates much finer. I should have known not to try to trick your palate."

"You should have. Tsk, tsk. I've never known you to take a shortcut."

"Just don't tell Marks about the Parmesan, okay? It'll be the end of my career."

They talked politics for a while, agreeing and sparring and playing devil's advocate. Inevitably the conversation turned to the campaign.

"I'm glad you're running for office," said Meredith. "It seems right for you. In fact the first time Tara met you," she added, referring to her best friend, "she said you should go into politics, that you'd get everything you wanted."

"Everything, huh?" Wes held his hands up in mock surprise. "And to think, all this time, that's all it took. What a shame I didn't run for office years ago."

Meredith grinned. "You should have consulted Tara earlier. She always has all the answers."

He laughed. "You know I don't need Tara for that. You've already met my mother."

His mother. Catherine sighed inside. The following day, they were visiting his parents; Ethel, Helen, Grady, and Olivia would be there, too. Catherine didn't want to share them. She wanted to be the only one.

"I'll forgive you the Parmesan," said Meredith. She turned and smiled at Catherine. "That's how happy I am to see you and meet your family."

"I owe you one," he replied. "If you ever run for Senate, all your cheese secrets will be safe with me."

The Kellys stayed in their guest room that night. Catherine made sure they had everything they needed. She knocked on the door timidly on her way to her bedroom, a neat stack of towels in her arms.

Meredith emerged in her pajamas—plaid flannel pants and a soft pink tank top. Her hair had been pulled back into a ponytail. She closed the door behind her and spoke quietly to Catherine.

"Nick's trying to get Gabe down," she explained.

"That's okay," said Catherine, handing her the towels. "I just wanted to give you these."

"Thank you so much, Catherine." Meredith took the towels and offered Catherine a kind smile. "And thank you for having us here. I know it must be difficult, with the new baby. It's hard to take care of yourself with a newborn, much less a house full of guests."

Catherine smiled politely. "Amy's a pretty easy baby," she said. "She's still at the age when she sleeps all the time."

"How are you adjusting? Are you getting any sleep? Everyone always says to sleep when the baby sleeps, but I know that's not always practical."

"I'm probably getting about as much as I can expect. It really isn't so bad."

"That's good. I'm glad to hear it." Meredith's face turned serious. She shifted her weight and relaxed her stance. "I had a really hard time postpartum. No one had told me how hard it would be. It came as a total surprise, and it made me feel so alone. I just like to tell new mothers that it's okay to be worn out and to have some trouble adjusting. I think knowing you don't have to be perfect is so important for new moms."

"I don't think I have to be perfect. I'm not really having trouble adjusting." Catherine felt irritated in spite of herself; who was this stranger telling her how she felt? "I love being a mother. It's the greatest experience of my life. I haven't had any post-partum depression at all. At least, not for that reason."

Meredith's eyebrows rose inquiringly.

Catherine frowned. She felt sorry for being mean to Meredith. She'd never been mean to anyone in her life. She didn't like any of these feelings. It was bad enough that she was doubting her marriage—she didn't want to doubt who she was, too.

"Thank you for your advice, Meredith," she said. "Sometimes I do feel a little down. It's good to know I'm not alone."

Meredith smiled. "I hope you don't think I'm presumptuous for saying all this. I just remember how much pain I was in, and I don't want anyone else to go through what I did."

Catherine wasn't interested in talking about new motherhood; she had so many questions about Wes, and she had a feeling Meredith would answer them. But she couldn't bring herself to ask. They hugged goodnight and turned in for bed.

As she walked down the hall to her bedroom, Catherine almost laughed. It was all just too darn comical. Meredith was genuinely a nice person, and her reasons for being there were benign and sincere. Catherine couldn't even find a reason to be mad at her. Which made her mad at her all the more.

THEY WENT to Sarah and Charles's house the next morning. Sarah and Meredith had a tearful reunion, hugging and rocking and laughing with joy. Sarah showed her a gift Meredith had given her, some sort of signed copy of her father's book. They fawned over and complimented each other, catching up enthusiastically like old friends do.

Meredith talked with Ethel, Grady, and Helen, and doted over little Olivia. They were happy to see each other. Catherine sighed inwardly for the hundredth time that day. She shouldn't have been surprised. How could anyone not get along with the Bickharts?

Meredith pulled her aside and confided in her privately.

"I always loved the Bickharts," she said. "For the longest time, I didn't get along with my parents. Things are much better now. But the Bickharts made me feel loved."

"I understand," said Catherine, feeling more warmly, and smiling. "They make me feel loved, too."

"How about you, Catherine? Do you get along with your family?"

Catherine blinked a few times, unsure what to say.

"I suppose I do," she said. "But they aren't very nice to me, sometimes."

Meredith's eyes grew soft and sad. "I'm so sorry to hear that."

"It's okay." Catherine looked here and there, then forced herself to meet Meredith's gaze. "They mean well. I think they're just trying to help."

Meredith took her hand. "Well, you're a sweet, delightful person with a good life and a thriving business. You don't seem to need very much help."

Catherine bit her lip. Meredith bent to tend to Gabe, who had toddled toward her and hugged her legs. As she stepped away, having been called away by Sarah, Catherine took a moment to regroup and to calm her nerves. The thing was, she'd been thinking a lot about her parents; she'd been wondering if they'd been right. Her father's gentle reproving, her mother's quiet criticism—it seemed that it was well founded, that she'd messed up after all.

At least Sarah completely approved of her; of that much, Catherine was sure. She'd done everything she could to push her and Wes together, and she'd even expressed her adoration to Meredith's own father.

Her thoughts were interrupted by Wes, who approached with a smile and an arm extended, and Nick, who was holding Amy. Wes wrapped his arm around her and kissed the side of her face.

"How are you, sweetheart?"

"I'm good, I guess," she murmured absentmindedly; she was watching the other side of the sunroom, where Sarah and Meredith seemed deep in conversation.

What was it that Helen had told her? About why Sarah thought she was a good match for Wes?

Sarah says you're just perfect for Wes. You're very different from Meredith and his ex-wife Claire, and you're a much better fit. That's what Sarah says, anyway.

What had Helen meant by this? What did Sarah see in her that she didn't see in Meredith and Claire?

And suddenly, it hit her.

I've been with women like myself. And when I think about the failure of those relationships, I can only theorize that opposites must attract.

Catherine felt weak and cold, like a ghost had passed right through her: she'd finally realized something that had eluded her all this time. Like Wes, Meredith and Claire were bright and bold —professionals with backbone, who had no qualms about asserting themselves. They were sharp-witted and smart. They were intellectually stimulating. *If opposites attract*, thought Catherine, *then what does that make me?*

FOR THE FIRST time since meeting them, Catherine was desperate to leave the Bickharts. She felt as if she'd been left out of a secret, and that the secret was about her. After suffering through two of her son's difficult breakups, Sarah had wanted for him someone simple, someone plain, someone easy. She'd sensed

Catherine would unquestioningly adore him, and she had been right. The only problem was, that wasn't the kind of woman Wes truly wanted. Now that she knew the secret, she wished she could have remained ignorant. She wanted to go home, to cuddle with Amy, to sit in a dark room and mull over her thoughts in quiet.

They finally left just after lunch. Catherine watched Meredith and Sarah emerge from the house arm in arm, and left them alone to say their goodbyes. There were lots of tears, lots of hugs, lots of promises to keep in touch. Catherine rubbed her cheek against her baby's, turning away from the emotional scene.

They waved out the window as the Bickharts faded from view. They returned to Wes and Catherine's, where the Kellys prepared to leave.

They all stood in the front yard, Nick and Meredith's bags behind them. Nick and Wes shook hands and hugged, clapping each other on the back. Nick then leaned in and hugged her, his eyes crinkling kindly, and thanked her for her hospitality. Meredith thanked her profusely, hugging her close and rubbing her back, making her promise to bring the family up to Maine one day soon. They buckled Gabe into the car, and Nick placed the bags in the trunk. The three of them stood there in a kind of awkward silence. Catherine excused herself and headed inside. Nick was letting them have their moment; Catherine gathered she should do the same.

She watched from the bedroom window. Wes and Meredith embraced for a time, then separated, faced each other, and spoke. They stood straight, with serious expressions, and quite a bit of distance between them. Finally, they embraced again, more quickly. Then Meredith backed away and climbed into the car, closing the door with a wave.

Wes stood still until the car had pulled away and disappeared down the street. He then turned and walked slowly back into the house.

CATHERINE HAD to decide what she was going to do next. She loved him, and she knew on some level he loved her too. But she just didn't think she could share him; she couldn't keep living a lie. Or could she? Darn it, she just didn't know. Part of her was willing to make that sacrifice, if it meant she could stay in his life. She hated herself for feeling like this; she felt sad, and degraded, and weak. *But I love him*, she thought, hot tears rolling down her cheeks. *Isn't that enough reason to fight?*

Her world had been turned upside down; her mind was swirling and swaying. She didn't trust herself to make any decisions. She needed to be told what to do.

She texted Maeve and Hei, both at the same time.

Meredith just left. Wes is still in love with her. What do I do?

She stood and waited anxiously for them to reply. She heard the door open and close, and silently prayed they'd be quick.

Her phone buzzed, and Catherine jumped. It was a text from Maeve.

Does he love you?

A text from Hei immediately followed.

Of course he loves her. That's not a question.

I'm just saying. It makes a difference.

I can't believe we're even talking about this.

Catherine sighed. She heard footsteps on the stairs.

He's coming upstairs right now.

A moment later, her phone blew up with texts.

Maeve: *Believe it or not, I wasn't trying to be difficult.*

Hei: *I didn't think you were.*

Maeve: *It was a hypothetical question. I know he loves her.*

Hei: *Then why are we arguing?*

Catherine tapped her foot on the ground impatiently.

He's coming down the hall.

She turned toward the window to await the responses.

Maeve: *Is he having an affair?*

Hei: *Of course he isn't! It's just not nice to say he is.*

Maeve: *It isn't about being nice. If he is, denial helps no one.*

Catherine texted back as quickly as her fingers would move. *He's not having an affair.*

Hei was the first to respond.

It's not over, honey. Talk to him. And come over for coffee tomorrow.

And a moment later, Maeve followed.

What she said.

Catherine stared at her phone, then texted her response.

You two actually agree.

Her phone buzzed several more times, but it was already in her back pocket. Her eyes met Wes's as he stood in the doorway, his hand on the frame, watching her.

She stood tall and straight as he entered the room, and stiffened when he rested his hands on her shoulders. He kissed the top of her head, and lingered, then patted her hips and sighed.

"Wes," she said. "We have to talk."

PART II
MEREDITH

CHAPTER FOURTEEN

"I have the fever."

"Then stay away from me."

Meredith grinned slyly over the laundry she was folding as she sat on a couch in her best friend Tara's suburban Philadelphia living room. Tara was lounging on the other couch, her auburn hair piled into a high messy knot. Tara's baby daughter Celeste was sleeping in a vibrating chair just on the other side of the doorway into the next room. Tara's older daughters, Evelyn and Ginger, were playing with dolls in the center of the room; their chatter and laughter, along with the Disney movie playing on the television behind them, provided cheerful background noise.

"I mean baby fever," said Meredith.

"Oh. In that case, I have the solution for all your problems."

"I know. I need to talk to Nick."

"No, you can babysit for me so Tom and I can escape. Er, I mean—"

"You mean escape."

"Yes. Yes, I do."

Meredith placed a pile of clothes neatly into the basket and stood, basket resting against her hip. She approached Tara and leaned down to kiss her forehead.

"Of course I'm babysitting for you," she said, straightening and heading toward the stairs to put away Tara's laundry. "I thought that was a given."

"I love you," she heard Tara calling on her way up the stairs.

"I love you too," she called back, disappearing around the bend.

When she came back downstairs, the girls had run off to play outside on the swing set, and Tara was sitting up on the couch, looking tired.

"I was hoping you'd be asleep," Meredith said on her way to the kitchen. "Why don't you lie back down?"

"I'm too stressed out to lie down."

Meredith made her way to Tara's kitchen and heated up some meatballs from the previous night's dinner, then shoved them into a roll and placed the sandwich on a plate, along with some baby carrots. She filled a glass with water and brought it back to the living room, where Tara was leaning against the arm of the couch, her feet tucked beside her.

Meredith handed her the plate. "Here you go," she said. "Eat up."

"You're an angel sent directly down from heaven."

Meredith sat on the adjacent couch and propped her feet up like Tara. She settled in comfortably and picked up the cup of coffee she had left on the end table.

"So where do you want to go on your date?" she asked, bringing the coffee to her lips.

"I don't know," Tara mumbled through a bite of meatball sandwich. "Somewhere adult. Somewhere adult and quiet."

"You could try the new Indian place you've been talking about."

"I was thinking more along the lines of an island in the Caribbean."

Meredith chuckled. "Can I go with you?"

"Sure. We could leave the kids with the men."

"Never mind. Can you imagine the mess we'd come home to?"

"Who said anything about coming home?"

Both women laughed.

Tara swallowed another bite. "So you've got baby fever, huh? Too many babies in your line of vision lately?"

"Yes." Meredith sighed ruefully. "First Amy, and now Celeste. To say nothing of Julia," she added, referring to her brother Vince's baby daughter. "I'm surrounded by baby girls."

"You'd better watch it. You know these things happen in threes. How quickly you forget how hard the newborn stage is."

"I know." Meredith directed her gaze at Celeste and pouted. "But they're just so sweet."

"They're not so sweet at three o'clock in the morning. You'll be falling asleep during tutoring sessions."

"That's the beauty of tutoring. I can make my own schedule or scale back if need be. The same goes for catering. I can take some time off, then pick it back up again."

"What about the new Building for Hope chapter you two are starting? I guess you can strap the baby to your back while you're out building houses."

Meredith laughed. "It isn't even off the ground yet. We still have to contact the organization to find out how to jumpstart a local affiliate. Besides, I'd be taking care of the business end. Nick would be the one out there building stuff."

"Well, if anyone can do it all, you can. More power to you."

Meredith leaned back against the couch and stared thoughtfully at the floor. "I think I'll bring it up with Nick."

"Oh, well that settles it. Nick will do anything you say. Congratulations on your new baby."

"Well, first I have to decide for sure it's what I really want. Every time I think I'm ready, I remember my postpartum depression and shudder."

"I hear that."

Meredith reached her hand across the end table toward Tara. Tara took it and squeezed.

"I just don't know why this is so hard for me," said Tara, her eyes turning red and glassy. "It's my third time doing this. Everyone said the transition from two to three would be easy. But I just can't catch my breath. Look at me now. I can't even talk about it."

"It's totally understandable, Tara."

Tara took a deep breath and sat up very straight, then flashed her hand in front of her face. "I'm okay," she said. She brushed the crumbs off her lap. "Thanks for the sandwich, Merry. And the laundry. And the babysitting."

"It's no problem. Why don't you go jump in the shower before Nick comes back to pick me up?"

"I get a shower, too? Is it my birthday?"

A tiny hiccupping cry interrupted their chatter.

Meredith stood and turned to Tara.

"I've got her. You go."

"Thank you, Merry." Tara rose and pulled Meredith in for a warm hug. "You're a lifesaver." Meredith heard her sniffle a few times before continuing shakily. "I just really needed a break. I was so…And you just…"

Meredith shushed her and rubbed her back. "You've done the same for me a thousand times. I can never repay you for how you've supported me all these years."

Tara bounded up the stairs for her shower, and Meredith hurried over to baby Celeste, who by now was red-faced from shrieking.

"Oh, no, no," cooed Meredith, unbuckling and removing her from her seat. "We didn't forget about you, little doll." She laid the baby over her shoulder and bopped up and down in an even rhythm, holding her close and shushing her. The baby's cries calmed to whimpering, then to soft gurgles. Meredith rested her cheek against the baby's fuzzy head, inhaling the dreamy scent of newborn baby. She closed her eyes and sighed longingly.

"You are so little and lovely," she whispered. "Aunt Merry is here for you."

The doorbell rang. Meredith glided to the door and swung it open with her free hand. On the other side stood Nick, firm and tall, eyes crinkling kindly, blond hair made golden in the warm July sunlight.

She smiled sweetly. "Shh," she whispered, her finger at her lips.

Nick smiled back, his finger at his own lips, and stepped inside.

"Where's Gabe?" Meredith said softly as she closed the door behind him.

"Your mother put him down for a nap. Playing outside wore him out."

"That means he had fun." She rose to her tiptoes to accept a kiss, then rocked back and forth, her hand on the sleeping baby's back, as Nick took a seat on the couch. "Tara's in the shower. We can go as soon as she's done."

"No rush."

Meredith sidled closer, kissing the baby's head. "Look how sweet she is, honey."

"She's adorable."

"Have you ever seen anything quite so beautiful?"

"No, I haven't. And the baby is beautiful, too."

Her face softened. His eyes crinkled with a smile as he looked at her, and she melted, as she always did.

They chatted quietly until Tara came back downstairs, looking clean and refreshed.

"Hey, Nick," she said, meeting him for a hug. "If you're here for Merry, you're going to be disappointed. I refuse to surrender my minion."

"I could take the baby with me," Meredith suggested, only half joking.

"Sorry, Merry," said Tara, taking Celeste from Meredith's arms and coddling her into her chest. "You know I love you. But I can't let you take the baby. Tom would ask questions."

"Okay." Meredith sighed and waved at baby Celeste. "Aunt Merry will see you soon. I enjoyed our snuggle."

"Merry, you're so good with babies, and you love them so much. You and Nick should totally have another one." Tara looked at Meredith from under raised eyebrows, and winked in an exaggerated manner.

Meredith shook her head at Tara's characteristic candidness. She pursed her lips, suppressing a grin. "Very subtle," she whispered, leaning in to kiss her friend's cheek.

"I've got your back," Tara whispered back, returning the kiss.

Nick and Meredith said goodbye to the girls in the backyard, then drove the short distance to Meredith's parents' house, windows down, hair blowing, faces smiling.

THEY STROLLED hand in hand up the walkway of the Becks' elegant old stone colonial, then stepped inside the foyer, its formal white wainscot-paneled walls made bright and cheerful by the sunlight pouring in through the windows. Meredith kicked off her shoes and walked barefoot into the kitchen, not unaware of how much more comfortable she was in her childhood home than the last time she'd visited, more than two years before. The difference was so stark and so much of a relief, she'd felt it every time she'd walked through the door the last few days, ever since she and her little family had arrived from Wes's house.

The kitchen was spacious and well equipped, with granite countertops, cherry wood cabinets, and top-of-the-line appliances. Meredith sighed inwardly: it was her favorite room of the house.

Her mother was sitting at the kitchen table by the window, sipping a cup of coffee.

"Hello, dear," she said. "How was your day?"

"It was good. I just feel awful that Tara's having such a hard time."

"Poor girl. You'll help her, and she'll feel better."

"I hope so." Meredith looked around the room, finding only Nick, who had followed her. "Where's Dad?"

Patricia tipped her coffee cup ever so slightly toward the doorway, and lifted her chin. "See for yourself."

Bewildered, Meredith walked down the hall toward the living room. There, on a love seat, sat her father, a book in hand. Gabe lay sleeping on his chest, his little hands fallen to his sides, his little mouth hanging open.

"Oh," Meredith whispered, her hand at her heart. Tears sprang to her eyes.

Nick stopped abruptly just behind her and stared at the unexpected scene, silent but wide-eyed.

"Shh," admonished Harold, eyebrows lowered crossly. "You'll wake him up."

Meredith stepped softly forward, unable to take her eyes off them. "I can't believe you let him fall asleep on you."

"Of course I did. He wouldn't sleep any other way, and you had made your nap instructions clear. I shudder to think of the hell I'd pay if he missed his nap." To prove his point, he literally shuddered. "The horror."

"I suppose you had no choice," said Meredith, stifling a knowing grin. "Clearly, it was quite a sacrifice for you."

"Don't patronize me."

Meredith's grin softened. "My apologies." She put her hands up and backed away. "I'll leave you to your book."

"Good. And if he won't sleep again tomorrow," said Harold, his eyes now twinkling with mischief, "I suppose I'd be bound by duty to do this again."

As Meredith and Nick tiptoed from the room, Nick put his arm around Meredith's back.

"It's so nice, how good things are now," he said. "That he would even do that for Gabe."

"It really is. I just wish it didn't have to come with the defenses, that he could simply enjoy it and openly admit it."

"He will, beautiful. Give it time."

After a quick kiss and a squeeze of the hand, Nick walked outside to sit on the patio, and Meredith returned to the kitchen to pour herself a cup of coffee and sit with her mother.

"How has your day been?" she asked Patricia, bringing the coffee to her lips.

"Uneventful."

Meredith hoped her mother would say more, but she was silent.

While Patricia sipped her coffee and stared out the window toward the rhododendrons and azaleas, Meredith took a moment to study her. Her mother's chestnut hair was swept upward, showing off her elegant drop earrings. She wore gray three-quarter slacks and a gray silk blouse with a pattern of large red orchids. She was slim-framed and delicate; she had feminine, fragile features. But one mustn't, thought Meredith with a smile, mistake delicate features for a delicate heart. In the sharpness of her eyes and the lift of her chin, one could see that Patricia Beck was not a woman to be trifled with—indeed, her quiet, unassuming disposition was the source of her power.

"Mom," she said, her heart fluttering—even though Gabe's birth had inspired Meredith and Patricia to work toward reconciling after years of estrangement and misunderstandings, the years had trained Meredith to tread carefully around her mother, and a small part of her remained intimidated by her. "I was thinking that it might be nice for you and me to have lunch together, just the two of us."

"Sure."

Meredith continued watching her, waiting for a sign of enthusiasm; for a brief moment, the old disappointment rose from deep within.

Her mother placed her coffee cup on the table and knit her brows together thoughtfully. "We could try high tea at the new tea house." She looked at Meredith, and a little smile crossed her lips. "That would be lovely for a mother and daughter. Wouldn't you say?"

Meredith returned her smile, warmth encompassing her heart. "I completely agree."

"I'd like you and your husband to have some time to yourselves, as well. Take tonight off; go have a nice dinner. Your father and I will tend to Gabe."

"That would be great, Mom. Thank you."

Patricia smiled briefly again from behind her cup as she sipped her coffee. "Tell me more about your trip to Virginia," she said, her hand now wrapped around the cup as it rested on the table. "Did you enjoy your visit?"

"Oh, it was great. I'm so glad Wes and I have been able to remain friends. He was exactly the same, only more relaxed. Moving back to Charlottesville definitely was the right decision for him. He seems genuinely happy."

"Catherine seems like a sweet girl."

"Yes, Catherine is the sweetest." Meredith smiled as she remembered Catherine's kind face and gentle manner. "She seems a little shy." She chuckled. "Maybe that's best. Wes and I were too stubborn for each other. We dig in our heels, and we argued too much."

"How were Sarah and Charles?"

"Sarah and Charles were wonderful," said Meredith, her eyes brightening. "Charles made a huge, indulgent lunch, of course. And Sarah was her usual gracious, sunny self. The whole family was even perkier than they normally are. They're all geared up for Wes's campaign. He seems on track to win."

"They're a lovely family. Though I imagine it must have been awkward to see them."

"Oh, not at all. I've actually really missed them, and I was happy to have that closure."

Patricia brought her coffee cup to her lips. "That's nice," she said, gazing once again at the flowers outside.

"Well," said Meredith, gesturing with her hand and tilting her head a little, wrinkling her mouth with thought, "there was a little something."

Patricia looked at her over the rim her cup. "Oh?"

Meredith took a sip of her own coffee. "It wasn't a big deal," she said. "It's just that…"

Patricia watched her in silence, with a nearly imperceptible rise of her eyebrows.

"It's just that Sarah said something to me, something that maybe suggested that Wes…well, that he might still have feelings for me. I think."

"Do tell."

Meredith sighed. "Sarah told me I looked very happy and that Wes needed to see that. I asked her what she meant, and she said that Wes is too gracious to say it, but that a mother always knows." She paused, looking carefully at her mother. "Was it wrong of me to go down there?"

"No, dear. I don't think so. Wes is married now, with a family. You had no way of knowing."

"It's obvious how much he adores Catherine. They seem to have a truly loving marriage. I wonder if Sarah was wrong."

"I suppose it's possible."

"Do you think I interpreted her comment correctly?"

Her mother's slender shoulders rose and fell. "It was rather vague."

Meredith watched her. "You talk to Sarah occasionally. What do you think?"

"I barely know him, dear. It's hard for me to say. Sarah hasn't mentioned it to me." She paused in the act of bringing her coffee to her lips once more. "You were just there. You interacted with him. What do you think?"

Meredith shrugged. "Everything was pretty normal. I didn't feel uncomfortable." She paused thoughtfully. "Then again, Wes is nothing if not refined. He wouldn't give anything away. It's hard to tell with him."

Patricia swallowed her coffee and set her cup on the table. "I wouldn't worry about it. You never really know what's in another person's heart."

"Very true."

Meredith rubbed her lips together, her heart fluttering a little as she debated whether to tell her mother about the look on Wes's face as they had said goodbye on his front lawn, how he'd appeared to want to say something, and then decide against it. Maybe it had just been her imagination, the power of suggestion after Sarah's confidential comment. She looked out the window and sipped her coffee, remaining silent.

"What do you have planned for the rest of your trip?" asked Patricia.

Meredith shook off her thoughtfulness and turned back to her mother with a smile. "Well, Nick and I will have a nice night out tonight, thanks to you."

The corners of her mother's lips turned upward slightly.

"Maybe you and I can have our lunch tomorrow. And I told Tara I'd babysit for her and Tom, too."

"That's a lovely idea. I'm sure Tara will appreciate it."

"As much as I did, last year, when you first babysat for Nick and me."

Her mother's smile warmed, making her eyes tender and

bright. Meredith met her mother's gaze, and the two shared a silent, meaningful moment. That day had marked the start of this new era in Meredith and Patricia's relationship. Meredith remembered how much it had meant to her that her mother had made that effort, that she'd extended her hand to help at a time in Meredith's life when it had mattered the most.

"Nick and I would like to go to the arboretum, too. We went years ago, when we first met, and we've been meaning to visit again. On the way home, we'll stop in New York City. Nick's never seen it, and I...I have unfinished business there."

The sound of pattering footsteps interrupted their conversation. Meredith turned to find her little son toddling toward her, his hair mussed from sleeping and his face wearing a bright smile.

"There you are, little love," said Meredith, scooping him up into a hug as he wrapped his arms around her neck. "Did you have a nice nap with your granddad?"

"Da," said Gabe, pointing to Harold, who had followed him into the kitchen.

"Let the record show that the child's first word was 'Grand-dad,'" said Harold, his finger in the air, his other hand on the handle of the coffee pot.

Meredith put her hand to the side of her face and spoke quietly to her mother, but loudly enough for her father to hear. "Should I tell him that 'da' is the only thing Gabe says?"

"No," said Patricia, her coffee cup back at her lips.

"Well, it's the only thing he says because he loves me just that much." Harold poured his coffee and leaned forward so as to be eye-level with the little boy. "Isn't that right, Gabe?"

"Da."

Harold gave him a thumbs-up. "See that, now? I rest my case."

They smiled and nodded in greeting as Nick returned, his skin flushed and glowing from sitting out in the sun. He went to Meredith's chair and rubbed her shoulders; Meredith smiled and patted his hand.

"Dad, it looks like you'll get another opportunity to fulfill your grandfatherly duty sooner than you thought," she said. "Mom's offered to babysit tonight so Nick and I can have some time to ourselves."

"Ah," said Harold, draining his coffee. "Happy to oblige. Give me an hour or two first, though, will you? I'm exhausted. I'm going upstairs to rest."

"I thought you just had a rest with Gabe."

"No, I need to lie down."

"You've been tiring more easily," said Patricia, turning to him. "Perhaps it's the heat."

"I can take the heat. I'm just old." He held up his hand in leaving. "Be good, family. I'll be upstairs."

After he had left, Meredith stood and brought her cup to the sink. "Well," she said, her hands on her hips, "I think I'll take Gabe back outside for a while. It'll be good for him to get out some energy before Nick and I go out."

"You should walk to the park down the street and let him play on the playground."

"That's exactly what I was thinking." Meredith smiled and bent down toward her son. "Gabe, go give Grandmom a hug goodbye."

The little boy ran to Patricia, who greeted him warmly in a big bear hug. For a few moments, her face transformed, becoming unguarded and expressive. Meredith watched her, struck again by how beautiful her mother was.

She and Nick waved and followed Gabe out the front door and down the street. He wobbled ahead, looking about his new surroundings with excitement. Nick and Meredith held hands and breathed in the sweet summer air, watching as Gabe ran into the playground and began exploring, stopping here and there to admire a caterpillar or a patch of buttercups.

"This brings back memories," said Nick, squinting against the sunshine.

"Yes." Meredith looked around, locating the spot. "It was right over there."

Nick turned in the direction of her pointed finger. "Oh yeah," he said, and grinned. "Our first kiss."

It was Christmastime, four years before. Nick and her brother Vince had come down to stay with her while they worked a job in Philadelphia, when their parents were overseas. Vince had left them for the night and gone off to his own devices; they'd walked down to this park and talked about snow, and Maine, and poetry.

She chuckled. "I still can't believe you threw that snowball at me, deferential and shy as you were."

"You were so unsuspecting. I couldn't resist." He stifled a snicker. "It was worth it, to see the look on your face."

"And ultimately, it got you kissed."

"It got me more than that."

She nudged him with her elbow, and he nudged her back. She slid her arm across his back, bringing her other arm around his waist. She rested her head on his chest, and he pulled her close, kissing the top of her head and rubbing her shoulder.

"It was the snowball fight that did me in," she said, grinning. "It was the first fun I'd had in a year, the worst year of my life. And then there you were, entering my life out of nowhere, with your quiet, rugged sexiness and your poetic commentary on the Maine night sky." She shook her head. "I couldn't resist all that. I still can't."

"I'm glad it worked." He patted her arm. "I spent the first two days trying to come up with excuses to talk to you and worrying that you would catch me staring. Then I threw that snowball, and my life changed forever."

"I think I knew even then. Even three days in."

"Me too."

She sighed happily and let him hold her, closing her eyes a moment in perfect bliss.

"I like being back here," he said. "It's good to remember those early days."

"And how much better things are now," she added eagerly. "The idea that I can sit at the kitchen table and have a conversation with my mother, that she could offer to babysit and we could be planning a mother-daughter tea. That my father would be—*affectionate*." She shook her head in wonder. "I can't believe how much they've come around. I didn't think I'd ever see the day."

"A new baby will do that to people."

Meredith nodded solemnly. Growing up, she'd felt her parents push her ever harder and ever firmer, no matter what her accomplishments, always requiring more. Her father was a well-known, well-respected journalist, a professor and education advocate. He and Patricia had set impossible standards, and Meredith had striven to meet them—and while she'd been happy in her life and her decisions, the coveted approval of her parents had always eluded her. After a difficult time in her life, through which she'd yearned for, and missed, their support, she'd grown estranged from her parents—until Gabe was born. Visiting her in Maine, and meeting her husband and baby son for the very first time, they'd been softer, more accessible, more willing to meet her half-way. It had culminated in an honest heart-to-heart between Meredith and Patricia, during which Patricia exposed her own fears and insecurities, and finally showed Meredith the love she'd sought for so long.

In the year that had followed, the changes had been tentative, but certain. Meredith enjoyed having real relationships with her parents—asking for advice, planning visits, calling to tell them about her week. It felt shockingly, pleasantly normal. And though they'd always be themselves, proud and sharp and a little standoffish, they'd even been gentler with each other, and the new intimacy between them warmed Meredith's heart.

"A new baby." Meredith's eyes turned wistful. "Julia's already six months old. It's been a while since I've been around newborns," she said, glancing at him sideways to ascertain his reaction. "You don't realize how much your own child has grown until you see a child who's just been born. It's amazing. It almost makes you want to go back in time."

"I was thinking the same thing."

She turned to him. "You were?"

"Well, sure. It's hard not to."

"So," she said, her voice quiet, bringing her hand up around his shoulder, where her fingers lingered over the strong, tight muscles of his arm, "do you really think you might want to?"

He looked at her. "Want to what?"

"Want to have another baby."

His eyes widened. "No. No," he said again, and laughed, a little nervously. "That's not what I was thinking at all."

"What were you thinking?"

"That I've realized how big Gabe is. Compared to the babies."

"Oh." Meredith frowned, and her hand dropped over his back.

He continued watching her. "Merry."

She looked at him again, forcing a smile.

He tucked her hair behind her ear, his eyes crinkling kindly in the corners. "Are you disappointed that wasn't what I was thinking?"

Meredith swallowed and smiled in earnest. "A little."

He leaned in and kissed her forehead, rubbing her back as they watched Gabe examining some flowers.

"I'm sorry," he said tenderly, his fingers tracing soft lines on her back, making her melt inside, in spite of her disappointment. "I just don't want to have another baby."

"Ever?" she asked, her voice rising a little as she tried to conceal the subtle swell of panic.

"Maybe. Probably. I don't know. Can we talk about something else?"

"But why not?"

He retracted his arm and shoved his hands into the pockets of his jeans. "We had such a scary pregnancy, Merry. I was terrified and stressed out for months. And then you had postpartum depression. You weren't even the same person. I don't want us to go through any of that again."

"But this time would be different. I know what to expect. I could put things in place for myself, and head it off at the pass."

"It wasn't any different for Tara."

Meredith was silent, frowning.

His face softened, and he offered a rueful smile. "Look, nothing's set in stone. Maybe we can talk about it later."

Meredith sighed inside and nodded, watching Gabe as he ran this way and that. "Okay," she said, making herself brighten; it appeared there still was hope. "We can talk about it later."

They took each other's hand, gathered Gabe, and walked back to Harold and Patricia's house to prepare for their night out alone.

THEY ENJOYED A RELAXING, fun-filled, pleasant few days. Meredith was delighted to spend time with her parents and with Tara, who seemed somewhat rejuvenated by her visit.

"Thank you, honey," Tara told her as the two hugged goodbye. "For the help and the company. I can never ever repay you."

"Don't be silly. You're my best friend and my sister, and you've been there for me a thousand times. I'm repaying you."

Her mother invited them to return for Thanksgiving—no small thing, as for years her parents had spent their holidays abroad or on vacation with friends.

"I'm so glad," said Meredith, hugging her mother as they stood outside with their suitcases. "It'll be a cozy family holiday."

"Yes, dear. It will." Patricia kissed her daughter's cheek. "Thank you for coming."

"You're my parents. I love you. I'm grateful for the invitation."

Meredith squeezed her hand, and Patricia hugged her once more.

"We'll see you in Maine for Vince's wedding, though, before that," Patricia said.

"So many good things," said Meredith happily. "We're all so very fortunate."

Harold stepped toward Gabe, then crouched low in his trousers and dress shirt. "Thanks for being my nap buddy. Can I get a high five?"

The little boy met Harold's palm with his own, and everyone laughed and cooed.

Harold straightened, and Meredith leaned in to hug him. He patted her back, tersely, then nodded in acknowledgment with a not unkind face. Meredith would take it: he was trying.

They drove away with big smiles and full hearts. Meredith patted Nick's thigh and kissed his cheek. He smiled and squeezed her shoulder, then relaxed in his seat for the drive to New York City.

MEREDITH STARED out the window at the tall buildings and busy streets. She had decided to be kind to herself, to release the need to make sense of all her feelings. She'd been here only once since Adam died. It was on the way home from Nick's house, when she'd visited him after he'd left her, to try to convince him to come back. Back then, she'd been recovering from the tragedy of Adam's passing. She'd had the light switched on inside her by a bright new love, one who'd reminded her of simple beauties, whose pure heart had restored her peace—only to lose him, too. Today, after a long journey, she was married to him, with a son and a house and the most beautiful life she could ever imagine. It was surreal, like going back in time, only it was no longer her life. She was no longer the same person. She was simpler but more complex. She valued different things and took pleasure in new ways. She was harder now, and stronger, and also more aware. But she was more at ease, ironically—or maybe not ironically at all.

"New York is nice," said Nick as he pushed Gabe's stroller down a tree-lined street of brownstones and apartment buildings.

Meredith looked at him, raising her eyebrows and grinning. "'Nice?' That's your assessment of the greatest city in the world?"

Nick chuckled. "It's pretty intense. I can see why people love it. I don't think I could live here, though."

"I couldn't, either. Not anymore."

She took his hand and stopped before a brick building with brown steps and a rounded archway door.

"Here it is," she said.

They stood and looked together, moving backward to let throngs of people walk by.

"It's funny," she told him. "Part of me can't even believe I ever lived here. It feels that long ago. And yet..."

She faltered as she searched for words she knew would never come. He put his hand on her shoulder but said nothing, letting her have a moment.

She sighed and shook her head. When Adam died of cancer, before they'd had a chance to get married, before they'd had a chance to do anything—she thought she'd never find love again. It was difficult for her to parse her feelings about Adam, now that she had a new life—one she wouldn't trade for anything, not even for the chance to go back in time. She knew her feelings were normal and expected. She knew Adam would be glad, that he'd want for her exactly what she had now. What was it she was feeling, then? It wasn't regret; it wasn't quite guilt. It was simply the weightiness of having moved on, of being happy, of knowing this was the natural flow of the universe. It felt wrong and it felt right, all at the same time.

One thing definitely felt right, however: coming back here with the family she adored, confronting the past, releasing the ghost and completing the journey. She blew a kiss and imagined it flying upward, into the bright sunny sky; then she reached up to kiss her husband, who'd willingly granted her this time. Nick rubbed her shoulder, and they continued on, back toward the car, back to Maine, back to the life they were grateful for every moment of their lives.

CHAPTER FIFTEEN

"So what do you think?" asked Jenny.

Meredith looked out the passenger's window at the small 19th-century cottage house. It was one of several on this street, which was on the other side of town, which was still only a couple of minutes' drive from Meredith and Nick's house. It was a quiet, cozy street—though most of the streets in Dearham were. This particular street was just on the other side of the woods, not far from the old granite quarry. The house was painted gray, with a little front porch and ample back yard, and pretty dormer windows upstairs. The scene was peaceful in the muted light of the October evening, the trees bare and still, their crumpled leaves now carpeting the lawn.

"It's cute," said Meredith, assessing the house, which she had to admit was charming. "I like it. And I say this as a person who doesn't want you to move."

"I know." Jenny's eyes grew sadder. "I'm sorry, Merry."

"Don't you apologize," said Meredith, patting Jenny's hand and smiling. "This is the way it should be."

Meredith sighed and looked at the house again. She could see Jenny and Vince here, and little baby Julia. Her brother and his family had lived for months in the apartment addition of her own house. Meredith had been foolish to think they'd stay forever. Now that they were finally getting married, it made sense for them to find a house of their own.

"Well," she said, "you've found the perfect house, unfortunately. When are you putting in the offer?"

Jenny pursed her lips and shifted her eyes, looking guilty.

Meredith's eyes widened. "You already put in the offer."

"This morning. We didn't want to wait. We were worried it would slip away from us."

Meredith grinned and shook her head. "Sneaky, sneaky."

"I didn't have the heart to tell you. I thought I could get away with keeping it from you so it didn't ruin our night out."

Meredith reached to the side and wrapped Jenny in a hug. "You couldn't ruin anything. I'm so happy for you both."

"Really?"

"Truly."

Jenny pulled away, and Meredith saw tears in her eyes. "You've been so good to us, Merry. We'll still help out with Gabe whenever you need us. And we still want to be part of Building for Hope. Vince is excited to paint and to work with Nick on construction."

Meredith put her hand on Jenny's and smiled. "It's okay, Jenny. Please, you don't have to explain."

"I just hate to leave you."

"I know. I hate to see you leave. But you're only a couple of miles away, right? We'll see you all the time."

"Promise?"

"Promise. You can't get rid of us just by moving away."

Jenny smiled. "I'm so glad you like it. Your opinion means a lot to me."

"And you mean a lot to me." Meredith dabbed at her own eyes, then shook off the emotion and clapped her hands. "So let moms' night out begin."

~

THEY PULLED into the gravel driveway later that night under a sky full of stars that reached from the bottom of the open field to the woods on the other side of the house, disappearing into the darkness.

It was a modestly sized house, with a boxy shape and white paneling, the apartment addition jutting from the side toward the open field. It was the only house on the street, an old farmhouse a couple of miles from downtown Dearham, which wasn't much more than a post office, hardware store, ice cream shop, and a few various other small places of business. The house sat between the open field and the woods, as it had for many decades; under the clear night's sky, the moon watching from above, it looked settled and comfortable, a natural part of the landscape.

They'd seen the glow of the fire pit from the down the street: Nick and Vince were sitting outside in hats and sweaters, leaning back in their Adirondack chairs as they swigged a couple of beers.

Meredith smiled as she climbed out of the car and shut the door.

"Hey," called Vince. "You two have fun?"

Meredith and Jenny stepped toward the men. Meredith inhaled the deep, smoky scent of the fire, enjoying the brisk autumn air on her cheeks and the peace she always felt upon returning to the simple house she so loved. The fire hissed and crackled in front of them. Beside each man was a baby monitor, silent as Gabe and Julia slept.

"As always," she said, leaning down to kiss Nick, who'd extended his hand. She sat sideways on his lap, and he hugged her close.

"What did you do on your night on the town?"

"We went to dinner in Asterfield, then moved to a café for coffee." Meredith settled in, grinning under the cover of darkness as Nick stroked her thigh with his fingers. "Jenny also took me to see your house."

"Did she, now," said Vince, looking over at Jenny, who was sitting in the chair beside him, watching Meredith and Nick. "You told me you were sad about showing her."

"I wasn't sad about showing her, just about telling her we put in an offer."

Nick's head turned to Vince and Jenny. "You put in an offer?"

It was Vince's turn to look sheepish. "Well," he said, patting the arm of his chair, "yeah. I was going to mention it eventually."

"We've been sitting here for an hour!"

"Well, well," teased Jenny, kicking Vince's foot. "I'm not the only one."

"It looks like Vince doesn't want to leave us, either," said Meredith, shaking her head with mock sadness. "I guess that means you two have to stay."

"Sorry, Merry," said Vince, taking a swig of his beer. "As much as I've enjoyed living in your apartment like a frat boy, it's time for us to move on. I'm going to be forty. Even I have to grow up, at some point."

"Then why didn't you tell Nick?"

"I was sad, too. Come on, Merry. I'm not dead inside."

They sat in silence a few moments, absorbing the brisk autumn air and contemplating the changes ahead. Meredith gazed into the vast open field, thinking of unlimited possibilities. Her eyes drifted up to sky. It still amazed her, how much bigger it looked here in Maine, how many more stars were visible in this remote little town.

"I can't believe my big brother's getting married," she said wistfully.

"For real," said Vince. He stood and leaned forward to stoke the fire; embers rose and flickered about, seeming to dance like fairies in the smoke. The sight looked magical in the darkness, the faces of her family half-lit by the shifting glow. "Looks like Hell finally froze over. Someone was actually able to civilize me."

Meredith watched her brother as he relaxed against the back of his chair and swigged his beer, staring out into the open. With his thick dark hair, chocolate puppy dog eyes, and suave, stylish good looks, he'd been too charming for his own good; with his love of shenanigans and his short attention span for women, he'd spent years chasing mischief and instant gratification. Studying him now, sitting next to his fiancée, baby monitor at his feet, Meredith couldn't help but smile.

"Times sure do change," she said. "I thought I'd never see the day."

"Well, you know," Vince said smugly, settling into his seat and crossing his arms, "sometimes the world has other plans for you."

"And sometimes your one-night stand gets pregnant," Jenny muttered with a snicker.

"And sometimes it's the best thing that possibly could have happened to your life."

Jenny looked at him, and he met her gaze. He held out his hand, and she took it, turning shyly back toward the fire.

"It is amazing all the wonderful things a baby brings to your life," Meredith agreed. "Gabe was unplanned, too, of course. But where would we be without him?" She nudged Nick beneath her, then played with his hair a little with her fingers. He tilted his head back and closed his eyes. "I'd like to have another, but I have to convince Nick. He's not sold on the idea."

"You mean you don't want to be sleep-deprived and covered in spit-up again, Nick?" said Vince. "You don't want to bring ten bags of stuff everywhere you go? Navigate your wife's hormones for nine months? I'm shocked."

"Oh, stop, Vince. You're not helping."

"Sorry, Merry. I feel you. And I love Julia, but man." He shook his head. "I don't know if I can do this again."

"Just wait six months until she's toddling around like a big girl. Then you'll see."

"How come you don't want another?" asked Jenny.

Nick opened his eyes and shrugged. "I don't want another high-risk pregnancy."

"But it all worked out in the end, right?"

Nick didn't say anything, but closed his eyes again as Meredith brushed his hair back and gently squeezed the back of his neck. She decided not to push him to talk about it; she shouldn't have brought it up in front of Vince and Jenny in the first place.

"So you'll be married in just twenty-two days," she said, changing the subject.

Vince smirked. "But who's counting?"

Meredith turned to him and grinned. "Sorry, I can't help it. I'm a planner."

"I'm grateful," said Jenny, holding out her hand for Vince to pass her his beer. She took a swig and passed it back. "I've been so overwhelmed by the wedding and the move. And seriously, the fact that you're catering has been a huge weight off my shoulders. I couldn't be doing this without you, Merry."

"Well, I think you could, but I'm thrilled to be able to help. There's no reason to do it by yourself if you don't have to."

"That reminds me," said Jenny, standing and stretching. "I have an appointment with the seamstress early tomorrow. I'm headed to bed. Vince, are you coming?"

"Yeah."

Vince and Jenny waved and walked back toward the apartment, leaving Nick and Meredith by the fire, which by now was reduced to a slumbering smolder of embers. They sat together cozily, Meredith's head resting on his, his arms around her, gazing into the open field, listening to the wood crackling in the fire pit.

"Merry," he said.

Meredith lifted her head and looked at him. He was watching her with a serious expression, his eyes intent and his lips straight.

He rubbed her back, and his eyes softened. "I hope you understand. About the baby."

His eyes were crisp, clear, and blue, even in the darkness; his earnestness undid her, as it did every time.

She sighed and rested her head on his once more. "I understand. I just..."

"I know. I'm sorry."

She was silent a moment or two. "You never put your foot down about anything," she teased. "Why do you have to do it when it's about something so serious?"

"That's the most important time to do it."

She felt sadness creep into her face. "I just never saw myself having only one child."

"I was an only child. I think I turned out okay."

She kissed the top of his head and squeezed him tight. "You turned out better than okay."

"And Gabe will, too."

"But it's not only about Gabe, really."

He patted her thigh and looked up at her again. "I know. And it's not just my decision to make. Can we just wait a while and talk about it again later?"

"I suppose that's reasonable."

They met in a kiss, and Nick slipped his hand under her jacket, splaying it across her back and pressing her in close. She brought her hand to his face, burying her fingertips in his hair and stroking his temple with her thumb. The Maine autumn air around them was brisk, but his lips were soft and warm, and at the slow, even movements of his jaw beneath her hand, all disappointment left her heart, flying upward into the dark night sky.

He pulled back, concluding the kiss with a few tender pecks, lingering long enough for his breath to fuse with hers. Meredith's blood tingled as he took her face in his strong, rough hands, kissing her one last time, with more boldness, tugging her lips with his own.

"Let's go inside," he said, in his soft-spoken way. Meredith grinned as his thumb sneaked under her shirt, caressing the bare skin of her waist. "The fire's gone, anyway."

"I think the fire's better than ever."

"I knew you were going to say that."

They smiled, stood, and put out the remainder of the fire, then walked hand in hand toward the house. Upstairs, in their bedroom, with its hardwood floors and modest furniture and simple, cozy white linens, the earthy smell of the fire remained, seeping in through the windows and clinging to their skin and to their hair. In his arms, bathed in moonlight, Meredith closed her eyes, the vision of embers lingering, the feel of his skin like magic on a star-kissed night.

VINCE AND JENNY were married three weeks later. The wedding took place at an inn in nearby Asterfield, a quaint, posh town that sat just over the causeway and was home to cafés, antique stores, and gift shops. The ceremony was outside, in a gazebo nestled in a small English-style garden, which at this time of year boasted the more modest blooms of heather, witch hazel, and candytuft. Jenny carried a colorful bouquet of red fall crocuses and chrysanthemums and wore a simple cream-colored dress; Vince wore a chocolate-colored suit and tie, with a white dress shirt. It was a small wedding in an intimate, picturesque setting, a couple of dozen friends and family members in the converted Victorian house to celebrate a union a long time coming.

Harold and Patricia were there. They'd arrived that morning and were staying a few days at the inn. Meredith didn't have much time to speak with them before the wedding; she'd been occupied in the kitchen with her food. But during the informal reception, which took place in the inn's cozy banquet room, they mingled with guests and coddled their grandchildren, taking pictures by the fireplace and doing their bests to assimilate into their grown children's lives. It was something she never would have imagined, even a year before, though she'd dreamed of such moments for as long as she could remember.

Meredith felt overcome. She approached her mother and took her hand, then kissed her cheek. Her mother smiled and squeezed her hand in return.

"I'm so glad you're here," said Meredith.

"We wouldn't miss it. Not after we weren't there for yours."

Meredith's smile faded. She looked at her mother sadly. "I'm sorry. I think about it all the time."

"It wasn't your fault, dear. We gave you no choice."

Meredith was silent, remembering. She and Nick had married during a period of estrangement from her parents, in a courthouse ceremony in Dearham, with only Vince and Tara in attendance. It had been a joyous, perfect day, the simplicity of the wedding enabling her to focus on the significance of that happy event in her life. Still, she'd felt her parents' absence.

"Well, it's good that things are better now," she said. "All we can do is move forward, I suppose."

"Indeed."

Meredith brushed off her moment of thoughtfulness and perused the room of guests.

"Where's Dad? I haven't seen him in a while."

"Oh," said Patricia, appearing to brush some dust off her arm, uncharacteristically flustered. "He went upstairs to the room to lie down."

Meredith turned to her, brow furrowed. "What?"

"The long trip up here exhausted him. He just needed to rest."

Meredith frowned. "Is everything all right?"

"We're just getting old, is all."

Meredith studied her mother warily, not quite believing her

explanation. As her mother declined to say more, however, Meredith decided to let it go for now, and to focus on her brother's wedding.

At the end of the night, everyone kissed goodbye until the morning; Vince and Jenny were staying in a hotel for the night, then would have breakfast at Nick and Meredith's house, where they'd pick up Julia and take her to Florida for a quasi-honeymoon. Meredith left the inn happy, fulfilled, and exhausted. She hugged Vince and Jenny, then her parents—who seemed especially tired by that hour, and even a little withdrawn—and headed home, a dozing Julia in tow. She put the children to bed in Gabe's nursery, then fell into her own bed with Nick, snuggling close, whispering a few sweet words, and falling promptly to sleep with a smile on her face.

The next morning, Nick and Meredith were up early with the children. They buckled the kids into high chairs and fed them Cheerios and yogurt, waiting for her family to arrive.

"I hope my parents get here soon," said Meredith, glancing at the clock on the wall. "If they don't, they'll miss Vince and Jenny."

"I'm sure they'll be here any minute," said Nick. "They won't want to miss sending them off."

But Vince and Jenny arrived to pick up Julia, and Harold and Patricia still weren't there.

"Hey, we've got to go," said Vince finally, after waiting around for almost an hour. "We're going to miss our flight."

"Okay," said Meredith, frowning fretfully, and glancing at the clock once more. "I just can't understand why they wouldn't be here."

"Looks like they haven't really changed. I should have known it was too good to be true."

"Let's not make any assumptions," she replied, but inside, a tiny part of her worried he was right.

Her parents rang the doorbell an hour later, just before lunch.

Meredith was annoyed, and wanted to ask why they'd missed Vince and Jenny, but decided against it. She had so been enjoying their new relationship; she was frightened to ruffle their feathers.

"Can I get you something?" she asked them as she met them in the doorway, gesturing with her hand that they should join her in the kitchen down the hall. "I have fruit salad, potato salad, and sandwiches."

"No, no, I'm not hungry," said her father, tossing his hand up and looking around distractedly. "Where's Gabe?"

"He's already taking his nap. He can't make it past noon."

"Oh." Harold frowned and rubbed his throat. "Say, could I get a glass of water?"

"Of course."

Meredith went to the kitchen to fetch her father some water. She thought he'd follow her, but when she turned to give it to him, he wasn't there. She walked back to the hallway and found him staring at the wall, where she'd hung pictures of her family in long, neat rows.

He pointed to a photo of Gabe. "I've never seen this one. When was this taken?"

Meredith looked at the picture and smiled. "That was at the spring solstice fair near Aspen Woods Mountain."

He stared a moment longer. "Make me a copy of it, will you?"

"Sure."

Patricia was in the living room fondling a blanket thrown over the back of a chair.

"This is new. It's very pretty."

"Thanks. My friend Jamie made it for Gabe's birthday."

Patricia smiled mildly. She took a sip from the coffee cup she'd brought in with her, and said nothing.

"No one wants to eat lunch?" she asked.

"I've already told you, no," said Harold. "We had a late breakfast at the inn."

Meredith sighed inwardly, her heart dropping as doubt crept into her heart. The tension was all too familiar. Vince had just gotten married—she'd been hoping today would be a joyous day, that the family could sit together as a whole and celebrate with smiles and laughter. Her parents' coldness, their defenses and their refusal to engage, brought all the old feelings up in a rush. She couldn't understand it; while she hadn't seen much of her father the night before, her mother had seemed fine. Meredith bit her lip, trying to calm herself, hoping her high emotions were making her misinterpret.

Nick approached and rested his hand on her shoulder.

"Let's make them some sandwiches," he whispered. "They'll sit down with us if it's already done."

She looked at his face—his expression was serious, but a smile was crinkling the corners of his eyes. She nodded and took a deep breath.

"Thank you," she replied, releasing her breath, smiling a little as his hand found her back and guided her into the kitchen.

They made sandwiches and set the table. Patricia joined them a few minutes later.

"Can I help?"

"I think we're done," said Meredith, looking around. "Why don't we all sit down."

The four of them took their seats at the kitchen table. It was a clear November day, and muted autumn sunlight filled the room. It poured in through the window over the sink and the glass doors by the table; it brightened the white cabinets and tile floor, and fed the potted plants that rested on shelves and countertops.

"So Vince and Jenny got off just fine," said Meredith cheerfully, picking up half a sandwich. "They're on their way to Florida by now."

"What are they doing in Florida?" asked Harold; a plate of food sat before him, but he hadn't touched it. "He never even told me. Are they going to Disney World?"

"No, they're going to Miami to sit on the beach. They want to wait until Julia's a little older before they take her to Disney." She swallowed a bite of sandwich and smiled at her father. "I have an idea. Maybe next year, we can all go. You can join us. Wouldn't that be fun?"

Harold and Patricia looked at each other.

"I don't know, Meredith," said Patricia. "That's a long time away. Let's see where we all are this time next year."

Meredith stopped chewing a moment, then swallowed with effort. "Okay," she managed to respond, looking down at her plate and mindlessly spearing a strawberry with her fork.

Harold whistled a few notes and drummed his fingers on the table. "Nick, how's business?" he asked.

Nick swallowed a bite and cleared his throat. "Business is good," he said, nodding. "Construction jobs tend to slow down this time of year, but I'm doing all right."

"'All right,' eh? What does that mean, exactly?"

"Better than all right." Nick shifted in his seat and smiled. "I'm doing well."

"Nick will never tell you how successful he is," said Meredith, with a fond little grin. "But he has more clients than he knows what to do with, and they all love him."

"Ah," said Harold. "That's what I like to hear." He turned to Nick. "You need to start tooting your horn, Nick. Don't be so bashful. If you want to grow your business, you're going to have to show some confidence."

"He's very confident, Dad," said Meredith. "He's just modest."

"Modesty gets you nowhere in business. I don't want to see him become stagnant. What will you do if work slows? How will you win new clients? How can you convince people to hire you, if you can't tell them you're the best guy for the job? How do you get anything you want if you don't insist on your own self-worth? Isn't that why you two split for a while?"

Patricia elbowed him discreetly, and he was quiet.

"Dad," Meredith murmured, her face turning red, her heartbeat picking up speed. "That's a little much."

"It's too much that I care about my family? That I want to make sure my daughter's taken care of?"

Meredith was dumbstruck. Her eyes darted to Nick, who appeared surprised but composed: his brow had lifted, but his body was relaxed in his chair.

"It's not too much, sir," he responded gently. "I've learned a lot since then. I'm smarter now, and I'm doing everything I can to provide for this family. I promise."

"You're a good, honest man," said Harold. "You mean well. But you can't blame me for worrying about my daughter."

Meredith's voice was flat and cool. "Dad, Nick is a wonderful husband and provider. He's the hardest worker I know. What you're talking about was years ago. We've all grown in that time. I've let it go, and you should, too."

Nobody said anything. Meredith pushed the food around on her plate, then forced herself to take a bite, barely even tasting it.

"Vince is probably going to quit his job and team up with Nick," she said finally, trying to lighten the mood. "Everyone's really excited."

"Now, I'm not sure that's a good idea," said Harold, appearing troubled. "Doesn't Vince already make pretty decent pay?"

"Well, yes. But so did Nick, when he worked there, too. They can bring in a lot more clients together. And Vince wouldn't have to travel anymore."

"A lot of good it'll do him if he's got no experience. What the hell does Vince know about construction?"

"Actually, he knows more than you'd think," interjected Nick, his voice bright, his arm on the table, leaning forward casually. "He's been at the painting company for years. When I went out on my own, he came with me on a few jobs. He's a pretty fast learner. I think he'll do just fine."

"'Just fine' just isn't good enough. Not when you have a wife and a child."

"It's just a figure of speech, Dad." Meredith was controlling her anger with effort, ordering the tears not to come. For so long, she'd wanted her parents to think she was enough; for years she'd defended her life and her choices, tolerating the judgment, brushing off the criticisms. The last year had felt like a dream, in which she'd begun to believe it would be different. Their visit together only a few months before had been so heartwarming and fulfilling. She should have known it wouldn't be long before their relationship regressed to its default.

She braved a glance at her parents. They were whispering together, faces stern, appearing to argue.

"What's wrong?"

Neither Patricia nor Harold answered her question; they faced forward, though her mother looked away.

"I was hoping to see Gabe," said Harold, looking at his watch. "When do you plan on waking him, Meredith?"

"I wasn't going to wake him," said Meredith, warmed that her father had so taken to his grandson, but frustrated by his crotchety mood. "He'll be up soon enough."

"When are you two going to have more children? Gabe's over a year old now. What's taking so long?"

Meredith's face fell, and she looked at Nick before she could help herself. His face expressionless, he was avoiding her gaze.

"Um, I'm not sure, Dad," she said, neatening her napkin on her lap nervously. "We may not have any more kids."

"What?" Harold barked, eyes wide, hands in the air. "How can you say such a thing? Children are a gift, Meredith. A blessing. Gabe is a delight and a miracle. He's going to grow into a fine man one day. He's the only thing carrying on your legacy, the most important contribution you will make to this world. How can you not have another? It's selfish, Meredith. It's just selfish."

"Dad," cried Meredith, mouth hanging open, abandoning all

her self-restraint. "Why are you doing this? You're completely overreacting."

"Overreacting, am I? By simply stating my desire to have another grandchild? Before it's too late? Before the chance is gone forever?"

"Stop," said Patricia.

Everyone looked at her with shock. She was calm and stoic as ever, but her eyes were soft, almost warm. In an unusual gesture, she placed her hand on Harold's. He jerked his body to turn to her, and frowned; the two seemed to share some unspoken communication, for he sucked in his breath and nodded.

"I'm dying," he said.

Meredith's eyes had been wide and alert; at his statement, they narrowed, and her face creased with confusion.

"You're dying...to have another grandchild?"

"No, Meredith. I'm dying."

Meredith stared at her father, her eyes frantically searching his face for any sign that she had misheard or misunderstood him. She opened her mouth to say something, but closed it.

"What...but what do you..."

"Your father's been diagnosed with pancreatic cancer," said Patricia. "We wanted to tell you in person. Anything is possible, of course. Realistically, however, we're probably looking at a year."

Meredith's breath left her; the room began spinning.

"It's why we didn't want to see much of Vince before his honeymoon," Patricia continued. "We didn't want him to have that hanging over him."

Meredith continued staring at her in silence. A sick, heavy feeling had begun encroaching her heart, but her mind was frustratingly blank. She shook her head and turned to her father. He wouldn't look at her. He was staring at the table like a child in trouble, his jaw set and his eyes dark and lost. She looked at Nick, whose eyes were already on her—they were wide and sharp, and his lips were drawn downward. He held out his hand for her. She took it, numbly, barely registering what was happening.

"Harold, I'm so sorry," said Nick. "I don't know what to—"

"No," said Meredith.

They all turned to her.

Patricia spoke first.

"I know this must come as a—"

"Damn it, I said no."

Nick squeezed her hand, then lifted it and kissed it. Meredith was breathing heavily, rubbing her lips together, desperately trying to keep a grip on her emotions. If the tears never came, there was no reason to shed them; if she didn't feel it, it wouldn't be real.

Finally Harold lifted his gaze, his face looking almost annoyed. "Believe me, I'm shocked too," he said with a snort and a morbid half grin. "Imagine how I—"

"No," she said again, through an abrupt, shaky sob. She wiped her eyes with her hands, resisting the urge to fall into Nick, who had moved his chair closer and brought his arm around her back.

"I'm sorry, dear," Patricia said, leaning across the table and touching Meredith's arm. Meredith came undone. She let Nick embrace her, and let the tears fall, allowing the words to reach her, surrendering to the truth.

MEREDITH STOOD outside under the stars, bundled up in her coat, gloves, and scarf, staring out into the open field. She watched her breath unfurl and escape into the cold November evening, finding a strange calm in its rhythm. She was in her backyard, which was really an extension of the field itself; though it was carefully domesticated, with a large, orderly vegetable garden, a shed, a swing set, and neatly mowed grass, it was situated beside the untamed space, which seemed to stretch on into the horizon.

On her other side was a thick expanse of woods, which stretched on for miles, past the little cemetery up the road and onward to the sea. Meredith loved her house and her yard, the way they were hugged by the Maine landscape. There was a kind of peace in the openness, a feeling of being part of the larger universe.

She turned as she sensed someone approach. Nick was stepping out through the glass doors in the kitchen. He closed them behind himself and went to her, rubbing her back and kissing her forehead, then standing beside her with his hands in his pockets.

"Your parents are getting ready to go back to the inn," he said. "I thought you might want to say goodnight."

"Thanks, honey. I'll go see them in a minute."

He faced the field with her, watching the still scene in silence.

"I'm sorry for what he said to you," she told him, in the tumble of emotions feeling that one needed addressing first. "I wish he'd left you out of it."

"He was just upset. It's okay."

"It didn't make you feel bad, did it?"

"No, honey, I'm fine." He looked at her and smiled. "I didn't take it personally."

She returned his smile and leaned toward him. He brought his hand around to her shoulder and pulled her in close.

"Merry, I don't know what to say," he said then, from above her. "About your father."

She sighed. "It's okay. There's really nothing to say."

He kissed the top of her head. "I know this must be even harder for you because of Adam."

She felt a tickle behind her eyes and in her nose, recognizing an oncoming rush of tears. She cleared her throat and took a breath, and looked back into the open field.

"Thanks," she whispered, patting his chest. "That really means so much to me." She closed her eyes and sighed. "You've been through it, too, with your parents."

He was silent a moment or two. "It isn't easy."

He held her in silence, resting his head on hers.

"It's just that things were finally getting better with my father," she said, willing her voice not to shake. "After so long, he was in my life, in a satisfying way."

"I know."

He rubbed her shoulder, and she nuzzled her head into his chest.

"So much time was wasted," she said.

"Well," he said, "you'll both just have to make good use of the time you have left."

She said nothing, but wrapped her arm around his waist, taking comfort in his warmth and his strength. The sound of the glass doors opening again made them straighten and look up: Harold was now emerging from the house, in his black pea coat and hat.

"I was just on my way in," said Meredith, pulling away from Nick. "I'm sorry I kept you. I guess I lost track of time."

"It's fine," said Harold. "But I do want to talk to you before we leave."

"I'll meet you two inside," said Nick, leaning in to kiss her. He walked away, leaving Harold and Meredith alone.

Harold walked slowly until he was beside her, but stood at a distance, looking out into the open field.

"Pretty scene," he said. "I don't blame you for loving it here."

Meredith's breathing had quickened; she was struggling with what she should say. Words now seemed petty and meaningless, or cruel. She took a moment to watch him as his gaze was directed elsewhere. His expression was serious in silhouette, his eyes fixed and contemplative. He was not a tall man; he was slim in stature and firm in posture. She'd spent many years feeling intimidated by him, and to a certain extent, she still was. She imagined the conflict underway inside him, the staunch, immovable soul in a body that threatened to vanquish him.

"You know, Meredith," he said, still staring straight ahead, "I have to admit I'm scared."

He finally met her gaze. He'd said it matter-of-factly, and his expression was stern, as usual. But there was sadness in his eyes, and acceptance. Her own eyes watered as she felt his loss, and her own.

"Of course you are," she whispered, wiping a tear from her cheek. "You're only human." She grinned then, before she could help it. "Despite what you might believe."

His expression lightened marginally; Meredith sensed him repressing a grin of his own. "You're going to kick a man when he's down, are you? You always were so droll."

"I learned from the best."

A humorless chuckle escaped him. "Yes, I suppose you did."

They stood in silence a few moments. Meredith's cheeks were bitten with cold, and her fingertips were growing stiff. It seemed to capture the feel of the conversation, mimicking the seriousness and urgency of the moment.

"Listen, Meredith," he said then, turning to her again, and stepping a little closer. "I need you to do something for me."

Meredith faced him and waited at full attention, ready to hear what he had to say.

He spoke softly, but his voice was firm. "I don't have a lot of time."

Meredith swallowed and bit her lip, fortifying herself.

He met her eyes with his own, and went on. "I want to write a book about my life. A memoir, of sorts, but an opinion piece, too. And I want you to help me write it."

Meredith's lips parted, and her eyebrows rose with surprise. "Oh," she said. "Yes, of course."

"I'd like you to help me organize it, do a little research where necessary, talk to people I've met over the years. I may even have you write some passages. Take a little dictation, maybe. Toward the end."

A low pressure amassed in her chest, but she soldiered onward, refusing to submit to it. "I'll do whatever you need, Dad. You just lead the way."

"You'll share my byline, of course."

"I don't care about that."

"Well, you should."

Neither spoke for a moment or two.

"I can confidently say, Meredith," he said, gazing out into the field, "that I've accomplished a lot in all my years. I taught at Columbia and NYU. I've written seven books and thousands of columns. I've met countless officials and heads of state. I've seen dozens of countries around the world. And for all my flaws and my sour disposition, I somehow raised a couple of damn good children." He cast her a serious look, then faced the field once more. "This will be my final project, my curtain call. My message to the world as I go out, for better or worse." He paused. "And we'll see it through together."

Meredith watched him a moment, then turned back to the open field, a spark of excitement twinkling deep inside her, despite her heartache. This book would be a way for her to connect with her father, to get to know him in a way she never had. She would stand beside him, in a sense, helping him achieve his final accomplishment, compiling for the world the sum of his brilliance. Though she and her father had a rocky personal history, she'd always respected him for his beliefs and achievements; this book would immerse her in his mind, would give her perspective she'd never had before. In the darkness of his illness, this book would bring her light.

She reached out and took his hand, and he looked her in the eye. They then stood for a time with their eyes on the open field before them, contemplating life, thinking about unlimited possibilities.

~

TWO DAYS LATER, they voted in the midterm election. Meredith was following Maine's, of course, and several others, but none more anxiously than Virginia's. She was brushing her teeth that night when her phone lit up. She picked it up from the counter-top: it was a news alert. Election results were in.

She hurried from the bathroom and held it out for Nick, who had already climbed into bed.

"Wes won," she told him with a grin. "It wasn't even close."

CHAPTER SIXTEEN

*M*eredith sat at the kitchen table, a cup of coffee and a pile of notes beside her laptop, the sky outside overcast and gray. After her parents had left the previous weekend, Harold had wasted no time, sending her outlines of chapters and little treatises on a variety of political topics. Her job was to edit and insert them appropriately, verifying details and fact-checking along the way. Her father had been very specific about how this was to be done. She was to take individual passages and meld them together, matching opinions to life events as she saw fit, unless he first specified a particular preference. She was to add outside voices when necessary, utilizing interview scripts or personal accounts when he shared them with her, and contacting acquaintances when he had not. She was to cite all her sources, strictly adhering to the style guide he'd provided. She was free to elaborate on points related to culture or politics, provided she checked with him first. The personal details he'd write himself.

His method surprised her; she thought he'd approach the book chronologically, in a logical, organized way. Instead, he tossed at her dozens of mismatched, half-finished journal entries and diatribes, in no particular order, evidently with the expectation that they'd coalesce by magic. It was unexpected, but she understood. He had to pinpoint and bring to life everything he knew and every belief he held dear, while watching the hourglass, to boot. The chaos of the passages probably mirrored the chaos of his mind.

She shuffled through the papers with a frown. There was no rhyme or reason to what he'd sent her. Her mind didn't work like this. She decided to form a blueprint.

But first, she needed to know where he was going, what he wanted the overall arc of his story to be. She straightened in her chair, squared her shoulders, and began typing a questionnaire for him to answer.

1. What are three lessons your life has taught you?

She bit the corner of her lip and studied the screen, then began typing again.

2. What are three lessons you would like to impart to the world?

She held her chin in her hand and thought for a moment. She ought to be more specific. She needed to discern how particular events shaped him; she needed some kind of roadmap that led to who he was.

The front door opened, and Meredith heard little feet scampering down the hall. Gabe ran inside and spotted her at the table. He went to her with his arms out. Meredith smiled and scooped him up, and kissed him.

Nick soon followed, striding casually behind.

"Hey, honey," he said. "Gabe's hungry. I'm going to make him some lunch."

"Okay," she said, setting Gabe down and watching as he began playing with some trucks from a bin in the corner. "How's the scarecrow coming?"

"Great." Nick smiled as he pulled some cheese and fruit out of the refrigerator. "Gabe helped me fill him with straw. Didn't you, buddy?"

From the corner, Gabe nodded in an exaggerated fashion as he pushed his truck back and forth on the floor.

Meredith looked with fondness from her son to her husband. "What are you going to name him?"

Nick slowed a moment as he thought about it. He turned to Gabe. "What do you think we should we name our scarecrow?"

"Da," said the little boy.

Nick stood behind her chair and rubbed her shoulders, and she reached backward and patted his hand.

"What are you working on?"

"I'm writing a questionnaire for my father," she said. "I'm trying to tie events in his life to his beliefs and opinions."

"That's a good idea. Do you need any help?"

"Sure. Can you think of any questions I should ask him?"

"Hmm," he said, leaning forward and looking over her shoulder at the screen. "You could ask him about his favorite politicians, who he thinks has done a good job."

"That's a good idea, but I think I already know all that." She flipped through his papers again. "He's sent me some things to think about, and I've read all his books and columns."

"I'll think about it some more." He returned to the countertop and put some food on a little plate. "In the meantime, maybe Wes would know."

"Maybe."

Meredith watched as Nick sat Gabe in his booster seat and placed the plate in front of him. She hadn't told Nick what Sarah said to her that day, and she still wavered as to whether it was the right decision. On the one hand, she kept no secrets from him. On the other hand, she had doubts as to whether Sarah had been right—she didn't even know if she had understood Sarah's meaning. Wes's behavior had been completely upfront and appropriate, and he clearly loved his wife; though Meredith tended to err toward caution, it seemed silly to make Nick uncomfortable or jeopardize her friendship with Wes for no good reason.

"Maybe I will call him," she said. "He can offer a political perspective."

"I hope he can help. Tell him I said hello."

Meredith poked around her father's notes, taking some notes of her own in the margins to the happy sounds of her little family. She gave Gabe a cookie, kissed his head, and waved as Nick took him upstairs for a nap.

When the room was quiet, she picked up her phone and called Wes.

"Hi, Meredith," he said upon picking up. "How are you?" There were some noises on the other end, what appeared to be muffled chatter. "Could you hold on a moment?"

Meredith waited patiently while he took care of whatever he was doing.

"Is that Catherine?" she asked when he'd returned.

"Yes, it is. Just so you know, I only have a minute."

"Oh." Meredith's face fell. "If that's the case, I'll call back another time."

"No, no. Don't do that. What's on your mind?"

"Well," she began, "it's not really something I can explain in a minute."

"If it's that important, I've got all the time you need."

Meredith hesitated. "Are you sure?"

"Please, Meredith."

She sucked in her breath, and let it out slowly. "Have your parents talked to my father, by any chance?"

"Not that I'm aware." He paused. "What's going on?"

Her heartbeat picked up speed; it was so hard to say the words out loud. "My father has cancer," she said.

"Oh," said Wes, in a long, drawn-out sigh. "Oh, Meredith, I am so very sorry. What's the prognosis?"

"It isn't good."

She heard him take a breath. "This is devastating news. God damn it."

She nodded and pushed her lips together, fighting back tears.

"I just can't believe it," he said at last. "Harold Beck."

She sighed and rested her head on her hand. "I still can't believe it myself."

"I know you've just begun to renew your relationship. That must make it much harder. You must be reeling."

"That part is very painful," she agreed shakily. "Thanks, Wes. I appreciate it."

"You have all my love and sympathy. Tell me, what can I do?"

"There is something, actually," she said. "It's the reason I'm calling."

"I'm all ears."

She told him about her project. He listened attentively for several minutes as she explained her father's ideas and what he had asked her to do.

"So now I'm trying to think of some questions for him, just a set of guidelines I can use to plan and organize. Inspiration has been slow in coming."

"I'd ask him why he never ran for office himself. He's one of the most fearless, knowledgeable voices of our time. What made him go into education instead? I'd be curious to know what influenced that decision, to start."

Meredith's eyebrows rose. "You know, I'm just realizing now that I don't know why he chose that direction, either. My grandfather was a city councilman. In all these years, I never thought to ask my father that question."

"You could also ask him whether he thinks politics has changed over the years. That might serve as the framework for

your outline, if he indicates there's some sort of historical timeline that follows his own."

"That's brilliant," she said, typing into her laptop. "How are
you coming up with these so quickly?"

"It's not so hard. I'd like to know the answer to that, myself."
Meredith sensed him smiling. "I'm just imagining what I'd ask
him if he and I sat down for a drink."

They brainstormed for some time, Meredith typing quickly to
keep up with his train of thought.

"This is fabulous, Wes. Thank you so much." She finished
typing and sat back in her seat. "If you think of anything else,
please let me know."

"Will do. I can ask my mother, too, if you'd like. I'm sure she'll
have some ideas." He paused. "May I share this news with my
parents? Or is it not common knowledge yet?"

"I'm going to take it upon myself to say yes. Now that Vince
and I know, my parents are going to start getting around to telling
their friends and other family. It might be good for you to tell
them. It'll be one less time my parents have to break the news."

"Okay. I'll tell them right away, though I'm not looking
forward to it. It's going to break them."

"I know. Thank you for taking care of it. I'll let my parents
know you told them."

They said nothing for a moment or two.

"You know, Meredith," he said, "I can only imagine how you
feel about this book. It must be exciting for you, in some ways,
though I suspect it's going to be painful at times. It's quite a
burden on your shoulders. And as much as I revere your father,"
he added, a grin in his voice, "something tells me working with
him will have its challenges."

"That's a smooth, tactful way of putting it. What are you, a
politician or something?"

Wes chuckled quietly. "In all seriousness, though. I'm sure it's
going to be tough on you, and on him. But I have to tell you, I

can't wait to read this book. It's going to be fantastic. And I'm proud of you for doing this. This book is doing things and going places."

"Well, whatever else it does, I hope it brings him some peace."

"Amen."

She heard Nick's footsteps on the stairs, then watched as he entered the room. He saw her on the phone and smiled, then went to the sink for a glass of water.

"Anyway, on to happier subjects," said Meredith. "Tell me all about the Senate. When does your first session begin?"

Wes talked for some time about the election night celebrations and his preparation for his first session of the General Assembly.

"And you?" he asked afterward. "I hope you've been well, otherwise."

"Well, my brother got married. It was a really nice event, quiet and sincere. And everyone loves Jenny."

"Ah, so Vince finally settled down, did he?" Wes said slyly. "Good for him. Please congratulate him for me."

"Thanks. The other big news is that Nick and I are starting a local chapter of Building for Hope."

"Are you really!"

Meredith could hear the surprise and appreciation in his words, and she smiled, pleased by the encouragement to say more. "We have everything ready to go—we've registered our chapter, opened the bank accounts, and recruited the other board members. News spread fast, and we have several wonderful volunteers. We're holding our first meeting next week."

"That's fantastic. So what will you do? Build houses? I assume Nick will run the construction?"

"He'll supervise, yes, on weekends. We'll bring in volunteers to help build, and we'll choose a low-income family to receive the house. But we'll also do repair work and painting for the disabled or the elderly—fixing roofs, building wheelchair accessible ramps. Things like that. It's going be great. We're really excited."

"This is incredible. It's outstanding of you to do this, Meredith. I have to say, I'm floored."

He asked after Nick and Gabe, and she updated him on Gabe's new accomplishments and abilities.

"And how's little Amy?"

"Oh, she's just marvelous," he said, and Meredith had to smile at the intensity and wonder with which he said it. "She's rolling over now, and trying to sit up. She's got this soft tuft of honey-colored hair. She just looks at you with those big brown eyes. I still can't believe she's mine."

"That's wonderful," Meredith said, smiling widely, eyes sparkling. "A baby will melt your heart."

"Well, she's melted mine, that's for sure. I have no defenses with that little girl. I'm putty in her hands."

"As it should be. How is Catherine?"

"Catherine? Catherine's good. I'm in awe of how quickly she recovered and got back on her feet. She's been a huge help at my office. And she's making her chocolate again, luckily for me. She and Helen have a babysitting arrangement."

"That's great. Good for her. Have you two been able to spend any time together, just the two of you? I think that's really important with a new baby."

"We've been out a few times. Amy's grandmothers push us out the door so they can watch her."

Meredith laughed. "Can I say hello to Catherine?"

"I'm sorry, she's not here. She took Amy for a walk long ago."

"Oh. Well, maybe next time."

They passed a moment or two in silence.

"Thank you again for sharing your ideas, Wes," she said. "I can't tell you how much I appreciate it."

"I'm happy to help you. And please keep me posted when you can. Let me know if there's anything else I can do."

They said goodbye and hung up.

Meredith placed her phone on the table and stood, stretching her arms into the air.

"Well, that was helpful," she said to Nick.

"Did he have some good advice?"

"Mmmhmm," she murmured with a smile as she approached him where he stood at the counter and rubbed her hands up his chest. He wrapped his arms around her waist, and she leaned against him, soaking in the comfort of being enclosed in him. "I've done my required work for the day. Now I just want to put it out of my mind for a while."

He squeezed her tight and kissed her forehead. "I can supply a distraction, if you need one."

"I need one."

A clap of thunder startled them. Nick kissed her once more, then separated from her and headed for the front door. "I'll be right back. I should bring that scarecrow inside."

"Okay. Hey, honey? Before you do that, there's something I wanted to tell you. About our trip to Virginia."

He turned to face her, eyebrows raised. "Oh? What's that?"

She looked at him thoughtfully. "Sarah said something strange to me. Something about how Wes needed to see me happy and how a mother always knows." She hesitated. "I think she was trying to tell me he still had feelings for me."

Nick stood still, watching her, his expression unchanged. "She did?" He paused a moment. "Well, does he?"

Meredith shrugged, her eyes soft. "I don't know," she said honestly. "I mean, I don't think he does. Did anything in his behavior make you think twice?"

"Not at all."

Meredith shifted her weight. "Our conversation just now was fine. He's head over heels in love with his family." She shrugged again. "I think maybe Sarah's reading too much into things. That's why I haven't said anything about it before. But it didn't feel right not to tell you."

"Merry, I trust your judgment. If you think it's fine, then it's fine. I'm not worried about it." He smiled, the corners of his eyes crinkling kindly. "Thanks for telling me."

"Thanks for understanding. I love you."

"I love you, too." He kissed the air and started down the hall. "I'll go grab that scarecrow."

Meredith watched him walk away, then turned back to the kitchen, feeling warm and happy inside. She ate a quick lunch while she waited for him to return, then snuggled with him on the couch until Gabe woke from his nap. The family spent a cozy Saturday together, playing games, walking in the open field, and enjoying Meredith's home-cooked dinner. As she fell asleep that night, the curtains open to the big Maine sky, like every night, she was grateful—for her life, for her son, and for Nick—who always centered her and brought her home, who was always her light in the darkness.

CHAPTER SEVENTEEN

*M*eredith, Nick, Vince, and Jenny packed the kids in their cars and drove down to Philadelphia for Thanksgiving. Meredith had sent her mother her shopping list, and her mother had ordered the groceries for Meredith to make the family meal. Meredith had been looking forward to a joyous holiday with the whole family. Instead, it was tense and dreary, no one addressing the most obvious subject: Patricia had told them Harold did not want to discuss it, and had explicitly warned them not to bring it up.

Meredith had had the unpleasant task of breaking the news to Vince upon his return from Florida.

His eyes had widened, and he'd sat down on the couch before she'd finished her story, leaning forward, his head in his hands.

"Jesus fucking Christ," he'd muttered, shaking his head as it hung toward the floor.

Meredith had sat beside him and rubbed his back as he took in the news.

"What the hell, Merry," he'd said then. "Just, what the hell."

Meredith hadn't known what to say. As contentious as her

relationship with her father had been, Vince's relationship with him had been worse. Vince had inherited his father's explosive temper, and the two had butted heads more times than one could count. To Harold's great disappointment, Vince had quit his teaching job to become a painter. And he'd gotten a near stranger pregnant, inspiring Harold to call him a "lascivious hooligan." Vince hadn't had the groundbreaking heart-to-heart with Patricia that Meredith had; he'd benefited by proxy from their newfound intimacy, but civility always seemed to hang on by a thread.

"I'm sorry, Vince," she'd said, because it was the only thing that made sense. He straightened and leaned in to hug her, and Meredith knew he'd be feeling a hundred shades of pain.

Now they sat around a beautifully prepared dinner, all together as a family for the first time in months. But the elephant in the room was inescapable, and the conversation was stilted and shallow. Meredith felt it incumbent on herself to try to make this holiday normal.

"There are rosemary sprigs in the potatoes," she said, pointing. "I brought them down from our garden. Doesn't it all look pretty?"

They nodded and murmured in agreement.

"It looks lovely," said Patricia.

"Tastes great, too," added Nick, with a smile.

The silence resumed. Meredith searched her mind desperately. "Nick and I had our first board meeting last week."

"Your mother told me," said Harold, picking around on his plate. "You have six board members. You met at your house."

Meredith watched her father, chewing slowing. She knew he'd been undergoing treatment. He was looking awfully thin. Probably he'd lost his appetite.

She bit her lip and took a breath, leaning on the table, attempting casualness. "Gabe's eating turkey now," she said, smiling at her son as he clumsily speared little nibbles from the tray of his high chair. "For the longest time, he wouldn't eat any meat."

Her father threw his napkin on the table, pushed back his chair, and stood. "Well, this is just silly." He gestured toward Meredith with his hand and headed toward the hallway. "Meredith, come with me."

He exited the room, leaving everyone dumbstruck.

Meredith placed her napkin on the table and went to follow him. "Excuse me," she said softly, nervousness tingling her belly.

She followed his footsteps to the living room. He was standing by a rolltop desk, arms crossed, rocking back and forth on his heels.

"What is it, Dad?" she asked him, stepping toward him until she was standing at his side. "Did I say something to upset you?"

"For God's sake, Meredith," she said, his mouth open, face long, expressing impatience and disbelief. "It isn't easy for me, you know. To have to make pleasant conversation, now—it's brutal."

"Was your conversation ever pleasant?"

Harold raised his eyebrows and studied her. Meredith's heart pounded. She hadn't intended to make this joke—it stood to reason that she should be kinder, more patient with her father, now more than ever before. She wasn't sure why she'd been more inclined to joke with him like this lately; it was something she never would have dared to do before.

He did something then Meredith didn't think he'd ever done in response to something she'd said—he laughed. "I've met my match in my daughter," he said. "Hell of a shame I'm just realizing it now."

Meredith suppressed a grin. She watched as he rubbed his face in his hands.

"Look, let's cut to the chase," he said. "The book. What do you have to show me?"

"You want to see it? You mean right now?"

"Yes, right now. Let me blow off some steam. Then we'll go back to small talk."

"Okay," she said. "My laptop's upstairs."

"I'll come with you."

They walked up the curving staircase to the upstairs hallway, where Meredith led him into her room. It had been her room in childhood, but now it was completely transformed; it boasted a Persian rug, an embroidered white quilt and white curtains, and well-maintained antique furniture, the epitome of taste and elegance.

She pulled her laptop from the case on the floor and placed it on the dresser so her father could read. She opened her notes and stood back, waiting.

He scrolled through the document, murmuring to himself.

He gestured toward the screen with his finger. "I like what you did here, with the bit about the Treasury." He scrolled a moment more. "Why didn't you follow that up with what I said about Hamilton?"

"I thought it might be nice to talk about Hamilton in the introduction. You have plenty of examples to follow the Treasury passage. This one goes a little deeper than that."

"No, no, no." He scrolled further, more quickly, shaking his head. Finally, he closed the laptop and faced her. "Put that passage after the Treasury. It needs to be in the spotlight. Attention spans are not what they used to be. No one gives a damn about intro-ductions these days."

Meredith bristled but forced a smile. "Okay."

"And send me the file, will you? I'll take a closer look at it later."

"Sure," she said, already bracing herself for his comments. "Have you finished my questionnaire yet?"

"I can't answer the questionnaire. I have to do this my way."

A couple of seconds passed in silence.

"Thank you for doing this, Meredith." His jaw tightened. "I'm a cranky, cantankerous old grouch, but I'm still capable of gratitude."

Meredith's smile softened from plastic to sincere. "You don't have to thank me. I'm happy to help." She swallowed and laid her heart on the line. "I think it's a good way for me to get to know you better."

"Be careful what you wish for."

He patted her back and guided her out of the room, back to the Thanksgiving table.

"WELL, THAT WAS FUN," Vince said as they all walked out toward their cars the next day, having hugged their parents goodbye and promised to go down again for Christmas.

"It was awful," said Meredith ruefully, snuggling her face into Gabe's. "I wish they'd let me stay." Meredith had begged them to let her stay a few extra days and fly home later—her father would be undergoing treatment that week, and Meredith couldn't bear the thought of not being there—but they'd refused.

"Hey, I'm sorry," said Vince. He wrapped his arm around his sister's shoulder as they ambled down the walkway. "I shouldn't make jokes. I don't handle these things well, at all. I always say the wrong thing."

"It's fine." They reached their cars and stood facing each other. "Is there even a right thing to say?"

"I guess not."

They both sighed.

"You know what I wish, Merry?"

Meredith looked up at him expectantly, surprised by the vulnerability in his voice.

He took a deep breath. "I wish he'd let down his guard a little. You know, bring us in, show some affection. Just be our dad." A flash of pain crossed his eyes but was gone a moment later. "I mean, it's now or never, you know?"

"I know. I was hoping this book would bring some of that about, but I'm not sure he's capable of it. We'll see."

"It's up to you, Merry. Tear down that wall."

Meredith tried to smile, but failed. "He's just so defensive. I guess I understand it; he has to deal with this however he can, to get through it. I just hate to think of them here without us, going through these treatments all alone."

"Let's work on them for next time. If they let us, I'll come down, too."

Meredith smiled in earnest and pulled him into a hug. "That sounds great. Maybe if we badger them together, they won't be able to resist."

"It'll be my pleasure to badger Mom and Dad."

They waved and climbed into their cars, then headed back home.

AUTUMN CREPT TOWARD WINTER. The last remaining leaves drifted toward the earth, leaving the trees scraggly and bare, standing straight against the darkening sky like warriors preparing for an oncoming battle. The first snowfall came, and with it the promise of quiet nights by the fire, heartwarming home cooking, and the sweet, woodsy smell of the Christmas tree. Meredith loved this time of year, under normal circumstances; she enjoyed winter baking and all the quiet comforts of being snowed in with the ones she loved. But this year, she was troubled by the muted sunshine and the shortened days. The growing darkness seemed to mimic and mock her, and to accentuate the darkness of the task at hand.

She and Nick left Gabe with Vince and Jenny one day, and headed to the mountains for a brisk winter hike. They bundled up and drove off with excitement to Aspen Woods Mountain, their favorite hiking spot, eager to escape and to spend some time alone together. The day was cleansing and rejuvenating. There was nothing like physical exertion in the winter, she thought. She loved the feel of her heart pumping against the cold, the rosy glow of her cheeks and the adrenaline high that followed. Nick had grown up in the mountains and was most at home when outdoors; his instinctive knowledge of nature, and his reverence for the earth, was one of the reasons she'd fallen in love with him. It had centered and calmed her in her darkest time, had reminded her that beauty lay waiting all around her. Their incorporating nature into their every day was something she appreciated most about their life in Maine. But in the chaos of the last couple of months, she and Nick had been hiking less than they normally would. It was wonderful to be back in the woods and the mountains, her special place with him, to accomplish the climb together and to return to the simple pleasures that had been the foundation of their relationship.

"I am so glad we did this," she said happily, holding his hand as they descended the final slope, ready to head back home. "It's been way too long."

"We need to mark it on the calendar. We should make sure to come out here every couple of weeks, at least."

"Definitely. I can't believe how much better I feel. I feel like I can conquer the world now."

They arrived at Nick's truck. It sat alone in the little parking lot on this cold December day. The trees around them were lightly dusted with snow, their brown bark peeking through. They reminded Meredith of fawns, with their soft nut-brown fur and white spots.

He held her close and kissed her before they climbed into the truck. His lips were lush and tender after the hike. Meredith wrapped her hands around his neck and smiled, enjoying the last moments of the day.

"Where do you want to grab dinner?" he asked her once inside the truck. He flipped on the heat and pulled onto the road, the truck bumping on the rocks and gravel.

"How about that little place in Oaktown we like?" she said, pulling out her phone.

"Sure, sounds good."

She glanced at the screen, and horror filled her. "My father called me fourteen times. Oh, my God. Something happened."

Nick looked at her with concern as she quickly called her father, every second that passed like torture until she knew what was going on.

"Meredith," said Harold upon answering. "I need to talk to you. Why haven't you been answering your phone?"

"We were hiking on Aspen Woods, and there was no service. What's going on? Are you okay?"

"No, Meredith, I'm not okay. What the hell's going on here on page thirty-two?"

Meredith froze, her eyes widening with disbelief.

"Hello? Meredith? Are you still there?"

"Yes," she said, trying to recover from her speechlessness. "I'm sorry. My heart is pounding. I thought something had happened to you."

"Well, something did. I read your alterations to my thoughts on the Cold War and almost dropped dead right on the spot."

Meredith closed her eyes and leaned against the back of the seat. She took a deep breath, trying to calm her heartbeat. "What's the matter with it?"

"Are you in front of your laptop?"

"No, we're in the truck, in the middle of the woods."

Her father released an exasperated sigh. "Just call me when you get home, okay?"

"That's fine, but it won't be for a while. We're going to have a quick dinner first."

"Can it wait? I need to talk to you. I've been working all day, and I'm on a roll."

Meredith looked at Nick again, hesitating.

"What is it?" Nick whispered.

She sighed again. "Hold on, Dad." She pulled the phone from her ear and spoke quietly. "He's upset about something in the book. He says he's on a roll and that he wants to talk about it right away."

"Oh." He watched the road for a moment. "We'll just go home, then. It's fine, Merry. This is really important."

"Are you sure? I'm so sorry, honey."

"Don't apologize. I understand."

"You're wonderful," she said, placing her hand on his thigh and leaning in to kiss his cheek. She brought the phone back to her ear and faced forward. "Okay, Dad," she said. "Now what's the problem?"

"So anyway, Dr. Heines wrote me a prescription. Now I just have to fill it."

"Why haven't you?"

Tara took a long sip of her cocktail and licked her lips. "I don't know. It just seems so final. Like, do I really want to go there?"

"If it makes you feel better, why not?"

Tara drained her drink. Watching her, Meredith did the same. They'd been sitting at a table at this bar in Asterfield for about a half hour. Tara and her family were visiting for a long weekend and were staying in Nick and Meredith's apartment now that Vince, Jenny, and Julia were living in their new house. Vince had dropped Tara and Meredith off at the bar and was going to pick them up later—Meredith had enlisted his help so they wouldn't have to worry about driving.

Their waitress came over and took their next drink order.

Meredith turned back to Tara and leaned forward a little, her expression serious.

"There's nothing wrong with taking an antidepressant, Tara. Do what you have to do to survive. Is it better to feel miserable, to not be able to live your life?"

"I don't know. It just makes me feel like I've failed, somehow."

"It's the opposite. It means you've done what you had to do to take care of yourself, so you can take care of your family."

Tara's eyes brimmed with tears. She managed a sad smile and sniffled, then clicked her tongue and dabbed at her eyes with her napkin.

"Damn it, Merry. I got all dressed up to have a grownup night, and I'm going to spend it crying. You always know the right thing to say."

"Here come the drinks," Meredith said as the waitress walked toward their table, two cocktails in hand.

"See, what did I tell you? Always the right thing."

They clinked their glasses.

"Have you been catering lately?" asked Tara. "I haven't heard you talk much about it."

Meredith shook her head as she sipped her cocktail. "No, I've been too busy. My dad's book is taking a lot more time than I'd thought it would. I had to put catering on the back burner."

"No pun intended."

"Right."

"What's going on with your dad, anyway? Is there any news?"

"My dad." Meredith's face grew more somber. She sipped her drink and relaxed in her chair. "No, there's not much news since I talked to you last. It's still very hard to accept. I think the book is going well, though we're still disagreeing a little about how to go about it."

She talked about the difficulty of her father's treatment plans and the dreariness of the updates from her mother regarding his health. She then related some details about the book, how her father had been calling her with various tasks and the pressure he was under to complete it.

"Bless your heart, woman," said Tara. "No wonder you brought me to a bar. You need this even more than I do."

"Let's just agree it's well deserved on both our parts."

Meredith glanced down as her phone rang on the table.

"Speak of the devil." She picked it up and went to answer it. "I'm sorry, Tara. I'll only be a minute."

"Take your time," said Tara, with a smile.

Meredith held the phone to one ear and put her finger on the other. "Hi, Dad. Are you okay?"

"I'd be much better if I knew what your plans were for my essay on the 2008 election."

Meredith was silent for a moment or two. "The 2008 election? We haven't even gotten there yet."

"But my comments on the '90s inform that essay. It's all related, Meredith. Events don't occur in a vacuum."

"I know that." Meredith was beginning to feel irritated, and was unbearably ashamed; she reminded herself that her father was living through the most difficult experience of his life and that this book was meant to be his crowning achievement. "Look, I really want to do this the way you'd like, and I want to take the time to work it out with you. But I'm not home now. Tara's here, and we went out for a few hours. If you don't mind, I could—"

"Meredith, I'm not going to be here forever. This has to be done now. Take out a piece of paper and write down my thoughts. I'm on a roll here, and I don't want to forget."

"Well, why don't you write it out yourself, then send it to me? Wouldn't that be easier?"

"Do you not want to do this for me? Is it too much to ask?"

Meredith frowned and firmed her jaw, hurt. "Please don't be so accusatory. You know I want to help you." She swallowed. "I love you."

A few moments passed before Harold spoke again. "Sending it

to you won't work. I want to hear your thoughts as I write it. I don't have time to go back and change it. You don't understand, Meredith." His voice had become tense, his words short. "I have too many thoughts in my head."

Meredith sighed. "Okay, Dad. Hang on."

She apologized to Tara and stepped outside, where she sat on a bench and took a dictation. She assured him she'd accommodate this request and that, promised to call him tomorrow, and returned to the bar to spend precious time with her dearest friend.

～

"'THE BUTTERFLY and I had lit upon, nevertheless, a message from the dawn.'" Meredith looked up from her book at her student, who was seated next to her at the kitchen table. "So what's the message?"

Emma furrowed her brow and bit her lip. "Um, the flowers?"

"That's right," said Meredith, smiling brightly and squeezing Emma's hand as it rested on her book. "Can you go a little further? What message is Frost saying the flowers sent the narrator?"

Emma stared at the page for several moments, then pointed with her finger to a particular stanza. "Well," she said tentatively, "I'm not sure, but I think it has something to do with not being alone."

"Right again. What was the narrator feeling before?"

Emma scanned the top of the poem. "It says up here that he felt alone."

"Good. So why doesn't he feel alone now?"

"He says he felt 'a spirit kindred to my own.'" Emma paused. "I think the narrator feels less alone because...they're bonded by their love of the flowers?"

"You got it."

"Wow," said Emma, laughing, and leaning back in her seat. "It's actually not as hard as I thought it was."

"That's because you're a thoughtful person. Poetry may look hard, but it's really no more than feelings. There's no need to be intimidated. You did a great job."

Emma was grinning with pride. "Thanks, Mrs. Kelly. Can we do another one?"

"Sure. How about this one, 'Mending Wall'?"

They were interrupted by the sound of Meredith's phone ringing from across the table. She glanced at the screen and frowned.

"Emma, I'm so sorry. Will you excuse me just a minute? It's my father."

"Sure, no problem."

Meredith answered the phone and walked into the hallway.

"Hi, Dad. Is everything okay?"

"Well, I'll tell you, Meredith," he began, and Meredith closed her eyes. "I know I gave my approval on the way you organized the third chapter, but I've been having second thoughts. I think you need to take what's at the end and put it in the beginning. Just reverse the whole damn thing."

"That's fine, but do you mind if I call you back later? I'm in the middle of a tutoring session."

"It'll only take you ten minutes, Meredith. I'm on a roll here. Go ahead and take care of it right now."

"It'll take more than ten minutes. And even if it doesn't, I can't take ten minutes out of my session." She forced her voice to be firm, but anxiety tugged at her gut. "I get paid by the hour."

Her father sighed. "Very well," he said. "But call me when you're done. This has to be fixed today. I'm moving on to chapter four tomorrow."

"Okay. Don't worry, we'll get it done today."

"I'll be waiting for your call. Goodbye, then."

He hung up.

Meredith inhaled deeply, then exhaled slowly with her eyes closed. Shaking off the conversation, she returned to the kitchen, eager to dive back into Robert Frost's poetry.

"So I have a list of potential donors," said Meredith, pulling up a file on her laptop. She was in a small conference room at the library, along with Nick and four other board members, volunteers who had stepped up to help their cause. "These are residents and businesses we've reached by word of mouth. I think we should set up interviews, both to go into more detail about what we intend to do and to hear more about their interests and why they'd like to donate."

"I agree," said Ellen, a bank manager. "And I was thinking we should set up a table at the fair in March. We may get some more donations that way, not to mention volunteers."

"We don't have anyone assigned to social media," said Jamie, a nurse, and Meredith's friend. "I'd be happy to take that on."

"That's fantastic. Thank you." Meredith turned to Nick. "Nick, why don't you tell everyone about the floors."

"Right," said Nick. "I have a client renovating an old hotel near Asterfield. They're basically gutting the place, including the floors. The wood's in great condition, beautiful old oak. They've agreed to donate it all for the house."

There was gasping and clapping among the board members.

Jean, a teacher, spoke next. "Let's talk to big box construction stores. I'll bet they'd donate some cabinets, or at least sell them to us at cost."

"Great idea," said Meredith. "Do you want to take charge of that?"

"I'd be happy to."

"We need to start gathering volunteers," Meredith continued. "Anyone have any ideas on how to make that happen?"

"We should have an information night," said Liam, a local shop owner. "We could set it up right here at the library. That way it'll go out in the library's flyers. And we can post about it in town."

"I know a couple of guys who have already said they'd like to get involved," said Nick. "These are other carpenters, so they'll really be able to help. They can come out and look at the sites with us, too. Just to offer another opinion about which will be best to build on."

"Perfect." Meredith was delighted. She checked the discussed items off her list. "Now the biggest question, of course, is which family we should choose. We have three complete applications, with all the required material. When do we want to schedule home visits?"

Her phone rang, vibrating on the table. She glanced at the screen and squared her jaw.

"Will you excuse me a moment? So sorry."

She rose from the table and hurried out of the room.

"Dad," she whispered, once on the library floor. "I can't talk right now."

"Why are you whispering? Where are you, in a library?"

"Actually, yes. I'm in a Building for Hope board meeting. We're making some big decisions, and I need to get back in there."

"I'm making big decisions, too. And I'm on a roll. Come on, Meredith. They can function without you."

"Dad," she said, preparing to get off the phone and trying her best to keep her cool. "The meeting will be over in a half hour."

"Fine, call me later. Just answer me this. Why did you use my entire entry on the Pope? I rather expected it would be edited down to size."

Meredith spent a few minutes calming her father and explaining her decision, told him she'd call him later, and hung up the phone.

"I am so sorry," she told the board members upon reentering the room. "My father is sick, and he's been needing me."

Everyone murmured insistence that she not apologize. She thanked them and put away her phone, and moved on.

That night Meredith sat at her laptop for several hours, talking to her father, carrying out tasks in real time as he attempted to relay to her his train of thought. When she finally hung up the phone, her thoughts were jumbled, and she had several conflicting ideas about how to connect the revised essay to the following chapter. While Nick put Gabe to bed, she called Wes, who helped her brainstorm solutions. Nick came downstairs and waited for her to be through; ultimately he kissed her good-night and went to bed. Meredith crept into the room after midnight, slipped into bed, and fell asleep instantly.

MEREDITH, Liam, and Jean were walking up the steps of the apartment where the Henley family lived. It was a small duplex house, too small for the Henleys and their four children, and practically falling apart. As they climbed the rickety steps to the door, Meredith wished they could build houses for everyone, and was even more determined to make this project work.

They knocked on the door just as Meredith's phone rang.

She quickly pulled the phone from her purse, and her stomach sank.

"Hi, Dad. I—"

She halted suddenly. She was surprised, and horrified, to hear her father crying.

"Meredith," he moaned shakily, wracked with violent sobs. "I'm writing about my father."

Meredith closed her eyes.

The door opened, revealing a woman surrounded by four young children.

"Liam, Jean," she said. "I am so very sorry. Go ahead without me. I'll be in as soon as I can."

~

MEREDITH WAS cross-legged on the floor of the library, Gabe snuggled into her lap. Nick sat beside her, his arm around her back. Around them, a dozen other families sat scattered on the floor, watching the puppet show with their smiling children.

"Look, Gabe! It's an owl, your favorite," Meredith said, and kissed Gabe's face. "What does an owl say?"

"Who!"

Nick and Meredith laughed and hugged him tight.

Her phone vibrated in her pocket.

"Oh, no," she said as she looked at the screen.

"Hey, Merry?" said Nick, leaning close to talk to her privately among the chattering crowd. "Don't think I'm awful. But what if you didn't answer it?"

Meredith looked at him with anguish. "You don't think it would be wrong of me?"

His eyes crinkled kindly. "Honey," he said, his soft voice even more tender than usual. "If you need to answer it, please answer it. But I think if you didn't, just this once, it would be okay."

Her face softened, and she smiled. "Thank you," she said, surprised by a strong rush of tears. She hastily wiped her eyes, and he held her tight, kissing her forehead.

She declined the call, the sick pull of guilt in her gut. Then she turned off her phone with tears in her eyes.

I'm so sorry, Dad, she told him through space, then tried to put it out of her mind, focusing on her family and the joy in her little boy's heart.

~

Later that night, Meredith lay beneath Nick, crying out with every surge of his body, her desperation rising with every kiss he lovingly pressed into her throat.

His back rose and fell beneath her hands; his breath was hoarse and ragged. He moved vigorously, with urgency, groaning into her ear. Meredith almost couldn't stand it. He felt so beautiful in her hands, his body tight and hard, his movements even and strong. She wrapped her arms around him and lifted her hips to meet his, pulling him in as deep as she possibly could.

God, did she need this. More badly than she had known. They'd been so preoccupied, and it had been way too long. Now she forgot all her worries, letting his body and heart consume her, the perfect, blissful feel of him inside her pushing the world from her mind.

"Merry," he whispered, his breath heavy on her neck. "Merry, I love you."

"I love you," she breathed, and cried out again as a telltale tingling amassed where he filled her. "Oh, God...I love you."

His lips trailed up her throat to her ear, planting firm kisses as they went. He held her face in his hands, and his lips met hers; Meredith sighed as their breaths mingled, taking him in fully, and rushing toward ecstasy.

The ringing of her phone made them both jump and swear. Meredith covered her face with her hands, then reached for it on the nightstand.

"No, no, Merry," Nick gasped, his hand on her arm. "Please, please, please. I'm begging you."

She moaned as he pushed smoothly into her, and the tingling spread through her thighs. Panting, she forced her arm to move again toward the nightstand.

"I have to at least see who it is."

She looked at her phone, and her eyes widened.

"It's my mother," she said, panic seizing her. She answered the phone breathlessly. "Mom? Is Dad okay?"

"I'm fine, Meredith, just a little pissed off."

She slapped her head with her hand and closed her eyes. "Why are you calling on Mom's phone?"

"You never called me back tonight. I was worried you wouldn't answer if you knew it was me."

She shook her head. Nick was looking at her questioningly, his breathing still fast and deep.

"Dad," Meredith murmured, suppressing another moan as Nick quietly resumed his movements, his hand on her breast and his fingertips toying with her nipple. "I can't talk right now."

"It's the middle of the night. What are you doing in the middle of the night?"

Meredith flushed and made a bold choice, on a whim. "I'm having sex with my husband," she ground out, blood boiling. Above her, Nick's eyes bulged, and he shifted off her and onto his side.

There was silence on the other end, and Meredith waited in agony.

"Well, that's a valid excuse," Harold said finally, his voice now calm. "I suppose I'll accept that. Just call me tomorrow, will you? Make me another grandchild."

And with that, he hung up, leaving Meredith holding her phone, mortified.

After a moment had passed, she replaced it on the nightstand. She turned to Nick, who was on his back, staring at the ceiling in silence.

"I know that was weird," she told him, shrugging. "I had a hunch it would frighten him off the phone."

"Looks like you were right."

Neither of them said anything for some time. Meredith touched his foot with hers, and they played footsie under the sheets.

"Do you want to try again?" she asked finally.

He said nothing for a moment, then sighed. "You know what, honey—we should probably just get some sleep."

Meredith nodded and stared into space, then turned onto her side when he snuggled up behind her. They cuddled together, pressed close, his arm around her waist and her back against his chest. She lay awake for a while thinking, then fell into a troubled sleep, from which she woke feeling frustratingly unrested.

THE WEEK OF CHRISTMAS, Meredith prepared for her family to travel to Philadelphia once more. They were all packed up, most of the bags sitting ready by the front door. Nick and Meredith were snuggling on the couch in front of the fireplace, sharing a glass of wine. Their Christmas tree sat in the corner, twinkling with lights, full of a motley collection of ornaments they'd collected together over the years.

"I don't know if I'm excited about this trip or dreading it," she said, and let a sip of the full-bodied red wine flow smoothly down her throat. She swallowed and closed her eyes a moment, relaxing. "There are just so many emotions. I want to see them. But I know my father's going to give me hell over this book. And knowing that every time I see him, there aren't too many more times..." She stopped and took a breath, heading the tears off at the pass. "It's just hard."

"I know," he said, tucking her hair behind her ear and kissing the top of her head. "It reminds me a little of what we went through with my father. Only this is so much worse."

Meredith looked at him. "Nick, I'm so sorry. I'm sure this must be hard for you, too." Besieged by guilt, her eyes watered. "With all my worry over this book, we've barely talked about that." She sniffled and pressed her lips together, holding back a sob. "I feel awful."

He wrapped his arm around her and hugged her, rubbing her

back. "Honey, that's not what I meant. Not at all. You have nothing to feel awful about."

"I feel so selfish."

"You're the opposite of selfish. This is a very hard time."

She sighed and tried to recover, taking comfort in the warmth of his arms and of his lips as they brushed against her temple.

"Your parents both went through long illnesses," she said at last. "And you had to watch it over years."

"Yes, but I didn't write a book with my father."

"And he was gentle and kind with you."

Nick said nothing for a time, then kissed her softly.

"Merry, I'm sorry he's putting you through this," he said. "I don't like talking like that about him, especially now. But you've really endured a lot from him."

"I know. It's been tough. I want to give him slack, because I know he's living a nightmare. But..."

"But you're still a person."

She gazed at him and couldn't help but smile. His eyes were the brightest blue, and crystal clear. She felt they looked right into his soul, the purest soul she'd ever known.

"Thank you for saying that." She let him hold her and sighed. "It's such a simple statement, but it's everything."

"I love you, Merry. I just want to help."

"You do more than help. You're my lifeline."

They sat for a while in silence, passing the wine back and forth and listening to the fire hissing and crackling.

"Nick?" she said quietly.

"Hmm?"

Nervousness unsettled her stomach, and her heartbeat picked up speed. "Can we talk about having another baby?"

He hesitated a few moments. "Now?"

"I think now's the perfect time. With everything going on, it might bring a little brightness to our lives."

"I don't think that's a reason to have another child."

She stared at him. "Why not?"

"Because you have to be ready. Otherwise it's not fair to the baby."

"Well, I'm ready."

He frowned and averted his gaze, looking distinctly uncomfortable. "I just think…We have so much on our plates right now. And we don't even have time for that. Adding a baby to the mix, it just…" He shrugged and looked at her. "It doesn't feel right."

"It feels right to me."

He stared forward. Meredith waited for him to say something else, but he didn't.

Meredith didn't want to feel irritated; he was so good and so well meaning, and he couldn't help how he felt. She didn't know if the source was stress, or sadness, or her biological clock, but something inside her was bubbling up, something that looked remarkably like resentment. She tried to focus, to prioritize, to remember what a big decision this was.

She placed her hand on his shoulder. "Honey. Most of your worries are about how I'll handle it—the high-risk pregnancy, the postpartum depression. I've been thinking for a while about changing doctors. That'll help. If I assure you I'll be fine, then what's the problem?"

"That's not really fair. This affects both of us."

Meredith's face fell. "I know."

"No, you don't." He turned to her with an unusually dark expression, and she raised her eyebrows, surprised. "Last time, the worry almost killed me. Every day, every second, I worried about losing you and the baby. And then after Gabe was born, you were crying every day. I couldn't do anything to make it better. Whatever I did, nothing helped. And now you're dealing with your father having cancer. It'll only be worse this time, I know it. Just ask Tara. You tell me you'll be fine, but what if you aren't? I can't go through that again, Merry. I just can't."

"Nick." She brought her hand to his shoulder, touched and

aching. "I know you were worried," she said gently. "I don't blame you for having these feelings. But—"

"Meredith, please." His voice was growing firm and agitated, and Meredith was taken aback. "Please don't ask me to do this. I'll do anything in the world for you. I'd die for you. But I just can't do this. It's literally the one thing in the world I just can't do."

"Well, maybe—"

"*Please*. I've asked you now three or four times. Just...please, stop."

Meredith sat in shock as he stood, kissed her forehead, and stalked out of the room.

CHAPTER EIGHTEEN

"What's this nonsense I hear about you quitting your job?" demanded Harold as Vince strode into the room, Julia in his arms and Jenny on his heels.

"I did quit my job, and it's not nonsense," said Vince. "Nick and I are a team now. It's pretty awesome."

"What could possibly have motivated you to make that decision?"

Vince sat his daughter on the floor at his feet so she could play with her new blocks. Next to her was Gabe, who was absorbed in a new puzzle. He then took his seat on the couch next to Jenny, leaning forward and folding his hands, watching the little ones, the perfect pretext for avoiding his father's gaze.

"Well," he said, with what sounded to Meredith like forced cheer, "Nick and I agreed that the time is now. He's doing so well that he can't serve all his clients at this point. Together we'd expand his business even more and make twice the money." He spread his hands, then clasped them again. "That's really all there is to it."

"Do you feel qualified for this job? What have you done to ensure you can do it?"

"Well," said Vince again, the brightness in his voice now dimming, and Meredith discreetly shook her head at him, alarmed, "I wouldn't be doing it if I didn't think I was qualified. Only someone completely brainless would do that. I've followed Nick out on a ton of jobs, and I seem to have a knack for it."

"I've heard nothing about your working on any job. You've told me nothing about this."

"Just because I didn't tell you, doesn't mean it didn't happen. I don't tell you everything, you know."

"It's no wonder why. You know I'll ask questions."

"If by 'ask questions' you mean insult my intelligence and tell me I'm not good enough, then yeah, that's why I don't tell you."

"Dad," said Meredith, determined to intervene before the situation exploded, "I think I mentioned to you once before that Vince has been thinking about this for a while. It isn't a decision anyone made lightly."

"Still, it defies common sense. I have concerns, Meredith. Concerns about my children and their families."

"I think we need to give Vince credit. He's bright and hard-working. He's not going to make any decisions that will put his family at risk."

"Forget it, Merry," said Vince, scooping Julia off the floor and standing. "You're wasting your time. I was really hoping things would be different, you know?" He shook his head. "I don't want to fight with you, Dad. Not now. I'm going to take Julia for a drive." He motioned to Jenny. "Do you want to come?"

Jenny rose and looked around the room. "I'm sorry," she muttered, fiddling with her hair. She and Vince left the room, their footsteps echoing down the hall and out the front door.

Patricia and Nick had been cleaning up Christmas dinner; upon hearing Vince and Jenny leave, Patricia joined the others in the living room.

"Where are they going?"

"Who knows. Vince is mad at me."

"Oh?" She drew a wool flannel blanket from the back of the couch and proceeded to wrap it around Harold, who was sitting in his old leather chair by the fire. "Why is that, dear?"

"I dared to question him on a half-baked decision that'll affect the rest of his life. I'm just trying to help, Patty. He doesn't believe me, but it's true."

Patricia was silent. She tucked the blanket around Harold's slim body.

"There now. Comfy cozy."

"Like hell. My mouth is sore, my body aches, and I've got precious little control over the contents of my stomach."

"Is there anything else you need, dear? Some water, perhaps?"

"No, not right now. Yes, actually. Oh, never mind, what difference does it make."

Patricia straightened. "I'll make you some hot water with honey. That will soothe your mouth sores."

Composed and calm, she glided from the room. Since Meredith, Vince, and their families had arrived the night before, Meredith had noticed her mother soothing and coddling her father, with unlimited patience in the face of his outbursts. Her mother's openly demonstrating affection was reason enough for Meredith to know that things were bad. But even if she hadn't picked up on this unusual behavior, her father's appearance would have made it impossible to ignore. In her mind's eye, visions of Adam materialized; she was pulled back in time to those desperate, troubling days, when the person she loved most dearly seemed to dwindle away, becoming a ghost of his former self. The memories tormented her, reopening the wounds and serving as reminders of what was about to come. Meredith glanced at her father. He was thinner now, his face growing gaunt, and his salt-and-pepper hair was now coarse and gray. A crushing feeling ached her heart every time she looked at him. He looked older, and so much more fragile. But his eyes were alert as ever. She had to smile. He still could shoot daggers with those eyes.

Meredith rose from her chair and leaned toward her father, placing her hand on his.

"I'm going to go help Mom. Is that okay?"

"Don't talk down to me, Meredith. And no one needs help heating up water. If you want to go talk to your mother, just say so."

Meredith picked up Gabe, straightened, and left the room, glancing over her shoulder on the way out. He was gazing into the fire, frowning.

She sighed and met Nick and her mother in the kitchen, where Nick had just finished wiping down the counters.

"Thank you so much, honey," she said, lifting her chin to meet him in a kiss. "You're a lifesaver."

"No problem."

Gabe struggled to escape Meredith's arms. She set him down, and he ran from the room, babbling happily.

"Why don't I take him outside to play in the snow?" Nick suggested. "It looks like he could stand to get out some energy."

"That would be wonderful," said Meredith, regarding him gratefully. Nick smiled and followed Gabe out of the room.

She turned to her mother, who was just pouring water from the kettle into a handmade mug.

"He's been using that mug ever since I can remember," said Meredith, nostalgia warming her heart for a fleeting moment.

Patricia turned. "Oh. Yes, he has."

"He bought it in Italy, right?"

"Italy. Yes."

Meredith went to the pantry for the honey and handed it to her mother. Her mother swirled a little into the mug, then stirred it a few times with a spoon.

"All right, then." She took the mug in her hand and looked at Meredith knowingly. "Pray for me."

Meredith watched her walk from the room, then poured two cups of tea from the remaining water in the kettle. By the time her mother returned, Meredith had set the table with two cups of tea and a plate of Christmas cookies.

"How lovely," said Patricia. She sat in her chair and sipped her tea. "Your father is already asleep. I suppose we'll know when he awakens."

"I think you're right."

They sat in silence for a few moments, letting the peace seep in.

"Your husband is a very kind man," said Patricia.

Meredith smiled. "Yes," she said softly. "He is."

Patricia's lips turned upward into the faintest hint of a smile. She sipped her tea, her slender finger crooked upward.

Meredith studied her over the rim of her steaming tea. "How are you, Mom?" she asked, hesitation in her voice, and gingerly took a sip.

Patricia blew on her tea, her delicate features even more lovely, somehow, in that gentle gesture. "I'm surviving. You know."

"You've been so good to Dad in his illness."

"Well, he is my husband, dear."

Meredith watched her and frowned. "He's having a hard time."

"Yes." Patricia went to sip her tea, but paused. "It's to be expected, of course." She took a small sip. "But he still has a personality."

Meredith took a cookie in her fingers but didn't eat it. She toyed with it a moment, then rested it on her plate. "Mom," she said, "can I ask you a question?"

"Of course."

"Why did you marry Dad?"

Patricia's eyes shot up. Meredith worried she'd gone too far, that her mother would chastise her for her rudeness—but Patricia merely pursed her lips and looked at her, as if considering how to respond.

"Well," Patricia said, placing her cup on the table, "I suppose it's because I loved him."

"Loved? As in, past tense?"

Patricia gazed out the window at the rhododendrons and azaleas that were now bare and covered with snow. "Love is so difficult to pinpoint, isn't it?"

"No, I don't think it is."

Patricia's fingers grazed the handle of her teacup. "When I met your father, I was at Wellesley, as you know. He was a reporter covering Vietnam War protests at the Seven Sisters schools. He'd recently earned his Ph.D in political science from Harvard." She nibbled at a cookie. "He was bright and ambitious, nice-looking and confident. As young as he was, he was ruthless in his quest for the truth. He didn't let anyone off the hook, no matter how powerful. When the congressman came to town, a large group of us went to see him. Your father was there." Abruptly, she laughed, and Meredith smiled. "Oh, he was brutal. He insisted on having an answer to his question, instead of the roundabout diversions politicians usually respond with, you know? He was Harvard-educated and socially aware—he understood what he was talking about, and he wouldn't be ignored. I had never seen anyone so passionate. He was very charismatic in those days, you have to understand. He was on the right side of history, and he knew it. He was brilliant, Meredith. I was very impressed."

Meredith's eyes were tearing, and warmth had encircled her heart. She had never known her mother to be so animated, had never seen her eyes sparkle as they did as she remembered.

"You ran into him at a coffee shop, didn't you?" she asked.

"Yes, it was later that afternoon. I had gone there to study, and I found him at a table in the corner, poring over his notes. I don't know what made me approach him; he was clearly engrossed in his work. He didn't even notice me until I was right in front of his table."

Patricia's eyes turned sly; a slight smile touched her lips.

"I just stood there, waiting for him to look up. When he did, it was like lightning struck me in the heart."

Meredith vaguely knew the circumstances of how her parents met but had never heard the story from start to finish, and never with so much enthusiasm.

"I would have thought," she said, "that it would be hard for me to imagine sparks between you and Dad. But I can feel it."

Patricia sipped her tea. "Well," she said, lowering the cup, "there's never been an occasion to imagine it, I suppose."

Meredith was silent, pondering her mother's words.

"So what happened?" she asked finally. "What did he do when he looked up?"

"He seemed rather surprised to find someone standing by his table. He leaned back in his seat and assessed me. He wore thick black glasses and a tweed sports jacket."

"And a bow tie. Please tell me he had a bow tie."

"Oh, yes. His affection for bow ties developed long before I arrived."

"What did he say to you?"

"Have patience, dear. I wasn't through describing what he looked like just yet."

Meredith pursed her lips, suppressing a grin.

Patricia straightened in her seat and stared out the window once more. "He was handsome, but not gorgeous. He wasn't a Hollywood actor or an all-star athlete. He was a reporter, and a good one, and his intellect shone in his eyes. He had jet black hair, slicked back. He was small-framed, but not weak; I could tell he could defend me if necessary. When he leaned back in his seat, his jacket fell to his sides. I don't know what it was about that movement that intrigued me so. It felt to me distinctly masculine. And yet, in a strange way, it made him vulnerable, too. It's these little things. You understand?"

Meredith's face softened. She understood, and she nodded.

"He watched me for a moment, then gestured with his hand. He said, 'Well, don't just stand there. Have a seat, why don't you.'" Patricia smiled. "He'd never seen me in his life."

Meredith's lips parted, then closed again as she sighed. This vision of her father, young and fresh-faced, the whole world before him and his future wife across from him at the table, made him seem softer to her, more human.

"We talked for hours at that table. I must have drunk ten cups of coffee. We shared a pastrami sandwich and a slice of blueberry pie. I'd thought I had nothing else to learn when it came to politics. Boy, was I wrong. Your father knew everything. Simply everything. And he had no qualms about telling me. I know your father can be a blowhard. He's pretentious and difficult and maybe even pompous. But the fact is, dear, that your father's a genius. I didn't care that he lectured me, that he showed me the shallowness of my opinions. I was flattered by it. It meant that he thought I was worthy of hearing it, that he found me compelling enough to teach." She shrugged. "I suppose that isn't very feminist of me. But I found it attractive, at the time."

"It's okay," said Meredith. "I think I can understand that."

"Your father showed me a whole new perspective. He made me see layers of policy I'd never imagined, described people and places I never knew existed. I was from a small town in Massachusetts. He was from New York City. His world seemed smart and glamorous, full of interesting things. What can I say. I fell for it."

Meredith sensed darkness in her voice; it had grown flat and hard. Her mother was still staring out the window, her elbow on the table, her chin in her hand. In profile, she herself looked smart and glamorous. Meredith pressed gently.

"Why do I have the feeling you say that with regret?"

Her mother inhaled; her slender chest rose. "Because, you see, Meredith," she said, turning to her—Meredith was shocked to see tears in her eyes, "I was already engaged."

Meredith's eyes widened, and her mouth dropped open. Her heart and mind were racing. She closed her mouth and sat speechless, stunned.

Patricia by now had recovered, the mask in place once more. Her hands were wrapped around her teacup, and she sat straight, her elbows on the table, her head held high. "Yes, dear, your mother has a past." Patricia cast her daughter a sly look. "His name was Cary Hudson. He was a mechanic I'd met at a bar the year before when I'd gone out with friends from school. My God, it's so cliché." Patricia rolled her eyes, but there was warmth in them when she met Meredith's gaze.

Meredith tried to speak several times before the words came out. "What happened to him?" she choked out finally, unsure whether she wanted to hear the answer.

"It's your rather basic story, really. I met your father several more times, and we grew closer, as was wont to happen. I suppose I understood the risk going in, but justified it, telling myself he was merely my teacher, my friend. Eventually I called off our engagement. Cary was drafted. I never saw him again."

Meredith gaped at her. "That's it? That's all you're going to tell me?"

"What else is there to tell? I chose your father. The rest is history."

"What was he like? What did he say when you called off your engagement? Did he make it back home from the war?"

"Meredith, dear," said Patricia, closing her eyes. For a moment, Meredith feared she'd offended her, and she braced herself to be quieted. But when Patricia opened her eyes, they were tearful, and her lips were lifted into a soft smile. "He was the kindest, most gentle, most decent man I've ever known."

Meredith leaned back in her seat, nearly breathless. The conversation had begun to upset her. She shook her head incredulously, trying to clear it.

"Cary and I used to have picnics on the banks of the river, by the bridge," said Patricia, turning her cup in her hands. "We wrote poetry together and talked about philosophical things, things you don't learn in school. He had the heart of an artist. He drew beautiful landscapes on my notebooks, and he'd sign them with romantic messages. That man got me on a bicycle." She chuckled. "We rode together along the trails outside town. I was timid, and he always waited for me. Or he'd fall behind a few feet, to make sure I was okay." She returned her attention to the azaleas outside, gazing wistfully. "It was a passionate relationship."

Meredith bit her lip. "Then why..." she began, and stopped.

"Then why did I leave him?"

Meredith frowned and nodded.

Patricia sighed. "Your father had what I needed at the time. Or rather, what I thought I needed."

"When did you realize it wasn't?"

"Dear, the honeymoon period never lasts long. Eventually we sink back into who we are. Your father was no exception."

Meredith waited for her to continue. When she didn't, she probed gently. "Was Cary terribly upset?"

"Yes."

Patricia said no more, but stared out the window, her features now hard.

Meredith took a moment to process all this. "What did Dad think of the fact that you were engaged?"

"I downplayed my relationship with Cary. You know." She waved her hand dismissively. "In any case, it wasn't his concern."

Meredith's heart was breaking. She was stunned, and sympathetic, and disappointed, as yet unsure how this would affect her vision of her parents. She had so many questions, but her mind struggled to process them.

"Have you ever thought about him?" she asked, her voice almost a whisper.

Patricia turned to her then, with a stiff, disbelieving look. "Would you?"

Meredith swallowed. She was breathing heavily now, and she looked away, unable to meet her mother's gaze.

"Cary made it home safely from the war," said Patricia, though Meredith still wouldn't look at her. "I know this because I called the local newspaper every week until the war was over." She paused. "I haven't searched for him since then. I don't know what became of him."

Meredith closed her eyes, taking a moment to breathe.

"Meredith."

She squared her jaw and calmed herself, and looked at her mother.

The lines in Patricia's face seemed more visible now, as if reliving the emotions had aged her. "I want you to know I made this choice of my own volition. I alone am responsible. I don't feel sorry for myself. What's done is done, and nothing I do now can change that." Her shoulders rose as she took a breath. "Your father gave me a decent life. I've never wanted for anything. He's taken me all over the world, and I've seen many places, places I'd never see otherwise. I've made lifelong friends through your father's connections. If it's been a little cold at times, well, nothing is perfect."

"I'm glad you can cling to that. Honestly, Mom...you've just never seemed happy."

"Happiness is difficult to pinpoint, too, I suppose."

Meredith wanted to disagree, but she knew it wasn't her place. And she refused to speak ill of her dying father. She felt unable to breathe; she rubbed her face in her hands. "I'm sorry if I seem speechless. I'm just stunned. But it does give me a fuller picture, of the way things have been with Dad."

At Patricia's silence, Meredith straightened. Patricia was staring into her now empty teacup, mindlessly fidgeting with the rim.

"Mom?"

Patricia looked at her. "I'm worried, Meredith."

Meredith's eyes softened with sympathy. "I know, Mom. You're bearing the brunt of Dad's illness."

"No. What I mean is that I worry about you and this book."

Meredith lifted her brow, then furrowed it. "Why?"

"Has your father talked about his childhood yet?"

"Not really. It's mostly been politics. Why?"

Patricia firmed her jaw. "Your father didn't become who he is in a vacuum. No one does. There are some things that have troubled him. If he hasn't recounted them to you, he soon will. And when he does, I anticipate it will be difficult for you to hear it."

Meredith's heart sank to the pit of her stomach. "But why? What happened?"

"Unfortunately, it's not my story to tell. I can't protect you from that. He needs to tell his story his way, or the book won't be his. I think it's silly, to be honest. I'd much prefer he expend his last remaining energy on the positive aspects of his life. But he insists he needs to do this, and I won't stand in his way. But I worry, Meredith. Just take care of yourself. It's going to grow more demanding. I hope you're prepared."

CHAPTER NINETEEN

*W*inter grew darker and colder. The once freshly fallen snow was now iced over, becoming, for the moment, a fixed part of the landscape. The open field beside the house was an endless ocean of white, pure and sparkling, untouched save for the scampering footprints of wild Maine creatures. Meredith usually avoided walking in the open field when it was covered in snow, preferring not to mar its perfection; any disruption she caused to the snow would remain until spring, or at least until the next snowfall, and would detract from its awesome beauty.

This year, however, it troubled her. It caught her gaze every time she drove by on the way to her driveway. It was a blank slate in need of a human touch. It tormented her with its arrogance.

On a Sunday morning, Nick had taken Gabe to clear some snow from the driveways of some elderly people in town. She stood at her bedroom window, staring, and the temptation this time was too much.

She bundled up in her winter gear and trudged outside in the snow. She walked around the open field, in wide circles and swirls, laying her footprints, making her mark. It would be only temporary. The snow would melt, then cover the field once again. But for now, in this season, it would reflect her actions; it would be an opportunity taken. And for as long as the season lasted, until the next turn of the cycle, it would be undeniable evidence that she had been there.

HAROLD'S NOTES were becoming more personal. Meredith braced herself, remembering Patricia's warning. As she learned more, as she delved further into his life, she tried to remain objective, in the interests of the book. She had to see his anecdotes as pieces to be fit into a puzzle; emotions would do her no good. But objectivity became impossible as he related previously undisclosed details about his childhood, as his recollections offered her a vision of her family that was completely at odds with what she had imagined before.

"Oh, my God, Vince," she murmured one Saturday morning as the families sat together at the breakfast table. She had printed out some anecdotes her father had sent her and was sifting through the pages to get a sense of what she was in for today.

Vince looked up from his plate. "What is it?" he mumbled through a mouthful of toast.

But Meredith was speechless. She met his gaze, wide-eyed and open-mouthed, then returned her attention to the papers, running her fingers through her hair.

Her father's personal essays were matter-of-fact, without much outright editorializing. He related the facts as he remembered them and described how he had felt at the time. Every so often he'd offer an opinion he had formed in hindsight. But there was no self-indulgence, no self-pity. He assessed the situation, suggested the resulting effect on his growth, and no more. He seemed to take responsibility for his actions, even when perhaps the responsibility wasn't his to take.

Meredith tended to work on these personal essays during the day, when Nick was at work and Gabe was asleep or playing with his toys on the floor. They were somber, introspective times that often left her thoughtful and upset.

In order to understand my father, one must remember that he was not a large man, in stature. He was, however, healthy and fit. He tended to his body the way he tended to his business—with utmost precision, careful analysis, and disdain for excess. To say he was well-regimented with his diet would be an understatement. He kept records of every morsel that passed his lips and inspected every ingredient my mother used in her cooking. He exercised vigorously, and he made me join him. Unlike my father, I had no interest in sculpting my body. Masculine bravado meant nothing to me. I was perfectly content to read my books or a newspaper, or to talk with people about the goings-on in the world. My father enjoyed doing this, too, but he wanted to be the best man in the room while he did it.

On my thirteenth birthday my father woke me at five o'clock in the morning.

"You're a man, now, son, and you're going to act like it."

Thus began the first morning of what would become my living hell, comprised of three-mile runs, fifty-pound kettle balls, and countless push-ups, all of which would become familiar parts of my daily schedule. I learned quickly not to complain and not to falter. Complaining meant I was weak, and would earn me more push-ups or rings on the dumbbell; faltering meant I was lazy, and would earn me a rendezvous with his fist. But worse still was the disappointment in his eyes, the lowness of his voice as he banished me to a chair in the corner to sit with my face in the wall. Why would I care about the opinions of a monster? you might ask, and

*your question would be warranted. Well, my answer, dear reader,
is that the monster was my father....*

Meredith lifted her eyes from the page in an attempt to stave
off the sick feeling that had begun churning in her stomach. She
took a deep breath, rested her elbow on the table and held her
head in her hand, and read on.

*I have often reflected on this phenomenon, my desperation to please
a man who undeniably was not to be pleased. A stronger man
might have resisted. But I was tender-hearted, a student of history
and literature. I accepted that my father had correctly assessed my
weakness, and, shrugging my shoulders, I doggedly moved on....*

She laid the papers on the table and pushed her seat back,
then rose and stepped outside through the kitchen door, into the
cold. She stared out into the open field until the nausea subsided.

*Inevitably it occurred to me that, had I wanted to, I could have
overpowered him. I could have made it stop. He had decided to
make his son strong, at all costs, and he had succeeded. He, too,
must have known a confrontation could, theoretically, take place.
He seemed to understand that it would not, and he was right. I
never could bring myself to stand up to him. Somehow, I knew
that my father was hurting. When he died, I felt regret but no
sadness. I ponder, sometimes, what could have been had I resisted.
At the time, I only knew I was obeying, that I was acting the part
of a dutiful son. He had, through his relentlessness, told me I
deserved it, and I believed him. But now I'm old, and I've traveled the world for decades. I've seen ungodly acts of subjugation
and flagrant abuses of power. I've come to feel that I failed his test,
that he was waiting for me to prove my worth, to pull the sword
from the stone. I did the best I could, as young as I was—though
the specter of the confrontation that might have sent away the*

demons, thus blocking them from permeating my psyche as a husband and father, has haunted me for years....

"I don't know that I can do this," she said, voice shaking, to Nick one night after dinner. "These images of my father. They're breaking my heart."

"Honey, I'm so sorry. Is there anything I can do to help?"

"I don't think so. I just have to push through it."

"I hate that you're going through this. And it just seems to get worse and worse."

"My grandfather," she moaned, her face in her hands. "I always regretted that I never got to meet him. If only I had known."

If there's one thing politics has taught me it's that everyone has a vice, and my father was no exception. Drinking transformed him from a drill sergeant to a tyrant. How many times did I hold ice to my mother's bruises? How many times did I cringe at the snapping of the belt or the cracking of his knuckles....

"I always blamed him for being so cold with me. I thought it was a reflection of him, and of his feelings for me. I will never get over the guilt for resenting him for so long."

"Honey, you had no idea. He never told you any of this. Please don't be so hard on yourself."

"I can't help it," she cried, leaning against him as he wrapped his arm around her shoulder and brushed away a few tears. "It's something I'll have to live with."

I never wanted children.

Meredith's face hardened. She glanced over at Gabe, who was sitting at his little table with an art project. It was a quiet Monday afternoon, and snow had begun falling, draping over the trees and beginning to obliterate her footsteps in the open field. Seeing that

Gabe was settled and happy, she turned back to her papers, a heavy feeling already weighing in her stomach.

Having a family seemed lazy and bourgeois, something that would distract me from my work and get in the way of my having real accomplishments. I wanted to transcend the mediocre. In addition, the dysfunctional nature of my own family had made me cynical at an early age. As hard as I'd fought to resist becoming my father, when I looked in the mirror, I saw him. I was sour and impatient, and I'd inherited his proclivity for regiments and routines. I didn't want to repeat the cycle. What was the point?...

"He goes on to say that having children was 'what one does,'" Meredith told Nick when he called her on his lunch break a couple of hours later. She had walked out of the room where Gabe was playing; she couldn't hide the anger and disdain in her voice. "He says he realized having a family would help him relate to important people in social situations and that the optics of being childless weren't good for his career. That's almost a direct quotation."

"Look, honey, I didn't want to say this. But I think what he's doing to you is wrong. He's got to know how it's going to affect you. I know he wants to write this book, but it's like he doesn't care about your feelings at all."

Meredith frowned, and she took a deep breath as tears rose and threatened to overwhelm her. "Thank you, honey. I hear where you're coming from. But what can I do? He's dying."

"I know that, and I feel terrible, and I know that he's your father. But you're my wife. And as much as I care about your father, my number one concern is you. I see how depressed this is making you. I think you should tell him you've done all you can do."

Frustration rose in her and mingled with the hurt. "Nick, you know I just can't do that. I appreciate your concern. But I have to ride this out until it's done. I could never live with myself knowing I didn't do this for him."

"Merry, please, just please take care of yourself. Take a step back if it gets to be too much."

Meredith thanked him, told him she loved him, and politely hung up the phone. She walked back to the kitchen slowly, taking deep breaths, refusing to succumb to anxiety. She knew Nick was trying to help. She didn't want to tell him he was making it worse, that his telling her to quit was just another demand, that it made her feel that she couldn't satisfy anyone.

Making matters worse was the fact that she'd been through this before, the worst experience of her life, and had thought she had put it behind her. After Adam died, it had taken her a year to rejoin the land of the living, and it was many years after that before she wasn't constantly relating everything that happened to her, to his loss. She would never fully recover, would never be the person she had been before. But the urgency, the frustration, the sense of racing against the clock—this was the stuff of night-mares, nightmares she'd never wanted to have again.

"What do you say we take a break?" asked Harold in the early weeks of March, as Meredith tucked him into his chair in the living room. She and Vince had flown down for a long weekend after one of his treatments, leaving their families back up in Maine.

"That would be wonderful," Meredith practically sang, her face crinkling with relief. She laughed. "Honestly, Dad, it's been very draining. I mean, I'm happy to do it. But it's a lot."

"Oh, there's more," he assured her, closing his eyes. "I need some time to prepare myself. But don't get too comfortable. There's more."

That night she and Vince met Tara for drinks. Harold had been declining, and the mood among them was solemn. Tara listened attentively as Meredith and Vince updated her with the details.

She shook her head when they were through. "I love you two," she said, with tears in her eyes, and reached across the table to hold their hands. "I'm here for you, whatever you need."

A few tears were shed around the table. Vince brought his hand around Meredith's back to her shoulder, hugging her close. Meredith sighed and thanked him, relieved by her big brother's presence.

"I'm sorry, but I have to ask," said Tara, leaning back in her seat with her glass in her hand. "About this book. Isn't it kind of personal? Does he really want all this out there for the world to see?"

Meredith nodded knowingly. "I've asked him that question on a number of occasions. He's a pretty private person, and this lays him out flat." She shrugged. "He's insistent that it be done this way. For whatever reason, he wants it all out there. He says he's going out with a bang."

"I can kind of see it. Your father's always enjoyed shocking people." A crooked grin crossed Tara's face. "Showing his soft side is the best way to do that, I guess."

Meredith laughed and wiped a tear from her eye. "That's an excellent point. And it totally makes sense."

"I don't know how you do it, Merry," said Vince, draining the last of his beer. "You have the patience of a freaking saint."

"The guilt of a saint, is more like it."

When Vince and Meredith returned home, Meredith felt more able to breathe knowing she had at least a week or two before resuming her work on the book. During this time, she threw herself into her Building for Hope work, delighted to drown out her anxiety with some charity work and to put some positive energy into the universe.

They held a fundraiser at a community center. Meredith enlisted a couple of friends to help her cater. They picked a spring theme and found a local band to play music for free, and with the excitement of the project and the joy of the oncoming nice weather, the event was a huge success.

In addition, site preparation for the Henleys' house had begun. Nick, as site supervisor, was occupied for much of the weekend. He and Vince often went together, during which time Meredith and Jenny entertained the kids.

By the end of March, Harold was ready to continue, and Meredith's Building for Hope work was put on pause.

"Are you almost ready for the board meeting?" asked Nick one evening when he returned home from work. He stood at the kitchen counter scarfing down reheated dinner.

"Honey, I'm so sorry. Can you go ahead without me? I told my father he could call me. I wasn't even thinking about the meeting."

Nick stared at her. "Are you sure? It's interview night."

"Oh, that's right." Meredith rubbed her face in her hands and groaned—the board was meeting a candidate for manager of the Building for Hope thrift store. "I guess I'm just going to have to leave it in your capable hands."

Nick watched her silently as she returned her attention to her laptop, then set his glass of water on the counter and approached.

"You must really be exhausted," he said as he began massaging her shoulders. "I don't think you've forgotten anything in all the years I've known you."

Meredith stretched back in her chair, reaching up toward the ceiling, then contracted with a sigh. "Tell me about it. This book has turned me inside out." She lifted her chin as he leaned down and kissed her, then moaned a little he massaged the back of her neck.

She was spending more time on the phone with her father, now that the structure of the book was taking shape. He had sent her most of his essays and notes, but promised her "the big finish" was coming.

"I have some things to say, Meredith, things that may surprise you."

Meredith braced herself. She'd had a few weeks to mentally prepare, and she felt ready for whatever he sent her. She was determined to work hard and persistently, to keep the process moving with his demands. Time was of the essence. There wasn't any room for faltering.

"Let's go out to dinner tonight, just you and me," said Nick one Sunday evening in the middle of April. "Vince and Jenny will watch Gabe. I've already asked."

Meredith's eyes brightened marginally. She turned her head from her laptop and looked out the glass doors toward the open field. The snow was gone, but the ground was still marshy, slowly drying out in the still-timid Maine sun. The trees looked cheerful with their fresh green buds, their branches extended wide as if they were showing off their brand new attire.

She sighed and turned back to her laptop, shoulders sagging.

"Honey, I would so love to. But I really need to finish this for my father." She looked at him. "You don't by any chance know the procedural details of committees in the House of Representatives, do you?"

"No, I don't. And it can wait until tomorrow, Merry. It's fine. He'll understand."

Meredith peeked out from behind her hands, which had been rubbing her face to work out the exhaustion. "Have you met my father?" she asked, with a dark, humorless grin.

Nick had been at the kitchen sink drinking a glass of water. He faced her now with a frown. "Merry," he said gently, his soft voice heavy, his blue eyes earnest. "You've been working all day. You're allowed to take a break. Your father..." His jaw worked as he appeared to choose his words. "Your father needs to cut you a little slack."

"Nick, he doesn't have time for slack."

"Merry..."

He didn't finish his thought. Meredith raised her eyebrows. "What?"

"Nothing."

"No, tell me."

He took a deep breath as he looked at her, his chest rising and falling. "It's just that…This isn't all that new, Merry. I mean…It's just his personality, to a certain extent. I really think a lot of the pressure he's putting on you, he'd put on you no matter what."

Meredith bristled, her blood seeming to turn to ice. "Let's forget it," she said, pushing her hair behind her ears and turning her attention to her laptop. "I can't have this conversation."

"Why are you getting so upset? You know it's the truth."

"Maybe it is and maybe it isn't. He's dying. It isn't right to talk about him like this."

"Merry, I love your dad. He's always been good to me. But—"

"Please. Please stop."

The panicked feeling had come out of nowhere. If she didn't intercept it, it would destroy her. She closed her eyes to calm herself. Neither said anything for a moment or two.

"Merry, I just want to help. I don't mean to upset you even more."

"It's not your fault," she muttered. She met his eyes, and seeing the compassion and concern there, she relaxed somewhat. "I'm very stressed out. I'm sorry."

"It's okay, Merry. I am, too."

Her face softened, and she attempted a smile. "You're always the peacemaker. Now you're telling me I'm being too nice."

"I just see what this is doing to you. And I want you to feel like you're allowed to have fun."

She sighed and closed her eyes, resting her face in her hands.

"Come to dinner with me, Merry. Please."

She didn't say anything. Her mind felt numb.

"Do it for me, then, as a favor," he went on. "I've been working on the site all weekend. I've barely seen you at all. You didn't even come to bed until I was asleep last night. I want to spend time with you. And it would make me happy to see you enjoying yourself."

"Nick, I just can't. I'm sorry. This has to be done tonight."

He sighed and turned to the sink to wash out his glass, shaking his head.

Meredith watched him with annoyance. "Please don't add to my stress by being mad at me, too."

"I'm not mad at you, Merry," he said, his back still turned. "I'm just disappointed, is all."

"Oh, no. Please let's not go there. I'm being pulled so many ways right now." She felt the stress rise in her chest; her heartbeat was already speeding. "You can't possibly imagine how much pressure I'm under, writing this book and mentally preparing for my father's death, all while trying to reconcile these tragic things I'm learning about his past and all his dark feelings. Then there's the board, and the guilt I feel for shirking my responsibilities when I want so badly to be more present. Then there's Gabe, and you, and Vince, and my mother, and the fact that despite it all, I can't stop dreaming of another baby that probably won't ever happen. It's just so much. Can you try to understand how much pressure that is?"

"Understand it? You mean like when you were on bed rest and I worked my job and grew my business, then came home and took care of you and the house and prepared for the baby? And all the worry that went along with it, knowing we could lose the baby, then trying everything I could to help you feel better once he was born? And to top it all off, knowing you won't be happy unless I agree to do it again? Believe me, I understand."

Meredith shrank back. "You know how appreciative I was and how badly I wanted to help. That's really not fair of you to say."

"I'm just saying, I know about pressure, too. I was happy to do it all. I wanted to do it. But don't say that I can't understand."

"Look, Nick. Writing a book is very hard. Especially something like this, with the complexities of politics. It's just very complicated. I can't possibly explain it to you."

"You don't have to explain it to me," he said, his voice tight.

Neither said anything more for some time. They looked to the side, away from each other.

"I know you're trying to help," she said. "But I don't have a choice. And your disappointment makes me feel guilty, and that doesn't help."

"I'm just not sure what you expect me to do, Merry. I'm not going to just sit here and watch you fall apart without saying anything."

"Well, I'll tell you what I definitely don't expect," she said, her voice tensing as she swallowed back the hurt, "and that's for you to turn my desire for another baby into something stressful. It's a totally normal feeling. I shouldn't have to defend it."

"I just can't believe you continue to bring that up. In the middle of everything, after all the times I've told you how I feel about it. How do you think we can manage a baby right now? We can't even go out to dinner. This book has taken over our lives."

"I don't have much time," she said wearily, holding her head in her hands and closing her eyes. "Once he's gone, it'll all be over, and I'll never have to do this again."

"I worry about you in the meantime. And after. The emotional effects of this, I mean. Having worked with him on this, and seeing it all in print. Things he said about your family. Are you going to be okay with that?"

Several moments passed in silence.

They were startled by brusque knocking on the front door, then the sound of it opening right after.

"Hey, hey," called Vince, with cheer in his voice, striding toward the kitchen; Jenny and Julia soon followed. "The babysitters have arrived! You two get the hell out of here."

He stopped short when he took in the scene.

"What's the matter? Merry? Did something happen?"

"No, nothing happened," said Nick, leaning against the counter and turning to Vince. "We're not going out. Thanks anyway."

"What? Why not?"

"Because I have work to do," said Meredith, firmly. "I wish I didn't, but I do."

"Seriously, Merry? No way. You need a break."

Nick looked at her pleadingly. "Are you sure you don't want to go out to dinner?"

She stared at him longingly, regret pulling her heart to the ground. "I do want to. I just can't."

His face firmed, and he nodded slightly. "All right, then. I guess I'll let you get back to work." He approached her chair, kissed her head, and headed toward the door.

"Where are you going?"

"For a walk."

"Wait up," said Vince. "I'll come with you."

Vince and Nick left, the door closing with a thud.

Jenny turned to Meredith. "You should go out tonight. You really, really should."

"Not you, too."

"I'm not trying to be a pain in your ass, Merry. I just know you need to do this."

"Jenny, I just can't." Meredith was exhausted; she had no energy to argue. She pulled her laptop closer and opened her eyes wide for a second or two in a feeble attempt to feel more awake.

"You and Nick are the closest couple I know," said Jenny. "You're like my role models. It kills me to see you two arguing."

"It's a very stressful time," Meredith replied wanly. "We'll be okay."

"Is there anything I can do to help?"

"There is." Meredith looked at Jenny, her eyes blurry with tears. "Would you mind watching Gabe so I can finish this essay for my father?"

Jenny bent and took Gabe's hand, and the little boy stood to follow her. "Yes, I will, Merry," she said. "You know I will. And if you change your mind and you decide to go out, just let me know. I'll take Gabe all night."

"Thanks so much, Jenny. You're a good friend."

"I love you, Merry. And as a friend who loves you, I'm going to tell you one more time that you need to take a break and go out to dinner with your husband."

She smiled knowingly, then took the children out.

Meredith laid her head on the table and allowed herself a minute to decompress. She lifted her head and ran her fingers through her hair, then rubbed her face in her hands and shifted in her seat, ready to get to work.

She was researching congressional committee procedures when her phone lit up with a text.

We're all at Vince's, wrote Nick. *We're ordering pizza. I hope you'll come over and join us.*

Meredith sighed, warmed by his thoughtfulness but frustrated by his evident lack of appreciation for the enormity of her task.

Thanks, honey. I promise I'll do my best.

She took some pages in her hands and flipped through them with a frown. Her father's notes had become more and more disjointed, and harder and harder to follow.

She sighed. "I can't understand any of this," she muttered, throwing the pages on the table.

She leaned back in her chair and crossed her arms. The house was so quiet, and probably would be so for hours. She could finish the section tonight if only she had the information she needed.

She glanced at the clock on the wall. It was after six o'clock. Wes would probably be having dinner with his family. But maybe he wasn't. Maybe he could help her, and she could put this essay to rest. Then she'd take a break tomorrow, and she and Nick could spend some time together.

To hell with it, she thought, and picked up her phone to call Wes.

"Meredith. Hi. How are you tonight?"

"I'm well, Senator Bickhart. And yourself?"

"I'm great, couldn't be better."

"Wonderful." Meredith smiled. "I want to hear all about how things are going. But first, do you have a couple of minutes to answer a politics question?"

"Of course. What do you need?"

"Really, you don't mind? You're not in the middle of dinner?"

"Just tell me what you need. Is this for the book?"

Meredith explained the situation and told him what she needed to know. Wes promptly answered the questions, giving her sources for further reading and offering advice on how to work the information into the manuscript. Meredith felt the stress seeping out of her chest with every word he said. As she typed his answers into her file of notes, asking follow-up questions and nodding as he elaborated with more details, she could perfectly imagine what the final essay would look like. She saw a path forward, and she felt like she could breathe again.

"This makes so much sense now," she said, finishing up the last few sentences, then leaning back in her seat with a sigh of relief. "My father's notes at this point are practically incoherent. And God forbid I ask him for clarification."

"No, I suspect you can't. It's just heartbreaking. I'm sorry."

"Seriously, Wes, I just don't know how to thank you."

"It's no problem, Meredith. Helping you is its own reward."

Meredith felt tears rise, and she closed her eyes. "This experience has been devastating, to be honest." She took a few shaky breaths, opened her eyes, and continued. "I've really tried to put on a brave face, as much as I can. For my own sake. If I let emotion take over, I can't do the job. But I'm not going to lie. It's been hard."

"I understand. But you can let the brave face fall, you know.

Let it go, recharge, then pick yourself up and get back to work. You're allowed to be human. I don't think repressing it is going to help you in the long run."

"I sort of feel like I have to," she said, the image of Nick's disappointed expression making her heart ache a little. "Nick's been very concerned about how this is affecting me. But I have to keep doing it regardless. I feel like the brave face will make him less worried, which means he's less likely to tell me to stop."

"Has he told you to stop?"

"Yes. And I get it. But..."

"You don't have to say it."

A couple of moments passed in silence.

"Nick just wants you to be okay," Wes said then. "You do know that, of course."

"Yes, I do." Meredith swallowed back tears. "I do know that."

"In his shoes I'm sure I'd feel the same way."

Meredith smiled sadly. "I'm sure I would, too."

"That isn't to say I don't agree with you," he went on. "You're between a rock and a hard place, and you can't please everybody. But if this book is going to happen, it has to happen now. Making sacrifices and hard choices now, knowing the end is in sight, is how I'd handle it, too."

"Thank you," said Meredith, wiping her eyes with her hand. "I can't tell you how much I appreciate your saying that. I feel so guilty about everything, like I'm letting everyone down."

"Sweetheart, they'll all be okay. You do what you need to do."

They talked for a while longer, changing the subject to lighter matters. Meredith listened with fascination as he told her about his first session in the General Assembly. He spoke with eloquence and enthusiasm, and Meredith was delighted.

"You seem to love it. It's the perfect job for you. I'm so proud of you for doing this."

"Thank you. I do love it. Engaging in the process, really

offering my input, it's all immensely gratifying. Frankly, I'm still flying high."

"Do you think you'll run for Congress one day?"

Wes laughed. "I don't think so, but who knows. One step at a time."

"And how are Amy and Catherine?"

"Meredith, Amy is divine. What a personality she's got. And Catherine's doing great."

They updated each other on their children and families, then talked books and politics for a few minutes. Meredith looked at the clock and started—she needed to finish the essay.

"Wes," she said, "thank you for helping me. And for cheering me up. I feel so much better, and I enjoyed the diversion."

"I'm so glad I could help. I'm always here if you need me."

She thanked him again and hung up, then opened her laptop and got back to work.

SPRING WAS in full bloom in Maine. The tall grasses of the open field now swayed in the fresh May breeze. The sky was a cheerful periwinkle, and the forest was alive with chirping and scurrying of woodland creatures. Meredith, despite her many obligations, had made the time to wake up her garden, and young buds were sprouting with the promise of flowers and vegetables. She left the windows open and breathed in the sweet northern air, feeling rejuvenated, like the cycle of life was beginning anew.

In addition, her father's notes—and his manner of speaking to her, and to her mother—had grown softer, kinder, more philosophical. Now that he'd related the most troubling aspects of his life, he seemed ready to examine them, to find ways in which they shaped him for the better. It was as if a burden had been lifted, and he was free to create lessons that would comfort him—lessons he could pass down to his children and grandchildren.

I was hard on my wife Patricia. There's no point in denying that now. Though I tried—Lord, did I try, growing comfortable, perhaps, in her silence—I could not avoid falling into the psychological backdrop planted for me by—whom? By "God"? By my DNA? By my father? Unfortunately, I believe in free will, and I don't believe in God....

I made her follow me on my grand, ambitious quests, and follow me she did, to the ends of the Earth, quite literally. I suppose I always knew she felt relegated to the shadows, and though it never was my intention, I suppose I let it be. It was never personal, mind you. Quite the contrary, I've loved my wife fiercely, perhaps with too much fierceness and not enough tenderness. In truth, she was a perfect wife, or the perfect wife for me. I was blustery and self-indulgent, and she listened to my tirades, and she let me stand on my soapboxes. Talking to Patty was heaven for a man like me. Even as I'm eaten away, I find myself grinning as I think of her, the way she gave me exactly what I needed, without my even knowing, without my realizing her sacrifice. She had a sharp, discerning mind, and endless patience. She could insert a sentence into my diatribe, and it would be so on point, it could actually blow your mind. She made me feel like my diatribes mattered, that I was right, that someone understood. In her quiet way, she told me everything, and she gave me the confidence to take that passion and that bluster out into the world. Therefore, it's been no surprise to me that she is sending me to the next world in a similar fashion, tending to me in my illness with extraordinary grace and selflessness, even when I've exhausted her with my dourness and exploited her compassion....

She never knew any of this, of course. I never told her. She stood by me of her own motivation, whether that be love, or sense of obligation, or indifference, I do not know. I have many regrets. It's futile to fixate on them now, but perhaps my sentiments will mean some-

thing to her one day. If nothing else, I hope I gave her the world; I hope she has enjoyed at least that much of her time with me. She deserves at least that much. I think of my mother, confined to the kitchen, never allowed to make use of her mind, never seeing anything other than the daisy-patterned wallpaper, and I believe I can rest assured that I never chained my own wife to such anti-quated walls....

Like all of us, I've made many mistakes. But I have dedicated my life to fighting for education, for children, for the equal rights of every human being. I believe everyone should have that chance, to see, to study, to make a difference, and that we must speak up for the silent. Despite any hardships I thought I might have had, I've lived a golden, privileged life. Now I'm leaving the world my children and their children. My life has grown warmer since the birth of my grandson, and my granddaughter after, and it's given new life to my relationships with my children. Fear once made me doubt my ability to be a real father. It took decades, and grandchildren, and cancer, but I'm free of fear at last. I look at my grandchildren and I see the future, and it's bright and eager and willing to take naps on your chest. Little did I know that all this time, that was what I was fighting for....

Meredith knew it would be a long time before she could reconcile all she had learned about her father and all she had learned about herself. Like her father's notes, her thoughts were many and garbled, and the pressure of making sense of them before the hourglass was empty made clarity feel all the more elusive. But she was grateful for this understanding of her father, grateful that he'd trusted her with the most important project of his life. He'd known that she was up to the task, that she was the only one who could do it; it had brought him some peace, and she was honored that after their stormy, complicated relationship, she had been the one to achieve that for him.

PART III
CATHERINE AND MEREDITH

CHAPTER TWENTY

"The voices of angels," said Catherine. "The intermingling of hearts."

She locked eyes with Amy and smiled. They were sitting together on a blanket on the front lawn, under their favorite hawthorn tree. Amy was staring at her wide-eyed and open-mouthed, her little body swaying as she balanced herself.

Catherine inhaled and closed her eyes, letting Brahms's wrenching melody flood over her soul. It was wrenching, wasn't it? Wasn't everything beautiful a little bit wrenching? Wasn't all love?

The balmy June air filled her lungs—the fragrance of sunshine and flowers, grass and happiness. If the fragrance were a color, it would definitely be yellow—yellow like daffodils, or lemon meringue pie.

An excited noise escaped Amy's throat. Catherine opened her eyes and turned to her.

"You like Brahms, do you? Mommy likes him, too. He almost makes me feel like dancing."

She turned the volume up, then rose to her feet and stretched tall, her hands up high in the air. She stood on her tiptoes and lifted one foot, bringing it in toward her opposite thigh. Her 1930s high-waisted floral skirt with the lace ruffle and green ribbon trim stretched outward and fell over her knee. She extended her foot a few times, toes pointed, then bent at the knee in a makeshift plié.

Her attention was drawn to the house. Wes was standing in his study window, watching her with a wide, warm smile. He waved when she turned, and his smile grew tender.

Catherine's heart pattered pleasantly, and she tingled all over. She waved back shyly, returning his smile, and continued dancing, aware of his gaze.

She turned to Amy with slyness in her eyes.

"Daddy is watching. Let's show him how lovely we are."

Arms still lifted, she turned a few times, feeling her skirt spin out around her knees. She glanced down at Amy: she too had her hands in the air, reaching toward the sky, her belly stretched, her face rapt with excitement.

"What a good little student you are," said Catherine. She lowered her voice. "Is he still looking?"

Amy bopped up and down with glee.

"Shall I take that as a 'yes'?"

Amy's eyes followed something behind Catherine. She began giggling and flapping her hands.

"He's right behind me, isn't he."

"Yes, but please don't let that stop you."

He took her waist from behind and spun her around to face him, eliciting from Catherine a delighted shriek. He clasped his hand with hers and danced with her under the hawthorn tree, prancing with her across the grass, the blossom-heavy branches like a magical canopy above them.

Catherine closed her eyes, enjoying the feel of the breeze in her hair and the warm support of his hand on her lower back.

"You always were such a marvelous dancer," he said, his lips grazing her ear. "Elegant and graceful, like a swan."

"Schiaparelli once wore a cape of coq-feathers in honor of Anna Pavlova, who had a pet swan."

"And who was Anna Pavlova?"

"She was a ballerina famous for her performance in *A Dying Swan*—fitting, seeing as she died halfway through her tour. Schiaparelli earned so much praise for her homage that she began using feathers on everything—hats, gloves, and the like. It sparked a whole movement."

"I adore your movement."

"I see what you did there."

The music tapered to an end, and he dipped her so her back was arched and he was leaning over her. Catherine felt her hair brush the grass; above her, his face was a silhouette in the sun. He pulled her up and kissed her, and they both bowed for Amy, who was watching them with wide brown eyes.

"Look at her face," he said, with a chuckle. "She's in awe."

"Yes," said Catherine. "What did Meredith want?"

"Oh." Wes placed his hands on his hips and exhaled, fatigued from dancing. "She had a question for the book. Something about protocol at White House press conferences."

"I thought the political part of the book was all done."

"Well, it mostly is. But Harold's remembered a few things he wants to add. He's nearing the end now. It's a desperate rush to get it all in."

Catherine offered a little hum of acknowledgment, but said nothing more.

Wes took her shoulders in his hands and kissed her. "Thank you for the dance, sweetheart," he said, his voice low and gentle. "How did I get to be so lucky?"

Catherine was going to tell him it wasn't luck, but rather a fortunate series of events mutual to their two families, but she didn't have time; he stifled her words with a kiss, tilting her head toward the sunshine, making her weak and breathless, right on the front lawn.

"Well, shall we go?" he said brightly, patting her hips. "I think we have a date at the park."

"Yes, I'm ready. I'll just grab Amy's things."

"Are you sure that's what you want to do on your birthday? You don't want something a little more indulgent?"

"No, I'm looking forward to a nice quiet family day. I feel like I haven't seen you all week."

"You haven't." He kissed her again. "But we'll correct that right now. Then we'll have a nice birthday dinner for you, just the two of us."

"I can't wait." She smiled and made to walk toward the house. "I'll just go get Amy's things."

"I'll do that, sweetheart. You just relax. I'll be back in a flash."

"Okay." She watched him pull the blanket and music player from the ground and swagger toward the house. She then turned her attention to Amy.

"She must be sad about her father," she said. "We should be understanding and let it go."

Amy flapped her hands in the air, too hard, and fell backward onto the blanket, her little legs straight up in the air.

Catherine giggled and picked her up. "Well, let's put it out of our minds," she said, and kissed Amy's rosy round cheek. "After all, what choice do we have?" She walked inside and prepared to take Amy to the park.

After Meredith and her family left last August, Catherine had confronted Wes again. She had told him it was evident that he still loved her. He'd once again insisted that this was false. She'd reiterated her point, offering evidence as to its obviousness, and she had asked him how it was possible for him to live with one woman and love another. The earnestness in his eyes as he assured Catherine of his feelings for her had been so convincing as to make her falter, and she'd been silent, reliving events in her mind in order to determine whether she had once again misinterpreted.

"Sweetheart, you're the most important woman in the world to me," he'd told her, tenderly rubbing her shoulders. "Well, you and Amy." He'd smiled, his eyes twinkling. "I truly love you, with all my heart and soul."

"I know," she'd whispered as he kissed her forehead, his lips so soft on her skin. "There's just something, though. My mind won't let it go."

"Your happiness is my greatest concern, Cat. I want you to know you have nothing to worry about. That being said, if it would make you feel better, I'll cut off all ties with Meredith."

She'd looked at him, brow crinkled upward. "You would?"

"In a heartbeat."

It had, in fact, made her feel better. She'd offered a wan smile as he kissed her and walked away, somewhat relieved, but confused.

Bullshit, Maeve had texted when Catherine told her what had happened. *Of course he doesn't want you to worry.*

But he said he'd cut off all ties. He said he'd do it in a heartbeat.

That doesn't change how he feels. And he could be bluffing.

Catherine had sat back and thought about this.

But what if I misinterpreted? I'm notorious for that.

Well, yeah, but you're not stupid.

So what should I do?

I say take him up on his offer. Tell him you don't want him talking to her anymore.

Hei, not surprisingly, had a slightly different take.

"I don't know, Catherine," she had said one morning over coffee as the two sat relaxing in her kitchen. "It seems to me that it would make her the forbidden fruit, or something."

"Then what should I do?"

"Honestly? Maybe you two should go to some couple's counseling."

It wasn't a bad idea, but Catherine instinctively knew it would never happen. Wes was far too busy; though the General

333

Assembly session had ended in February, his law practice with Grady was jumping, and he had many commitments to various committees and charities, in addition to his duties as senator. And besides, the image of Wes in therapy was almost laughable. Catherine could perfectly picture it—his charming smile, chipper disposition, and persistent declarations of love for his wife. Catherine had no doubt any therapist would wonder what he was doing there. And she herself would only look foolish.

Catherine had decided to take her time making up her mind. There wasn't any need to rush. She loved her life, she loved her house, and she loved him—and he treated her with kindness and respect. She'd keep an eye on things and ask for advice from Maeve and Hei as situations arose. She didn't really want him communicating with Meredith—but thankfully, their conversations had been infrequent, and they no longer seemed to affect his mood. Catherine had begun to feel a little more secure.

Then, in November, Meredith had called to inform Wes that her father was ill and that she was helping him write a book. She'd had some questions she thought Wes could help her with. Catherine was disheartened, as it meant Wes and Meredith would be in more frequent contact. However, she couldn't very well prevent Wes from helping Meredith perform the final requests of her dying father. And besides, she felt sympathy for Meredith. Meredith had been nothing but courteous during her visit. It had seemed to Catherine, even through the fog of her anxiety and uncertainty, that Meredith had gone out of her way to be tactful and inclusive. She imagined herself in Meredith's position, and her heart ached. She'd be devastated to learn this news about her own father. And she'd do everything she could to ensure that his final wishes were fulfilled.

So she kept silent about Wes's calls with Meredith. He hadn't given her any reason to believe the calls were secretive or inappropriate. He seemed perfectly willing to take them in front of her. As a result, she usually chose not to be present. As compassionate and understanding as she wanted to be, she had a visceral reaction to following along with their conversations. An unpleasant feeling churned in her gut—not exactly anger, not exactly fear, but something ugly, like mustard or olive green—and a nervous chill ran up her spine. It was better at these times to take comfort in Amy, to remove herself and forget it, and move on with the pleasantries of her life.

"What an exquisite day," she said as they pulled Amy's stroller from the trunk and strapped the baby into it. Catherine held her hand to her forehead to block out the sun as she looked around the park. It was full of life, the leaves swaying in the breeze as families strolled along the trail and children scampered about on the playground. Catherine placed a bonnet on Amy's head and smiled as Wes kissed her forehead. Then the little family began their walk around the park, the path shaded with trees and lined with bright spring flowers.

They were rounding a corner by the pond when Catherine stopped short, her hand on Wes's arm.

"What is it?" he asked, watching her inquiringly.

Catherine could barely speak. She blinked, and the object of her fright was gone.

Wes looked in the direction of her gaze. "I don't see anything."

Catherine's heart was hammering. "I thought I saw Rick Tremaine," she said, her voice low and shaking, "but I don't see him anymore."

Wes said nothing while he looked around the park, his eyes sharp, his expression stern.

"I don't see him, sweetheart," he said finally, rubbing her back. "Are you sure it was him?"

"I don't know," she said absentmindedly, trying to fend off the rising nausea; she'd begun to doubt herself, but she couldn't shake the feeling of being on high alert. "I...I was positive I saw him. But maybe I was wrong."

"I think it must have been somebody else. It's a beautiful day at the park, and happy people are enjoying themselves. That's not Rick's scene at all."

Catherine attempted to smile at the joke, but her heart wasn't in it. "Let's leave," she said, tugging at his arm. "I don't feel comfortable here anymore."

"Sweetheart, are you sure? We could take the other path, if you'd like. I'd hate for this to ruin your day."

"It didn't ruin my day. It just ruined my walk. I can't relax if I think he could be here. Let's go."

They turned and walked back toward the car. Catherine didn't look back, but she didn't feel safe until they had secured Amy in her car seat and driven out of the parking lot.

"I don't like that man," she said with a shiver. She took a deep breath, calming herself. "I can physically feel the dislike. I don't know what it is about him."

"I know exactly what it is. He's a lecherous, brutish, conniving scoundrel who's harassed you with unseemly comments, once when you were pregnant. I would wonder about you if you didn't have that reaction."

"I've met unpleasant people before. They've never affected me like that."

"He's rather more unpleasant than most. I'd say your instincts are working just fine."

They drove off toward home. The sun was shining, her husband was beside her, and she was looking forward to an elegant birthday dinner. Her life was good. The cloud of unease gradually lifted.

Later that day, they dropped Amy off at Sarah and Charles's house and went to Le Paon, one of Catherine's favorite restaurants in Charlottesville. For the occasion, Catherine chose a 1930s black lace dress with a deep v-neck, fitted waist, and flowing long skirt. As the dress was sheer, she wore a vintage black silk slip underneath, and slim stiletto back heels. She completed the look with a generous swipe of bright red lipstick.

"This might be my favorite of all your dresses," he told her as he held the door for her to pass through. His hand on her back, he guided her into the restaurant. "You're a bombshell, sweetheart. A goddess."

Catherine grinned and thanked him, little prickles tickling her blood like sparkles. They reached their table, and he pulled out her chair. She sat and thanked him again, smoothing her hair.

He took his seat across from her. Catherine felt breathless—he looked so handsome in his suit and tie. He shook his head. "I love when you get all dressed up," he said, and the fond smile on his face made her heart melt. He reached across the table for her hand, and she took it. "And I love you."

Catherine sighed and smiled, the rushing of her blood making her giddy and warm. She clasped her fingers together under the table, and squeezed, relieving some pressure so she could sit still.

They perused the menu and ordered their wine. When the waiter had walked away, Wes dug into his pocket.

"I was going to wait until later for this, but I want you to have it now." His hand emerged with a black velvet box. "Happy birthday, sweetheart."

Heart pattering, she took the box from his outstretched hand and lifted the lid, revealing a dramatic brooch in a luscious swirl pattern, with crystals along the sweeping half circles.

She gasped. "Oh! So beautiful! Is it—"

"Yes, it's Schiaparelli." He laughed good-naturedly. "No one can match your eye, sweetheart."

"It's just so beautiful." She unhooked it from the backing and brought the clasp to her dress. "Oh, it's perfect!"

"It looks perfect on you."

She patted it in place and looked at him with a sigh. "Thank you so much, Wes," she said, her voice heavy with emotion. "This is such a thoughtful gift. The thought is even more beautiful than the gift itself."

"And it's nothing compared to you."

They enjoyed dinner, wine, and dessert, then drove home under the richly colored summer evening sky. When they reached the door of the house, Wes stopped her.

"Catherine," he said, rubbing her arm, a wicked little grin on his face. "You need to be warned about something."

Catherine crinkled her forehead with confusion—his words had made her instantly nervous, but they didn't match his expression.

He was looking at her with a smile in his eyes. "Inside the house are all our friends and family. They're going to yell 'surprise' at you as soon as I open the door."

Catherine's mouth dropped open. "Everyone we know is in our house?"

"Yes."

"They're here for my birthday?"

"You got it."

Catherine's heart was pounding painfully. "Is this a surprise party?"

"Yes. But I know how you hate surprises."

Catherine's eyes darted toward the house; he was silent as she took a few moments to let her mind settle.

"Then it's really just a party."

"Let's call it an unsurprise party."

Warm affection filled her as his hand found her back. "You planned a surprise party," she said, her voice shaking—though with tears or laughter, she wasn't sure. "Then you told me about the surprise. Just because you know I hate surprises."

"Well...yes," he said, and laughed. "It does seem a little silly, doesn't it?"

"It's the sweetest thing anyone's ever done for me." She laughed, too, her eyes glistening. She ran her hands up his chest and looked into his eyes, which glimmered in the moonlight. "Thank you for being so thoughtful."

"Thank you," he said, between playful little kisses, "for being the sweetest, most wonderful wife." He offered his arm for her to take. "Let's go inside for your unsurprise party, shall we?"

～

"Happy birthday, darling," said a radiant Sarah, leaning in and kissing Catherine on the cheek. "My, how stunning you are."

"You look just like an old-time movie star," said Helen. "Like Katharine Hepburn. You even have the same name."

"She looks more like Grace Kelly," said Ethel.

"I agree," said Sarah, admiring the finger waves Catherine had painstakingly pinched and curled into her hair. "Her look was much softer, wouldn't you say?"

"You're all wrong," said Wes, coming up from behind, resting his hands on her hips and kissing the back of her head. "Neither of them can hold a candle to her."

"Right as usual, darling," said Sarah, holding up her glass in a toast. "And cheers."

There was cake, and there were cocktails, and there were Glenn Miller and Billie Holiday playing in the background. Catherine took a picture with all her most important women, just like at her wedding. Only this time, her daughter was in the picture, too.

"Some party," said Maeve, nursing a cocktail. "Is there anything he can't do?"

"That man really loves you," said Hei. "I mean, look at all this, you know?"

It was impressive; Catherine had to agree. Her house was filled with love and well wishes—and roses, her favorite flower. Catherine walked around sniffing them where they sat on tables, mantels, and bookshelves. She danced a little to the music. She mingled with her friends and family, grateful, but growing exhausted.

"Where is Wes?" she asked Hei at one point, realizing she hadn't seen him in a while.

"Did he put Amy in bed?"

"No, Amy's over there, with my mother."

She walked around the house for a time, but he was nowhere to be found, not even in his study. She was just walking into the foyer, smiling at the ivory roses that hung in garlands from the banister, when she saw movement outside through the window. Squinting to discern who was standing there in the darkness, she recognized Wes.

She opened the front door to find him standing there on his phone.

He turned to her and smiled, listening to whomever was on the other end. He mouthed an apology and held up his finger, suggesting he'd only be a minute.

Catherine stood there and waited, but he didn't get off the phone. It took only a moment of listening to the conversation for her to understand who it was.

All the joy she'd been feeling instantly vanished, replaced with a churning mass of anger and pain. It was dark and heavy in her gut, like a boulder on fire. It was clear she would never escape this; his deference to Meredith would cloud their marriage, no matter how wonderful and good. It would hang there, like a shadow, elusive and omnipotent. It would always be greater than the tangibles of their lives.

She shook her head and walked inside, then went right upstairs to her bedroom to panic in private. She closed and locked the door and sat on her bed in the dark, hugging herself as she rocked back and forth, letting the wrenching sobs come. It wasn't just that she would never be enough; it wasn't just that he was completely at the mercy of another woman's needs. It was that he insisted it wasn't so, that she must be imagining it; it was that, intentionally or not, his continued denial exploited her lack of faith in her own intuition. It was that he had opened her up to darkness, that he had made her know anger and rage. The change it had wrought in her filled her with resentment and hate. And the confusion of loving him so much regardless made the torment intolerable, burning and slashing and ripping her apart from the inside out.

CHAPTER TWENTY-ONE

"*S*o, without further ado, let's build this beautiful house!"
The assembled volunteers cheered and applauded.
Meredith, holding Gabe, stepped aside, turning the platform over
to Nick, who as site supervisor would offer directions and instruct
everyone what to do next.

She joined her friend and fellow board member Jamie where
she stood to the side.

"Great speech," said Jamie. "I'm so excited."

"Me, too," agreed Meredith, watching the scene with a wide
smile. "I can't believe it's actually happening."

"Amazing." Jamie wrapped her arm around Meredith and
pulled her close. "You did good, my friend."

"As did you. This wouldn't be happening without everyone
involved."

They watched the peppy scene for a time, volunteers hopping
this way and that, everyone smiling and eager to work.

"Where's your wrap?" asked Jamie, tickling Gabe's belly,
making him giggle. "You usually try to have two free hands."

"He's really too big. He doesn't like it anymore."

"You'll have to save it for the next one."

Meredith murmured agreement, but her smile dimmed.

Jamie studied her. "Still no progress there, huh?"

"No." Meredith kissed Gabe's cheek. "I'm not sure I'm going to be able to convince him."

"I think you will. Just keep trying."

Meredith watched the hustle of the workers, her eyes lingering on Nick—he was easy to spot, tall and strong, with a head full of golden hair.

She gazed with longing, then turned back to Jamie with a frown.

"It's been a little tense at home," she said. "I need to put the conversation on hold for a while."

"Oh, no. What's going on?"

Meredith sighed and shrugged. "It's nothing in particular. It just feels like we're two ships passing in the night. He's at the site all weekend, and even when he's home, I'm working on my father's book."

"How's that been going?"

"It's good, I guess. It's taken a lot out of me, though. I'm sprinting toward the finish. Nick wishes I'd slow down, but now's the time for me to give it all I've got."

"It'll get better," said Jamie, rubbing Meredith's shoulder. "It's a very stressful time."

"I know it will, eventually." Meredith smiled gratefully. "Thanks."

Their chatter returned to the subject of the house. They talked about plans and upcoming events, enjoying the lively cacophony of the build.

"Okay, I'm going to take Gabe home," said Meredith, hitching her son up on her hip. "Keep me posted on how things are going."

"You mean you're not going to stay, on the very first day?"

"No, I don't want Gabe at the site, at least in the beginning. Vince and Jenny really wanted to be here today, and I don't want to stop them."

"Oh, Merry. I'd be happy to take him so you can stick around."

Meredith smiled kindly. "That's so sweet of you, Jamie. But it's just as well, anyway. I'm expecting a call from my father. He's in the middle of an important chapter, and he doesn't want to wait."

"Okay." Jamie hugged her again and smiled. "If you get done early and you want to come back, just call me."

"I appreciate it. Thank you. Have fun!"

She waved to the volunteers and headed home with her son.

SHE LET Gabe run around in the open field for a while; she knew he'd been aching to stretch his legs at the site. The summer sun was high and bright, its warmth like kisses on her skin. Gabe stopped to play with some grass, and Meredith looked around. Standing in the center of the field, she appeared to be adrift in an ocean, but her feet were planted firmly on the ground. It was a strange, comforting feeling, being surrounded, yet alone. She closed her eyes and took a deep breath, the freshness of the air cleansing her lungs and her mind.

They tromped back to the house, and Meredith gave Gabe his lunch and put him down for his nap. Then she gathered her notes and her laptop and took her seat at the kitchen table, preparing for her father's call.

She waited and waited, but her phone never rang. Her heart had begun pounding, and her foot tapped nervously on the floor. Finally, she picked up her phone and called him herself.

"Hi, Dad. Did you fall asleep?"

"What? Who is this?"

Meredith said nothing for a moment or two. "It's Meredith, Dad. Are you okay?"

"Meredith?"

"Yes." Meredith rested her head in her hand and rubbed her

lips together, the dark pull of dread growing stronger and stronger. "Do you know who I am?"

"Don't push me into the grave yet. Of course I know who you are. For chrissake."

Meredith laughed and ran her fingers through her hair, staving off tears. "Okay, I'm sorry."

"Now, about my essay on the Korean War."

Meredith crinkled her eyebrows. "You don't have an essay on the Korean War."

"Don't joke with me, Meredith."

"I'm not joking with you." The panic that had seized her and fizzled away had instantly returned. In desperation, she scrolled through the file on her laptop, even though she knew that no such essay existed. "Do you mean the little section of the introduction, where you talk about diplomacy?"

Her father made an exasperated sound. "It should be right there, toward the beginning, between the anecdote about my father's bridge club and the op-ed I wrote for the *New York Times*."

"Dad, the bridge club passage is all the way back in chapter four. The *Times* op-ed is in chapter twenty-two. They're miles apart."

"But how can that be?" he countered, and Meredith imagined him with his hands in the air. "The *Times* op-ed is all about Korea. It's the heart of the message of the bridge club passage."

"No, Dad." Meredith was very close to tears, and she felt her defenses failing; though they'd had troubling conversations before, and though she knew his condition had been deteriorating, something in this conversation told her there would be no going back. She made her voice firm. "The *Times* piece was about Dodd-Frank. How could it be about Korea? You were only a child during the war."

"All right, forget about Korea. Where are we with the congressional hearing?"

"Which congressional hearing?"

"You know. The congressional hearing. The one from chapter six."

She rubbed her face in her hand. "There's no congressional hearing mentioned in chapter six."

"There's not? Well, then add it."

"But which congressional hearing do you mean?"

"The name escapes me. I'm sure you can figure it out. Get on that, will you? Thanks."

Before she could answer, he hung up the phone.

Meredith sighed and placed her phone on the table. She turned to her laptop. Chapter six was about national intelligence. She presumed her father was referring to the Church Committee hearings.

She read over chapter six and began the long, arduous task of research gathering, then emailed her father to ask what he wanted to say. A half hour later, he emailed her back, telling her he'd meant chapter sixteen, not six.

Frustrated, and out of patience, she pushed away her laptop and picked up her phone, but not to call her father.

CHAPTER TWENTY-TWO

*C*atherine sat in a chair by the window of Wes's study, Dorothea snugly in her lap, watching the swaying of the trees. The sunlight was dappled through the branches of the hawthorn tree. She was lulled by the ever-changing patterns on the grass, the way the shade shifted with the breeze.

Wes was dozing on the love seat. He was lying on his back with his feet up on the pillow, his arms folded across his chest and his head lagging to the side. It was a bright, cheerful Saturday. She had planned to take her family to a concert at the park, but she'd changed her mind—she wasn't in the mood. She'd told him she preferred to stay at home, and it hadn't taken much to convince him. He'd promptly kicked his shoes off and retreated to his study to read, inviting Catherine to join him. It hadn't been long before the book had dropped to the floor. Catherine wasn't surprised. He'd been working endlessly, as always, and for once, Catherine didn't mind. She'd resigned herself to her current situation, aware of her weakness, and hating herself for it. Now she needed time to adjust, to work through her acceptance for as long as it took. The less she had to see him as she did that, the better.

Her thoughts were interrupted by the vibrating of his phone.

It was sitting where he'd left it on his desk. She glanced in his direction. He was still sound asleep, not budging at all.

Before she knew what she was doing, she'd removed Dorothea and stood up straight. She swept toward the desk and glanced at the screen, already suspecting whose name she would see.

When she saw that she was right, she was infuriated, but not surprised. She glanced back at Wes, her heart pounding hard. He didn't even hear it; he wouldn't even know. She looked back to the table at the vibrating phone, watching in wonderment as her hand slowly reached out as if of its own accord. As her fingers grazed the sides and pressed the phone into their grasp, it suddenly felt so personal, such a secret part of him. She picked up the phone and quietly stepped from the room, closing the door behind. It was voyeuristic, almost, an invasion of his privacy. And somehow, in a way she couldn't quite understand, it was for exactly this reason that she did it. It was a defense, an insistence, a way of reclaiming her intimacy with him. She answered the phone with a stern, steady face, though the rushing of her blood made her very nearly breathless.

"Hello," she said, bracing herself for her voice.

"Hello," was the response. "Catherine?"

Catherine stood straighter, unnerved: Meredith was crying. She hadn't expected that. She'd only wanted to remind her of her existence; she wasn't prepared to comfort her. *Darn it*, she thought, frantically looking at the closed study door. What was she supposed to do now?

"Meredith," she said, walking down the hallway. She cleared her throat. "I'm very sorry about your father."

"Thank you." Meredith sniffled and took a breath. "So sorry to be calling. So sorry to be calling you crying." A nervous-sounding laugh escaped her. "Um, how is Amy?"

"Amy's perfect." She didn't know why that sounded like the wrong response.

Meredith's voice was calmer now. "Yes, she is," she said; she no longer appeared to be crying.

"How is Gabe?"

"Gabe is wonderful. Thanks."

Neither said anything for a moment or two. Catherine waited for Meredith to tell her why she was calling.

"Listen, Catherine," Meredith began. "I know it's Saturday afternoon and that you're probably spending time as a family. But by any chance, would you mind if I spoke with Wes for a minute? My father's making no sense, and Nick is—"

"Meredith, you need to stop calling."

Instantly there was silence. Catherine didn't know if she was sorry she'd said it or not. It had slipped out, without her barely realizing, and for a moment she wondered if her thoughts were somehow seeping out of her mind. She wasn't even sure if she'd actually said it, or merely thought it with a lot of feeling, until Meredith spoke once more.

"I..." she said, and then stopped.

Catherine still said nothing. She was breathing rather heavily; she wondered if Meredith heard her, or whether she'd managed to sound like she'd meant to speak the words out loud. *Well, this is awkward,* she told herself, for once not chastising herself for it. *But I suppose I've already said it. I might as well make the most of it.*

"Meredith," she repeated, impressed with the firmness of her voice. "I think you need to stop calling."

Meredith seemed stunned into silence, and Catherine couldn't blame her. She'd grown used to calling whenever she wanted; she'd thought nothing of asking for her husband's emotional energy. There was something exhilarating in asserting that the entitlement was her own. There was something empowering in standing up for herself.

"Okay..." said Meredith, sounding confused. "Can you just tell me why?"

Catherine felt like she was hyperventilating; she was worried she'd actually pass out. *Because he's my husband and he's in love with you*, is what she wanted to say. She closed her mouth to force herself to calm down, and commanded that her thoughts align.

"Because I'm not comfortable with it. Not anymore."

The silence now was deafening. Catherine waited anxiously for Meredith to respond.

"I'm so sorry," Meredith said finally, her voice now utterly different. Catherine grew a little frantic; she had no idea how to read her. She had no idea what her next step should be. Was Meredith genuinely sorry? Was she being defensive or ironic? It was like being in a pitch black room, and having to guess the direction of the door.

"It's okay," she said, because that was what one said when one was told someone was sorry. "I'm sorry again about your father." *There*, she thought, feeling good about her performance. She hadn't been harsh, merely truthful. She'd ended with an expression of sympathy. She straightened and held her head higher, satisfied.

A few moments passed before Meredith spoke again.

"Have a good evening," she said softly. And then, just like that, she was gone.

Catherine turned the phone over in her hand a couple of times. Wes's phone, black and immaculate. She stared at it in wonder, the vehicle through which he conducted business, made connections, organized his tasks and routines—a microcosm of his entire life. Holding it made her feel powerful, like she'd regained some lost control. Her conscience told her she shouldn't have done it. But her heart was proud, was cheering her on, was finally healing from a thousand silent wounds.

She reentered the study and replaced the phone on the desk. Then she retrieved Amy from her room and walked barefoot outside to the lawn, where she played in the grass with her baby, the sunlight dancing in their hair.

CHAPTER TWENTY-THREE

*M*eredith lowered the phone from her ear and laid it on the table. Then she sat for a moment, her eyes wide, a sick, slow pulling in her stomach.

Catherine had chastised her. Shy, sweet Catherine. And over her friendship with Wes.

Meredith replayed the conversation in her mind, over and over. She must have misunderstood.

But no. It could not be denied. Catherine had made it quite clear.

There were so many facets of this. So many complexities, so many conclusions.

But right now, at this moment, it was only the repercussions that mattered.

She stared straight ahead, already resigned.

That's it, then, she thought. *I'm truly on my own.*

There was no time for thoughtfulness, no time for emotion. She shook off her shock and sucked in her breath. She pulled her laptop closer, and she got back to work.

AFTER LONG DELIBERATION, Harold decided he wanted to self-publish the book. The quickness of the process meant there was a chance he'd actually see it published. And the lack of editors and middlemen meant he wouldn't have to do what anyone else said.

"It's brilliant, Meredith. Just brilliant. I can leave it exactly as it is. My words, my thoughts, my vision. No muss, no fuss. And the best part is, it's a big middle finger to The Man."

"Don't you think you'll sell more copies with a book deal?"

"Not if it's done right."

"But I don't know anything about self-publishing. Where do you even begin?"

"I believe you mean, where do *you* even begin?"

Thus Meredith's responsibilities grew wider, as she now added "publisher" to her already many hats.

"There are so many decisions to make," Meredith lamented to Nick one evening as she resumed her work after dinner. "I can't believe how many details go into publishing."

He turned to her from the sink, where he was finishing up washing dishes. "Like what?"

"Everything. Literally everything. What trim size do I want? What's the name of my imprint? Where should I advertise? Do I buy my own ISBN?"

"What's an ISBN?"

"International Standard Book Number."

"What's the advantage of buying one?"

"I seriously have no idea."

Nick turned off the water, dried his hands, and stepped behind her, taking her shoulders in his hands.

"Goodnight, honey," he said. "Try not to stay up too late."

"Okay," she said, meeting him for a quick kiss, then briefly watching him walk away before turning back to the laptop on the table.

As work on the book began to draw to a close, she was also tasked with obtaining recommendations and reviews for the book, as well as for Harold's previous books—Harold thought it would help the book sell more copies.

"Meredith, I'm sending you a list of a few people to contact," he said. "Please ask them to write a little something."

To Harold, "a few" was a couple of dozen. Meredith found herself calling educators, congresspeople, former Cabinet members.

"Meredith," he said one Saturday afternoon in July. "Do you think Wes knows Senator McNair?"

"I don't know, Dad." She gave Nick an apologetic look; they were hustling around the house, preparing to take Gabe fishing at Pierce's Cove, near Aspen Woods Mountain. "Why?"

"Because Senator McNair is Secretary McNair's daughter. I need an interview with Secretary McNair."

"But who is Senator McNair? And why would she know Wes?"

"She's a Virginia state senator. Her father the Secretary's grown old and reclusive. He never talks to anybody anymore. I think maybe he'd talk to me. I need you to call Wes."

Meredith froze. "I'm not sure I can do that."

"Why the hell not? It'll take you five minutes."

"You're friendly with Sarah and Charles. Why don't you call and ask?"

"Meredith, I'm on a timeframe here. And I don't want to talk about the goddamn cancer. If I call Sarah myself, I'll never get her off the phone. She'll ask me questions and fuss over me. No, I can't call Sarah."

As loath as she was to admit it, she knew her father was right. "Well, maybe Mom can call, then."

Her father was beginning to sound frustrated. "It won't be any different with Sarah. In fact, it'll be worse. I'll still be showered with sympathy, only I won't even be speaking for myself."

"Maybe Mom can send her a text? Or an email?"

"Meredith, please." Her father's voice was anxious, and for a moment, she thought he might weep. "You can take care of this without any drama. I can't talk to the Bickharts right now. I just can't." He paused. "Can you try to understand?"

Meredith bit her lip. "Okay," she said. "I'll call him. But I can't do it right now. I'll call him tonight and get back to you."

"Fine," said Harold. "It's a deal. And Meredith."

"Yes?"

"Thank you."

Meredith hung up the phone. She held her face in her hands and rubbed at her eyes, anxiety making her nauseated. She'd have to live with the nausea all day, the fear of offending Catherine—and she still hadn't reckoned with the reasons why Catherine would feel so adamantly about her calling. But in the meantime, she intended to enjoy the day out with her family. She'd deal with the Bickharts later.

CHAPTER TWENTY-FOUR

*C*atherine's slender fingers held the brush just so, delicately painting the innermost design of the mold with purple-dyed chocolate. It was a swirling ranunculus, with layers and layers of petals. It would be surrounded by a lavender oval, which would rest atop a white chocolate square. The square would be filled with lavender-flavored nougat. She was making these chocolates for the Charlottesville gift shop, a special collection just for summer. It was her second batch of these special chocolates: the first batch had sold out in days.

Brahms serenaded her in the background, the melodies swirling like the petals of the ranunculus, interweaving and repeating, and coming together at its center. It was rather like marriage, she mused. There were so many layers, seeming always to miss each other, never to meet. But it always made sense in the end; they always shared a common core. Catherine listened to the music she knew by heart, knowing in the end, the melodies would converge. She wondered if the melodies of her life would converge, as well, whether people worked like music, or whether music was an ideal, a fantasy, like art tended to be.

She worked for several hours, finishing her task in the peacefulness of her studio. She then cleaned up her work and took one last look around her workshop. Everything was orderly and clean. She nodded, satisfied, and walked back upstairs, where Dorothea ran to her and snuggled against her legs. Catherine scooped her up and brought her to her carrier, prepared to go drop off a sample at the gift shop before heading back home.

"I have some exciting news, Dorothea. We're going out to dinner tonight." She kissed the paw that extended through the grate. "Then, we're staying in a fancy hotel. Grandma Lois is watching Amy overnight. Isn't that nice?"

Indeed, it was nice, and Catherine was looking forward to it; she felt they needed a night to themselves. Now that she'd made a conscious effort not to pursue him, it seemed she and Wes barely saw each other. Anxious and confused, she tended to retreat to her workshop, as she was today. And by stepping back to collect her thoughts, she'd unwittingly learned how much of their inter-action was the result of her efforts. He was never cold to her, never neglectful; he kissed her goodnight and asked her about her day, all with a smile that still made her melt. But there was a sadness in her joy now, a sense that he wasn't hers. It was growing harder for her to feel motivated. Though she loved him deeply, her enthusiasm was dwindling.

She gathered her things and picked up Dorothea's carrier, then headed to her car and drove to the gift shop downtown.

She took Dorothea into the shop and spoke a few minutes with the owner, who cooed and clapped with delight over the samples Catherine had brought her. Catherine waved goodbye and carried Dorothea back outside, eager to go home and prepare for her night out with Wes.

As she stepped out of the store, her eyes detected someone leaning against the wall. She cried out with fright, and her heart seemed to leap out of her throat. Looking right at her was Rick Tremaine.

"Well, well," he said, with a cheerless grin. He stood straight as she emerged from the store. "If it isn't Mrs. Bickhart. What an incredible coincidence. You're looking very nice today, Catherine."

"Why are you here?" she asked, desperately looking around.

"I need a gift for a friend."

"I don't believe you." A violent churning in her stomach, she backed away without even realizing it, as if they were opposite poles of a magnet. "I think you were waiting for me."

He held up his hands with professed innocence. "You don't believe I'm the kind of guy to buy gifts? I'm offended."

She pointed at him accusingly. "You were at the park that day."

"I don't know what you're talking about. You must be imagining things."

He took a step toward her, and Catherine jumped back.

"You sure are a skittish little thing," he said, with a laugh that made her want to wretch. "Did your cocky husband tell you not to talk to me? I keep trying to be friends, and you keep brushing me off. That's not very polite, Catherine."

"Go away. Leave me alone. And leave my husband alone, too."

Shaking with terror, she ran to her car, looking over her shoulder more than once. She hastily put Dorothea inside; then she scrambled into the driver's seat and sped down the street like lightning.

SHE DIDN'T EVEN REMEMBER DRIVING HOME; she had no idea how she arrived in one piece.

She burst through the door and down the hall to Wes's study, where she found him at his desk with some paperwork. He stood promptly as she ran into the room, his eyes wide with curiosity and concern.

She told him what happened, hysterically crying; she was barely able to speak the words.

He was holding her shoulders, listening intently, his eyes alert and following every change of her expression. With every sentence, his face grew darker—but his eyes remained soft, making his compassion plainly clear.

He held her close and rubbed her back, shushing her gently and kissing her face.

"Sweetheart, you're okay now. You're home, and you're okay. I'm so sorry this happened to you."

"Wes, I'm really scared. I really think he's following me. He never even went into the store. And I know he was at the park that day, too."

"I've had enough of his skulking around scaring you. We're not going to stand for it. I'll talk to Grady. It might be time to consider a restraining order."

"Yes, please, anything. I want him away from us for good." Her voice caught. "It makes me not even want to go out tonight. It makes me not want to go out at all."

He continued to hold her in his arms until her shaking had stopped and her breathing had slowed. Despite her fear, for those wonderful moments, she felt protected and safe, as she always did with him. She leaned against his chest and took in the pressure of his arms around her sides and her back. She felt her anxiety loosen with every kiss he planted on her forehead.

"I'll tell you what," he said softly. "Let's try not to think about it tonight. I'll look into it first thing Monday. In the meantime, let's enjoy a nice night out together. What do you think, sweetheart?" he asked when she was calm. "Should we start getting ready to go?"

"Okay," she said, meeting him for a kiss. "I have been looking forward to this."

"I have, too. What a treat this is. A night away, just the two of us."

"Mmm," she breathed, with a tentative smile. She sighed, relaxing somewhat. "I can't believe I actually have you all to myself for the entire night."

He chuckled and kissed her again, more deeply, a delicious preview of the night ahead. "That's right. I'm all yours. Nothing can take me away from you tonight."

That evening, Lois and Fred arrived to pick up Amy. Catherine's stomach was in knots. Suddenly, she didn't want to leave her. Her heart was fluttering nervously as she handed her parents Amy's things and finally waved goodbye. She stood in the doorway after they'd left, for several minutes, closing her eyes and breathing evenly, trying to calm herself down.

Is this normal? she texted to Hei, fanning her face with her hand.

Completely, was the response. *Are you okay? Do you need me to come over and help you?*

No, I think I'll be okay. Catherine inhaled again, then exhaled purposefully. *But thank you so much for your offer.*

Catherine dressed in the crimson suit she'd worn on their very first date. She attached the brooch Wes had given her on her birthday, then turned to face Wes, who was just slipping into his suit jacket.

He was so dashing and handsome it almost reduced her to tears.

He regarded her curiously as he put on his cufflinks.

"What's wrong, sweetheart?"

Catherine was inexplicably overwhelmed. She shook her head, her throat seeming to constrict with emotion.

His face softened as he approached and stroked the side of her face with his fingers.

"Sweet, lovely Catherine," he said, with the kindness and charm that had drawn her from the start. "We're going to have a wonderful time tonight."

She smiled and nodded, and held his hand as it caressed her

skin. He kissed her and took her hand, and they walked downstairs to prepare to leave.

He was picking his keys up from the table in the foyer when his phone rang.

"Hold on just a minute, sweetheart," he told her, glancing at the screen.

"Is it Meredith?" she asked, before she could stop herself.

"Yes, it is. She must have another question for her father. I promise, I'll make it quick."

"No."

He looked at her with surprise, his brow raised. He put the phone to his ear. "Hi, Meredith. Hang on a second, okay?" He muted the phone and turned to Catherine. "What's wrong?"

Catherine's heart was pounding; something in her had broken.

"You're not going to talk to Meredith. Not tonight."

He stared at her, expressionless, for a moment or two. "Does it really bother you?"

"Yes. Yes, it really bothers me. Especially since I told her not to call you again."

His eyebrows rose higher. "When did you do that?"

"A few weeks ago. You were sleeping. I answered the phone and told her to stop calling."

"Why?"

"Because you're still in love with her."

His face went dark. He took the phone off mute and held it to his ear once more. "I'm going to have to call you back. No, it's okay. I'll call you right back."

"No," she said again, and swallowed. "You're not going to call her back."

He slipped his phone back into his pocket and watched her then in silence, appearing unsure how to respond. His brow now crinkled with thought, and his jaw set tight.

"I've tried to hide what it does to me," she said. "The anxiety. The fear of not being enough. I didn't want you to see all that. I haven't wanted you to see me so weak." He opened his mouth to respond; she held up her finger and continued anyway. "But I'm stronger than that. And I don't deserve this." She took a breath, steadying herself. "If you call her back, tonight, of all nights, I will take the bag I packed and stay the night at my grandmother's house."

His expression now lightened somehow, perhaps in disbelief. "That's a little dramatic, don't you think? I told you before, Cat. I'm not in love with her."

"You are!" she now shouted. "You are, you are, you are. You keep saying you're not, but you are. I may not catch everything. I may not be the sharpest. But I'm not stupid. And I won't let you treat me like I am."

His eyes were shifting across her face, trying to take in what she'd said. She'd never known him to be speechless, had never known him to not understand. It was frustrating, and satisfying, all at the same time.

He began to say something a couple of times, but was carefully choosing his words.

Finally, he spoke gently, his face soft with sympathy—and something in that sympathy angered her even more.

"Cat, I know I'm not home that much, but I give you damn near everything."

"It's completely beside the point." It was all so clear now, the root of the problem. Though it broke her heart to recognize and expose it, it was such a relief to finally understand it. "It's easy to throw a party. It's easy to buy a brooch. What's not easy is being honest. What's not easy is committing your heart."

He seemed to inhale and step back slightly, clearly affected by what she had said. It hurt her to hurt him, but she was spurred further by the fact that she was actually getting through.

"I feel like..." she said, and then the tears hit. She swallowed and wiped her eyes, determined to go on. "I feel like you're over-compensating. You give me the perfect life. But it's almost as if you're making up for the fact that...that I'm not the woman you want."

"Sweetheart, no," he said, and approached her once more. He rubbed her shoulders and smoothed her hair, his expression so sad she almost backed down. "It breaks my heart that you feel this way."

"Well, it breaks my heart that you love another woman more."

His chest was rising and falling; his expression was unreadable. There he was, in his stunning black suit, with his beautiful face and his impeccably neat sandy hair; it was the man she'd fallen in love with the first moment she'd met him, who had made her feel special and made her feel safe, who'd defended her and comforted her and offered her things she never knew she'd needed. He'd given her a daughter, and a family full of happiness. He'd been a shining light of courage, a pillar of strength fighting for justice and fairness.

But it wasn't enough. She needed a partner, not a savior; she needed him to love her as much as she loved him.

"I need to think," she whispered shakily, pushing away his hand as it wiped away her tears. "If you need me, I'll be at my grandmother's."

She picked up her bag from the floor and walked out the door.

SHE HAD NEVER WORKED in her workshop this late at night before.

The atmosphere was very different at this time of night. It was summer, and the sun still lingered in the sky, but its light was dim, the promise of darkness present in the air. The equipment around her sat in shadows, and the walls felt danker. She switched on a lamp, and the room brightened, now cast in an effervescent glow. She turned on her music and settled onto her stool; she'd changed from her suit into a blouse and worn vintage jeans. It was peaceful and quiet, a kind of quiet only the night can bring. Activities of the day were ending. Soon, the world would be asleep.

She dipped her brush into the lavender-colored chocolate. A sound above her made her pause and lower her hand.

She turned down the music. Footsteps coming toward the door.

She should have been glad he had come back for her. But something about the gait was wrong.

The door of the workshop opened. Footsteps creaked on the stairs.

Catherine stood. Her heart was hammering. It wasn't him. It was somebody else.

Shoes appeared, then legs. Not his shoes, not his legs, not his face.

Rick Tremaine.

She screamed and flew backward, knocking into her stool.

"Now, now," he said, walking slowly toward her. "That's no way to greet a guest."

"How..." she gasped, dangerously close to fainting. "How did you..."

"You left the door unlocked, Catherine. Not a very smart thing to do, unless you want visitors."

She closed her eyes against the vision of him. She let out a little whimper, trying not to cry.

"What is it about me that makes you so frightened?" She opened her eyes; he was following her as she stepped sideways around the room, her back to the countertops, her hands gripping themselves. "I'm really a nice guy, Catherine. I keep paying you compliments. Why don't you give me a chance?"

"Please stop saying my name."

"Well, what should I call you, then?"

"Don't call me anything. Just go."

He shook his head with a smile, reaching into his jacket. "I'm not going anywhere."

AMANDA GALE

His hand emerged holding a handgun.

She pulled in her breath and bit her lip, unable to stop the tears. *Amy*, cried her heart. *My sweet baby girl.*

"Please." Her voice was a shaky whisper. She cleared her throat and made her face firm. "Please just take what you want, and then go."

"Oh, I intend to take what I want," he said, and the smoothness of his voice made her skin crawl. "You didn't think this was a robbery, did you?"

Catherine looked around desperately. The carver might work...or the pick...

"Don't even think about it." He was suddenly on her, his hand gripping her arm; she cried out from the force of his fingers digging into her flesh. The head of the gun was pressing into her chest, and she froze, afraid even to breathe.

"That's better," he murmured, his lips now at her ear. "You know, you don't have to do this, Catherine. You don't have to rebuff me out of obligation to him." His lips grazed her neck, and she winced at the saccharine assurance in his tone. "And I'll give you some advice: you shouldn't tease. The thing about teasing is that teasing has consequences." She shivered and recoiled, the heat of his breath like poison on her skin.

Sweet Amy, I love you. I'm going to try to come home to you, love.

Catherine picked a spot on the floor, and concentrated on it. This was the spot on which she'd focus, the spot she would cling to. She was going to be raped. He was going to do it. Her only task now was to make it out alive.

He pushed her away from the countertop and against a nearby wall. He pressed himself against her, his heavy bulk trapping her and crushing her lungs. His hand went between her legs, where his fingers probed roughly. She winced in pain, but said nothing, preparing herself for what was coming.

The front door above them opened and closed, and footsteps marched toward the workshop.

Rick and Catherine looked up in unison. Then Rick's big hand was clamped down on her mouth.

"Don't say a fucking word."

Catherine's eyes looked frantically toward the stairs.

Go away, she ordered him, praying his mind would hear her. *Go away and be there for Amy.*

The workshop door opened, and he hurried down the stairs. And then there he was, still in his suit and tie.

"Catherine! Jesus—"

Rick turned and extended his hand, pointing the gun at his heart.

Wes raised his hands and sucked in his breath. He looked at Catherine with wide, frantic eyes.

Her own eyes crinkled. *I love you. And I'm sorry.*

"You've really fucked things up now, Senator," Rick spat. "You should have just stayed at home."

"Let her go." He'd nearly choked on the words. He swallowed and stood straight and tall, his chin raised and his face calm. "Just let my wife go."

"You're so fucking full of yourself," said Rick. "You've just got to swoop in and be the hero. Why do you keep getting in the way? You're always in the damn way."

Wes took a step toward her. Rick pushed the gun closer, and Catherine sobbed.

"Stay the fuck away! I'm trying to think what to do with you."

Everyone was silent, their heavy breathing the only sound.

"Rick," said Wes, his hands still in the air. "Just tell me what you want. Tell me what I can do to make you let her go."

"You can shut the fuck up for once, to start."

"Please." His voice was cool, but there was terror underneath. "Do whatever you want with me. It's me you have the problem with, right?"

"There's going to be a problem if you don't shut up!" Rick

bellowed, and his voice reverberated through the basement walls. "I swear to God, you just don't know when to shut up."

"At least let me go to her. Okay? Just let me go to her."

Catherine shook her head from behind Rick's sweaty hand. Her eyebrows were raised high; her eyes were round with panic. *No,* she told him through her mind. *I want you by the stairs. Be quiet, now, and just do what he says!*

Rick turned his head to face her and pressed his hand harder, making her head hurt as it crunched into the wall. "You be quiet," he snarled through his teeth. "Don't you shake your—"

In that moment, Wes had lunged for him, but Rick turned back too quickly. A furious scuffle, then an ear-splitting shot, and Wes flying backward toward the wall.

His eyes were wide, disbelieving. He sank to the floor, a bloody wound in his chest.

Catherine screamed and ran to him, barely noticing Rick escaping up the stairs.

"Oh, my darling, no, no, no..."

She snatched her phone from the countertop and dialed 911.

"My husband's been shot, he's bleeding from his chest..."

She hastily wiped away tears, and took his face in her hands.

"I love you, Wes. I love you so much..."

His eyes were searching hers, darting here and there. His mouth was open, but he wouldn't speak.

She lifted his suit jacket. Blood, there was so much blood. She cradled him in her arms and rocked him, his strong body limp against hers. She kissed his face and patted his cheeks, moaning and crying and trying to be strong.

Sirens sounded on the road outside. Catherine kissed him and held him close.

His eyes had stopped moving; they seemed to look right through her.

"Help is here, my darling...Help is here, just please hold on..."

The door burst open, and the paramedics surrounded him,

filling up her workshop and ushering her aside. Someone wrapped a blanket around her shoulders. She looked down at herself: she was drenched in blood.

She watched as they swarmed him; she could barely even see him. She sensed someone soothe her, but she couldn't hear the words. In a terrified haze, she followed them outside, then into the ambulance, where they strove to pull him back to the light.

CHAPTER TWENTY-FIVE

*M*eredith and Jenny sat in the backyard with their feet up on the table, basking in the heavy summer sun. The air was sweet with the sounds of the children playing in the sandbox, birds fluttering in the trees, and ice clinking in their lemonade glasses. Meredith leaned her head against the back of her chair and adjusted her wide-brimmed hat and sunglasses. She was taking a break, and she refused to feel guilty about it. The heat felt so good as it pounded into her skin. Jenny's company was so refreshing after days of dreary work.

"I almost feel like I'm on vacation," she said lazily, watching as Gabe reached out to a passing butterfly.

"Lord knows you need one. How's the book going?"

Meredith nodded. "It's going." The truth was, it was almost done. Most of the work she did now related to the publishing. She was proofreading and formatting files, and she'd hired a graphic designer to work on the cover. "It's really taking shape. It's pretty incredible."

"I'll bet you'll be so happy when it's finally done."

"Mmm." Meredith frowned and took a sip of her lemonade. Oddly, the approaching completion of the book made her sad.

Her phone rang on the table beside her. She was surprised to see not her father's name, but her mother's.

"Hi, Mom," she said, the phone at her ear. "How are you?"

"I have to be honest, Meredith." Patricia's voice was shaking. "I'm calling to tell you something, and it's going to upset you."

Meredith's heart dropped, and she sat upright. Beside her, Jenny straightened. Meredith reached out, and Jenny took her hand.

"What is it, Mom," she said, bracing herself for the news.

Patricia was silent, and Meredith waited breathlessly.

"Your father's decided not to continue his treatment."

Meredith squeezed Jenny's hand, her eyes tearing behind her sunglasses.

"It could be a couple of months. But we'd like to see you now."

"I'm there, Mom," said Meredith, her voice heavy and firm. "I'll be there by the end of the day."

NICK AND VINCE came home early, Nick to kiss her goodbye and Vince to pack. Meredith and Vince didn't know how long they'd be gone. Meredith guessed it would be about a week. They were taking Gabe with them. Meredith thought he might cheer her father.

"I guess I'll keep you posted," she said as Nick held her in the driveway; Vince had thrown their bags in the car and now was saying goodbye to Jenny and Julia. "I wish I had a better idea of what I should expect. Unfortunately we'll just have to play it by ear."

"Whatever you need. Just do what you have to do."

She pulled him close and pressed him tight, letting his strength and comfort seep into her bones.

"Okay," she said reluctantly. "I guess we'd better go."

Nick held Gabe's head in his hand and kissed him firmly on the head. "I love you, little buddy. You be good for Mommy."

Meredith looked at Nick, her vision clouded by tears. "I love you, honey. I'm going to miss you."

He kissed her softly, his hand on her face. "I'm going to miss you, too," he said. "Just let me know if you need me to come down."

He kissed her again, and they all waved and parted. Meredith, from the passenger's side, regarded Vince, his silhouette straight and serious. The years had become visible on his face. She patted his shoulder, and he turned to her and smiled. But the smile soon turned sad, his eyes filling with tears. They sniffled and blew their noses, and looked at each other meaningfully. Then they hurried down to their parents' house, bracing themselves, and gathering courage from each other.

CHAPTER TWENTY-SIX

Catherine had never seen so many wires and monitors in one place. It was overwhelming and oppressive. Everything was beeping, everything was hooked up to something somewhere else. It was a labyrinth of equipment, determining life and death. Catherine hated this room. She was completely out of control here.

She turned to Wes, who was covered with wires, who had things sticking out of him everywhere. He lay on his back, his skin dull and sallow, his chest buried in bandages. Even worse than being attacked was seeing Wes so fragile. She knew that she was traumatized, that what Rick had done to her had changed her forever. She'd already had nightmares, had already jumped when a doctor or family member had come up behind her and said her name. But there just wasn't any time to think about that now. Her mind had compartmentalized; it had set it aside for later. Every day, every moment, was spent being thankful that he was alive. It was spent praying with all her might that he'd wake up and be okay.

Catherine closed her eyes and relived that horrible night. She couldn't prevent it from tormenting her, couldn't make the images go away. The events repeated themselves, in vivid detail, over and over and over again, and she suffered through them, her fingertips at her temples, silently begging them to stop.

"I can feel his breath on my neck," she'd whispered from within Hei's arms as she held her.

"I know, sweet friend, I'm so sorry," Hei had cried, hugging her tight and rocking with her back and forth.

The sound of his footsteps on the floorboards above, the look on his face when he'd pulled out the gun, the taste of his hand as it clamped down upon her lips. It kept coming back. But what had happened next was worse.

Catherine opened her eyes and looked at Wes. His eyes had been closed for days. He'd mumbled a few times, and everyone had scrambled, their hearts in their throats—but it had never amounted to anything. And so they waited, and waited.

When she thought of the ambulance all she saw was blood. Blood on his chest, blood on their clothes, blood on her hands and in their hair. The red contrasted with the white of the ambulance, in a ghoulish, ghastly way. As they'd raced through town toward the hospital, they'd called in for blood—he would need a lot of blood. They'd hooked him up to an IV and a chest tube, they'd given him oxygen, they'd done all sorts of things she couldn't even remember. He'd been so helpless, so open and exposed. He'd been reduced to his humanness, in all its carnal, physical gore.

That vision of him would haunt her forever. She already knew it; it had already become part of her. She didn't know how she'd get over it. She saw it in her mind's eye constantly, without end.

He'd suffered a collapsed lung and rib fractures and had undergone hours of surgery. They'd tried to keep her updated when they could. He was active and fit, and in excellent health. Thankfully, the surgeries had gone well.

"He's very lucky," the surgeon had told her. "The bullet missed the vital organs. If it hadn't, I'd be telling you a very different story."

"Quintessential Wes," Grady had said from behind her, his lips trembling as he'd held back more tears. He let out a nervous laugh and allowed the tears to come; Helen, standing beside him, rubbed his back. "My brother's a hell of a fighter. He always pulls through. He could dance with the devil and still survive."

"It appears," the doctor had said, "that that's exactly what he did."

They'd moved him to this room in the ICU, where he'd remained ever since. He'd graduated from critical to stable condition. Still, he'd spoken not a word. He'd remained unconscious for more than three days. Catherine was at her wits' end.

It was on the fourth day that it happened. Sarah had been with her, as she'd been most of the time. She was taking a break with the rest of the family; they'd gone down to the cafeteria for coffee and lunch. Catherine couldn't eat and had remained behind.

She'd been dozing in the chair by his bed, holding his hand. Suddenly, his fingers twitched in hers. She opened her eyes to find him turning his head.

"Catherine," he whispered, so softly, his eyelids struggling to open. He closed them tight, and his whole face crumpled. "I'm so thirsty."

Catherine scrambled to the table for water, then held the straw to his dry, parched lips.

He drank like a man who'd been lost in a desert, then leaned back and sighed when the cup was empty.

"Thank you," he said, just barely, his voice quiet and hoarse.

She patted and kissed him, careful of the wires. She couldn't speak through her tears. She wiped her eyes with her sleeves and rested her forehead on his.

She held his face and looked at him through glassy eyes. He looked so gaunt and tired, his cheeks more hollow and his lips parted, as if the effort of keeping them closed was too great to bear. But his eyes were sharp, and dark with emotion. Catherine's tears wouldn't stop. She hadn't known if she'd ever see those eyes again.

"I love you," she managed to utter, and he lightly touched her arm. "I'm so glad that I can tell you that."

"Sweetheart," he whispered, his eyes taking her in. "I love you, too."

Catherine rang for the nurse, who came rushing in with a smile. She texted Sarah, and the crew returned in no time, everyone hugging and crying with joy.

"Oh, my God," cried Sarah, smiling through tears with her hand on his face. "You gave me such a scare."

"I'll bet." He grimaced as he tried to shift. Catherine adjusted his blankets and pillow. "I'm sorry, family. You must have been living in hell."

"You're the one who's a pincushion, darling." Sarah frowned, and her tears renewed. "You just get better and don't worry about us."

Maeve knocked on the door. "Catherine," she said, waving her hand to draw Catherine near.

Catherine made to follow her. Wes's hand on hers stopped her.

His eyes were now wide, his lips long and straight. Catherine furrowed her brow. What was it she saw in his face?

"I'll be right back," she assured him. "I promise."

The divot between his eyes had creased and risen; his lips had parted and turned down. His eyes on hers, he lifted his hand. She glanced back at him as she approached the door. He was watching her, his face like that of a frightened child.

Her heart was flooded with sympathy, the weight of it aching in her gut. She smiled sweetly and waved, then exited the room to find Maeve.

Maeve was holding Amy, standing with Lois a couple of feet off. Upon seeing Catherine, the little girl reached out.

Catherine took Amy and sighed as her little arms wrapped around her. She held the back of her head and rested her cheek on hers, and for a moment, she forgot where she was. Oh, this feeling, of holding innocence so dear. It was bright and pink and sparkling, a color unmatched.

"Catherine."

Her sister's serious tone brought her back. "What is it, Maeve?"

"I just wanted to tell you. They arrested Rick Tremaine."

Catherine gasped, and Lois brought her hand to her back. "Oh my! That's wonderful news. Where was he? How did they know?"

"Mr. Jensen next door heard the gunshot and took pictures of him leaving. They found him at a girlfriend's house near Richmond."

"So you don't have to worry," said Lois, kissing her daughter's temple. "He won't hurt you again."

Catherine shivered and buried her face in Amy's hair. She couldn't think of Rick now without imagining that gun, the way his fingers had grabbed her, the smell of his breath in her face.

"Hey, Catherine."

Catherine once again looked at her sister. Maeve was wiping away a tear. Beside her, rubbing her back in little circles, Lois was sniffling into a tissue.

"I'm just so relieved that you're okay," said Maeve.

Catherine leaned in and hugged her, and Maeve squeezed her tight.

"The idea of not having you in my life," Maeve said shakily. "It's the worst thing I can imagine."

"I love you," said Catherine, her tears mingling with her sister's.

"I love you, too. I'm so glad you're my sister."

"And I'm glad you're my daughter," said Lois, hugging both

daughters close. "I'm just so very proud of you." She paused for a moment as she choked back tears. "You've been so brave, much more so than I could have been."

Maeve nodded. "You're kickass in every way possible," she said, blowing her nose and sniffling.

They stood like this for some time, until Sarah came out to reclaim her. Catherine smiled at her sister and mother, who had made her feel much better. Sometimes bad things made good things happen, too.

WES'S RECOVERY would be long and trying. It could be a year, she'd learned, before he was back to where he was before. He'd need physical therapy and pain control, and possibly more surgery. They listened to the news in silence, trying to take it all in. It was impossible to imagine the road ahead, to understand the extent to which it would affect all their lives.

But he was here, and she was grateful, especially since he so needed her. Catherine had noticed that he never wanted her to leave the room. His eyes would grow sad, almost desperate. Sometimes he begged her not to go.

"Please," he'd whispered, when she'd told him she was going to talk to the nurse.

"I'll only be a little tiny minute. Then I'll be right back."

"Catherine. Don't leave me."

There'd been terror in his eyes. He'd looked so powerless.

She'd been unable to bear leaving him. She'd sat back down.

"Okay," she'd said, and his face had flooded with relief.

The first few days, he'd tire so easily. He'd speak a few words, and he'd need to rest. As the days went on, he was able to tolerate a little more. He'd cracked a couple of jokes. The old Wes seemed to be returning.

But Catherine felt he wasn't quite the same. Though his wit was the same, and his eagerness to get strong, she couldn't shake the feeling he was putting on an act. His smiles seemed hollow, and his laughs were too short. He was gentler, calmer, quieter. The pensiveness in his eyes made him look always ill at ease. Catherine knew the rib injuries made moving and speaking, even breathing, very difficult. However, it was more than that, something much deeper than the physical pain. She wondered if anyone else had noticed.

Toward the end of the week, Wes was allowed to go home. Sarah and Charles set up an intercom to make it easier for Wes to reach Catherine anywhere in the house. The family also decorated the house with balloons and a "Welcome Home" banner, and he seemed cheered and appreciative of their efforts. After they helped him get situated in the bedroom, they left him in Catherine's care. He watched her as she puttered around the room, bringing him blankets and placing a glass of water on his nightstand. He held out his hand for her to join him.

She stopped what she was doing and went to him, squeezing his hand and kissing his lips gently.

"You have been so good to me," he told her. He shook his head. His face looked very serious. For a moment, she thought she saw tears in his eyes. But the glistening was gone before it got started, and she assumed she'd only imagined it.

"Well, that's because I love you," she said. "I want you to get better."

"Me, too," he said, more adamantly. "And I'm going to, sweetheart. I really am."

Catherine offered a sober smile. "I know you are. And I'm so thankful."

They locked eyes for several moments, so many words unspoken. He looked so tired, his face so weighty with thought. Catherine wanted him to confide in her, to talk to her about all he was feeling. She was afraid to ask how this had affected him. He seemed staunchly closed-lipped, unwilling—or unable—to explore that just yet.

"It's really good to have you home," she told him. "You belong here. I'm so glad to be out of that horrible room."

"I can't tell you how glad I am to be home, sweetheart. There just aren't any words."

He watched her for a moment. Then his face turned serious once more.

"Sweetheart," he said. "I have to ask you a favor."

"Oh, anything," she told him. "Anything at all."

He took a deep breath, still holding her hand. "I need to see Meredith."

Catherine felt the color drain from her face, and her heart seemed to turn into ice.

"Why?"

"I can't tell you. Not yet."

She pulled her hand away. She felt like she would faint. The fury inside her transcended reaction; it ate her alive and left her with nothing.

"I know this isn't ideal for you," he said, in an understatement that would have been funny in any other circumstance. "But I need to do it anyway."

She looked to the side, avoiding his gaze.

"Please," he said, taking her hand back.

She didn't respond; she closed her eyes. *This is it*, she thought. *This is the line I draw.*

She turned her head to face him.

"Fine," she said. "I'll call her."

CHAPTER TWENTY-SEVEN

*I*t was after nine o'clock, and Meredith's father had gone to sleep long ago. He'd been sleeping most of the day, as his pain medication made him tired. Gabe, too, was sleeping, in Meredith's old bedroom. Vince, Patricia, and Meredith sat in the living room, each holding a glass of wine.

Vince and Meredith were leaving the next day and would visit again within the next few weeks. It had been a long, difficult day, full of planning and remembering and coming to terms. Now the three of them were relaxing together, commiserating with each other and finding strength in each other's presence.

Meredith's phone rang, and she glanced at the screen. She raised her eyebrows, surprised.

"Hi, Wes," she said upon answering, clearing her throat, trying to sound chipper.

"It's not Wes. It's Catherine."

"Oh." Meredith's brow furrowed; since their conversation, Catherine was the last person she expected to hear from. "How are you, Catherine?"

"Well, I'm not all that good. Wes has been shot."

"What?" Meredith cried, mouth hanging open. She placed her

wine glass on the table and stood, startling Vince and Patricia. "Did you say he was shot?"

"Yes," said Catherine. "In the chest. It happened last Saturday."

"I can't believe this." Meredith paced back and forth, her hand on her forehead. "Is he..."

"He's alive, thank goodness. He was incredibly fortunate."

"Oh." Meredith now put her hand on her heart, choking back tears. "Oh, thank God. Is he going to be okay?"

"It's a long road ahead, but the prognosis looks good."

Meredith whispered the news to her mother and brother, who had been staring at her with concern. They gasped and started, expressing their shock, then sank back in their chairs to let her talk to Catherine.

"Who did this?" asked Meredith. "How did this happen?"

"The man who shot him is named Rick Tremaine. He's an attorney Wes has had some run-ins with before. He was trying to attack me. Wes came in and saved me."

Meredith shook her head. "Oh, Catherine, I'm so sorry. Are you okay?"

"Yes, I'm fine. Just upset and shaken up."

"Did they find him? Is he still out there?"

"They've arrested him."

Meredith sighed with relief. "I'm so happy to hear that. Thank you for letting me know."

"There's more."

She waited anxiously, wondering what more there could be.

"Wes wants to see you," said Catherine.

Meredith froze. "He does?"

Catherine didn't say anything for a couple of seconds. "Yes. He didn't ask for anyone else. Only you."

Meredith turned from Vince and Patricia and took a few steps into the hallway. "Do you know why?"

"Yes," said Catherine. "It's because he's still in love with you."

Meredith's heart seemed to skip several beats; then it pounded relentlessly, making it hard to breathe. "Why do you...what makes you..."

"It doesn't really matter." Catherine's voice now sounded angry, like she was holding emotion back. "Just please come down here and talk to him."

"Wait, Catherine," said Meredith, beginning to recover, and sensing that Catherine was getting ready to hang up the phone. "Are you okay with this? I don't want to cause trouble."

"It's too late." Catherine was yelling now, and Meredith felt she would be sick. "You've been causing trouble since the beginning. In fact, he was shot because of you."

Meredith leaned against the wall and sank down until she was crouching. "What do you mean?" she asked, her head between her legs to stop the dizziness.

"We were supposed to go out that night. Then you called him. After I'd already asked you not to. I told him not to answer it, or I'd leave. He answered it, so I left, and that's when I was attacked."

Meredith rubbed her face in her hand. "Catherine, I'm so sorry. I never meant to hurt you. My father that night, he—"

"Honestly, Meredith, I really don't care. I'm probably going to leave him, so it doesn't even matter."

"No, Catherine. You're leaving Wes?"

"Well, maybe I won't leave him," said Catherine, more calmly, until her voice turned angry again. "It just goes to show how much I love him and how stupid I am."

"No, Catherine, no. You're not stupid. You—"

"Just come down here. He almost died, and he wants to see you. I promised I would tell you, and I did. Oh, and Meredith."

"Yes?"

Catherine was crying, a tormented, defeated sound. "If you want him...you can have him."

She hung up the phone, leaving Meredith stunned and silent.

~

MEREDITH WALKED SLOWLY BACK into the living room, her eyes red and harried, arms wrapped around herself.

Vince and Patricia looked up as soon as she entered the room.

"So what happened?" asked Vince. "Is Wes going to be okay?"

Meredith related the details numbly as they listened with rapt attention. When she got to the part about Wes wanting to see her, and why, they stared at her in silence.

"Wow," said Vince finally, leaning back in his chair. "To think that all this time, he's carried the torch."

"Vince, please. Not helpful."

"I'm just saying. It's a long time. Are you going to go?"

"How can I go?" asked Meredith desperately, throwing up her hands. "I'm visiting my father, who's just ended his cancer treatment. I have Gabe with me. I just found out his wife thinks he's in love with me."

"Yeah, but he's just been shot. I don't know if you can say no."

"Well, I can't be away from home any longer. And I don't want to cause them trouble. Besides, there's Nick to consider. What am I going to say to him? 'Hi, honey, I haven't been home in a week, but I'm going to Virginia to see my ex, who his wife thinks is in love with me.'" She shook her head. "It doesn't sound too good."

"Maybe Tara would go with you."

Meredith considered. "Maybe I'll call her and see what she thinks."

She turned and walked out, then went up into her father's study.

Meredith called Tara and told her what had happened.

"Well, if you end up going, I'll go with you," said Tara. "Tom can stay with Evelyn and Ginger. I'll bring Celeste. I could use a road trip, and you could use the company."

"Do you think I should, though? That's the big question."

"I see this both ways, Merry. Call Nick and ask him."

Meredith's fingers shook as she hung up and called Nick. Her heart was beating painfully as she began to tell her story.

"Of course, you should go," he said, before Meredith had finished. "Maybe send Gabe home with Vince, and you can fly home later."

"I was thinking of taking Gabe. Tara said she'd go with me."

"Good idea. Whatever you want to do. You've been helping your dad all week, and now this. Maybe you could use some time with Tara."

"Hey, Nick. Just hold on. There's more."

"What is it?"

Meredith took a deep breath. "Catherine says Wes is still in love with me."

Nick was silent, for a rather long time.

"Are you still okay if I go?" she asked, when he didn't say anything more.

"I mean..." he said. "Not really."

Meredith's chest was constricting. She closed her eyes and nodded.

"But what am I going to say."

Meredith opened her eyes. "Look, honey. If you're not comfortable, I won't go."

"I don't know, Merry. It's an impossible situation."

Meredith nodded again. "I know."

"It kind of changes things, you know? I guess it's just a lot to process all at once."

Meredith said nothing, letting him think it through.

"But," he said, and sighed. "He was shot. You should go. And I trust you."

Her eyes filled with tears. "Thank you, honey."

"Just keep me posted."

"I will. I love you."

"I love you, too. I miss you."

They talked a few more minutes, and Meredith hung up the phone. That night in bed she felt lonely and scared; she missed Nick desperately, yearning for him to hold her. She tossed and turned, wishing he were beside her. She lay awake for hours, thinking about the past, and worrying over the future.

VINCE DECIDED to stay a few extra days, and then he and Meredith would drive home together as planned. Tara picked her up the following morning. She had baby Celeste in the back. Meredith installed Gabe's car seat beside her.

"Where are you staying?" asked her mother, as she and Vince stood in the driveway to send them off.

"We're going to stay at Sarah's. Catherine texted me last night. It was very cold." Meredith frowned. "I'm very nervous about seeing her."

"I can't say I blame you."

They stood in silence for a moment or two.

"Listen, Meredith," said Patricia. "Be careful."

Meredith looked at her. "What do you mean?"

"I can't say I think this is a great idea, to be honest." Patricia looked her in the eye with a strange expression; Meredith couldn't tell what she was thinking. "I'd hate to see this cause tension between you and Nick."

Meredith stared at her, taken aback. "Nick says he's okay with it."

"Still."

Meredith was unnerved, but she thanked her mother and hugged her goodbye. She climbed into the passenger's seat of Tara's car, and the two took off down the road toward Charlottesville.

"I AM SO NERVOUS," said Meredith, looking out the window at the great rolling blue mountains, a scene familiar, yet part of a whole different life.

"I'm nervous for you. This is a pretty big deal."

"I'm so glad you're here with me."

"I am, too."

They listened to the music, in mellow, comfortable silence. Meredith looked at Gabe and Celeste, both slumbering in the backseat.

"They're so cute," she said quietly, smiling.

"Yes, they are." Tara glanced briefly at Meredith. "So let me ask you this, Merry. Is there any part of you that still has feelings for him, too?"

Meredith's jaw dropped. "No! Of course not. How can you even ask me that?"

"It wouldn't take away from your love for Nick, you know. These things are very complex."

"Tara, I'm telling you. There is nothing, absolutely nothing there. Please don't ask me that again."

"Point taken. Consider the subject closed."

Meredith stared forward, annoyed. "Do you have feelings for any of your exes?"

"No, but I can acknowledge that some of them are hot."

Meredith rolled her eyes, her anger already dulled. "You're supposed to be helping, not making me more stressed out."

"Sorry, Merry. I'll turn in my best friend badge."

"No, you will not." Meredith playfully slapped her arm. "I'll forgive you, provided I get extra Celeste snuggle time."

"That I can help you with."

They arrived in Wellbourne midafternoon and pulled into Sarah and Charles's driveway as they were preparing lunch. After hugs and introductions, they all sat down to eat. They caught up on each other's lives, and Meredith listened eagerly as they told her about Wes's condition. The family laughed at Tara's quick quips and raucous sense of humor. Meredith smiled gratefully: she could always count on her friend to help dispel the darkness.

As lunch came to a close, Meredith's stomach clenched into knots. She became unable to contribute to the conversation, and unable to keep herself still. She was relieved when they stood and cleared the table. She turned to Sarah once they'd finished cleaning up.

"What's a good time for me to see him?" she asked. "I have to be honest. I'm incredibly nervous."

"I have no doubt you are." Sarah rubbed her arm. "It's upsetting, isn't it? To see someone you care about, so helpless and hurt."

"Very."

Sarah watched her carefully, her eyes narrowed with thought. "You know, darling..." She paused, then shook her head. "Never mind. We'll talk later." She sighed and ushered her toward the door. "Come on, now. Let me take you to Wes."

MEREDITH FOLLOWED Sarah up the walkway, the same walkway she'd first seen a year ago, the walkway that almost had been hers.

The tension in the air was palpable. Meredith's heart was pounding frantically with dread. She didn't want to see Catherine. She felt hurt, and guilty, and tired, and she was still processing her visit with her father. She didn't want to have to defend or explain herself. She didn't know how much further she could stretch.

Sarah opened the door, and the two of them stepped inside. Meredith was struck again by the beauty of the house, its elegance and grace. Catherine was standing there waiting. Her face was stony, her posture straight. She accepted a hug from Sarah, then turned to Meredith and extended her hand.

"Hi, Meredith." Her voice was calm, but full of emotion; she was on the verge of tears, and Meredith's heart broke for her. "I hope you had a good trip. Can I get you anything?"

Meredith took her hand and shook her head, incapable of speech. She locked eyes with her, hoping the other woman could sense she felt her pain.

Catherine retracted her hand and took a breath. "Okay, then." She nodded. "Wes is upstairs."

She went first, then Sarah, then Meredith. The three women walked down the hall to the master bedroom. Meredith put her hand to her heart, hoping to steady it.

The room was bright and airy, with mint green walls and soft white linens, a four-poster bed in the middle, atop a Persian rug. Wes lay in bed, half-sitting under the blankets, in classic blue button-down pajamas. Catherine went right to him; she gave him a kiss and bent low, whispering to him, clearly checking on how he felt and whether he needed anything. She reached for a little cup containing some pills, then passed him some water and helped him take them. After she'd stepped aside to clear away some dishes, Sarah approached him and hugged him as carefully as she could, kissing his temple with closed, mournful eyes.

Meredith hung back, afraid. The scene was so personal, so intimate; she felt out of place, an intruder.

Catherine approached with an awkward smile.

"Please go right in," she told Meredith, gesturing with her hand toward the bed. She looked at Wes, and her face firmed slightly; she was his nurse now, and she was clearly comfortable being in charge. "I'll be downstairs if you need me."

Sarah blew him a kiss and left the room, and Catherine followed a moment later. She put her hand on the doorknob and paused a moment. Then she shut the door quietly, and then she was gone.

Meredith turned to Wes. He was looking at her from across the room.

"Well, come on in, stranger." While his words were cheerful, his voice was somehow quieter. He waved his hand toward himself. "Have a seat, and stay for a while."

Meredith walked slowly toward the bed. She sat down beside him and put her hand on his.

"Wes, my dear friend." The tears had risen already; she'd been trying to hold them back. "I'm so sorry to see you like this."

"Ah," he said, in that more tempered voice, tossing his hand up as if it were nothing. "It looks worse than it is. I'm going to be okay."

She smiled and squeezed his hand, brushing away tears with her other hand.

"Are you in much pain?" she asked.

He tilted his head, seeming to consider. "I could say no, but I'm too tired for sugarcoating."

She exhaled and took a deep breath, already out of words.

"Meredith," he said. "It's going to be okay. This"—he held his hand out and gestured downward toward his chest and then outward toward the room—"it's small potatoes. It could have been much worse. I'm grateful that it wasn't. I'm just happy to be here."

Meredith nodded and smiled in earnest. Then she laughed. "I can't believe you're comforting me. That's not how it's supposed to work."

"Have you ever known me not to take the lead?"

Meredith shook her head and laughed again. "No. I guess it fits."

He was looking at her, his eyes on her face. "Tell me, how is the book?"

"Oh," she said, tossing her hand up and blowing her nose with a tissue she'd picked from the nightstand. "It's fine. I don't want to talk about that."

"Is your father much worse?"

She nodded, fighting off a renewal of tears. "Yes, he is."

He exhaled slowly. "Meredith. I'm sorry."

She sniffled and attempted to shake it off. "What a year it's been."

"Amen."

She took a moment to collect herself, and indulged in a deep, calming breath. When she lifted her gaze, he was still studying her. She smiled, a little bashfully.

He took a deep breath, and his face turned serious. Meredith settled where she sat, sensing the conversation was beginning.

"You know, Meredith," he said, fidgeting with something on the blanket, "as you can probably imagine, this has given me a lot of time to think. And oh, have I been thinking. Too much, probably, if you want to know the truth."

Meredith listened patiently, waiting for him to continue.

"I've been thinking about that night, of course, and how terrified I was."

"Of course," she whispered, her face soft with sympathy. "You must be traumatized."

He lifted his eyebrows in agreement, then sighed. "I wish I could say that was the worst of it. The thoughts about myself, about my life." He closed his eyes a moment. "They torment me."

"Wes." She placed her hand on his once more. "Something like this is bound to do that. I'm sure it's so very normal."

He was watching her in silence, his expression grim. "I have some things I need to say to you." He closed his eyes and swallowed, then opened them and looked at her once more. "Please. Hear me out until I'm through."

Meredith nodded, her eyes wide.

He looked at her for some time in silence, his jaw working as if he was gathering his strength to speak.

"Catherine's been a little upset," he said. "She says I'm still in love with you."

Meredith said nothing. Her heart seemed to stop beating.

"She's been insisting it's true for quite some time. I've denied it, of course."

Meredith couldn't hold his gaze. She looked downward at her hands, nearly dying of suspense.

Her eyes lowered, she heard him speak.

"She isn't wrong."

She sat completely still, save for the rising and falling of her chest. She dared to lift her gaze upward. His eyes were so gentle, she nearly lost her breath; he was looking at her so tenderly, and she flushed, overcome.

"Wes—"

"Please. Just listen."

Meredith looked around desperately, unable to meet his eyes. Her lips parted as she struggled to catch her breath.

"Meredith, please look at me."

She closed her lips and swallowed, and forced herself to look.

He was smiling sadly, his eyes now warm. "It's true. I never stopped loving you. I lied to my wife, many times." He took a breath. "After I told her I always keep my promises."

Meredith was determined not to speak. She waited for him to continue.

"I loved you," he said, "the very first moment I saw you. You remember?"

She suppressed a sly grin. Sure, she remembered. She'd just moved in across the street from him outside Washington. She'd been gardening that day, and had soaked herself with the hose. When she looked up, he'd been standing there, staring at her from his porch.

A little grin touched his lips. "We had good times, back then."

Meredith nodded, more comfortably now. She took a deep breath and let him go on.

"After you left, I tried to move on. I moved down here hoping it would help." He shook his head. "It didn't. Nothing did. Not even meeting my future wife."

Meredith thought of Catherine downstairs, the sweet, kind woman she'd inadvertently hurt.

"I knew I had to let go," he went on. "What was the point in not moving on? It was over between us. I would never have you back." He closed his eyes for a moment, then opened them and continued. "I went through the motions of living my life. I pretended everything was fine. But I was living a lie. I thought of you, always. I knew it was wrong. I knew I was hurting my wife." He shrugged. "I want to say I couldn't help it. But I can't absolve myself of the responsibility. Now's not the time to make excuses." He closed his eyes again. "Please give me a minute. I'm sorry."

Meredith watched him in silence. His chest rose and fell. She had promised she wouldn't speak, but was worried he was in pain. She was about to ask if he needed something, when he opened his eyes and went on.

"I allowed you to be an unwilling player in this. I got you involved. All because I couldn't let go, or wouldn't. I apologize for that."

She rubbed her lips together, looking at him with sympathy.

"All that being said."

A few moments of silence passed.

"A brush with death will make you get a grip real quick. I see now that it's all smoke and mirrors. The pedestal's an illusion. It isn't real." He was watching her intently, his eyes now serious. "I know you and I could never make it."

She inhaled and exhaled, waiting for more.

He looked at her warmly, and his voice grew even softer. "You, Meredith—you're the only thing that's ever made me come undone. From the first time I saw you. I was so used to being in control. And with you, I rushed decisions. I lost my self-control. So much so, that I jeopardized my marriage, and my life." He inhaled deeply and swallowed, and his eyes grew glassy with tears. "And that's why I have to say goodbye to you."

Meredith's eyes widened, then lowered to the bed as he took a moment to collect himself. She focused on her breathing, even and deep; she was grateful for those moments, in which she calmed her racing heart.

"What happened to me last Saturday." He shook his head. "It's made me realize how ridiculous I've been. All this time, when I could have been truly happy. When I had everything I needed. What the hell have I been doing? Because Catherine"—he gestured toward the door with his finger—"she's the real deal, the true love of my life. I'm at my best with her. I'm not afraid. There are no games. She does that to me. And she doesn't even realize she's doing it."

Meredith's eyes now clouded with tears. She picked another tissue from the nightstand, and he gave her a minute to compose herself.

"Sweetheart," he said. "You made me come undone. But Catherine. She puts me back together."

Meredith smiled and took his hand. He squeezed it, and they sat there in silence, until he patted her hand and sighed.

"Thank you for sharing all this," she whispered. She cleared her throat and blew her nose. "It takes a lot of courage."

"I'm a coward, Meredith. I've always been. I'm trying to make up for lost time."

"No, you're not," she said, her voice a little firmer. "You're just figuring it out, like everyone else."

He was watching her thoughtfully. "Did you know? Didn't you have any idea?"

"You know, it's hard to tell with you." She smiled, her eyes glistening. "You always put on a good show." She turned more serious. "I think maybe I knew, on some deep level. Maybe I told myself you didn't, because it would have made it harder to be friends."

"I can understand that," he said, "especially if you didn't feel it, too."

Meredith's smile dimmed, and her heartbeat picked up speed. She felt her blood racing as her mind worked furiously.

And then, she let it happen—let a feeling rise from the deepest, darkest corners of her heart. It was a feeling she'd forced into the shadows, where it wouldn't be seen by anyone, not even by herself.

"Wes, Nick is my soulmate," she said, barely recognizing her own voice for its shaking. "He truly makes me whole, and I love him more than life itself. He's the only man in the world for me. I never knew there was love this strong." Her hands were mindlessly fidgeting; her heart was hammering in her chest. "Which is why"—she paused, choosing her words carefully—"which is why"—tears rose here, and she let them come—"which is why I can not say I feel it too, not even a little, in a tiny, hidden, sliver of a part of me—I can't say it."

He looked at her with a funny expression; then understanding reached his eyes. It was surprise, and eagerness, and pain—and for a moment, she regretted what she'd said. She'd been so careful to conceal it, to avoid complication and to preserve the purity of her one true love.

But no. This would be her only chance. She wouldn't admit it outright; she wouldn't grant it that strength. But she'd had to meet his honesty—she wanted to give him that.

They stared at each other knowingly, many unsaid words between them. He squeezed her hand and smiled, her words seeming to give him some life.

"You and Nick are perfect, you know." He was smiling brightly now, and the sight warmed her heart. "You really are. That's what's funny, is I couldn't even be upset. You were clearly so happy. And that was more important."

"Well, I think it all worked out."

He appeared to be very tired; he'd closed his eyes again. Meredith knew she didn't have much time left with him.

She asked the question that broke her heart.

"Will I ever see you again?"

He opened his eyes and looked at her; there was a long, thoughtful pause. "I'll tell you what, sweetheart. Let's not talk about that now." He grinned. "I'm not supposed to call you 'sweetheart.' My wife doesn't like it."

Meredith smiled tearfully. "I can't say I blame her. Maybe you should stop."

"I had to do it just one more time."

They sighed and looked at each other, preparing to part ways.

"Tell Nick I said hello," he said. "And give Gabe a little kiss for me."

"I will." She swallowed against the renewal of her tears. "I'm really happy for you, Wes. You have a beautiful family."

"Thank you. I'm really happy, too."

She leaned in and kissed his cheek; he lay still and let her do it. Then she squeezed his hand, met his gaze, and walked to the door to leave him.

She glanced over her shoulder at him one last time. He was watching her walk away, and he waved as she disappeared into the hallway.

CHAPTER TWENTY-EIGHT

atherine turned off the intercom when she heard
Meredith leave the bedroom.

She hastily wiped her tears on a napkin, sniffling and straightening and getting herself under control.

She heard Meredith's footsteps on the stairs; she stood from the kitchen table.

She met her in the hallway as she entered the room. The two women faced each other in silence.

"Thank you for coming," said Catherine finally. "I know it means a lot to him."

"Thank you for letting me. I'm sure it wasn't easy."

Catherine stared at Meredith, whose eyes were puffy and red. It was obvious Meredith was not trying to hide anything. Catherine had to respect her transparency.

"It wasn't as hard as I thought it would be," she said. She hesitated. "I'm sorry for yelling at you yesterday."

"No, no. Don't apologize. I completely understand."

Catherine's lips held the shadow of a smile. "Thanks."

Meredith looked very tired. Catherine knew the feeling.

Emotions were exhausting, especially hard ones. And it seemed more and more that all emotions were hard.

"Where's Sarah?" asked Meredith. "I should probably go."

"She's outside doing some gardening. I kill everything I touch."

"Well, you certainly seem to have done a good job with Wes."

Catherine smiled. "I guess that's true."

"He's a really lucky man, you know." Meredith's eyes were tearful. "It's obvious how much you love him. And Catherine." She shook and inhaled, appearing to stifle a cry. "He really loves you, too."

Catherine watched as she dabbed at her eyes with her tissue. She knew this must be difficult for Meredith; she knew she hadn't wanted this. The ugly dark feeling was fading. She felt the old Catherine return.

"I know he does. But I appreciate your telling me, too."

They hugged goodbye, and Meredith found Sarah outside. Sarah and Catherine chatted for a minute, then Sarah and Meredith drove off.

CATHERINE CLIMBED THE STAIRCASE. She walked to the master bedroom.

He was staring out the window, his head resting against the pillow. At her entrance, he turned. His face brightened, and he patted the bed beside him.

"Come here, sweetheart. I want to talk to you."

Catherine joined him on the bed. He rubbed her thigh and smiled. She snuggled closer, and he took her hand.

She looked at his face, and started: his eyes suddenly were full of tears.

"What's wrong?" she asked, her hand on his cheek, watching him take in every detail of her face.

"Catherine, sweetheart," he said, and inhaled dramatically as the first cries took him. "I am so sorry. I have not been fair to you."

She leaned forward and held him, and he wrapped his arms around her waist. He shook and gasped, and she let him, waiting patiently until he could speak once more.

"I lied to you. I led you on. I made you think it was all in your head. It was cruel of me, and selfish. I hope you can forgive me."

She closed her eyes and nodded, tears falling over her cheeks and nose.

"You are the greatest love of my life," he went on. "You are the culmination of all my searching. And I'm so blessed that it ended with you. I don't even deserve you. But I'm so grateful that of everyone in this world, you've chosen me."

Catherine sniffled and wiped her eyes, hugging him tighter and listening to his cries.

"Catherine," he said, and pulled back to look at her. She brought her fingers to his face and wiped away a tear. "You have my full heart. There is no one else but you." His eyes searched hers. "Do you believe me?"

"Yes." She nodded and cried, letting him pull her forehead to his. "Yes, I do believe you."

"Good. Because I love you, Catherine. I love you so much it hurts. I love you like...like Schiaparelli loves metallic threads woven through silk with a velveteen appliqué and an organza underskirt."

"That much, huh?" She laughed. "I'm just kidding. That doesn't even make any sense."

He laughed, too. "Your laugh. It's the most beautiful sound in the world."

"No, it's not. It's the sound of your voice, because it means that you're here."

He hugged her close again, and they said nothing for quite some time.

They pulled apart and sat together, holding hands and stroking each other's faces.

"Sweetheart."

She met his gaze and waited.

"I shouldn't have invited her to visit last summer. That was cruel to you. I'm so sorry."

Catherine smiled soberly. "Maybe you thought it would help to see her one more time."

Wes said nothing, but looked at her sorrowfully. Catherine took it as agreement.

"Wes," she said. "Do you remember when I asked if you were having an affair, and you told me you weren't? You said, 'May God strike me dead if I'm lying.'" She regarded him knowingly. "And look what happened. You got shot."

He smiled then, a beautiful sight. "Well, I wasn't lying, sweetheart. I wasn't having an affair. I guess getting shot and surviving was God's way of reminding me there are shades of truth."

They held each other in comfortable silence. Then he leaned back and sighed.

"I have to tell you. That night." He closed his eyes and shook his head, then spoke in a shaky whisper. "I can barely even talk about it."

"You don't have to right now, if you don't want to." She smoothed his hair, and he tilted his head in submission to her gentle touch. "But I think at some point, you should."

"I keep reliving it." He paused a few moments, his eyes still closed. "To see you like that, to think of him hurting you." He swallowed. "Then looking down the barrel of that gun."

She kissed his forehead and brushed her cheek against his head, letting him take his time.

"I just knew we were both going to die right in that workshop, that we'd never see Amy again. I'd never have the chance to apologize. I'd never have the chance to make it right." His voice choked, and he paused a moment. "And all I could think about was that it was my fault."

"No, it wasn't your fault." Her face crinkled, and she felt tears rise. "It was my fault, for not locking the door."

He looked at her then, with a gentle smile. "That doesn't make it your fault, sweetheart. An unlocked door is not an invitation."

She nodded, wanting to believe him.

"Rick Tremaine. I can't believe it came to this." He took a deep breath, and his face contorted. "I should have taken action sooner. I knew how scared you had been. You have to live with the attack forever. I'll never forgive myself for that."

"You should forgive yourself. You took a bullet to save me."

"I'll never forget the look on his face, or the look on your face as I walked down those stairs. And then after." She sensed the growing anxiety in him, and held him tighter. "Being dependent for the most basic needs. Being at the mercy of the pain." His voice shook. "The pure horror of it all, feeling ripped apart and mangled. It's very hard to take."

"I was thinking, Wes. You should talk to a therapist. We both should. This kind of psychological trauma won't go away by itself."

"I think you're right."

She knew they'd work this through together, for as long as it took to find peace. She smiled and looked toward the window, where sunlight filtered in through the curtains.

"I was thinking of something else," he said. He patted her thigh. "How would you feel about moving your workshop? It would be nice if you didn't have to leave to make your chocolate."

"I was thinking about that, too. I'd like to do it. And I don't think I could ever work in that workshop again."

"What would you like to do with your grandmother's house? We could rent it out if you'd prefer not to sell it."

"No, let's sell it. I think it's time."

After a few moments, he took her hand.

"That night," he said. "You told me you'd been hiding your anxiety. That you didn't want me to see it." Tears swam in his eyes once more, and he squeezed her hand tight. "Please don't think you have to hide it from me. I don't want you to do that. I don't want to be a source of your stress. I want to help you, by being involved and by being better."

"You were never a source of my stress, Wes. It was because I love you, because you always seemed so perfect."

"Well, clearly I'm not perfect. So I think we can let that go." He looked at her, his eyes studying hers. "Will you talk to me more, from now on? Please?"

She smiled sadly. "I will. I promise."

He paused a moment before continuing. "You also said you're not the sharpest, that you don't catch everything." He rubbed her hand, his fingers brushing with gentleness over her skin. "You don't give yourself enough credit. You caught more than you thought you did. But also..." He pressed his lips together and furrowed his brow, thinking. "Your outlook, your vision of the world." He smiled. "It's a beautiful thing. I aspire to have that, too."

"You want to be more like me?" Her skin tingled pleasantly at the soft touch of his fingers on her neck and jawline, and she closed her eyes, soaking in the shivers. "I've always wanted to be more like you."

"Don't you change a thing, sweetheart. I love you exactly the way you are. And I intend to spend the rest of my life trying to be worthy of you."

She leaned down and kissed him with his face in her hands. He tilted his head up, eagerly meeting her, and sighing as her lips moved with his. In that moment, the world was perfect. And so was he, and so was she.

CHAPTER TWENTY-NINE

*T*he ride back to Sarah's was quiet. Sarah comforted and sympathized with Meredith, and they talked a little about how hard it had been for the family. But largely they were silent, Meredith's sniffling the only sound.

They arrived at the house and entered the foyer. Meredith had been planning on excusing herself quickly; she wanted to check in with Tara and Gabe, and she desperately wanted to talk to Nick. But before she could climb the stairs toward her room, Sarah placed her hand on her arm and spoke to her quietly, in a confidential tone.

"What did he tell you?"

Meredith froze. "What do you mean?"

Sarah gave her a chastising look. "Darling, now's not the time to be obscure."

Meredith stared at her. "Are you asking if he told me he had feelings for me? Because if you are, then the answer is yes."

Sarah's face registered her understanding. She stood back a little and nodded. "I thought he might. I'm glad he did. This has gone on for far too long."

"What has?"

Sarah looked at her meaningfully, her jaw taut. She sighed. "You know, Meredith...I've always been torn. I suppose I was an idealist. I thought we could all be adults, we could all love each other, and everything would be magically fine." She waved her hand above her head and smiled. She then folded her arms, shifting her weight to one hip. "You know I've always been so very fond of you. And your father, well! It's been an honor to be his friend."

Meredith's face had begun to take on a rueful smile. She understood where Sarah was going.

"But..." Sarah sighed again and looked at her candidly. "Life...it intervenes, does it not?"

Meredith nodded and wiped a few tears from her eyes. "Yes, it sure does." She took a moment to collect herself. "Wes called me down here to say goodbye."

Sarah was watching her, her face warm, but sad. "Darling, as much as I adore you." Her eyes glistened with her own tears. "I think it's best."

"I understand." Meredith took her hand. "Of course, I'm very sad. Wes is a good friend, and I love your family." She squeezed her hand. "But if I were in your shoes, I would feel the same way."

Sarah clicked her tongue and pulled Meredith in close, and the two stood in an embrace for a minute before Sarah pulled away.

"I want to be updated in regards to your father," she said. "Please promise me you'll keep me informed."

"I promise."

Sarah sighed. "Life is hard, and wonderful."

"It definitely is both of those things."

They embraced again. Meredith took a moment to commit this feeling to memory—the joy of female friendship with this strong, smart woman, with her silver hair and eloquent voice; the comfort she provided, and the memories of how she'd acted as a mother when her relationship with her own mother was so complicated; and the warmth of the house in which she'd been

CATHERINE AND THE WIND

blessed with happy times. Then she went to her room, took out her phone, and called her husband.

~

"So how did it go?"

Meredith curled up on the chair by the window and looked out onto the front lawn. "It was good. Great, actually. We had a good talk." She paused. "We said goodbye. At least for a time. That's why he wanted to see me. He told me Catherine was right."

"Wow." He was silent for a moment. "Did you leave on good terms?"

"Oh, definitely." She couldn't help but smile. "It was very sad. But kind of a celebration, too. I mean, he's still alive. He's had a lot of time to think. It was refreshing to have an honest conversation, you know?"

"Mmm." Nick appeared to be thinking, himself. "Was it awkward at all? When he told you?"

"A little. But it wasn't too bad. It was all within context of his relationship with Catherine. And when the two stack up, there's no comparison."

"I guess something like this makes you put things in perspective."

"I guess so." Meredith's chest began tightening with emotion. "Listen, honey...with everything going on now, all the people I'm having to say goodbye to..." She felt the familiar rush of tears, and she didn't fight it. "It's just reiterated to me how fortunate I am to have you by my side."

"Merry," he said softly, waiting as she sniffled. "I thank my lucky stars every day for you."

"I do, too." She took a deep breath. "I can't wait to get home. I miss you so much. I just want to snuggle up close, or go for a hike on Aspen Woods Mountain, or have a picnic in the open field. To just have some normalcy again."

"I know. I can't wait. But I think it was good you went down there. Sometimes people just need closure."

"I hope it helped him. I think it did. I just wish it wasn't ending this way."

"Well, who knows. Maybe after enough time passes, you'll be able to talk again."

Meredith nodded and sighed.

"When I get home," she said, "I have to finish this book. I'd like my father to see it published, if I can manage it."

"Just let me know if I can help."

"You already do," she said, smiling through tears. "More than you ever could know."

MEREDITH AND VINCE went back to Philadelphia one month later. This time, their families joined them.

Gabe and Julia pattered around the house, their cheerful innocence contrasting with, and alleviating slightly, the somber mood. Patricia was composed and quiet, as self-possessed as always. But Meredith noticed that her eyes were often red, and the lines in her face looked more pronounced. Her hair, usually perfect, was a little more disheveled, and she seemed to have forsaken her jewelry. The year had aged her, as very well it should. Meredith worried about her mother being alone.

She discussed it with Nick. They agreed they should invite her to live in the apartment.

"I appreciate it, dear," said Patricia. "But it's out of the question."

"But why?" Meredith pleaded. "You'd be up there with all your family. You'd have nothing to worry about. You'd never be lonely."

"I like my house. And I have friends here. I won't be lonely, dear. But thank you."

Meredith sighed and let it drop. But she vowed to bring it up later, to see if she'd changed her mind.

Harold was drawn and tired. He tried his best to be cheerful for Gabe. And he always smiled when the little boy entered the room.

"Kids," he said, shaking his head. "You've got to love them. There's nothing like them to show you life goes on."

Nick and Jenny took Gabe and Julia outside so Harold could talk to Meredith and Vince. Meredith was glad Vince had this time with their father. It was honest, introspective time, during which they put many demons to rest.

Vince emerged from the room shaking with tears. Meredith hugged him and held him close, saying nothing, patting his back.

"I'm going to miss that cranky old bastard," he said, pulling away and rubbing his eyes with his hands. "I never realized how dependent I'd become on his hassling me."

"Did you get anything worked out, Vince?"

"Oh, yeah. For sure." He sighed and tried to smile. "Dad came through. And I think I did, too."

"I'm so glad to hear it." Meredith rubbed his arm. "I truly believe he's always been proud of you. I think he was so proud, he was afraid of it."

"That's exactly what he told me, Merry."

Harold wanted to see Meredith. Vince patted her back on his way downstairs. She straightened, braced herself, and entered the room, holding a special item behind her back.

The lights had been dimmed so Harold could rest. Meredith couldn't get used to the change in his appearance. His skin was wan, and his frame was thin and frail. And without the shock of black hair, he was barely recognizable as her father.

He was breathing deeply, but slowly. It was hard for him to be awake now, as the pain was always present. Meredith watched him for a few moments before he noticed her. How amazing he was, she thought. He'd hardened himself to survive, had made his heart inaccessible when it had continued to be broken. He'd refused to let down his defenses, sacrificing the warmth of his relationships to preserve the safety of isolation. Instead, he'd dedicated his life to fighting for those less fortunate, to speaking out fearlessly for those who couldn't speak for themselves. He'd tried to hold government and politicians accountable; he'd been a true defender. It was his way of vindicating the tender-hearted boy he'd been, of compensating for the softness he'd been forced to renounce. His Achilles' heel had been his grandchildren; he'd never been able to hold up the front with them. He'd treated his illness as just one more foe; it had put up its hand, and he'd told it, *Not yet.*

He was tortured and imperfect and overly rigid. But he had done his best. He'd never gone down without fighting. And he'd leave this world a better place than it would have been without him.

"I don't have all day, you know."

Meredith was drawn from her thoughts by his raspy voice. She stepped into the room and approached him slowly.

"Can I get you anything?"

"Just yourself. Sit down, daughter."

Meredith walked toward the chair by the bed.

Harold was watching her. "You're hiding something behind your back. The book, I presume." He gestured with his hand. "Might as well let me see it now. No reason to make it a big dramatic moment."

She sat in the chair and held it out for him. He looked her in the eye as he took it, then directed his attention to the book in his hand.

"'*Through My Eyes*, by Harold Beck and Meredith Beck Kelly,'" he read, perusing the cover. He turned to her. "You decided to share my byline."

"It isn't that I want any credit," she said hastily. "I—" She stopped. She hadn't expected to grow so emotional so soon. "I wanted a connection to the experience. Of working with you." She firmed herself. "Of being your daughter."

He flipped through the pages. "You don't have to justify it. You deserve it." He stared at it a moment longer, then rested it by his side. "My apologies for not being able to read. I'm so tired."

"I understand."

"It looks beautiful." He looked at her. "So do you."

Meredith's eyebrows rose. "I don't think you've ever said that to me before."

"Just in under the wire."

Meredith watched him watching her. For the second time, she waited for the man lying in the bed to empty his heart and his conscience to her.

"You really came through," he told her. "Thank you."

Meredith shrugged and smiled sadly. "I was happy to do it."

"I gave you hell. You took it admirably." He nodded in deference. "You're one hell of a woman."

Her smile softened. "Thank you, Dad. That means a lot to me."

"Hold my hand, Meredith."

Meredith scooted her chair forward and took his hand in hers. He brought it to his lips and kissed it, making Meredith shake with tears.

"Now, now. None of that. I've already been through that with Vince. You wouldn't think a rascal like him capable of tears, but that boy bawled like a baby."

"Vince is more sensitive than you'd think," she said, dabbing at her eyes with her other hand. "Just like someone else I know."

"Yes. So the secret's out. Your father, the great Harold Beck. A softie at heart."

"There's nothing wrong with that."

Her father was silent for a moment or two.

"This is the part where I'd offer you some reflections about my life," he said, "but you already know everything."

"You can say whatever you'd like, Dad. I'm willing to listen to anything you have to say."

"Yes." He took a few breaths as he studied her. "You have shown your willingness to do this, throughout your entire life."

Meredith offered a soft smile, but said nothing.

Her father went on. "Just because I didn't acknowledge it," he said, "doesn't mean I didn't see it."

Meredith's smile faded, and tears pricked at her eyes.

"You're a brave, smart, compassionate person. My greatest accomplishment."

She didn't try to control her tears. She blew her nose and smiled at him, squeezing his hand and meeting his gaze lovingly.

"I wasted so much time being abrasive," he said. "I have so many regrets."

"Your abrasiveness is part of your charm. I wouldn't have changed it."

A grin touched his eyes, and he chuckled a little, silently. "Well. It's good of you to say that."

Meredith turned serious once more. "It was an honor to work on this book with you. Thank you for entrusting me with this very important job."

"I entrusted you with it because I knew you could handle it. And me."

Meredith smiled. "I know."

"Thank you for being a good daughter. Even when I didn't deserve it." He paused for a moment, closing his eyes. "I'm sorry, Meredith. I'm so tired."

"No, no. You should rest." She tucked in his blanket and moved the book to the nightstand. "And you always deserved it."

"I love you, sweet daughter. I always have. More than you know."

Meredith kissed him and patted his hand. He was asleep almost instantly. Meredith tiptoed from the room, then walked outside into the sunshine in search of her husband and little boy.

~

BACK IN MAINE, Nick continued working weekends as site manager on the Henley home, and Meredith resumed her responsibilities on the board. It was a relief to be outside with the cheerful volunteers; it helped refresh and center her after the emotional upheaval of the previous couple of months.

Meredith also published Harold's book. The launch was a wild success. She'd contacted book reviewers and Harold's connections at the *Philadelphia Times*, and it hadn't taken long for word to get out. It was featured by every major outlet, to raving, stellar reviews. It seemed Harold Beck indeed was going out with a bang, and the support he received warmed Meredith's heart. She was grateful to have helped make his final project possible. She was relieved it was doing so well organically, without her having to put too much energy into promotion. And she was overjoyed that her father was alive to hear the good news.

"You did it yourself, just the way you wanted," she told him on one of her visits. "And people love you for exactly who you are."

"We did it together. They love you, too. And it pleases me that you'll reap the rewards."

She became in high demand; everyone wanted to hear about the writing of the book and her experiences with her father.

"The *Times* wants to interview me," she said to Nick as he walked into the kitchen one evening, her face in her laptop. "I think that'll really help, if I can find the time."

"Well, you don't have time tonight, because we're going out, just you and me."

Meredith looked at him with surprise—he was all dressed up, in dark slacks and a white dress shirt.

"And don't even try to tell me you have anything else to do," he went on, pointing his finger at her, but with a grin in his eyes, "because there's nothing you can do to get out of it."

"I can't remember the last time I saw you in anything dressier than jeans," she said, a smile creeping onto her face.

"I hope you approve."

"Indeed," she said slyly, eyeing him up and down.

At that moment, Vince and Jenny burst in, little Julia toddling behind.

"Let me guess," said Meredith, leaning back in her chair. "You're here to watch Gabe."

Vince scooped Gabe up from off the floor. "That's where you're wrong, Merry. We're here to take Gabe." Meredith watched as Jenny took a bag handed to her by Nick. "He's spending the night at our place. You two have a night to yourselves."

"Really?" Meredith couldn't help but brighten.

"Really," said Nick, approaching her chair. "I booked us a room at the Roseview."

Meredith's eyes widened, and her mouth opened. "Are you serious? That place is exorbitant!"

"It's also the most romantic place in town," said Jenny, smiling girlishly. "Isn't that exciting?"

Meredith had turned to Jenny; now she turned back to Nick. "I can't believe you did this."

"I did." He held out his hand. "So are you coming?"

Meredith's heart pitter-pattered with excitement. She smiled and took his hand. "Well, I can't very well say no."

THEY ENJOYED an elegant dinner in Asterfield. The restaurant sat right on the bay, and their outdoor table offered a delightful view of the docks, which were bustling with activity. Across the water were the tree-covered hills of the isles, including Dearham. She inhaled and exhaled, letting the placidity of the landscape seep into her soul. The raw, heady scent of the water filled her lungs.

Meredith leaned back in her seat and sipped her wine, her eyes appreciating Nick as he took in the scene. The setting sun cast shadows on the sharp features of his face; it illuminated his golden hair as it fell in crests over his temples.

He turned to her and smiled, holding out his hand. "Are you relaxed yet?" he asked.

She took his hand and returned his smile. "I'd say I'm ninety-five percent relaxed."

"How can I get the other five percent?"

"I'm not sure it's possible. At least, not for the time being."

They were silent for a moment or two, watching the boats on the water.

"Hey, Merry."

Meredith looked at him and blinked a few times—she was determined not to give in to tears tonight.

"I'm really proud of you," he said. "You did a great job on your dad's book." He squeezed her hand; his eyes crinkled kindly in the corners. "You pushed through, and you did it."

"Thanks." There was fondness in her smile, but sadness too. "You know, it's funny. While I was working on it, I just wanted to see it done. Now that it's done..." She frowned with thought. "It feels anticlimactic, like a letdown."

"I don't think it's anticlimactic at all. The book's selling really well. It's getting a whole lot of attention, which means your dad's thoughts are being heard."

"I know." She didn't know how to explain it; she didn't even fully understand it. "It's just that it was his final project. And now it's over." She shrugged, and the tears came, despite her efforts to stop them. "It's like...his life's work is now..."

He squeezed her hand and looked at her with sympathetic eyes. "It's not, though, Merry," he said softly. "Because it's out there now, forever."

A sorrowful smile touched her lips, and she wiped some tears from her cheeks. "It's not just that." She paused to catch her breath. "As hard as it was on me...I enjoyed working with him."

"Merry, there's nothing I can say to take that pain away. I love you, though. And I'm here for you."

Meredith was too overcome to respond. They held hands across the table as she rubbed at her eyes and composed herself.

"I know you are," she whispered. "That's the one thing I always know."

They looked out onto the water, which was choppy with the wake of boats on evening cruises. The waves glistened with the golden glow of the setting sun, which hung on the horizon, leaving darkness in its path.

"It just made me feel connected to him," she said finally. "And it made me feel important, like I was working toward a great accomplishment."

"It's not your only accomplishment, Merry. There will be lots to work toward in the future."

They smiled at each other. Meredith's heart lightened a little as they passed a few moments in meaningful silence.

"Thank you for seeing me through this," she said. "For being so patient and for always trying to help. I know I've been preoc-cupied, and probably not myself."

"You don't have to thank me. That's what we do. We're here for each other, right?"

After dinner, they strolled hand in hand through Asterfield, poking in shops and admiring the view of the bay from the docks. The little town was magical in the evening, its lights twinkling against the indigo sky, the soft, rhythmic sound of the water in the background. Meredith snuggled up against him as they walked up and down the street and through the park. He wrapped his arm around her and kissed her head; she leaned her head against his chest and smiled, grateful for this quiet time with him.

"It was nice of Vince and Jenny to take Gabe for us," she said as they wandered leisurely toward the Roseview. "It sure will be nice to get some rest."

"Who said anything about rest?"

She stopped and looked up at him with a raised brow, a grin spreading across her face. "In a bold mood, are we?"

"Yes," he laughed. He took her hips in his hands and pulled her close. "I've got you all to myself tonight," he said then, his soft voice now smooth as silk. He kissed her a few times, each lasting longer than the one before. "I'm not going to waste it."

A little hum escaped her as his lips claimed hers, moving so slowly, his hands now sliding along her back. "Rest is highly over-rated," she murmured hazily.

"Who needs it?"

She brought her hands up his chest, taking the time to admire his firm, lean strength. She let her fingers trail from his shoulders to his biceps. She imagined his arms holding her, his hands grip-ping her, and she sighed as her blood tingled with anticipation.

"I'm going to get that five percent," he said, nudging her, as he pulled his lips from hers. Meredith gazed at him, his handsome face now shrouded in the darkness of night: his eyes were full of mischief, and his lips were turned up into a playful grin.

"You know, I'm starting to believe you." She tilted her head as he kissed her neck, her eyes drifting shut and her hand slipping to the back of his head. "You've already gotten two or three."

"Then I've got it in the bag," he said, taking her hands and pulling her toward the inn. "I haven't even gotten started yet."

She laughed and let him lead her, warmth encircling her heart and prickling pleasantly at her skin. In the cozy inn on the beau-tiful isle of the home she so loved, she surrendered to happiness and gratitude in the arms of the greatest love of her life.

$\sim$

Harold passed a few weeks later. The families drove down to Philadelphia one more time. Meredith was to give the eulogy. The pressure of having to summarize her relationship with her father, and her thoughts on her father's life, proved too much to bear.

"It's like I'm living in a fog," she told Nick. "I can't organize any of my thoughts. There's just so much. Where do I even start?"

"I wrote that letter I read at my father's funeral," he said. "Maybe I can help."

"That's right." She looked at him with a tearful smile. "I'd definitely like to hear what you have to say."

"It wasn't exactly a eulogy. I just wrote about how I felt."

"It was beautiful," she said, pulling her laptop close. "What advice can you give me?"

Hundreds of people attended Harold's funeral. Meredith was amazed and overcome. Mostly, she was grateful for the many kind words they shared about her father.

"He was one of the greatest voices of our time."

"I read his column for thirty years. It was always the highlight of my week."

"He brought something new to journalism."

"I always knew that when Harold Beck said something, it had to be true."

Meredith greeted them and sat through the service in a daze. She managed to keep her voice steady as she delivered her eulogy; she found strength in the crowd—in their rapt attention, in their enthusiastic responses to her anecdotes, and in their sheer numbers, knowing they were there to respect the man she'd been honored to call her father.

She talked about how his bluster belied his sensitivity, how underneath the sharp words hid a tender heart committed to helping others. She talked about his high standards, the way he had intimidated her—but how she'd always respected and admired him, and how working with him on his book provided her with deep insight into just how much he'd actually loved her.

She took her seat with a sense of relief, the burden finally lifted from her shoulders.

Nick wrapped his arm around her shoulder and looked at her with tears in his eyes.

"You did great, honey," he whispered, kissing her head and holding her tight. "That was perfect."

She leaned against him and sighed, waiting for her heartbeat to slow. "Thank you for helping me." She took his hand. "I couldn't have done it without you."

As the service continued, she closed her eyes, taking a moment to feel her father's presence.

I love you, Dad. I hope I made you proud.

After the service, they held a reception at one of Harold's favorite restaurants. Meredith talked with Sarah and Charles, first and foremost concerned about Wes's wellbeing.

"He's doing just fine, darling," said Sarah, her arm around Meredith's shoulder. "He has to take it easy, of course. But you know Wes. He's finally back on his feet, and as peppy as ever."

"I'm so happy to hear that. Please send him my warm regards. And Sarah, please give him this."

She held up her finger and went to her purse. She retrieved two copies of *Through My Eyes* and returned to Sarah.

"This one is for you," she said, handing her one copy. "My father signed it and wrote you a message."

"Oh," Sarah gasped, her hand at her heart, her face contorted with tears. She opened the book and read Harold's message. "How beautiful." She took a moment before speaking again. She sniffled and shook her head. "I'm sorry. It's just, his handwriting."

"I know." Meredith's eyes watered as she looked at her father's slanted, masculine hand. Usually neat, it was shaky and uneven. "It's hard to look at. But he cherished your friendship, right until the end."

"Thank you." She hugged Meredith tight, then kissed the book and held it up to the air.

"And this one is for Wes," said Meredith, handing the second book to Sarah. "He was such a big help. I mentioned him in the acknowledgments, and I hand wrote him a personal message." She looked at Sarah knowingly. "I hope that's okay."

"Oh, that's lovely, Meredith. He'll appreciate that."

"I want to respect his wishes, and Catherine's. But this felt too important not to do."

"I agree. It's beautiful." She hugged Meredith again. "I know he was happy to help."

"Sarah," said Meredith, hesitating. "I hope things have settled. Between Wes and Catherine."

"Darling, it's wonderful." Sarah rubbed her shoulder. "Sometimes things have a way of working themselves out, you know. Of course no one wanted this to happen. But as long as it did—well, it's brought them much closer. They're meant for each other, and they know it."

"There's nothing you could say that would make me happier. I'm really so glad for them both."

"I know you are, darling. Thank you for helping it happen."

Meredith and Patricia made the rounds at the reception, comforting some mourners, accepting comfort from others, and listening to stories about Harold. Meredith was impressed with the elite crowd that had gathered to celebrate his life. It was a reminder of how widely he had traveled, of how many important connections he'd made throughout his life.

Patricia carried herself with grace and composure, her eyes glistening, occasionally dabbing a stray tear with her handkerchief. She was reserved and quiet, seemingly not fully present in conversations with guests.

"How are you holding up, Mom?" asked Meredith, rubbing her mother's slim back. "Do you think you need a break?"

"No, no. I'm fine." She sniffled and held up her chin, then smiled. "It's a lot to take in, you know."

"It is." She looked at her mother worriedly. "I wish you'd consider coming up to Maine. At least for a time. Or if nothing else, let me stay with you for a while."

"No, dear. I'm fine. You must live your life. And I won't mind being alone."

"The thought just breaks my heart. How can I leave you? I just—"

Patricia placed her arm on Meredith's to stop her. "I appreciate it. I really do. But I'd like to be alone. I promise."

What could Meredith do? She accepted her mother's answer, and moved on to the next guests.

That night, back at her parents' house, the mood was somber as they prepared for bed. Up in her old bedroom, Meredith snuggled Gabe until he was sleeping, then turned to Nick.

"Honey..." she choked out, and instantly was in tears.

He went to her and held her in silence, letting her cry against his chest. After some time had passed, she pulled away and rubbed at her eyes, then looked around nervously, her heart suddenly pounding.

"Merry?"

She met his gaze, her eyes warm with emotion. "I have to tell you something."

He raised his eyebrows in expectation.

She began crying again, softly, so as not to wake Gabe. "Honey...I'm pregnant."

His eyes widened, and his mouth dropped open. "You're..."

"I know this isn't what you wanted," she went on shakily, her face now wet with tears. "I can't even believe this happened. We're so careful." She paused to blow her nose. "I'm sorry. I'm a blubbering mess."

He was watching her intently, his hands rubbing her shoulders.

"I just found out a couple of days ago," she said finally, a little calmer now. "I didn't have the heart to tell you." She looked at him, trying to read his face. "I hope you aren't too upset."

"Merry, I'm thrilled."

She stared at him with surprise. "Really?"

"Yes," he said, smiling, his voice tense with latent excitement. "Yes, I really am."

She fell into him, absorbing the feel of his arms holding her tight, crying now uncontrollably. He kissed the top of her head and waited. She brought her hand to his face and shook her head.

"I was so afraid to tell you. I thought you'd be so upset."

"Of course I'm not upset." He tucked her hair behind her ear. "Is it what we planned? No, not really." He shrugged. "But come on." His lips turned up into a crooked grin. "I can't be upset about having another baby with you."

She smiled, her eyes now filled with tears of happiness. "It's going to be great, you know."

"I know."

"Everything was fine with Gabe."

He kissed her, then squeezed her tight again. "And everything will be fine this time, too."

She brought her lips to his, taking comfort in his closeness, putting the past momentarily behind her, and looking toward the future.

CHAPTER THIRTY

EPILOGUE

"*L*ook how sweet this is," Meredith cooed, her fingers grazing a baby girl's sundress as it hung on a little pink hanger. "Little strawberries with smiley faces."

Patricia turned and regarded the sundress. "Just precious." She removed the hanger from the rack and added the dress to her basket.

They were walking around Asterfield on a cheerful May day. Baby Aspen was due in July. Patricia had driven up to Maine all by herself to help Meredith prepare. She'd also been there for the Building for Hope ribbon-cutting ceremony: the Henleys' home was now complete. Meredith had been proud to share this moment with her mother. It was the culmination of all their hard work.

Meredith brought a hand to her six-month-pregnant belly and fingered through the pile in the basket with the other hand. "We need to put some of this back. I don't need all this."

"Yes, you do."

"But Jenny gave me all Julia's old clothes."

"I want you to have it. It doesn't matter if you need it."

Meredith accepted this answer without another word. She

placed her hand on her mother's back and kissed her cheek. Patricia leaned toward her to receive the kiss, then stepped toward the register to pay for the items in the basket.

They walked outside into the sunshine. Meredith treated her mother to ice cream, and they continued their stroll up the street, ice cream in hand.

"I wish you'd stay an extra week," said Meredith, licking her ice cream cone. "I could use the company now that Nick's supervising the new project. Besides, you drove all the way up here all by yourself. I'd love for you to relax a little more."

"I've been relaxing, dear. I've had some much needed time to think."

"I understand." Meredith watched her mother daintily scooping ice cream from her bowl. "I just hate to think of you in that big house all alone."

"Meredith." Patricia lowered her spoon and looked at her. "I miss your father." For a moment, her eyes glistened, and the hint of a frown crossed her lips. "Terribly, in fact. More so than I'd even expected." Her voice shook. She closed her eyes and paused a moment, then dipped her spoon in her ice cream and continued walking. "But I'm fine."

Meredith frowned as she walked beside her. "Well, if you insist, there's not much I can do. Won't you at least stay an extra day?"

"I can't."

"But why not?"

Patricia hesitated. "Because I have plans."

"Oh? Anything interesting?"

"No, not really. It's just that I'm making a stop on my drive back home."

Meredith regarded her with curiosity. "Where are you going?"

Patricia took a bite of ice cream and licked her lips. "I'm visiting a friend."

Meredith stopped walking. "A friend?"

Patricia wouldn't look at her. Meredith's brow furrowed. "Who is this friend?"

Patricia finally lifted her gaze. "Cary Hudson."

Meredith's mouth dropped open.

Patricia was nibbling her ice cream as if nothing had happened. Meredith stared at her.

"Is that all you have to say?"

Patricia shrugged, examining her spoon as it fiddled in her ice cream. "There isn't much to say. I had nothing to do one day, so I looked him up. His wife passed away several years ago, and he's eager for some company." While Meredith gawked, Patricia glanced casually about. "He lives in a cabin in Massachusetts. It's on the way home. Very easy to stop by for a chat."

Meredith finally closed her mouth. Her mother was nonchalantly tending to her ice cream. Meredith hoped she'd say more, but she didn't.

"That's nice," said Meredith. She lowered her voice. "Do you think you..."

Her mother looked at her. "He's an old friend, dear. I'm just stopping by for a chat."

Patricia smiled innocently and started walking. Meredith followed her, her heart a little lighter, a wide grin on her face.

CATHERINE SMOOTHED down the front of her 1930s cotton lawn sundress with the fitted bodice and large tie bow, drop waist, and long A-line skirt. She'd purchased this dress specifically for Amy's second birthday party: the colors matched the chocolate. The dress boasted a chevron pattern of mint, salmon, and cream. Similarly, the chocolate, of a mermaid theme, lay before her in a tempting array of turquoise and pink, with the occasional ivory starfish or toffee-colored seashell. Gold sugar pearls had been strategically placed upon chocolate seaweed or chocolate mermaid hair. Catherine, not to be outdone by her own creation, had adorned her ears with gold drop earrings, and around her wrist was a gold vintage bracelet.

She'd set up cake and chocolate on a table under the shade of a blossoming magnolia tree in the backyard, surrounded by fallen petals that perfectly complemented her ethereal feminine display. She closed her eyes and inhaled the delicate scent of the flowers, enjoying the warm July breeze in her hair.

"You're out of sand dollars, sweetheart," Wes said from behind her. He slipped his arms around her waist and squeezed her tight, then brought his lips to her neck and kissed her from her ear to her shoulder, making her tilt her head and smile. She hugged his arms as they held her, closing her eyes, breathing slowly against the steadily increasing rhythm of her heart.

"You can grab some more from the workshop," she murmured dreamily, only half knowing what she'd said.

"Whatever you say, ma'am." His voice was velvety smooth; Catherine felt him grinning as he kissed her. "I'm at your service."

He spun her around and kissed her, then smoothed her hair around her neck.

"Listen, sweetheart. I was thinking. What do you say you and I go away next weekend? We can leave Amy with one of the grandmas."

Catherine's eyes brightened. "That's a lovely idea. Let's not go too far away, though."

"Will you worry about Amy?"

"No, I'll worry about you."

His smile softened, and he kissed her again. "We'll talk to the doctor. He'll give us his blessing, and it'll be fine."

"Just the same," she said, grinning as he discreetly trailed his finger up her waist. "Better safe than sorry."

"Think about it. We could use it."

Catherine straightened reluctantly as they were joined by Sarah and Lois. Wes pinched her backside on his way toward the house, and Catherine pursed her lips in an attempt to hide a wide, dopey grin.

"Hi, Mom. Hi, Sarah," she said. "Have you had enough to eat?"

"Not yet," said Sarah. "We're here to devour your chocolates." Her eyes swept over the display on the table, and she clasped her hands together at her chin. "Darling, you've outdone yourself this time. I simply don't know how you do it."

"Have you thought about my suggestion?" asked Lois.

Sarah turned to her. "What suggestion is that?"

Lois smiled at her daughter. "I told Catherine she should consider opening a shop. Her chocolates sell so well at the gift shop, and she already fills so many orders from home."

"Oh, how delightful!" gasped Sarah. "Catherine, you must. You just must. It could have a 1930s feel."

"With vintage paintings in the background."

"And feather boas hanging on coatracks."

"It's a good idea," said Catherine. "I'm considering it."

"Darling," said Sarah, her hand on her arm. She looked at her intently, her sharp eyes full of excitement. "It's a fabulous idea. Take a risk. Share your talents. Live life to the fullest."

Lois picked a chocolate seashell off the table and took a little bite. "What a charming theme, and such pretty colors. I think this is your best display yet."

"Thank you," said Catherine. "It's a nod to the work of Australian illustrator Ida Rentoul Outhwaite, who often collaborated with her sister on children's books featuring her fairies, elves, and mermaids."

She abruptly closed her mouth and smiled awkwardly. "You get the idea."

"No, please do go on," said Lois. "I'm curious about your inspiration, and I'm sure Sarah is, too."

Catherine's smile warmed. She pointed to a mermaid. "Well, her delicate lines are reminiscent of Arthur Rackham and Kate

Greenaway. She was extraordinarily popular. She was inspired by a watercolor plate from *The Enchanted Seas...*"

Wes returned carrying a tray of chocolate sand dollars, which he helped arrange on the table by the cake. Catherine scooped up Amy and announced that it was time to sing "Happy Birthday." The partygoers gathered and sang to Amy, who then blew out her candles and clapped her hands, delighted to dig into a slice of her cake. Catherine and Wes took a picture with their daughter, then set her down to play on the lawn among her friends and family, who held plates of cake in their hands and chatted gaily on the lawn and among the gardens.

A group of family members collected on the patio. Wes stood beside Catherine, his arm around her waist, his hand holding her protectively.

"Glad to see you up and about, Senator," said Fred, patting Wes on the back. "You look good. Feeling well today, I presume?"

"Absolutely. Better every day. I have to tell you, it feels great to be back to work."

"I don't doubt it. Good for you. Any interesting cases?"

"Mostly the usual, but there is one thing." He tossed his finger toward Grady and grinned. "Grady and I are in talks with the county. We want them to petition the state to donate the surplus land that would've been the Munson site."

"We think it would make an excellent park," said Grady. "It's surrounded by residences. It's the most obvious solution for that space."

"Indeed." Fred folded his arms and regarded them with interest. "There's poetic justice in that. I wish you all the best."

Catherine soon fell into conversation with Maeve and Hei, whose children were playing with Olivia on the lawn.

"Wes wants me to go away with him next weekend," she told them.

"That sounds fun!" said Hei.

"Fantastic," agreed Maeve, gulping her punch.

"Not so fast. I don't know if I want to. I just think we should stay close to home for a while."

"Don't be silly," said Hei, nudging her with her elbow. "He's been back to work for what, a couple of months now?"

"He's fine," said Maeve, chewing on an ice cube. "Go away. Have fun."

Catherine stared at them. "You two agree. That hardly ever happens."

"Then that means you should do it," said Hei.

"What she said," said Maeve.

The party continued into the evening. Catherine stood with a glass of wine on the patio, her beloved house behind her, her entire life in front of her. With fireflies blinking and the stars twinkling, and the flowers bathed in moonlight, the scene was peaceful and magical, the most beautiful scene in the world.

Wes stepped toward her and gently pried the wine glass from her hand. He placed it on the table and took her hand in his, placing his other hand on her waist and dancing softly with her to the music.

He pulled her close and swayed with her, his cheek nestled against hers. Catherine slinked her arm around his waist and melted into his chest. She closed her eyes and rubbed her cheek against his. Electricity seemed to pass between them, and she inhaled, taking it all in.

"How long do you think we have to entertain these people?" he asked her, his voice like velvet in her ear. "I'm no longer in an entertaining mood."

"What kind of mood are you in?"

"Help me get rid of them, and you'll soon find out."

She let him hold and squeeze her, dancing under the stars. She smiled as he dipped her and hugged her tight once more.

"I know what kind of mood you're in." His hand was slipping downward, over her hip and backside. "It's a romantic mood, my favorite mood. It's a deep red mood, with just a splash of silver."

"Deep red, huh? Like crimson?"

"I think it's fair to call it crimson."

He spun her around and gazed at her, and her heart fluttered like a hummingbird. It was the face she had fallen in love with, a face full of good humor and charm. As he locked eyes with her, she saw it all, all that they'd been through together. It made his face even more handsome; it registered years that were hers.

"You always were such a magnificent dancer, sweetheart. You take my breath away."

"And you take mine," she whispered, and met him in a kiss.

THE END

MAEVE IN THE MORNING

She's been hiding a secret for decades. But in order to move forward, she'll need to reckon with the past.

Maeve Sheering is living fabulously. Fiercely independent, wickedly sharp, and infallibly stylish, the fortysomething crusader works as the communications director for a lawmaker passing a promising water safety bill. But now an insufferable scientist from her past has partnered with her boss to take down a local polluter... and it could jeopardize everything Maeve has worked for.

Forced into an unwanted collaboration with her former adversary, Maeve suppresses her frustration with his tactics—and the memory of how their rivalry years ago led to the worst night of her life. But as she gets to know him, she begins to wonder if their differences may be the very thing that binds them together.

Now Maeve finds herself confronting her past and lowering her defenses, risking her heart in the process. It's a risk that could lead not only to saving her community but also to a chance at healing and connection she never saw coming.

Easily read as a standalone novel or as the sequel to *Catherine and the Wind*, *Maeve in the Morning* is a story about facing vulnerabilities and learning to trust others—and about how self-discovery can come from the least likely of places.

THE MEREDITH SERIES

About Book One, *Meredith Out of the Darkness:*

She's created the perfect life. But when it doesn't turn out as planned, can she take what she's learned and find her way in the darkness?

Meredith Beck had it all: the love of her life, a thriving career, and an apartment in the excitement of New York City. Then tragedy strikes, leaving her adrift in a world that's suddenly lost its luster. Optimistic by nature, she desperately attempts to rebuild. But no matter how hard she tries, she just can't muster her former strength.

Then a light appears in the darkness: Nick Kelly, a quiet painter from a small town in Maine. Thoughtful and kind, and utterly without pretension, Nick is unlike anyone Meredith has ever known. She is drawn to his love of nature and is comforted by his purity of heart. Through his eyes, the world seems to hold limitless possibility, and as their romance blossoms, she's delighted to find herself on the road toward a simpler life, with a partner who reminds her of the beauty in every moment.

But it isn't as simple as it seems. As Nick's own demons surface, the life they're building threatens to unravel. Human fallibilities once again complicate best-laid plans. And it becomes clear that before they can embrace the future, they must confront the lingering ghosts of their pasts.

A story of love, loss, and the power of second chances, *Mereditib Out of the Darkness* is first in a slow-burn series of cliffhangers ending with a warm and satisfying happily-ever-after.

ACKNOWLEDGMENTS

My heartfelt thanks to Gina, Jessica, Jocelyn, Judy, Rusty, Terri, Sandra, Thien-Kim, Erica, Sandy, Jennifer, Melissa, Sarah, and April.

I'd also like to thank Janet, Marty, Maggie, Diana, Helen, Dave, Frank, Jocelyn, Phyllis, and Leslie for providing factual and professional information as I researched the many complex topics that went into the writing of this book.

Dez knows my characters as well as I do (perhaps even better) and understood where this story was going from the start. Thank you for holding my hand and for believing.

Made in the USA
Monee, IL
27 September 2024